THE
BLOODBOUND
KNIGHT

FRACTURE PACT BOOK THREE

MEGAN O'RUSSELL

Ink Worlds Press

Visit our website at www.MeganORussell.com

This book is a work of fiction. Names, characters, places, and incidents either are products of the author's imagination or are used fictitiously. Any resemblance to actual persons, living or dead, events, or locales is entirely coincidental.

The Bloodbound Knight

Copyright © 2023, Megan O'Russell

Cover Art by MiblArt (https://miblart.com/)

Editing by Christopher Russell

Interior Design by Christopher Russell

All rights reserved.

No part of this publication may be used or reproduced in any manner whatsoever without written permission, except in the case of brief quotations embodied in critical articles and reviews. Requests for permission should be addressed to Ink Worlds Press.

Printed in the United States of America

THE BLOODBOUND KNIGHT

Grace

Sweat dripped down Grace's back, joining the rain that still soaked through her shirt.

Beyond the sheen of blue light surrounding her cage, figures moved through the shadows.

A dozen. No, more.

All of them dressed in black. All of them moving with precision, like they had experience in kidnapping.

Grace bit her lips together, not letting them wobble even as tears streamed down her cheeks.

"Orders aren't up for debate." The gravelly voice came from the far corner of the room, behind the table where two of the kidnappers worked on computers.

Grace listened to the soft rumble of the reply but couldn't make out the words.

She twisted up onto her knees, edging toward the voices.

"Triumph requires sacrifice," the gravelly voice said. "From all of us."

One of the men at the computers tensed, the lines of his furrowed brow contorting his face in the dim light of his screen.

"I understand the importance of our mission." A new, lighter, female voice spoke.

Grace slid closer to the front of her cage.

"If the—" the gravelly voice began as pain shot through Grace's leg, driving all the way up into her spine.

She screamed, toppling forward, sending a surge of pain slicing up her arms. Spots sparked through her vision as the searing agony stabbed into her skull.

"Stop. Stop!" Gasping, Grace pushed herself up, her nails tearing on the cracked concrete of the floor as she scrambled forward, trying to flee the torment. But the pain didn't stop.

A fresh scream tore from her throat as the pain seized into a sharp-edged spasm.

She fell onto her side, cracking her head against the ground.

Cords of bright blue light wrapped around her wrists, the tethers stretching to two of the fist-sized jewels topping the wooden staffs that formed the corners of her cage.

The blazing glow of the cords pulsed, sending waves of pain through Grace's body, like every atom of her being had somehow caught fire.

She tried to twist away from the cords. Sparks joined the pulsing light, digging a new layer of agony into Grace's mind.

Her scream brought the taste of blood to her mouth.

She couldn't make herself stop.

"Move back to the center," a voice said.

Grace reached for the light on her wrist, paying for the movement with a fresh surge of white-hot agony.

"Crawl back to the center," the voice said. "Stay in the center of your cell, and the pain stops."

Sobs punched through Grace's chest.

"Move to the center, Grace."

Arms shaking, Grace slid herself back a few inches. The pain in her arms dulled just enough to give her hope.

She pushed herself to her knees, choking on her tears as she crawled backward a foot.

The pain in her leg eased.

And another foot.

Only the vicious ghosts of the searing pain still danced through her body.

The cords of light that bound her faded away.

"That's better." The voice came from behind Grace. Calm. Unfazed by Grace's pain.

Grace didn't dare turn toward the sound.

"Are you going to ask me what that was, Grace?" the voice said.

Grace took a shaky breath, ready to speak, but the pain had stolen all the words from her mind.

Footsteps cut around the side of the cage.

"What you just experienced was a very powerful spell." The speaker, a woman with short, blond hair, stepped into view. "This cell was designed to hold magicians."

The word wrapped fresh fear around Grace's lungs.

Magicians. A cage for magicians. People in uniforms capturing magicians.

Maree.

"No one here wants to cause you pain," the woman said. "But you will be staying in this cell. Keep to the center, and you'll be comfortable. Stray, and accept the consequences. Do you understand?"

No. Stop. Let me go home.

Help me.

Please help me.

Grace couldn't make her lips form the words.

"Grace," the woman said, "do you understand that, if you stray, you will be responsible for the pain you endure?"

Grace looked to her wrists. The skin was perfect, unburned, as though she'd only imagined the fiery agony.

"Grace?"

Grace's whole body trembled as she managed to nod.

————

Grace gripped the seat of her crooked folding chair, digging her nails into the patches of rust left behind by years of Florida damp. If the scent of bleach hadn't tainted the air, the humidity could have almost fooled Grace into thinking she'd made it all the way home.

With her eyes closed, and if the fiends stayed quiet, it might all have been a horrific nightmare.

She was safe in bed. Pops had put too much bleach in the wash again, that was all.

A normal, peaceful morning.

"Grace," Calla said. "I know you can hear me, Grace."

Grace opened her eyes.

Calla stood just outside Grace's cage.

The blue light of Grace's prison cast a strange glow on Calla's short, blond hair, gleaming off the strands as though she were more than plain human.

The other fiends all stayed in the shadows. Lurking. Waiting.

"Grace," Calla said.

The ones in the shadows...if they weren't plain humans. If they were feu—

I'd still be trapped.

"I need you to talk to me," Calla said. "I'm not your enemy."

Grace's cracked nails bent back as she tightened her grip on the chair.

"You're in a lot of trouble," Calla said.

Grace looked away.

Calla circled the cage, planting herself back in Grace's line of sight.

"In fact," Calla said, "I think you're in so much trouble, you don't know what to do."

A fresh knot of fear swelled in Grace's chest.

"You really only have two choices," Calla said. "You can talk to me. Explain how a high schooler from Florida ended up with a crew of criminals in Rhode Island."

The knot of fear punched up into Grace's throat.

"Or, you can refuse to communicate," Calla said. "You can hope things don't get worse for you or your friends while you waste time staying silent, and that whoever they send to talk to you after I fail will be compassionate in their questioning."

The knot grew. She couldn't swallow past it. She couldn't breathe around it.

"I promise you, Grace, I'm the best option you're going to get. I want to help you, but you have to let me. Tell me everything, and I promise you and I will work together to figure out how to minimize the damage you've caused to your life and your family."

A surge of anger shattered the knot, allowing Grace to draw a full breath.

"Your fathers seem like wonderful people, Grace." Calla gave her what should have been a kind smile. "I want to help them get their daughter back. But if you choose not to speak to me, there's nothing I can do for you. My commander will release me, and you will end up having to face someone who's been ordered to gain information by any means necessary. Do you understand what that will mean for you?"

Calla paused.

The fiends in the shadows behind Calla froze, like they were waiting for Grace to suddenly speak.

"Grace?" Calla said.

Grace nodded.

"Good. That's a good start." Calla smiled again.

Grace didn't smile back.

"You haven't had anything to eat since yesterday," Calla said. "How about you answer a few questions, and I'll get you a meal. I'll make them all yes or no so you can keep nodding, okay?"

Grace's focus flicked to her stomach. She hadn't felt any hunger pangs through her overwhelming terror, but with that one quick thought, her stomach began to growl.

She nodded.

"Let's start simple," Calla said. "Your fathers are both sombs. And since they filed a missing persons report, I'm guessing they had no idea you were going to Rhode Island. Correct?"

Grace's muscles tensed, her neck stiffening as her conscience took over her body.

But no.

Admitting her fathers knew nothing about the feu, let alone a plot to steal the heliostone, wouldn't be the same as telling Calla about Jerek coming to Florida to tell Grace she was a magician then convincing her to make so many terrible mistakes.

Keeping her fathers away from the feu...it was the right thing to do.

Grace nodded.

"Do your fathers know about you?" Calla asked. "Do they know you're a magician or anything about the feu?"

Clueless sombs.

Simple. Truthful. Proof of her fathers' innocence.

Grace shook her head.

"Thank you for answering me. You're doing a great job." Calla paused for a moment, as though giving Grace a chance to speak, before moving on. "I've looked through the security footage from the Museum of Magic. We've been able to identify one of the boys as a runaway and one of the girls from a previous criminal incident. But the rest, we're still working on."

Because Jerek changed their faces and tricked you all, you nasty, kidnapping, bridge troll.

Grace glared at Calla, narrowing her eyes and biting the insides of her cheeks, making sure her face didn't betray any hint of satisfaction.

"The girl we've identified is very dangerous," Calla said. "And she's involved with some people who are even worse."

Grace bit down harder on her cheeks, killing her temptation to scream.

"The others who were with you at the Museum of Magic," Calla said, "your friends, are they in danger?"

Danger.

The rest of the crew in danger.

Even without the hungry vampire and temperamental werewolf, just being near Jerek Holden put everyone in danger.

Feu, sombs, strangers, his friends. Everyone in danger, all the time.

Jerek pulled danger toward him.

And I'm the worst danger of all.

Grace's leg began to bounce. She rammed the bottoms of her feet against the floor, forbidding the movement.

"If your friends need to be rescued, we can't afford to waste time," Calla said.

Lock Jerek up. Protect the rest of the crew from him.

None of us are innocent.

We're all criminals.

Criminals don't get rescued.

"I need you to answer my question," Calla said. "Are your friends in danger?"

Grace shook her head.

"Good." Calla looked over her shoulder to the two men at the computers.

One of the men nodded to her.

She turned back to Grace. "That's very good. How about one more question, and we'll get you something to eat?"

Grace nodded.

"Where are your friends now?"

A hint of something almost like relief eased the weight on Grace's lungs.

"We need to find them." Calla stepped closer to Grace's cage.

The metal chair squeaked as Grace leaned back, buying herself another inch of distance between her and the Maree.

"Your friends are involved in some very dangerous things," Calla said. "Things no teenager, no matter the mistakes they've made, should face."

Grace stayed frozen.

"Where are your friends?" Calla asked.

Grace held Calla's gaze, tipping her head to the side in a deliberate non-answer.

"Do you know who the Knights Maree are?" Calla asked.

Grace peeled her right hand away from the seat of her rusted chair, ignoring the cramps in her fingers as she pointed first to Calla then to the shadows in the darkness.

"Very good," Calla said. "If you've figured out that we're Knights Maree, you must have realized your friends killed some of my people at the Museum of Magic."

The figures in the shadows shifted—straightening their

shoulders, stepping toward the cage, setting down whatever was in their hands—all moving as though answering some silent call to assess Grace as a target for vengeance.

"Right now, our orders are to apprehend and capture all those involved in the attack on the Museum of Magic," Calla said. "*Apprehend and capture.* But if we can't get to them soon, if your friends cause more trouble, that order will change. If my people are told to subdue your friends by any means necessary, how many of your friends do you think will die?"

Grace sat forward in her seat, mouth open, ready to shout, but swallowed her words at the last moment.

It's your people who will end up dead, Maree.

"From this moment on, if anyone gets hurt because of your friends, it'll be on you," Calla said. "If they attack innocent people again, it's on you. If our orders change from capture to kill, it's on you. How much blood do you want on your hands, Grace?"

Grace sprang to her feet, grabbed her chair, and hurled it at Calla.

The walls of the cage flashed bright as the chair ricocheted off the blue light and flew back at Grace.

Pain shot through her head before everything went black.

———

Grace clutched the musty blanket to her stomach, trying to make the rough material feel soothing, like she was buried in her comforter at home.

But the rat-chewed blanket wasn't soothing. Her sad shield while she peed in a bucket, yes. Her bed, yes. Her towel when her new interrogator had woken her up with a hose, yes.

But there was nothing soothing in the Maree warehouse from Hell.

She shoved the blanket aside, resorting to sitting with her knees pulled to her chest instead.

Focus on your safe place, Grace.

The voices of her flock of therapists blurred together in her mind.

Breathe, and take your mind to your safe place.

The beach.

The nice, flat spot on the rock wall. Sitting on a towel.

Steven sitting beside her. Looking at her instead of at the sunset.

A rumble of angry voices punched into the perfect scene.

Nope.

No angry voices. Just waves. The rumbling of waves.

The waves crashed against the jetty, fierce as they rolled in, like a storm brewed far out at sea.

"None of us want to risk word of this spreading," Calla's voice broke through the pounding waves.

Ari appeared on the water. Not swimming. Being borne on top of the waves like the Queen of the Sea.

"Pushing is too risky," Calla said.

"Your opinion has been noted, now stand down," Interrogator Zappy said.

Steven leaned forward, forgetting about Grace, his gaze locked on the perfection of Ari.

Shit.

Grace opened her eyes and dug her fingers into her hair, pulling at the roots, letting the ache in her hands carry her above the fanged vortex of panic that longed to swallow her.

You are being held captive, Grace Esther Lee-Weiss. This is not the time for crushes and jealousy. You are not allowed to panic.

Just keep breathing, dammit.

Interrogator Zappy stopped beside the two computer guys,

taking a moment to look at their screens. I.Z.'s face gave no hint of what he'd seen. He dragged his finger along the edge of the table as he cut around toward Grace's cage, like he was either desperate to get a splinter or concerned the table wasn't clean enough to be in an abandoned warehouse.

How the hell did you destroy your life badly enough to end up in an abandoned warehouse?

I.Z. stopped right beside Grace's cage, only a few feet away from her, close enough for her to watch the I.Z. engraved on his cufflinks glinting in the blue light.

If she could dive for him, if she could get through the shimmering wall, shove his glinting cufflinks into his hateful eyes—

"Have you enjoyed your rest?" I.Z. tapped on the cage, sending shockwaves of sparks across the blue barrier.

Remnants of the sparks streaked down from the corners of the cage, zapping along invisible cords to burn Grace's ankles and wrists.

"Shall I ask again?" I.Z. paused, turning his head slightly, as though listening for Grace's answer.

She didn't even shake her head.

"Have you enjoyed your rest?" I.Z. slammed his palm against the cage.

Sparks flared across the barrier, lighting the cords as they raced toward Grace.

She screamed as heat, like red-hot cuffs of iron, clamped around her ankles and wrists.

"Have you"—I.Z. shouted, then lowered his voice—"enjoyed your rest?"

Grace nodded, the shimmer in front of her blurring as her breath came in tiny gasps.

"Speak, magician," I.Z. said.

"Yes." Grace's voice cracked. "Thank you."

"Good girl." I.Z. smiled. Wrinkles pinched the corners of

his eyes, making the hate glinting in them even more terrifying. "Where is the rest of your crew?"

I.Z. lifted his hand, preparing to smack the cage.

"I don't know," Grace said.

"Where is the rest of your crew?" I.Z. pressed his palm against the cage, sending a steady line of sparks flowing down the cords.

"I don't know!" Grace scratched at her wrists, trying to pull the sparking blue cords away, but her fingers couldn't find anything to grip.

I.Z. leaned his weight onto his hand. "Where is your crew?"

Grace screamed, tearing at her wrists, trying to find something, anything she could rip away to make the pain stop.

"Where—is—your—crew?" I.Z. emphasized each word with a smack against the cage.

"I don't know. I don't know. I don't know!" Sobs muddied Grace's words.

"Perhaps you don't." I.Z. stepped away and tucked his hands behind his back, his smile still creasing the corners of his eyes, like he was enjoying his job.

The pain from Grace's bonds faded, but her breath kept hitching in her chest and her tears wouldn't stop.

"Why don't you know where your friends are?" I.Z. asked.

"I—I left them." Grace wiped her tears with the inside of her sweat-fouled shirt. "I wanted to go home."

"So, you just left?" I.Z. said.

"Yeah."

"Decided you didn't want to be a criminal anymore, and the rest of your crew let you walk away?" I.Z. stepped back toward the cage.

"Yes." Grace pushed herself up onto her knees. "They were pissed about it, but no one tried to stop me."

"After being involved in the deaths of Knights Maree at the

Museum of Magic, your murdering friends let you run back home?" I.Z. trailed his finger up the cage, sending a sting of warning zaps racing toward Grace.

"They even gave me money for a hotel and a bus ticket. Whatever you think you know about them, my friends aren't monsters. And Jer—" Grace froze, her muscles seizing like a deer waiting for the windshield of doom.

"Jer?" I.Z. pressed his palm to the cage.

Grace clenched her teeth and shut her eyes, trying to think past the pain. "Jersey!"

The pain stopped.

Shit.

"Jersey?" I.Z. said.

Breathe and think, Grace.

The ding of a phone snapped her thin shred of a brilliant lie.

"Speak, magician," I.Z. said.

A steady pulse of shocks pounded through Grace's bonds.

The phone dinged again.

"Jersey." Grace opened her eyes. "Jersey was one stop too far for me."

"New Jersey?" I.Z. tucked his hands behind his back again.

"Yes." Grace rubbed her eyes, hoping the shaking in her voice leaned more toward tears of betrayal than crying from fear of punishment. "I don't know where in New Jersey. Only that's where they're going next."

"Why?"

"I don't know." Grace dropped her hands, letting the pure terror of being locked in a cage take over her face. "I really don't. That's how things always were. We'd be halfway to somewhere before anyone told me where we were going."

"Interesting." I.Z. didn't reach for the cage.

"I've told you where they were heading," Grace said. "That's all I can do. So please let me go."

I.Z. laughed.

The people in the shadows shifted, but none of them made a noise.

"I can't tell anyone you kidnapped me," Grace said. "My parents are sombs, they'd never believe me even if I wanted to tell them. And I don't want to tell them because all I want is my life back."

"Your somb life back?" I.Z. said.

"Yes." Grace held I.Z.'s gaze. "I just want to go to high school and eat dinner with my parents and never think about magic or the feu again."

"You abandoned all hope of returning to that world the moment you were involved with the deaths of Knights Maree." I.Z. slammed his fist against the cage.

Grace screamed, scrambling to her feet, uselessly trying to escape the pain.

"We're going to start with the names of your crew and every person, both feu and somb, you've come into contact with since leaving Sun Palms." I.Z. drummed his fingers on the sheet of blue light.

Grace choked on her sobs but held I.Z.'s gaze.

"If you don't comply with the questioning, you will be punished. And believe me, it gets worse than a few sparks." I.Z. dragged his finger along the front of the cage then up the wooden shaft of the corner's staff. "Once I believe you've truly given us all the names you can, we'll start on why you targeted the Museum of Magic. And after that"—I.Z. grinned—"we'll see what other questions arise."

I.Z. gripped the blue gem at the top of the staff.

Crushing pain slammed into Grace's body, buckling her knees, stealing her sight.

Her scream didn't stop as she fell to the floor, slamming her side against the cracked concrete.

"What"—Grace spoke between gasps—"wha—what the hell is wrong with you?"

"I'm not the monster, magician," I.Z. said. "Ariel Love, Jack Swain, Grace Esther Lee-Weiss—those are the names of monsters."

A blurred shadow of movement caught Grace's eye, shifting behind I.Z. like the king demon had called the darkness itself to torment her.

"Give me the rest of the names." I.Z. flicked the blue gem, spiking white-hot agony that thrummed through Grace's bones.

"I can't." Grace forced the words through her scream.

I.Z. flicked the gem again.

"I can't!"

The shadow demon crept closer, drawn to the light of Grace's cage.

"Speak, magician." I.Z. pulled back his hand.

"Please." Grace's whole body shook as she pushed her sweat-and-tear-slicked hair away from her face.

The shadow demon kept coming, gaining three fellows as it stalked closer.

Four demons come to torture Grace for abandoning the crew.

I deserve a hundred.

"Speak," I.Z. said.

A flash of silver caught in the blue light, glimmering as it slashed at I.Z.'s throat.

"Ari!" Grace reached for the one wielding the blade, but the blond wasn't Ari.

It was Calla.

Calla wielding the dagger. Calla whose blow was knocked aside by I.Z.

I.Z. rounded on Calla, swinging for her stomach.

A man in a Maree uniform dove for I.Z., his knife catching I.Z. in the shoulder before I.Z. tossed him aside.

"Let me out!" Grace shouted.

But none of the fighters even glanced her way as more of the black-uniformed Maree joined the fight.

A scream came from deep in the shadows, cutting over the chaos of I.Z. fighting three at once.

"Someone let me out!" Grace scratched at her wrists, trying to feel the invisible, intangible bonds. "Let me out!"

A body slammed into Grace's cage, sending a shock of agony slicing through her. The body slid down the cage, leaving a red smear that sizzled away on the blue barrier.

"Lock down the exits!" A shout came from the back side of the warehouse, away from where her captors had always prowled.

Seven more people in Maree uniforms swarmed in through a side door Grace had never seen used.

A flash of bright red light came from Grace's left, but she couldn't make herself look that way, couldn't tear her gaze from I.Z. slashing his knife across Calla's stomach.

"No!" Grace scrambled forward as Calla fell. Pain shot into her ankles. "Stop!"

She pushed herself back to the middle of her cage as an arrow whizzed past.

"Stop." Grace spoke through her tears. "Please, just stop. Please, stop."

A wave of terror and rage swept through Grace, digging into her chest, surging heat out to her limbs.

"No, no, no." Sparks leapt from Grace's fingers, each tiny flicker of magic costing a shock of pain streaming through her bonds. "Breathe, Grace. Breathe."

But the flares of pain wouldn't let her anger die.

Another flash of red came with another terrified scream.

Flames dripped from Grace's fingers, sizzling on the concrete, lighting her blanket on fire.

"Shit. Shit." Grace's whole body shook from the blazing pain as she shoved her blanket away, pushing the flaming fabric into the corner. Her palms caught on a crack in the concrete, ripping through her skin.

Red smeared the floor, smudging the singe marks on the concrete, as she tried to push herself back to her knees. The hurt of the cuts didn't even flicker through the agony pushing deeper, burning into her bones. "Br—breathe, Grace."

"He's heading for the trucks," a woman shouted over the chaos.

Her fire devoured the blanket, its flames lapping at the corner of the cage, casting an orange light on the staff just beyond the blue sheen.

Four staffs, locking in a feu, a magician.

Wood and gems stealing her freedom.

"Your Ari sucks." Grace crumpled forward, pressing her bloody palms to the ground, focusing every bit of strength she had left into the flames flowing from her hands.

She leaned into the searing pain tearing through her body, letting the agony fuel her magic as she pushed the fire down. Down into the cracks in the floor. Down through the concrete to the dirt below.

Jagged pain squeezed around her lungs. She couldn't pull in enough air to scream.

You're feu. You're feu.

Her heart pounded in her ears. White spots danced through her vision, blocking her view of the flames as she pushed the blaze out, out, out through the concrete and dirt, reaching wide, as far as the cracks allowed...and let the fire burn.

The sounds of the fighting changed, surging away from her cage, the tones of the shouts gaining a fresh layer of fear.

As pain pulled her toward the relief of dark oblivion, Grace dragged in a breath, screamed, and let her magic burst out of her body.

Power. Heat. Flames.

Consuming her. Tearing through her.

Until the pain in her body snapped away, and only fire remained.

Better for it to end like this. Better to be taken by her own magic.

But she didn't fall into darkness.

A bright light drove the white spots from Grace's eyes.

Orange. Flickering. Growing every moment.

Flames had spread across the warehouse floor, driving the black-clad fighters back.

Grace fumbled to her knees, trying to flee the blaze, but there was nowhere to go. The flames born of her magic surrounded her, trapping her in a burning cage of her own making.

Gasping against the pain in her legs, she lurched to her feet. Her knees shook, threatening to buckle, but she stayed upright.

Flames lapped at her ankles, singeing the hems of her pants.

But their heat didn't burn her.

She slid her foot forward, giving the fire more flesh to broil.

"Go. Move!" a deep voice shouted.

Crack.

Grace spun toward the sound, ready to dodge some awful weapon.

Crack.

The flames had climbed one the staffs that made the corners of Grace's cage.

Crack.

The wood of the staff split.

Pain flared in Grace's wrist as the top of the staff tipped

back, its gem gleaming as it pulled against the other staffs, slanting the walls of Grace's cage, sending a fresh surge of pain through her left arm.

"Fall." Grace inched toward the damaged corner, not even noticing the flames around her growing, reaching up to her knees, melting her shoelaces. "Come on, just fall."

A terrible screech, like tearing metal, sliced into Grace's ears.

The flames wavered as Grace winced.

"No, keep going." Grace raised her hand, luring the flames higher, willing them to surround the jewel. The floor shook as a section of the roof fell, caving in near the door at the back of the warehouse.

"Please," Grace whispered.

Pop.

Such a tiny noise to greet salvation.

The flames surged, rising five feet high as the blue light of Grace's cage vanished.

A scream, gruesome and horrifying, carried over the chaos.

Grace ignored the sound as she stepped forward, holding her breath, waiting for the pain to come. But the tethers of light didn't appear.

The horrible scream stopped.

A terrifying moment of nothing seized Grace's mind.

Escape. She needed to escape.

Run away.

Run away from the monsters, Grace.

Go!

She turned and sprinted for the back door, moving as quickly as her still-shaking legs would allow.

Another metallic shriek came from above as part of the roof tipped, angling toward Grace.

She covered her head, dodging around the already fallen

debris, ignoring the flames, keeping her gaze fixed on the back door.

The invading black suits had left it open, giving Grace a clear path to the corridor beyond.

A thick haze of smoke filled the hall.

Grace stumbled to a stop, pulling her shirt over her nose, searching for a hint of what direction might offer escape.

On the right, flickering feebly, an exit sign on a barely burned wall.

Grace barreled toward the door, ramming her side against the push bar, bursting out onto a loading dock.

There were no cars on the crumbling asphalt—no people either.

She pressed her palm to the wall as she ran down the steps, leaving a line of fire trailing behind her, bidding the flames to rise, letting them nip at the roof.

Her foot fumbled on the last step. She crashed to the ground, her knees and palms splitting open as they smacked into the concrete.

Bursts of shouting came from the front of the building.

She dug her fingers into the ground, funneling every bit of fury—taken from her home, taken from her world, thrown into chaos, thrown into a cage—into the cracks in the asphalt, sending an inferno worthy of the demons toward their voices, before pushing herself to her feet and running into the dark maze of warehouses stretching before her, only glancing back when a boom shot a pillar of flames into the sky.

2

Lincoln

Ford held up a finger, silencing his four trained and deadly companions.

Lincoln eased away from the table where Ford sat typing on his tablet with one hand while risking his life shushing the sleep-deprived werewolf, who leered at Ford as though considering how best to kill him, with the other.

Jack pushed away from the plain brick basement wall and planted himself beside Ford. He placed his palms on the table, bending over to meet Eve's danger-laden glare.

Ari took Lincoln's hand, drawing him away from the trio to sit on one of the many dust-covered crates the archivist's basement had to offer.

"I don't know what's going on above my head, but it's distracting," Ford said.

"Nothing's going on," Jack said.

"Awfully sweet of you to say, but there's no need to lie."

Ford swiped open a new screen on his tablet and fell back into silence.

The earthy, vaguely damp scent of the basement scratched at Lincoln's mind, pulling him back toward panic.

The network of tunnels and cellars in the Maree compound had the same sort of scent, like time had forgotten the subterranean places and all the secrets that had been left to molder in dark corners.

Corners where Maree could now hide, waiting to attack fellow Maree.

Ari leaned forward, her hair falling over her shoulder as she caught Lincoln's eye. She furrowed her brow, like she was asking him some sort of question and he should know her well enough to understand what she meant.

Lincoln opened his mouth to speak, but he only had words of fear and panic to offer. He shook his head.

Ari bent low, brushing a kiss on the back of his hand.

A whisp of exquisite warmth flickered through his panic.

Guilt banished the warmth with a merciless stab through his chest.

"And"—Ford dragged out the word— "we're ready."

He pushed a baggie holding a set of earbuds toward Eve.

"Can I go?" Eve said.

"Please do." Ford passed an earpiece to Jack. "I'd like to savor a moment of success before someone else tries to kill us."

"Great." Eve bolted up the creaking wooden stairs to the first floor.

"Eve," Ari called after her.

Eve's footsteps paused.

"No risks," Ari said. "Ask for backup at the first hint of anything wrong."

Eve ran the rest of the way up the steps and slammed the door closed behind her.

"Now that I've switched things up to avoid being overheard by, well, whoever might care enough to try listening, whether they're murderers, or thieves, or feu, or Maree, or cops, or—"

"Ford," Jack said.

"Sorry. Long night. The point is we're ready to roll." Ford passed Ari an earpiece then grabbed her hand, holding on and making eye contact as he overenunciated the words. "Eve's all patched in with us and can hear everything we talk about in our meeting."

Ari nodded.

Ford tossed Lincoln the same earbuds he'd been using for days.

A second stab of guilt struck Lincoln's chest.

Days he'd been using the earbuds. Weeks he'd been helping with Jerek's plans to mend the Fracture.

Weeks to throw away a lifetime of vowed service to the Maree while jeopardizing the centuries of secrecy Maree had fought and died to protect.

The Maree are fighting now, fighting our brethren.

"Everybody set?" Ford asked.

"Mass chaos waits for no one," Jack said.

Lincoln slipped in his earbuds.

"Just checked on Jerek." Eve's voice spoke in Lincoln's ears.

"He's still out, but his breathing and heartrate are fine," Eve said.

"And Mariah?" Ari asked.

Lincoln's earbuds stayed silent.

Ari's face paled. She laced her fingers through Lincoln's, hanging on to him like he might actually be able to offer her comfort.

"She's alive," Eve said.

Lincoln squeezed Ari's hand.

"Her heart's going faster than Jerek's," Eve said. "But she's still breathing."

"She's a magician," Jack said. "That's pretty close to plain human. Can we take her to a doctor?"

"I don't think we can risk it," Ari said. "Even if we didn't have to worry about the Maree or LeBlanc or whoever else wants us dead showing up at the hospital. If we did it, if we really finally mended the Fracture, and if all the news stories about weird things happening really are being caused by magicians whose powers are flooding back—"

"Then sending Mariah into a hospital full of sombs could end up with a whole lot of people dead," Ford said.

Lincoln's gaze flicked up to the ceiling as a childish shock of fear shouted he'd find blood dripping down from the kitchen floor.

"Even if she didn't actually hurt anyone, a single levitated bandage could put the feu in danger," Ari said.

"If things go wrong and we could've saved her—" Jack said.

"Hospitals are off the table." Ari slipped her hand away from Lincoln's, squaring her shoulders, donning the mantle of the unshakable genius. "How's the roof, Eve?"

"It's a shit sunrise, but no signs of attack," Eve said.

"Good," Ari said. "We've got magic catching sombs' attention, a revolt at the Maree compound, Grace playing arson, and a dead body in the kitchen. Where do we want to start?"

3

Ari

None of the others spoke. Eve didn't even growl through Ari's earpiece.

"Okay." Ari closed her eyes, pushing her thoughts toward the blissful calm that surrounded her when she let herself dive deep underwater, out of reach of all the messes that came with surviving on land.

Gleaming, cool. Easy to breathe and think.

"Priorities. First, we need better protection for the house. Until we figure out how to move everything in the archives to a safer location, this is officially super squad headquarters. Ford?"

"Oh captain, my captain?" Ford said.

"There's a video doorbell, but we need more eyes than that, and keeping Jack and Eve on the roof isn't sustainable," Ari said. "I want cameras covering every approach to the house with monitors and software to match. Batch the purchases around the city to keep it subtle."

"We'll be up and running by noon," Ford said.

"Eve." Ari tipped her head as she spoke, like that would somehow help Eve hear her. "Does your grandmother have any magician friends?"

"Other than Jerek, no," Eve said. "Not since they all ignored the slaughter of my pack at Blood Mountain."

"Shit." Ari paced beside the table. "Jack, anyone on your end?"

"I could try asking Lydia," Jack said.

"I don't want to get her involved," Ari said. "Not until we know what hell we're looking at."

"Thank you." Jack reached for Ari's hand. "Truly."

She didn't fight as he pulled her into a hug and kissed her forehead.

She stayed in his arms as she continued. "I'll deal with feu chatter."

"We mended the Fracture," Eve said. "Other than waiting for magicians to scream *thank you*, why the hell do we care what they're saying?"

"Did all magic return at full strength to all magicians?" Ari said. "Or did we only mend part of the Fracture? Are the somb reports of unexplained weirdness just spikes in magic, or—"

"—are we looking at an entire world of magicians who've forgotten how to control their powers?" Lincoln said.

"Temporarily." Ari turned in Jack's arms, keeping tucked close to him while looking at Lincoln. "Magic flooding back into magicians after twelve years caused a massive shock to their systems. A blip like this was always a possible consequence of mending the Fracture."

"You knew this could happen? Why didn't you tell me?" Lincoln stood, the top of his head too close to the low ceiling of the basement, making him look far too large for the space as he dragged his hands over his hair and dug his fingers into his scalp like he was trying to keep his brain from ricocheting out of his skull.

"I didn't think anyone had to be told," Ari said. "If I'd kept your right arm tied at your side for twelve years, you wouldn't be playing baseball the day I cut the rope and freed you."

"Magic is being noticed," Lincoln said.

"We don't know that the flying cereal was caused by magic," Ford said.

"Really?" Eve said.

"Well, not *for sure* for sure," Ford said. "It could have been a really good prank."

"The ability to control magic atrophies," Ari said. "Once magicians realize they've gotten their powers back, they'll go to ground and wait out their recovery."

"You can't be sure of that," Lincoln said.

"We can't do anything about it, either," Eve said.

Ari shut her eyes as she listened to Eve, blocking out Lincoln's pale, worried face, not wanting to risk seeing anger in his eyes.

You can't keep everybody happy. You're here to save the feu, Ariel Love.

"Unless there's a magician phone tree I've never heard of," Eve kept talking, "we have no way of contacting every magician and ordering them to hole up at home, let alone the manpower to make sure they obey."

Keeping her eyes closed, Ari lined up the images from all the news stories that had pinged on her alerts, filing through them in her mind—one stack for high probability of feu involvement, another for solid maybes, then vague possibilities, then pranks, stupidity, and deep fakes.

"Flood the system." A hint of soul-saving, roguish confidence broke through Ari's fatigue.

"What?" Eve said.

"No one's going to care about flying cereal boxes if we offer them a flying car." Ari opened her eyes.

"You're brilliant," Ford said.

"A flying car?" Lincoln said. "Ari, even if Jerek wakes up and can find a spell to levitate a car—"

"No, not like that. Too much work." Ford flapped one hand at Lincoln while still typing with the other.

"I find better weird news stories," Ari said. "Deer with three heads, hundred-and-ten-year-old woman wins marathon, frat house vanishes in the middle of the night—and push those stories in the social media algorithms. I'll shove in some steamy political scandal a bigwig paid tons of money to hide and the latest celebrity gossip as extra clickbait."

"Your brain is equal measures terrifying and sexy, Ariel Love," Ford said.

"Once I snag the top spots in the algorithms, we send in a second batch of fake videos to flood the system with faux supernatural happenings," Ari said. "A specific spot on a dirt road that makes cars levitate. A storm that hovers over one condemned house for days. A girl who sets everything she touches on fire.

"Most people won't get past the real scandals and news. And the people who follow our supernatural breadcrumbs will be focusing on our carefully selected fakes instead of the real magician-made oopsies. Once people figure out how many of the videos are scams, they'll pan the sudden flurry of bogus videos taking over the internet. No one will be able to trust anything they see, even a legitimate video of a magician slipping up in the cereal aisle."

Ari dared to meet Lincoln's gaze. He had no anger in his eyes, just heartbreaking worry and fatigue. She left the comfort of being nestled close to Jack to take Lincoln's hand.

"We can't do anything about in-person witnesses to magic,"

Ari said, "but if we blur out the blips from last night, we can keep magic from going viral."

"If the problems stay blips," Jack said.

The creases in Lincoln's brow deepened.

"We're going to fix this." Ari smoothed the wrinkles beside Lincoln's eyes.

"What about the Maree?" Eve said.

"I haven't heard from my family." Lincoln turned his head, looking toward the empty stairs, freeing himself from Ari's touch.

"As much as that sucks, there's more in play than making sure your family's safe," Eve said. "A compound filled with an ancient order of knights who've decided to kill each other is a hell of a lot worse than flying cereal."

"I'd say we could warn the Council of the Feu," Jack began.

"We can't trust them," Eve cut in as Ari said, "It's too risky."

"Which is why I was going to say, 'but they could be worse off than the Maree, and I'm fairly certain they'd like to arrest all of us,'" Jack finished.

"Leave the Maree for now." Lincoln tucked his hands behind his back, shifting into the stance of a knight, like that could somehow help tilt the world away from chaos. "Ari sent messages to my family, and her alerts will ping when they message back. Until then, anything short of flying home to join the fight is useless."

Ari let out a long breath, banishing the creeping tendrils of fear that longed to strangle her. "Lincoln, if you need to go to your family, we'd—"

"My place is here," Lincoln said. "Whatever else has happened, it's my duty to protect Jerek. I can't leave him, and I can't walk away from the archives. This place in the wrong hands could destroy the feu. It has to be protected. Disgraced or not, there should be a Maree here."

"The Maree can—" Eve began.

"We're in a boobytrapped house filled with books on dark magic, records of awful family secrets, and a whole bunch of other nasty things." Jack spoke quickly, keeping his words loud enough to drown out Eve's voice. "We need to dig through everything. See if we can find anything useful or any fancy artifacts that might explode and kill us all."

"You start down here," Ari said. "Lincoln can start upstairs. Jerek and Mariah can help once they're awake."

"Wait." Ford set his tablet down. "If Ari and I are on computers, Eve's guarding the house, and Lincoln and Jack are searching...the house's things, what about Grace? We already have decent security footage of her running from the warehouse fire. Chances are there are more cameras in the area. I can start tracking her that way."

"Grace is on her own," Ari said.

"Which gives her more options for where to run. I'll do what I can from a thousand miles away," Ford said. "Hopefully, I can nail down a few options for potential Grace-friendly hidey-holes, and we can start searching from there."

"If she's smart enough to hide," Eve said.

"But once I find her, we'll have to send—"

"Grace is on her own." Ari cut across Ford. She stepped back, making sure she could see the boys' faces. "We can't worry about her next move. She chose to leave the crew. She's not one of us. She doesn't make the list of things that are our problem."

"Ari." Jack's fangs peeked below his lip.

"Who should we send to help her? You? Are you willing to leave us short a fighter while we're sitting on information that could either help rebuild or completely destroy the feu? What if there are spells in the archives that could hurt vampires? Spells that could kill your whole clan if they got into the wrong hands? That's what we're dealing with, Jack." Ari banished the tears from her cheeks, pulling their moisture in through her skin. "Even with Jerek and Mariah awake, who could we spare to hunt Grace down?"

Jack ran his tongue over his bottom lip, licking away the blood his own fangs had spilt.

"I'm not being petty," Ari said. "We're dealing with the future of the feu. We can't risk being down a member of this crew when shit hits the fan."

"Grace was a member of the crew," Jack said.

"And she chose to leave," Eve said.

"I told her if she walked out we weren't coming to her rescue. I made sure she understood the risk, and she chose to leave anyway. I hate it, but she's on her own." Ari held Jack's gaze, watching as his eyes shifted from anger to worry. One of the tendrils of fear won the battle to coil around Ari's throat as Jack drifted into resigned sorrow.

"What else is on the list?" Lincoln stepped closer to Ari, placing his hand on her back like he was trying to prove he, at least, didn't think she was a monster.

Ford raised his hand. "We need food. We ran out of pizza, and my abstract reasoning skills drop when I'm hungry. I would prefer to order delivery or go pick something up. But if that's too dangerous"—Ford nodded to himself as he let out a long breath—"I can be the one to fix breakfast."

"Which sweeps us to the last item on the doom of the day list," Ari said. "Who has a brilliant idea for getting rid of the corpse in the kitchen?"

4

Eve

The scent of death cut through the smell of fear that filled the kitchen. Shit and sweet-odored decay and burned flesh, the stench growing worse as the midday sun streamed in through the sliding glass door at the back of the kitchen.

"You're sure we can't wait until Jerek wakes up?" Jack said from the other side of the basement door. "If he's back to full strength, maybe he can do a spell to make the body go bye-bye."

Eve's gaze flicked to the corpse beside the kitchen table before she could stop herself.

His burned hands still clung to the heliostone, but the blood on his clothes had dried, darkening to a shade of brown she could almost pretend was dirt.

She should be on the roof. Things were better on the roof. Why the hell had she let them put cameras on the roof?

"I can already smell the body from down here." Ford spoke

through Eve's earbuds. "We can't keep letting him sit there decaying."

Hot sour rose in Eve's throat.

"I'm not wearing these things anymore." She yanked out her earbuds. "I can hear him in the basement and in my ears, and I can't think with your voices banging into my head."

"Harsh but fair." Ari pulled out her own earpiece. "I agree with Ford. We can't wait for Jerek to deal with the body. We don't know how long it'll be before he wakes up."

"I've got him on camera, and there's no sign of a change from the sick room." Ford's voice carried up from the basement.

"Ford says Jerek's still sleeping," Jack said, relaying the message for Ari and Lincoln, the two in the kitchen stuck with somb hearing.

And sense of smell.

Sour surged up into Eve's throat again.

"Ford put cameras in Jerek and Mariah's room?" Lincoln asked.

"Six cameras on the roof, four at street level, and one in the sleeping magician room," Jack said. "If I'd ever dreamt of becoming a spy, I would be having the time of my life."

"Go big or go home," Ford shouted up the stairs.

"I think Ford may have dreamt of being a spy," Jack said.

"Oh, he did." Ari pulled her hair back, twisting it into a tight bun. "He glued pictures of his face into comic books."

"That's adorable," Jack said.

"He keeps them in his closet." Ari pulled on rubber kitchen gloves. "Blue bin, back right corner. I moved the best ones to the top of the collection. You can thank me when you see them."

"What the hell are you doing?" A flare of anger punched through Eve's chest. "If you're going to brag about digging through your boyfriend's closet, take it somewhere else."

"So you want to pry the heliostone from the corpse's

hands?" Ari moved to peel off the gloves. "Because I'm just trying really, really hard not to think about what I have to do."

Don't bait friends, Evelyn, Gran whispered at the back of Eve's mind.

"Sorry." Eve shoved her hands into her pockets to hide their shaking. "I'm sorry."

"Great." Ari turned back to the corpse. "Lincoln, can you grab me a salad bowl, or, I don't know, whatever the hell I'm supposed to put the heliostone in to wash it?"

"Wash it?" Lincoln said.

"We can't leave dead guy on a priceless artifact." Ari closed her eyes, exhaled, and shook out her shoulders. "There's a box tucked into the side of the blue bin where Ford hid all the pictures he cut his face out of."

"Really?" Jack said. "Should we be worried?"

"I don't think so." Ari moved closer to the archivist, her sneakers making a horrible, bone-grating peeling noise as she stepped through his blood. "It would be really creepy if we didn't know why he'd cut himself out of the photos, but since there was such an adorable purpose, I like to think of it more as high defacement decoupage."

"But why save the pictures?" Jack said.

"He wanted to keep the other people in them." Eve turned away as Ari reached for the magician's hands. She clutched the two moonstone pendants around her neck, closing her eyes, willing her body to stay calm.

"You're giving him too much credit." Ari raised her voice to shout. "Ford, tell them why you didn't throw out the pictures."

Crack. Crack.

Two small sounds.

Crunch. Crack.

Eve pressed her forehead to the wall as a sound like breaking bones stabbed into her ears.

A tiny noise, like a swallowed whimper came from Ari.

"They were pictures from computer camp," Ford called up the stairs. "I hated sleepaway camp. I didn't want to remember any of those narcissistic pig-twits, but the computer lab was great, and I had learned more about hacking than a ten-year-old should know, so I hid the cut-up pictures and kept telling my mom how excited I was to go back the next year."

"And?" Ari said.

"And it was because of that camp that I had the skills to find Ari," Ford said. "So now I keep the pictures to remind me that sometimes you have to go through hell to find heaven."

"Damn right, you do."

The clang of stone on metal came from behind Eve.

Steeling her stomach for horror, Eve turned around.

Lincoln held a mixing bowl in front of him, his lips thin and brow furrowed as he looked down at the heliostone.

"It doesn't look like the spell damaged it." Ari tipped her head as she studied the monstrosity that had gotten them all into this. "There are some singe marks, but, as morbid as it sounds, I think we can get them with dish soap."

"Why the hell do we care about scrubbing the heliostone!" The shout clawed up Eve's throat, burning away the taste of bile. "Smash the thing. Dump it into the Hudson where no one will ever find it."

"Eve," Lincoln said.

"I watched the heliostone work," Eve said. "I saw the magic that thing can do, and it needs to be destroyed."

Lincoln stepped toward her, still carrying the mixing bowl that held the heliostone. "Eve, take a breath."

"I can't take a breath, the kitchen reeks of the guy I killed!" Eve swung for the wall, not even registering pain as her fist went straight through the drywall to crack a wooden support beam.

She pulled her hand back out. Blood coated her knuckles.

It looked the same as the archivist's had when she'd slashed her claws through his gut.

But the blood smelled different.

Hers smelled like a wolf's. Meant to fight. Made to survive.

His had smelled delicate. Easy to spill. Not made to clot and heal during battle.

"Eve." Ari stepped toward her, holding out her empty hands.

She'd gotten rid of her gloves.

Eve hadn't heard her take off the gloves.

"Eve, I found a closet. Front room, fourth floor," Ari said. "The shelves are packed with bottles and tins. The archivist had stashed a few potions books with them, too. I don't know if the books have anything on healing or what the hell good it would do us with our two magicians out of commission, but maybe if we get lucky there'll be something we can do to wake Jerek and Mariah up."

"Fine." Eve pushed away from the wall and bolted up the stairs, fleeing the mess she'd made like the worthless coward she'd become.

5

Ari

Eve's footsteps thundered up the stairs as she fled the first floor.

Ari watched the kitchen door swing back and forth, waiting until it had stilled before letting her mind shift from worrying about Eve to the grisly task at hand.

"I can take care of washing the stone," Lincoln said.

"We just need dish soap and a toothbrush." Ari turned to Lincoln, trying to ignore the sound of her shoes sticking in the dried blood. "If it's good enough for my mom's many engagement rings, it should work for the heliostone, too."

"One problem off the list then." Lincoln set the mixing bowl on the counter.

"We still need it." Ari pulled her gloves back on.

"What for?" Lincoln looked at her, genuinely asking the question, making her point to the damn thing.

The archivist's chest had gone completely white, like the

life had been syphoned out of him, pulled into the red gem still stuck in the flesh right above his heart.

"Do we—" Lincoln scrunched his eyes shut. "Do we need the stone?"

"It's an amplifier." Ari shifted her weight to her toes as her body begged her to sprint from the room and not stop running until she reached the river. "It's a tool and a weapon, and with the list of people we've pissed off, I don't think we can afford to bury it with the body. If we can even find a place to bury a body in Manhattan. Which the internet is wholly failing me on. All I can find is a list of places hidden bodies have been found. Which is a great list of where not to shove a corpse, but the lack of helpful suggestions of places to stash a body feels like a personal betrayal right now."

"We'll figure it out." Lincoln stepped toward her, stopping just outside the worst of the archivist's dried blood puddle.

"You say that with such confidence, but I've never actually hidden a corpse before."

"Only a fool would doubt you." Lincoln raised his hand, reaching for her like he'd forgotten Ari was wearing contaminated gloves.

She held her hands up, keeping them out of his reach.

"I'll get the amplifier out of his chest," Lincoln said. "You step back for a minute."

"It's fine, I can do it."

"I'm a Maree."

"I didn't know the Maree covered desecration of human remains in Knight school." Ari let out a breath, shook out her fingers, and reached for the red gem.

"I meant it's my duty to protect the feu. If that means protecting you from the trauma of—"

"I'm a trauma champion." Ari pinched the red stone. Panic pounded against the shield of calm that kept her from screaming. She closed her eyes as she gave the stone a hard tug. It didn't budge. "Dammit."

"Are you okay?" Lincoln stepped closer, braving the dried blood.

"Trauma and coffee. The combination explains ninety percent of my personality." Forcing herself to watch, she pulled on the stone again. "It's really stuck in there. Can you pass me a butter knife?"

"Are you sure you don't want me to do it?" Lincoln kept his feet in place as he reached for the counter, grabbing a knife from the dish drainer.

"I've already made myself accept the fact that I'm touching a corpse." Ari took the knife, not bothering to banish the tears that brimmed in her eyes. "It's just that this could have been Jerek. If you hadn't stopped him, his corpse would have looked like this. No gashes from werewolf claws. But his hands would have been burned, and his chest would have been this awful white from the amplifier eating him alive. And just looking at this stupid red stone makes me want to scream."

She dug the tip of the knife in on the side of the amplifier. The stone shifted ever so slightly. She planted one hand on the archivist's shoulder, using her weight to leverage the knife farther under the stone.

With a tiny pop, the gem flew free, hitting a cabinet with a soft thunk.

A wave of disgust rolled through Ari's stomach.

"I see it." Lincoln's shoes peeled out of the blood. The sound didn't stop as he crossed the room.

The amplifier had landed in the corner.

Lincoln started reaching for it before freezing.

"There are extra gloves under the sink," Ari said.

"It's fine." Lincoln snatched the gem from the ground,

holding it in his bare hand like it hadn't come close to killing his best friend.

"Put it in the bowl with the heliostone. I'll soak them both." Ari pulled her gloves off as she backed away from the archivist. She laid them on the edge of the sink before hopping up to sit on a clean part of the counter. "I spotted some bleach upstairs. Hopefully we'll get lucky and find a mop, too."

"I can look around." Lincoln placed the amplifier in the bowl and started the tap, letting the water from scrubbing his hands begin soaking the gems.

Ari peeled off her shoes, placing them bloody-side up on the counter. "Some rags would be great, too."

"I don't mean to be the asshole—"

Ari's heart rammed up into her throat as Jack spoke through the basement door.

"—but is it worth mopping up before we get rid of the dead dude? If we need"—Jack paused—"smaller pieces to dispose of, we'll just mess up the floor again."

A ping of panic punctured Ari's calm.

"If we have to mop up again, we'll mop up again," Lincoln said. "We can't just let this keep sitting here. It's bad enough that he's starting to stink. Eve shouldn't have to walk past it to get to the basement."

Ari stuck her hand under the tap, seeking a hint of salvation. She ignored the impurities of the chemically treated water, letting her heart settle back into a steady rhythm, allowing herself to whisper lies into her own mind, promising herself unflinching strength.

"I can get rid of the smell." Ari pulled her bloodstained shoes back on.

"Ford says he looked up the instructions for getting rid of a body with acid," Jack began.

"No acid needed." Ari hopped off the counter, not giving

herself time to think as she crossed through the archivist's blood and placed her bare hand on his chest.

Pushing past the cold of his skin, she felt for a hint of familiar freedom.

The water in his body had sunk into his legs, stagnant, trapped.

Her body screamed for her to back away.

You can't.

A spring. A clean, pure spring.

Ari painted the scene in her mind. Trees casting shade over the water.

Water she longed to touch.

That was the water she wanted. That was the water she tried to convince her mind waited just beyond her reach.

But the feel of the water was wrong. Foul. Tainted.

Stuck in a dead monster's body.

Her hand trembled as loathing thrummed through her being.

You've done worse things, Ariel Love.

She called the corpse's water to his chest. Pulling it from his veins, his fat, his heart—every trace she could find drawn to the hole the amplifier had bored into his chest.

Eyes still closed, she lifted her hand, hovering it an inch away from the terrible wound, luring the water out into the open, free from the horror of being trapped in the macabre tomb.

She pulled her hand farther away, moving slowly, carefully, not stopping until she couldn't feel the archivist anymore, only the water, pure water, free from its magician cage.

Letting out a long breath, she released her hold on the magic.

The water fell to the ground, splashing her shoes.

She didn't bother trying to hide the shaking of her hands as she opened her eyes and backed away from the desiccated corpse.

Mouth wide, leathery skin taut, the archivist looked closer to a mummy than a person who'd been breathing only a day ago.

"If you'll excuse me, I have to burn my shoes and scrub a few layers of skin off my body." Ari embraced the numbness that encased her mind as she walked out of the kitchen, leaving the rest of the mess for someone else to clean up.

6

Jack

Using his fingers to pry the lids off crates had never been on Jack's list of reasons he was grateful to be a vampire, but as he ripped the twelfth crate open, he had to admit it was a definite benefit.

Round, bubble-wrapped things took up the top layer of this crate.

"Perfect," Jack said.

"What's that?" Ford said.

"More bubble wrap." Jack picked up the table, carrying it to the crate.

"It seems a waste to unwrap everything." Ford didn't look away from his newly arranged bank of security camera monitors as he spoke. "Moving a massive amount of magical objects would be less of a nightmare if the objects were still wrapped."

"I'm happy to stop digging through this whenever you want." Jack lifted the first two things from the crate.

"We can't stop," Ford said. "That's the problem."

"How do you mean?"

The first bubble-wrapped item was a thing that looked like a green, spikey paperweight.

Jack snapped a picture on Ari's phone.

"We're a snowball," Ford said.

Jack watched Ford, waiting for him to keep speaking, but Ford stayed silent, completely focused on the monitors like he hadn't said a word.

"Can't say I've ever been called a snowball before." Jack pulled the bubble wrap off a carved wooden thing that looked almost like a tower.

Ford flipped open his laptop and began typing.

"Ford," Jack said, "why are we a snowball?"

"Because we started down the slope, and now we can't stop." Ford glanced at Jack. "And the farther down the hill we go, the bigger our collective snowball gets, which makes it even harder to stop."

"Until we crash into something." Jack set the tower aside.

"But is our snowball going to get smashed, or are we going to destroy everything in our path?"

"Neither." Jack abandoned the crate, refusing to feel guilty for the hint of joy that bubbled in his chest as he laid his hands on Ford's shoulders. "We're going to figure out how to save the world from our saving the world."

"And if that doesn't work out?"

"Then we sell all the artifacts in these crates and bolt for a country with no extradition treaties." Jack kissed the top of Ford's head.

"No extradition treaties and a good nightlife. I'll start making a list."

Jack gave Ford's shoulders a gentle squeeze before brushing away the butterflies in his stomach to go back to digging through crates.

The next mass of bubble wrap held a turquoise glass bowl that looked like it belonged in a fifties somb house.

"Are we sure the archivist wasn't just a hoarder?" Jack said.

"As far as I can tell, the archivist never even existed," Ford said.

"The corpse in the kitchen says otherwise." Jack pulled out the next package in the crate.

"I mean before he became *the archivist*. I've been looking through magician records, trying to figure out his real name, but he definitely wasn't a Manhattan-born feu."

"Maybe he ran away to the big city." Jack chose another item from the crate. The objects inside the bundle shifted as he unwrapped it.

"For the amount this house cost, he could have built a badass compound in the woods with much better storage space for nefarious magical objects."

The things inside the bundle had been wrapped in thick, black canvas, which had been tied closed with a leather strap.

"Maybe we're looking at protecting this stash all wrong," Ford said.

Jack untied the strap, running his thumb over a divot in the leather where someone had embossed a badly shaped *O* around a lowercase *t*.

"Don't move the party, rebrand the club. Same music, new bouncers, new DJ," Ford said. "It's such a bad idea, it might loop back around to brilliant."

Jack unrolled the canvas, laying it out on the table. "I think we should talk to Ari first."

"Obviously I'd have to run something this big by her."

"I meant about the bloody knives."

"The what?" Ford actually looked away from his monitors.

Using the bottom of his shirt, Jack held up one of the knives.

Blade broken, the knife looked like something from a film where the hero's weapon is shattered by the force of the villain's evil.

"Is that a crest on the handle?" Ford glanced back and forth between the monitors and the knives, like he was trying to give himself whiplash.

Jack turned the blade. A flaming shield marked the hilt.

"Not just any crest." Jack set the blade back down and re-tied the bundle. "All of these are marked with the crest of the Knights Maree."

7

Lincoln

The wood of the bathroom door hadn't been marred by the archivist's death or any other bloody, terrible thing. The light paint didn't even have any chips in it.

If he ignored the stench of cleaner that had thankfully replaced the scent of rot stuck in his nose, Lincoln might have been in a normal house, standing outside a normal bathroom, where a normal girl had just gotten out of the shower.

Lincoln raised his hand to knock...and froze.

Ari was on the other side of that door. Wrapped in a towel.

But would she even need a towel to dry off?

If she didn't...

"You're a Knight Maree," Lincoln whispered. "Act like it."

He knocked on the door.

"Did you find something?" Ari called.

A floorboard creaked as she stepped closer to the door. The knob turned.

Lincoln opened his mouth, trying to shout a warning, but his voice wouldn't work as Ari opened the door.

She'd wrapped a towel loosely around herself, holding the front of it with one hand, leaving the rest to droop behind her, showing the sides of her breasts.

And the length—no towel should ever be that short. Shorter than any skirt. Showing her legs, stopping barely below—

"Where's Eve?" Ari leaned to the side, peeking behind Lincoln to the closet of vials and boxes Eve had been ransacking.

That slight movement shifted the towel, showing even more of her breasts.

Lincoln pinned his gaze to the doorframe above Ari's head. "In the kitchen."

"With the archivist?" Ari let go of the door, stepping fully out into the small corridor that led from the bathroom to the bedroom.

A tiny space.

Too cramped for two people to stand together.

"Lincoln?" Ari tapped his chest.

He glanced down.

She'd loosened her hold on the towel, like she'd forgotten how incredibly important it was for her to maintain a firm grip on the fabric.

"I wrapped the archivist in a sheet." Lincoln forced his gaze back up. "I scrubbed down the kitchen, wrapped him up, and put him in a closet. I think Eve was waiting for me to be done. She kicked me out as soon as I'd rechecked the floor for any stubborn stains."

"You didn't have to do that by yourself."

"I didn't want it to fall back on you. You've already done enough."

"Hey"—Ari took Lincoln's chin, tipping his face down, making him look into her teal eyes—"thank you."

She leaned closer, brushing a kiss on his cheek. She didn't back away.

Heat flooded Lincoln's face.

"I'm sorry I lost it down there," Ari said. "I don't know if I can actually describe how awful reaching into his body felt."

Her shoulders tensed, she tucked her head onto his chest, rounding herself into him as though seeking comfort, or protection, or both.

Hold her, you fool. Just hold her.

Lincoln wrapped his arms around her. But her back was bare. The towel had drooped too low to conceal that glorious expanse.

She didn't flinch as his hands touched her divinely soft skin. She leaned against him, nestling into the embrace.

"Are you okay?" she whispered.

The weight of corpses and battles and family and broken vows crashed back down onto Lincoln's chest, speeding his heart as it pressed the air from his lungs.

"I have to be okay," Lincoln said. "We all do. We don't have a choice."

"I know." Ari leaned back, looking up at him. "But if you need to hide in the shower for a few minutes, I won't judge."

"Did it help?"

"A little. At least I feel clean."

"Good."

Say something better than good.

"Good," he said again.

"You should hop in," Ari said. "Before the next disaster."

"I might be too late," Lincoln said.

"Why?" Ari took a step back, angling toward the bedroom door as though waiting for an attack.

"Jack asked me to bring you to the basement." Lincoln held out his hand, like that offer of comfort could somehow ease the panic that flared in her eyes. "Then Eve said she was almost ready for you in the kitchen. I tried asking what for, but she looked ready to grab for her moonstones. I thought it best to just come upstairs to get you."

"Okay." Ari took his hand, closing her eyes for a moment. "I'll grab clean clothes and be right down."

"I'll see if I can find any coffee."

"Thanks."

A flutter flickered through Lincoln's chest as the tiniest of smiles lifted the corners of Ari's lips.

"I was going to steal some, too," Lincoln said.

Ari opened her eyes.

Stupid. How are you so stupid, Martel?

"I meant for letting me be not okay for a minute." She kissed the back of his hand. "Let me know when you need me to return the favor."

She squeezed past Lincoln and out of the little corridor, into the bedroom they'd stolen the mattress from the night before.

"Tell Eve and Jack I'll be right down." She crossed to her pink pack in the corner, the bottom edge of her towel teasing the tops of her thighs. "Close your eyes if you don't want a show, Maree."

She let go of the towel.

He dodged out of the room and slammed the door behind him. His heart raced, his breath catching in his throat as he leaned against the wall.

As he dug his knuckles into his eyes, trying to blur out the image of the most perfectly shaped bottom he'd ever imagined, he could have sworn he heard a faint laugh drifting through the door.

8

Eve

If she hadn't known the kitchen had belonged to an evil, murdering magician, she might have guessed she was pulling through the cupboards of a wannabe chef. The stash of colanders and strainers in the cupboards could've drained a spaghetti dinner for the whole pack.

She grabbed a strainer from the top of the stack, slamming the cupboard closed before she had a chance to wonder if the archivist had ever made dinner for the butcher who murdered her family.

"You okay?" Lincoln looked up from the coffee maker he'd been jabbing at, trying to make the rich people shit work.

"Are you really going to ask me that?" Eve dropped the strainer onto the counter with a satisfying clang.

"At the risk of you tearing out my throat, yes." Lincoln unplugged and replugged the coffee maker.

"Then no, I'm not." Eve snatched the wooden spoon off the

counter, forcefully gentling her grip as the handle threatened to snap. Focusing on careful movements, she stirred the bubbling contents of the stew pot.

"Want to talk about it?" Lincoln smacked the side of the coffee maker.

"No, I don't want to talk about how I left my pack to finally tear apart the monster who murdered my family and all I've accomplished is killing the only person I've found who might have been able to lead me to the son-of-a-bitch that blew up my little brother."

The spoon snapped in half.

"Sweet, naïve Eve." Ari pushed opened the swinging door, pausing to glance over the pristine white floor before stepping barefoot into the kitchen.

"Ari," Lincoln whispered as a rumble rose in Eve's throat.

Ari ignored him as she breezed over to the coffeemaker. "You speak as though by removing the archivist from the column of the living, you've also removed all his knowledge from the column marked *available to us.*"

"Death does that." Eve stepped away from the stove, pressing her hands to her thighs where she couldn't break anything but herself.

"In a non-digital world, maybe." Ari pressed a button on the coffee maker. She held it down for a count of two. The coffee maker beeped. She pressed two more buttons before speaking again. "If we only had the books and records in this house, our chances of finding something that could lead us to the mystery *they* and the butcher might have been iffy. But this is a digital world, and you've got Ford and me working on your side.

"We're not stuck, Eve. If anything, taking over the archives has given us too much information to comb through. But never fear, we're going to pursue every possible lead. We just need time and coffee."

With a bleep and a hiss, the coffee started to brew.

"That would have been so much cooler a second earlier." Ari frowned. "So what did you want to show me?"

"Right." Eve spread her fingers wide, making sure she could control her hands before stepping back toward the stove. "I may have a way to wake Jerek and Mariah up. For all I know, it could kill them, but I think the logic makes sense."

"*Could kill* is better than *will kill*." Ari started opening the cupboards. "So what's the idea?"

"Feu heal," Eve said. "Wolves, magicians, vampires, nymphs—we heal faster than sombs."

"Even divs get the healing mojo." Ari pulled down mugs. "Coffee for four, right?"

"The shit of it is all our bodies shut down while we heal," Eve said. "We get forced to sleep while the supernatural parts of us patch our bodies back together."

"Inconvenient but true," Ari said.

"But, as a wolf, I know that if I'm going to do something dangerous, shift first. If I'm going to do something stupid, wait for the full moon."

"Interesting," Lincoln said.

A flare of anger lurched through Eve's gut as instinct screamed for her to attack. Slaughter the Maree who seemed so interested in wolf business.

She latched her focus on to the pot simmering on the stove. "The stronger the magic running through me when I'm hurt, the faster I'll heal. I got gut shot in full wolf form once. I was healed before I finished tearing the hunter's trigger hand off."

"Fitting vengeance," Ari said.

"But most cryptids don't have the ability to up their power level like that. They have what they have, and that's it," Eve said. "It's the same with magicians."

"I have a feeling I'm about to really love this *but*," Ari whispered.

"But"—Eve leaned into the word—"the archivist seemed to like beefing up the little magic the Fracture left him with."

"Awfully sketchy for a guy who wanted to get rid of magic," Ari said.

"It gets worse." Eve pointed to the journal on the counter. "This handwritten shit was in with the other potion books. The most spattered and crinkled page was for the *stamina and vigor tonic*."

"I think I just puked in my mouth." Ari leaned against the counter, eyes closed, face contorted with disgust.

"Do we really need to discuss the archivist's"—blood rushed to Lincoln's cheeks—"activities?"

"You just made it worse," Ari said.

"But *vigor and stamina* sounds a lot like the kind of thing that could boost the power in a magician's body enough to speed up healing," Eve said. "Creeper had all the supplies in his closet."

"The stinky stew is the potion." Ari held her hair back as she leaned in to look at the contents of the pot.

"*If* I'm right," Eve said, "getting some of this into Jerek should help him wake up faster."

"Or it could interfere with his natural healing process and hurt him," Lincoln said.

"Kill him," Eve said. "Potentially. Watching that magic was bad enough. Actually performing the spell that mended the Fracture has to have done some pretty serious damage."

"Then we wait for Jerek and Mariah to wake up on their own," Lincoln said.

"For how long?" Eve rounded on Lincoln. "Do we let Holden sleep for a week? Two?"

"He could wake up on his own in a few hours," Lincoln said.

"Or he could sleep through the best chance of finding the butcher we have left." Eve let her anger flash through her eyes.

The Maree winced.

"It's great that there *might* be some information we *might* somehow be able to drag out of the archivist's hoard or digital life, but when the butcher finds out we killed the archivist, what are the chances he goes to ground?" Eve planted her feet, her weight on her toes, her body begging her to attack. "We cannot risk the butcher going into hiding. We have to find him now. Holden would agree."

"We can't trust Jerek to make decisions about his own safety," Lincoln said.

"Of course the Maree doesn't understand that some risks are worth it," Eve said.

"Enough, Eve," Ari shouted, like Eve had been shouting, too.

A growl rumbled in Eve's throat.

"You're right," Ari said. "Jerek would want to take the risk and try to wake up sooner."

"So I'll give him the potion." Eve turned back to the stove.

"Ari—"

"We just poured magic back out into the world," Ari said. "The butcher is a mass murderer who I'm willing to bet is a part of the *they* who wanted magic gone for good. *They* wanted magic gone, *they* like to murder people, and we just pissed *they* off. If the butcher starts killing people again and we didn't even try to wake Jerek up so he could help Eve hunt down the monster, I couldn't blame him for never forgiving us."

Lincoln dug his fingers into his scalp.

"It's not just about revenge," Ari said. "We have to protect whoever the butcher might go after next."

"Someone has to sit with him." Lincoln dragged his hands down his face. "If his heart explodes—"

"There'll be shit we can do about it." Eve grabbed a ladle from the drawer.

"He shouldn't be alone," Lincoln said.

A hint of worry and fear scratched the shield of satisfying anger encasing Eve's chest.

"We have to get down to see what Jack found," Ari said.

"I'll grab Holden and dose him in the basement," Eve said.

"He should be kept in a bed," Lincoln said.

"Nobody asked your opinion, Maree." Eve shut off the stove and headed upstairs, ignoring the itch in her fingers that begged her to let them become claws.

9

Ari

Ari fluffed the pillow under Jerek's head, like that could somehow make laying him on the concrete basement floor less bad.

"What did you need us down here for?" Lincoln asked.

"Four things." Ford frowned. "No. No, five things."

"Shouldn't we wait until after Eve doses Jerek?" Jack asked.

"It's going to take forever to dribble this down Holden's throat," Eve said. "Start talking."

"Well, I found—" Jack began as Ford said, "To start off—"

"Sorry." Ford went back to staring at his monitors. "You go first."

"Thanks." Jack stepped closer to the table. "I'm genuinely hoping these have nothing to do with any of our problems, but I've learned to accept that we're not that lucky."

He unrolled a piece of black canvas, pursing his lips as he displayed the seven broken knives inside.

"Those are Maree blades." Lincoln reached out to touch one.

"You probably shouldn't do that." Jack knocked Lincoln's hand away. "There's dried blood on them. Never touch a bloody weapon with your bare hands."

"Germs?" Ford said.

"Fingerprints," Jack said. "I figured they were Maree, what with the Maree crest on the hilts, but what I don't understand is why the archivist would hang on to these."

Ari left Jerek to kneel beside the table, getting a level view of the knives. "I don't think they're magic-wrought."

"They aren't." Lincoln knelt beside Ari. "But they are pre-Fracture."

"How can you tell?" Jack asked.

"The guard on the handle." Lincoln pointed. "After the Fracture, the Maree started using an Italian somb weapons maker. The new knives have a rounded edge on the guard."

"Any chance the blades on the old knives were known to shatter?" Ari asked.

"Not that I've ever heard of," Lincoln said. "The older knives are a point of pride for Maree who still have them."

"Which loops right back to who broke the knives and why ruined weapons were worth saving," Jack said.

Ari pressed her forehead to the top of the table. "Any chance Maree knives have serial numbers?"

They needed a lab. If Ari could find a forensic scientist, flirt or bribe her way into getting the blood on the knives tested...

To compare to what?

"A knife like that would be hard for even a cryptid to break," Eve said. "Why would someone bother?"

Lincoln sat back on his heels. "It could be mirroring a dishonorable dismissal from the Knights Maree."

"What does that mean?" Jack asked.

A weight, like a blanket of fatigue, seemed to settle on Lincoln, sinking his shoulders and dulling his eyes.

"Traditionally in the Knights Maree, if you received a dishonorable dismissal, your sword would be shattered," Lincoln said. "Maree swords used to be imbued with the kinds of magic that allowed knights to effectively fight feu. Losing their sword upon dismissal broke the dishonored knight's connection to the Maree and left them defenseless against the feu."

Ari slid closer to Lincoln, laying her hand on his leg as pain joined the exhaustion in his eyes.

"Since the Fracture, the shattering of the blade is no longer part of the banishment ceremony," Lincoln said. "There aren't enough weapons for any to be wasted by being intentionally broken. There aren't even enough magic-wrought weapons to go around. Most of the stockpile was lost during the quests to find the source of the Fracture. They didn't even issue me a proper weapon when I was assigned to protect Jerek."

"Seven knives that could possibly mirror an out-of-date Maree ritual," Ari said. "Great."

"What if they're someone's collateral?" Eve asked, spoon in one hand, Jerek's head in the other. "The blood on those blades came from seven different people."

"How do you know?" Lincoln asked.

"They smell different," Jack said. "Like the difference between dried apples and dried papaya."

"Not how I was going to describe it, but yeah," Eve said. "Seven bloody knives probably means seven corpses."

"Which points to a very busy murderer," Ari said.

Lincoln took her hand.

"I liked it better when we were going with *villain*," Ford said.

"The butcher of Blood Mountain is a mass murderer," Eve said. "Someone who stabs seven people and saves the knives—"

"Is a serial killer hoarding trophies," Ari said. "Shit."

"If a serial killer handed their trophies to the archivist, it would've been their collateral," Eve said.

"So, whether or not it's got anything to do with the Fracture," Ari said, "we're now morally obligated to figure out if one of the archivist's patrons is still stabbing people for funsies."

"Does it make me awful that I really, *really* hope these are LeBlanc's trophies?" Jack said. "Or at least the butcher's. Or that we can prove LeBlanc is the butcher. I don't want to add catching a non-Fracture related serial killer to our to-do list."

"*Seven dead* sucks," Eve said. "But they can't come before finding the butcher and the *they* who sent the butcher to murder my pack."

"She's right," Ari said. "We shouldn't have to look at body counts of bad guys—"

"But that's the shit hand we've been dealt." Jack flipped the canvas wrapping over the shattered knives. "I'll make a special folder in our photo archives for potential murder weapons."

"My turn?" Ford asked.

"Yes." Eve dripped more potion into Jerek's mouth.

"First of all"—Ford swept a hand toward his bank of monitors—"welcome to the Archives Defender 24000. Twenty-four thousand, because that's how much of Jerek's money this setup cost."

"He won't care." Ari stood, getting a better view of the screens.

"The video feeds are arranged to mirror the cameras' positions around the house in what I hope is an easy-to-follow manner," Ford said. "I will eventually pass out from fatigue, so whoever is going to take the next shift should have me walk them through how it works before I do."

"I can take the next shift," Ari said.

"Great," Ford said. "Start an invoice to hand in to Jerek now, because the second thing is that watching these monitors, trying to decide who's a somb going about their day and who might be coming to kill us, is paranoia-inducing, and there's no way I'll be able to pay for enough therapy to handle this trauma on my own."

"Noted," Ari said.

"Third," Ford pressed on, "I think I may have found the origin of our mysterious archivist, and none of you are going to be happy about it."

"Why will I not be happy about it, Ford?" Ari asked.

"Actually." Ford's shoulders tensed. "Let's circle back to number three."

"What?" Ari leaned over Ford's shoulder, trying to catch a glimpse of what he'd been looking at on his actual laptop screen.

"Hmm." Ford glanced up at Ari, winced, and looked back at his computer. "Okay, number four. I've figured out how to protect the archives."

"Oh no," Jack whispered.

"Congratulations may be in order." Ford raised his coffee cup to toast the air. "You're looking at the new archivist."

10

Ford

Ford held his breath, waiting for the room to explode.

"What the hell are you talking about?" Ari said.

"Why don't I have a turn watching the monitors?" Jack took Ford's shoulders, turning his chair around and making him stand to face Ari.

"Ford?" There was no excitement or intrigue in Ari's eyes.

"Okay." Ford held up his hands, backing away from the monitor bank to give Jack his place. "But please wait until after you've heard the whole idea to tell me you hate it."

"Fine." Ari folded her arms and sat on the table, right beside the canvas-wrapped, broken daggers.

"We can't move the whole collection," Ford said. "Not discreetly enough to protect the secrecy of the feu. If we try to do it all ourselves, there's no way we'll finish before we're caught. And even the highest-end concierge movers probably shouldn't be handling a crate with seven potential murder weapons."

"I'll accept that reasoning." Ari's tone didn't lighten.

"As this house shares walls with the neighboring properties, we can't move the whole house," Ford said.

"You actually looked into that?" Eve wiped dribbled potion off Jerek's face with the collar of his own shirt.

"I like to explore all possibilities." Ford shrugged. "But like I said, can't be done."

"And how did the shocking revelation that we couldn't move a four-story house with a basement out of Manhattan end with you becoming the new archivist, Ford Roscoe?" Ari said.

Sweat beaded on Ford's brow. "If the archivist's patrons keep thinking he's here, one of them is going to show up looking for answers as to why magic has suddenly popped back into the world. We can try to fight them off without attracting the attention of New York's finest, but if they survive—"

"They wouldn't," Eve said.

"No," Jack said. "No more dead bodies in the house."

An ass-cramping growl rumbled in Eve's throat.

"The point is"—Ford's voice pitched too high—"once the archivist's patrons start popping by, it's only a matter of time before they figure out the archivist is dead and a pack of teens is now in charge of their deepest darkest secrets, not to mention whatever other potentially cataclysmic power comes from having all the books and artifacts in this house."

"Patrons start whispering to other patrons, and we end up with a battle on our hands." Ari dug her fingers into her shimmering blond hair. "Very not ideal."

"A magical battle in Manhattan is the kind of catastrophe the Knights Maree have spent centuries trying to prevent," Lincoln said.

"Like I said, not ideal."

"Which leaves us with abandoning the archives," Ford said.

"No," Eve said.

"Or bringing the archives under new management." Ford spread his arms wide, making his smile endearingly bright while the others, except for Jack at the monitor bank and Jerek with his eyes closed, stared at him. "We quietly spread word that the archivist sold his collection to me. We can create a nice paper trail and everything. Make it painfully clear that the deal they had with the former archivist still stands. Cross me, and I'll expose your darkest secrets."

"We don't know what secrets people gave as collateral," Eve said.

"They don't need to know that," Lincoln said.

Ari shot a glare his way.

"We set up as much insurance for ourselves as we can and dare them to defy me. Convince the patrons the only chance they have of protecting their secrets is to protect their new archivist and the archives." Ford rocked back on his heels. "It can't be any of you, so that leaves me." He tried to smile again. "Your friendly new archivist."

"It's too dangerous," Ari said.

"Not any worse than sitting here waiting to get attacked," Eve said.

"Absolutely not." Ari shifted her glare to Eve. "Once we attach your face to the archives, it can't be undone."

"Ari, don't." Ford swallowed, taking a breath, removing the anger from his voice. "We can't afford to be naïve about this. If the Maree haven't figured out who the random somb with Jerek Holden's crew is yet, they will. My face is already attached to this."

"I can work the records," Ari said.

"It won't be enough."

"We can give you a doppelganger identity." Ari stood. "We'll set the Maree on the double's track."

"Maybe you could buy me time. But the Maree would find the real me eventually." Ford reached for Ari's hand. "I don't get to just fly home when this is over. Best case scenario, I end up being watched by the Maree for the rest of my life."

"No." Ari shook her head, sending her hair fluttering around her shoulders in an unhuman way. "I'm not going to let that happen."

"Too late, Love." Ford took her hand. "I'm all in."

Ari stared into his eyes for a long moment, testing him, begging him to give in. Finally, she pressed her lips to the back of his hand and nodded.

He tucked her hair behind her ear, kissed her forehead, and whispered, "Never forget this was my choice."

Blinking back the heat in his eyes, he stepped away from her to face the strangely silent group.

"On to more cheerful"—Ford winced and frowned—"cheerful's a bad word...less emotional turmoil-inducing news. Number five."

"What happened to three?" Lincoln stepped closer to Ari.

Ford let go of her, moving away as he gave a grand, sweeping gesture toward Jerek. "First, could someone with supernatural strength lay Jerek on the table?"

"I just finished dribbling potion into his mouth," Eve said. "We should leave him be for a while."

"Please indulge me," Ford said. "I promise, it will be worth it."

"I do swimming, not lifting," Ari said.

"I've got him." Eve scooped Jerek off the floor like he weighed no more than a blowup doll.

Ford carefully moved the bundle of broken knives aside while Ari placed Jerek's pillow.

As Eve lowered Jerek to the table, he groaned, like he was sleeping and someone had stolen his blanket.

Eve froze.

"Jerek," Ari said. "Jerek!"

He gave another sleepy groan.

"Eve," Ari said, "you may in fact be a genius in the realm of creepy potions."

"A skill I always wanted." Eve laid Jerek down, taking a moment to settle his arms by his sides before turning to Ford. "Are we back to thing three yet?"

"Almost." Ford pointed to the stretch of concrete where Jerek had lain only moments before. "Behold, the perfect place to dispose of a desiccated corpse. The plans and maps I've found all agree—there are no pipes, wires, or other things workers should have to dig for in that section of the basement. And, as Jerek so kindly demonstrated, it's the perfect length for laying out a body."

"But this is where I'm stuck all day," Jack said. "You're going to turn my daylight space into the Tell-Tale Heart?"

"People get caught with bodies hidden in their basement all the time in America," Lincoln said. "This would be the worst place to hide a body."

"Hmm." Ford pursed his lips. "I don't know what American media the Maree show their kids, but that's not accurate. People get caught with bodies in their basement, sure. But they have to screw up or move, or have someone track a victim's movements—"

"Or have their basement flood," Eve said.

"That, too," Ford said. "But compared to the rest of our options, that stretch of floor is our best body disposal site available."

"Shit," Jack said.

"Which leads me to thing three," Ford said.

"That wasn't three?" Ari said.

"No, that was five," Ford said. "Now we're looping back around to three."

"How are we still listening to him talk?" Danger glinted in Eve's eyes.

"That's great." Ford backed toward Lincoln and Ari. "Keep that rage, and direct it."

"What?"

"I found the archivist's real name. Patrick Davis. I've prepared a dossier on the late archivist." Ford pointed to the stack of papers on the desk beside Jack, using the excuse to take another step away from Eve. "Patrick was born in California but spent time in France and Italy studying magical antiquities."

"Fits with his hoard," Ari said.

"The last trace of Patrick Davis I can find is three years before the Fracture," Ford pressed on. "His last known location under that name lines up with one of LeBlanc's last missions before his missing time. They were in North Carolina."

Eve's face went white. "They were near my home. Those two bastards were near my home, and I can't make the archivist tell me why."

"If you could please direct your oncoming terrifying rage toward the concrete we need to break through, we could—"

The sound of Eve's fist smashing into concrete cut off the rest of Ford's words.

Grace

"Shit." Grace dug her hands farther into her pockets, trying to ignore the sooty texture that covered her clothes. "Shit. Shit."

A place to hide.

A place to hide.

How hard could it be to find a place to hide?

Grace kept walking, weaving her way through the rundown neighborhood beyond the warehouses.

See a fancy coffee shop, head in that direction.

See a drug deal, go back the other way.

Back to where, you stupid shit?

Not back to her parents.

She just scorched a warehouse of Maree.

I killed people. Holy shit, I killed people.

The Maree would never stop looking for her.

Even the somb police could be looking for her.

Arson. Murder.

No, self-defense.

Shit. It doesn't matter.

Panic pressed against the front of Grace's throat, cutting off her supply of air.

You can breathe, Grace. You know how to breathe.

In four, hold seven, out eight. In four, hold seven, out eight.

A mom with two girls got out of her car. The mom had a decent purse. Clean shoes. Both the girls had phones.

Grace followed them.

A place to lie low.

That was step one. Get out of sight, figure out what to do next.

But hotels wanted money. And homes had locks. And stores looked at the soot-covered girl like they were going to call the cops.

"Shit," Grace murmured. "Shit. Shit. Shit."

The mother and two girls stopped in front of a restaurant. The sign out front highlighted their açai bowls.

Grace continued in the same direction even after the mother and girls went into the restaurant where they would eat food. Wonderful food.

Food Grace didn't have money to buy.

You're a magician. Find a way to get the food without money.

By lighting everything on fire?

"Shit." She cut down the next alley, tucking herself behind a dumpster that smelled like rotted meat, risking taking a minute to think.

Going back to her parents was off the table. No way in hell she could put her dads in that kind of danger.

Tears spilled down Grace's cheeks.

She couldn't go to any of her friends, either.

Sun Palms was officially off limits.

No family. No friends. No home. No money.

No bed. No shower.

No food.

"Shit."

Jerek wouldn't have to hide behind a dumpster.

Jerek would have crossed state lines in the van and booked a hotel room where he could order tons of room service.

Grace's stomach growled.

"Shut up," Grace whispered.

Money. That made the difference between hiding in an alley and escaping to a hotel room.

Money is flammable, Grace. If you try to rob a bank, you'll burn the whole place down.

But Jerek didn't have to rob banks. He just had money and Ari to book the hotel reservations and a van to move his crew around.

"I'm an idiot." Grace hiccupped through her tears. "An impossible, doomed idiot."

A man on a bike whizzed down the alley, not even noticing Grace.

A bike. She could steal a bike.

"And ride to the corner store?"

She needed to find the crew. Find them. Apologize for everything. Beg for forgiveness. Hope they took her back. Hope they'd keep her safe.

The blast of a horn scared Grace from her hiding place. She bolted down the alley, heading to the road on the far side.

She cut left, sprinting past a storefront church and a bridal boutique.

A little boy stopped, pointing at Grace as she approached. "Mommy, what happened to her?"

"Don't play with matches, kid." Grace dodged past them,

cutting around the corner, stumbling onto the blessed normality of a mainstream mega store.

"Find the crew." Grace strode through the automatic doors into the airconditioned bliss. "That's only one task, Grace Esther Lee-Weiss. You can do one thing."

12

Jerek

The pounding in his head drummed through his thoughts, breaking them into pieces that didn't quite make sense.

Wake up.

He needed to wake up.

His heart thumped.

A happy rhythm. Lively. Visceral.

Heat.

He really should wake up.

Heat burned through his whole body.

No. Heat wasn't right.

Burned wasn't right, either.

Bright. Wonderful.

A radiant glow that flowed through him.

Filled his veins.

Pushed at his fingertips.

Driving against his palms. His hands.

Power pressing at the outermost reaches of his being, longing to break free.

Freedom. Bliss.

Letting the power go promised bliss.

"Jer—"

A noise cut through the pounding in his head.

"Jerek. Jerek!"

Light burned into his skull as his eyes flew open.

"You're awake." A voice, familiar but somehow terrifying, spoke from right beside him. "Take it slow, don't try to move. I'm not sure how Eve's potion affected you."

Eve. Potion.

The words didn't pair well.

"Can you hear me, Jerek?" Pale gold floated in front of his eyes, blocking the shimmering light above. "Jerek?"

Something touched his arm.

Something cold.

No. Fresh.

No.

Boundless and deep beyond all reason.

Cool and wonderful and freezing and deadly.

"Jerek?" The boundless being touched his cheek. "Jerek?"

"Unnnh." He made his voice work.

"Good," the boundless said. "Just take a minute. Let yourself wake up. We're safe for now. The archivist is dead—"

Awareness. The sharp, jagged need to understand stabbed through his mind.

"—mess I'll have to explain, which I'm not looking forward to," the boundless said, "but for now, just breathe."

He took a deep breath. Pain sliced through his lungs, clearing his vision.

Ari stood over him, worried wrinkles on her brow, her hand

on his arm. Her hand radiated the boundless joy—not joy, the yearning to explore and know and cherish all wound together into one soul-consuming need.

"Ari." Jerek scrunched his eyes shut, trying to shove the pieces of his thoughts back together.

"Take your time," Ari said.

"The archives...archivist." Jerek's eyes flew back open as panic snapped through his being. "The spell." He tried to sit up. Ari pressed her hand to his chest, keeping him down. "The spell to mend the Fracture. The archivist was dying, we had to—"

"Take a breath, Jer Bear." Ari took his hand, flooding a fresh wave of the boundless through his being. "Explaining the mess we're in is going to take a while."

"Mess?" Jerek looked around the room.

A dining room, where he lay on the table, stretched out beside Ari's laptop.

"Less literal in this part of the house," Ari said. "But the basement wasn't a great place for you to rest right now, so Lincoln and I carried you up here. We were aiming for a bedroom, but after the first flight of stairs, I thought we'd hauled you far enough."

"Where's Eve? Why couldn't she help?"

Ari wrinkled her nose. "Why don't I get you a glass of water?"

"I'm fine." Jerek pushed himself onto his elbows. "Where's Eve?"

"Eve's fine. But, based on the table I should hold off on throwing you face-first into the chaos." Ari pointed to the table beside Jerek's hand.

The wood around his palm shifted from orange to black to deep, deep blue.

"Take a breath." Ari stepped back. "Find your inner calm.

Just don't open any closets. I'm not sure which one Lincoln shoved the corpse into."

13

Ari

"Which is why Jack is going to keep digging through the crates as soon as he's done making sure Eve doesn't break through anything in the basement that might collapse the house on top of us."

Jerek leaned back in his chair and dragged his hand over the stubble on his chin, leaving a faint red hue behind. "How bad are the spikes in magic?"

"Worse than we'd hoped, not as bad as our nightmare scenario." Ari turned her laptop toward Jerek, pulling it just a few inches farther from him as his finger brushed against the table, leaving a streak of bright green.

"Anyone hurt?" Jerek asked.

"As far as I can tell, maybe a few stitches from a streetlight explosion in Atlanta," Ari said, "but I've done such a great job muddying the search algorithms with fake magic, I've made finding the real deal harder for myself. Not perfect, but tagging my own work would open the door for other hackers to figure out I'd been messing with search trends."

"And it's working?"

"You did spend about twelve thousand dollars making a beer-producing cow from Iowa go viral, but yeah. The fakes I've chosen are drowning out the real magic. There's shit I can do about eyewitnesses without shutting them up by ruining their lives to shove them off the internet, but since that's the kind of evil I like to avoid, I'm sticking with shunting traffic away from the truth."

"And if the spikes in magic don't stop?"

Ari turned her laptop back to her. "Then we come up with another plan."

"Are you all right?" Jerek reached for her, stopping with his hand hovering right above hers.

"It's okay if you turn my skin purple. It'll just go back to normal."

Jerek touched the back of her hand, leaving a teal fingerprint behind.

The teal faded into Ari's skin. "Just don't touch my laptop until you've got the finger painting under control."

"Of course." Jerek drummed his fingers on the table, making dots that changed with each tap. Purple, then yellow, then gray, then red.

"What does it feel like?" Ari asked.

"Like nothing." Jerek drew a swirl on the table. "Thoughtless. Instinctive. Like blinking or breathing. The magic is sitting right there beneath my skin, begging to be used. Before, it was like digging down, searching deep inside for a tiny grain of magic. Using every bit of control I could muster to focus that magic into something usable. But this"—he swiped his hand over the swirl, leaving a streak of sparkling gold behind—"is like

I've shed a thousand-pound cocoon and my body can finally function the way it should."

"It makes sense." Ari took Jerek's hand, letting him turn hers deep blue.

He met her gaze, true worry in his eyes. "Does it?"

"As a half-mer on dry land, yeah." A knot pressed on the front of Ari's throat. "It really does."

"Thank you. For getting us here."

She kissed the back of his hand.

His eyes widened, his chest bouncing with suppressed laughter as she pulled away.

"What did you do to my face?" Ari fought her own laughter.

"It's already fading." Jerek grinned.

"I was going to say something deep and meaningful about my contributions to our cause, but never mind." She kissed the back of his hand again, winking as Jerek laughed at whatever it was he'd done to her face. "But screw depth and meaning, just help me figure out what the hell to do with the rest of this mess."

Jerek's smile faded.

"We've already dealt with the corpse and viral floating cereal," Ari said. "So you're hopping onto clean-up crew at the right time."

"I know. And I am grateful, more than grateful, for all you've done."

"Don't you dare say *but*, Jerek Holden." The knot in Ari's throat sank, spreading into a nagging pressure on the front of her chest.

Jerek gave what couldn't quite pass as a wry smile. "*However*, I had never really put much consideration into what would come after mending the Fracture."

The weight on Ari's chest changed, becoming a fist that wrapped around her heart. "Because you were supposed to be dead."

"Considering the *after* of breaking the curse was dangerous for me. My vague assumption was that you'd contact the Council of the Feu to tell them what I'd done, use your hacking skills to force the Council to add protection for divs and rewrite the horrific feu hierarchy, then, utilizing your incredible powers of hope and persuasion, convince the younger generation of feu to strive for a better world."

"So I should just call the Council of the Feu?" Ari pulled her phone from her back pocket. "I obviously won't tell them where we're hiding. I'll keep it simple. *Hi, we mended the Fracture and flooded magic back into the world but there's a mysterious they we have to track down who we're pretty sure ordered the slaughter of werewolves, and there's a fairly good chance Callen LeBlanc fits somewhere in the plot to cause the Fracture, but we're not totally sure how. We also have a little problem with a dead body. So good luck with magicians all over the world dealing with their powers flaring, but I have to track down the origin of some serial killer Maree blades, okay bye.*"

"I was thinking more along the lines of the first-ever feu newsletter written by an anonymous source, informing the feu that the Fracture was mended and warning them of the shadow group that caused the Fracture in the first place," Jerek said. "But calling the Council works, too."

"There isn't a list of the email addresses of every feu," Ari said. "Even if I had weeks to comb the internet, I still couldn't figure out how to contact everyone."

"How many could you gather by tonight?" Jerek asked.

Ari shut her eyes, running through all the data she'd pulled from the feu message boards and Maree computers.

"At max, five percent of the feu," Ari said. "Probably more like two to three percent."

"And when people start sharing the newsletter?" Jerek

dragged his finger across the table, drawing a white triangle on the wood.

"The information keeps spreading while we move on to the next problem." Ari threw her arms around Jerek's neck. "Don't you ever even pretend I could've gotten through this without you."

Jerek wrapped his arms around her waist, pulling her over to sit in his lap, closer than she'd seen him hold anyone in so long.

He laid his head on her shoulder.

"I adore you above all others, Ariel Love." He kissed her cheek, smiling at whatever color he'd left on her skin. "You could've absolutely done it without me. But I am so grateful to be here."

"I love you too, Jer Bear." She kissed the top of his head.

The thunder of footsteps raced from the kitchen.

"I really hope Eve didn't tear out a support wall." Ari kept her arms around Jerek.

Ford bolted past the dining room door, heading toward the stairs.

"Are you okay?" Ari called after him.

Ford stumbled to a stop and whirled toward the dining room, blinking at Ari and Jerek for a moment like he was trying to make his brain work before speaking. "Glad you're awake, Jerek. Ari, your arm is violet, and I need to talk to you now."

"Sounds fun." Ari shifted back to her own seat. "Did Eve find an old dead body buried under the floor where we wanted to put the new dead body, or did some other proverbial poo strike the fan?"

"Worse than a body." Ford glanced up the stairs before coming into the dining room. "Jerek, could you give us a minute?"

"I'm not sure Jerek can stand," Ari said.

"Well, we could..." Ford looked to the stairs again. "It's just that this is going to sound really bad, and I don't want anyone to get upset. Or try to pummel my face."

"Ford, sit." Ari pointed to the chair opposite her.

"I'll go." Jerek pressed his hands to the table to stand, sending a shockwave of bright yellow across the wood.

"That's less than ideal." Ford stood behind the chair Ari had pointed to.

"I just need to adjust," Jerek said.

"That makes sense," Ford said. "Remove a strain from the system, and—"

"Ford, what did you need to tell me?" Ari said.

Ford glanced to Jerek.

"Don't worry about something sounding bad in front of Jerek. If his face twitches in a judgmental way, I'll tell you stories about him that will have him turning the whole house scarlet."

Jerek's head snapped toward Ari, a satisfying touch of horror in his eyes.

"Fine," Ford said. "But can the details of how I stumbled upon this...problem stay in this room?"

"Sure." Ari planted her elbows on the table. "Talk."

"Right. Sure." Ford nodded. "Easy."

"Ford."

"So, when you disappeared a few weeks ago, I just knew you'd run off to be with Jerek again," Ford said. "And I got worried. And in hindsight, I think we can all agree my worry was justified."

"Fair," Jerek said.

"I can decide when people should worry about me," Ari said.

"That's not actually how it works," Jerek said.

"Anyway," Ford cut in, "I knew I needed to find you. And I

did, by running down all his known aliases and tracking you to the hotel."

"The dummy hotel I had used to set a trap." Ari leaned back in her chair. "Just to be clear."

"You're absolutely right. But I was really, *really* worried, Ari." Ford glanced over his shoulder, looking back toward the hall.

"What did you do?" Ari asked.

"I created an algorithm to scrape the internet for anything that might lead me to you." Ford's lips flattened into one straight line.

"Your criteria?"

"There were combined filters and an extensive list of search terms," Ford said.

"What kind of terms?" The table beneath Jerek's hands turned a deep, muddy orange.

"Blond. Water. Mermaid. Fighting." Red crept into Ford's cheeks. "Beautiful. Goddess. Mystery. Magic. Love. There were six hundred and seventy keywords and about two thousand exact phrases."

"Did you get any hits?" Ari said while Jerek said, "You decided to stalk her?"

"A few vague matches before I tweaked the search terms." Ford's shoulders rounded as the red in his cheeks deepened. "When I found the hotel and joined the crew, I didn't cancel the search, just in case you disappeared again. And then things spiraled very quickly. I haven't thought much about it. I've gotten a couple notifications, but I just ignored them since you were with us. But one just popped up, and it's you."

An unfamiliar sense of frigid fear gripped the back of Ari's neck. "Me where, Ford?"

Ford glanced back to the damn stairs again.

"Me where!"

14

Lincoln

Kneeling beside the low table, Lincoln checked his hands for the fourth time before unrolling the scroll, careful to use only the necessary amount of force to manipulate the centuries-old treasure.

The document had been written in Greek. Not one of Lincoln's readable languages, but he knew enough to understand the words *wand*, *bone*, and *necromancy*.

Just as carefully as he'd unrolled it, Lincoln rerolled the scroll and placed it in line with the other four he'd laid out on his coffee table station.

He'd opted to move the antique, pearl-inlaid table from one of the adjoining rooms, placing it right next to the glass cabinet at the top of the stairs on the second floor of the archivist's house, minimizing the distance the precious documents had to be carried from the humidity-controlled case.

Lincoln turned to the notepad on the floor, adding the

general contents of the scroll to his list, marking the text as missing any mention of the Fracture or Knights Maree, before moving on to the next in line.

He checked his fingers again before handling the scroll—this one in French, detailing the escape of three witches during the Inquisition.

Lincoln added a note to his list and moved on to the next.

This one had an old, partially intact wax seal on it.

A thunder of footsteps came from downstairs.

Lincoln yanked his hands away from the scroll, stopping himself before he could accidentally grip the old parchment too tightly. He froze, listening for attack.

Quiet voices came from downstairs. Nothing panicked. No screaming.

No danger to tighten his grip.

He stayed frozen, listening for one more moment before shaking out his shoulders and going back to the document.

Tipping the scroll, Lincoln squinted at the seal, trying to make out the details with the subtle shifting of the light.

A line cut through an arc—annoyingly vague without the rest of the image.

Lincoln sat back on his heels, thinking through all the crests he'd seen in the Maree compound records. He couldn't recall any that were both so plain and so old as the one on the scroll he now held in his hands.

With the careful touch the Maree archivist had taught him, Lincoln unrolled the parchment.

The document had been written in Italian, easy for Lincoln to read, if not understand, its content.

From this solemn day, a record of the dissidents has been requested.

Upon the vote of the Lord Maree and his Council, mercy

for the cryptid has been granted in trade for peace from the magicians.

While the firm majority held in favor of releasing the beast back into the wild, a brave minority maintained their refusal to negotiate, demanding the vampire's life regardless of threats from the feu.

The names of the minority have been recorded below.

Percival Fitzwilliam

Edmund Wa—

"Me where!" The shout boomed up the stairs, startling Lincoln, making him pinch the scroll.

"Damn." Lincoln let go of the paper, leaping to his feet, backing away from the marred parchment while moving closer to the stairs.

"What video?" Ari's voice carried up to him.

Ford replied too softly for Lincoln to hear.

"What?" A bang, like a chair falling over, came with Ari's shout.

"It's not as bad as it sounds," Ford said. "Please don't panic."

"Why would you say that?" Ari said. "All that's going to do is make me panic!"

Lincoln crept down the stairs, keeping his back to the wall, testing each step for squeaks before transferring his weight, though he couldn't quite reason through why instinct screamed for him to stay silent.

"The video of the fight is the worst of it," Ford said.

"What do you mean by *worst?*" Jerek said, his words crisp and clear with no hint of residual fatigue from being out for an entire day.

"Her face is clear," Ford said. "Really clear, and people have cleaned up the images."

"Clear enough to identify?" Jerek asked.

"Pretty easily with the right access," Ford said. "The other two videos aren't as good. The rose garden video doesn't focus on your face."

"What does it focus on?" Ari said.

"Your legs wrapped around him," Ford said.

A sharp punch rammed against Lincoln's chest. He straightened his spine, steadying his stance, shoving the pummeling pressure aside.

"I don't think anyone but me would be able to tell it's really you," Ford said.

Two breaths of silence passed.

"I'm really sorry," Ford said.

"What's the third video?" Ari said.

Silence.

"Ford!"

"Someone caught you running across the pond," Ford said.

"Ari," Jerek said.

"The quality on the video is mediocre at best," Ford said. "And there's barely a glimpse of your profile."

"My profile?" Ari said.

"The hair from your wig sweeps in front of your face," Ford said.

"My profile!" A sharp bang punctuated Ari's shout.

"It's fine," Jerek said. "Everything is going to be fine."

"A video of me running on water isn't fine, Jerek."

Lincoln crept farther down the stairs.

"You've already been boosting fake videos," Ford said. "The running on water will get lumped in with that mess, and no one will think anything of it."

"Except for the Council of the Feu," Ari said. "And the Maree."

"We'll fix this," Jerek said.

"There is no fixing this," Ari said. "Just stop, Jerek. Stop. Once a video is out there, it's out there."

"I can help you," Ford said.

"Even if we manage to hide it for a day or a week, the Maree have got to be investigating what happened at Greenwood. And when they dig up a video of a div running on water, the only thing I'm going to be able to do is run like hell and hope when the Maree find me they kill me instead of throwing me in a dungeon."

"I won't let them touch you," Jerek said.

Lincoln reached the bottom of the stairs, stopping as he gained a view of the dining room.

Jerek held Ari by the shoulders, gripping her like he was stopping her from running.

Ford stood beside the dining room door, one arm out like he was preparing to catch her if Jerek failed.

"You're one of the heroes who helped mend the Fracture," Ford said. "Even if they don't know that now, they will soon. The Council will thank you."

"I won't be brought before the Council." Ari knocked Jerek's hands aside, breaking his hold on her. "If a wild animal misbehaves, you don't put in on trial, you put it down." She backed away from him. "I'm a div. An abomination of a beast. They won't give a shit what I did right."

"We'll make the Council and the Maree care, whatever it takes. We're going to get you through this." Jerek kept his hands out but didn't grab for her. "Let's just focus on what we can do right now. We mended the Fracture. We can figure this out. What's step one?"

Ari shook her head.

"Step one, Ariel," Jerek said.

She took a shaky breath. "If the videos are getting posted on a hosted board, we get the board shut down. Slow the circulation of the video."

"If we can get the thread shut down soon enough, we might be able to keep the Maree from finding the video," Ford said.

"Is Greenwood attached to the file?" Ari asked.

"Yeah." Ford's shoulders rounded like someone had yanked out part of his chest. "It is."

"Then we're talking buying hours, not days, before the Maree find it." Ari backed farther from Jerek. "I screwed up. I knew better than to risk it, but those knights were right behind me, and I had to get out."

"And we'll tell that to the Council of the Feu," Jerek said.

"They won't care," Ari said.

"We just changed the world." Jerek eased closer to her. "We don't know what anything will be like anymore. And if you're right and the Council won't listen, I'll buy or blackmail whoever it takes to keep you safe. We are going to fix this. But I need you here to do it, all right? I need you to stay with me."

Lincoln's heart hitched, his blood whooshing in his ears as Ari just stared at Jerek's outstretched hand.

"If it gets bad, I'll help you run before they find you," Jerek said. "I will not let them hurt you. I will not let them lock you up. Plan reef is always ready. I promise."

She still didn't take his hand. "Plan reef means you think I should run."

"Plan reef means you don't have to worry about running," Jerek said. "Everything is already in place. If things get that bad, you have a way out. You don't have to waste time thinking about it now. You can concentrate on how we fix this so you can stay with me."

She just shook her head.

Sharp, twisting panic locked around Lincoln's chest.

"The Maree attacked you." He cut around the corner into

the dining room. Ignoring Ford and Jerek, he walked straight to Ari, planting himself in front of her, taking her hands.

"Another reason to get rid of the div." Ari tried to pull her hands away, but Lincoln held on tighter.

"Maree aren't allowed to engage with feu in public unless there is already a risk of exposure or high fatalities." The words rushed from Lincoln, bursting from his mouth so quickly he wasn't sure they made sense. "The knights who attacked you went against the rules of the Maree. And if they're Chanler's guards, they could be in league with LeBlanc."

"It doesn't matter," Ari said.

"We will make it matter," Lincoln said. "They broke the rules of engagement. We'll make the blame fall on them."

"Shame the Maree into total amnesty," Ford said. "I like it, Ari. It's a clean way to fix this."

"What?" Lincoln glanced to Ford, still keeping hold of Ari.

"We're already sending out the very first feu newsletter," Ford said. "We include the video of the fight, show the Maree attacking a feu."

"A div," Ari said.

"Who is still feu," Jerek said. "We know there are Maree working for LeBlanc. Make the Maree look to the trouble in their own house."

"The Maree are already fighting each other in the compound," Lincoln said. "If you spread a video of Maree risking exposing the feu, you'd be throwing a match at a powder keg. I don't know who would get caught in the blast."

"It would show the good Maree exactly what they're fighting against," Ford said.

"And when feu start targeting honorable Maree?" Lincoln rounded on Ford, his grip on Ari loosening for just a moment.

She yanked her hands away.

Lincoln clamped his arm around her waist, holding her

close to him. "What happens if a feu needs help and they refuse the aid of the Maree? If a feu goes rogue and starts attacking sombs? Damaging the name of the Knights Maree helps no one."

"Except Ari." Ford gestured between Ari and Lincoln. "Have you forgotten the girl you're pinning to your side is in danger?"

"No." Lincoln tried to loosen his hold on her. He couldn't. "You have my word as a Knight Maree, I will keep her safe. I swear it."

"My flock of boys." Ari's tears vanished, leaving a soft shimmer of salt behind. She touched Lincoln's cheek. "All so convinced you can save me."

"You're perfectly capable of saving yourself," Jerek said. "It's saving yourself while keeping you with us you have trouble with."

Ari tipped her chin down, hiding her face behind the shimmering curtain of her hair.

Lincoln shifted his weight to his toes, ready to catch her if she tried to break away.

"I know every instinct is telling you to run. I know it would be easier to disappear," Jerek said. "I can't imagine how hard that need is calling you right now."

Ari tensed.

"But I am begging you not to go where I can't follow you," Jerek said. "Please, Ari. I don't know how to do this without you."

She nodded before looking up, meeting Jerek's eyes. "I'll try." She took Lincoln's hand, lifting it away from her waist.

Lincoln kept hold of her hand as she stepped away from him to face Jerek.

"I'll hold out as long as I can, Jer Bear. Promise."

"We need to minimize the damage done by the video." Jerek

looked to Ford, all trace of worry gone, his tone back to the normal Holden habit of issuing orders.

"I've nixed the visibility of the thread, but I can't stop people from starting new threads with the same videos," Ford said, barely a hint of fear left in his voice. "I squashed one thread, and a new one popped up a minute later. I can't actually stop people from posting."

"How do we get it done?" Jerek turned to Ari.

"Stop whoever is creating the new threads," Ari said. "It might take a little searching and bribe money and/or light blackmail, but if we can get them to stop posting, it'll be a hell of a lot easier to make people lose interest so we can blur the video in with the faux magic chatter we've been building."

"We've steered right back to the other part of this that's going to sound really bad." Ford glanced to Lincoln, his body tensing like he was preparing for a blow. "I don't think blackmail or bribery is going to stop the person who's posting."

"Why?" Ari stepped closer to Ford, still letting Lincoln hold on to her hand.

"It's Regi. Somb Regi," Ford said. "He's searching for the mystery girl who stole his heart in the shadows of Greenwood Gardens."

15

Grace

The ambulance turned the corner, the flashing of its lights disappearing as it cut around the community welcome center and out of sight.

Grace closed her eyes, trying not to worry what the sweet scent coming from the gravel beneath her hair might be, searching her body for the crackling rush of energy that seemed to precede every fiery disaster.

Her heart sped too fast. Tiny jabs of pain cut into her back from the rocks she lay on. A stress headache pinched between her eyes.

But no flood of chaos and doom demanded to pour from her body.

Grace opened her eyes, looking up into the undercarriage of the car beside her.

The shadows were too dark for her to make out anything but some pipes.

"Reason seven hundred and ninety-two I really wish I had a cellphone." She rolled onto her side, facing away from the car.

There were no people around the parking lot, at least not that she could see. She hadn't spotted any security cameras, either.

"Just a little bit." Grace fixed her gaze on her left pointer finger. "I just need you to catch fire a tiny bit."

Anxiety overwhelmed any embarrassment she might have felt at lying in a parking lot talking to her finger.

"Like a match. You can do that." Grace let out a slow breath, imagining the source of magic deep inside her pushing out to her finger. The energy started to crackle. She let out another slow breath.

Nothing.

Not even a spark.

"If you can burn down a warehouse, you can light your freaking finger on fire, Grace Esther Lee-Weiss."

A wave of disgust rolled through Grace's gut.

Her magic had burned people. Killed people.

The sound of their screams banged through her ears, tightening the pain between her eyes.

The energy lurking inside her was nothing better than a murder weapon. Violent, vicious, only capable of causing pain.

A wave of flames burst to life, engulfing Grace's hand.

"Shit." She rolled on top of her arm, ramming rocks into her skin as she doused the flames with her own body.

Heat burned her hand, but not the way it had burned the Maree. Not charring her, only singeing her enough to scream her failure to the world.

"You don't get to fail at this, Grace." She closed her eyes, picturing a solid shield of black locking around the crackling energy that fed the flames.

The heat stopped burning her hand.

"Good job, Grace. Nailed it."

She rolled onto her back.

"If you don't stop talking to yourself, you're going to start doubting your own sanity, Grace."

She held her finger up again.

A match. A flame as delicate as one dancing on a match.

She scrunched her eyes shut, trailing her mind along the black, searching for a hint of the energy that longed to destroy.

A thread, thinner than spider's silk, that was all she needed.

A knot of pain pressed against her chest, digging into her lungs, begging her to let her magic break free. She ignored the pain and pierced the black, plucking one tiny thread of power, drawing it out through her arm all the way to her finger.

Warmth tickled Grace's fingertip.

Slowly, she opened her eyes.

A perfect blue flame flickered on her finger. "Oh, hell yes."

Keeping her finger upright, Grace twisted back to look under the car.

Pipes. Engine stuff. Dirt.

"Damn."

Wincing from the jabbing rocks, Grace rolled over and got to her knees.

The parking lot was still empty.

She hunched over her lit finger, hiding the blue flame as she crept around to the next car.

She pressed on the door of the gas cap. It didn't open.

Lying down beside the car, she checked the underside but again found nothing but a filthy engine.

She moved carefully down the first row of twelve vehicles, checking for an open gas flap before looking beneath each car.

After the fifteenth car, the temptation to stay lying on the ground until someone hauled her away started scraping at her thoughts, adding to the weight of the fatigue that begged her to sleep.

The flame on her finger wavered.

"Five more cars, Grace. You've done fifteen, checking five more is nothing."

A rock cut into her elbow as she pushed herself up, slicing deep enough to bleed.

Tears burned down Grace's cheeks.

"Five more, then you can quit."

Car one. Nothing.

Car two. Nothing.

Tears caught in Grace's throat as she tried to open the gas flap on car three.

Locked.

She lay down beside the car, letting her mind sink into wondering if the somb police would agree to arrest her before the Maree captured her.

The blue light of her flame flickered beneath the car, giving depth to the rusted engine. A black rectangle caught Grace's eye—stuck to the undercarriage, coated in grime, a magnetized black box with a key-shaped logo on the front.

The flame on Grace's finger vanished.

She held her breath as she pulled down the box, a fresh wave of tears flooding down her face as something inside rattled.

She pulled at the top of the box, her hands shaking as she pried it open to find the most beautiful car key the world had ever seen.

16

Ford

"You don't have to be here." Ford opened his eyes, backing away from the powder Ari kept dusting across his face.

"Are you going to record yourself?" Ari rapped Ford on the head with the brush, making him close his eyes again.

"Jack can record," Ford said. "You shouldn't even be going into that room."

"We need this to have high production value," Ari said. "Jack has some amazing skills, but his tech mojo doesn't compare to mine."

"I'd never claim it did." Jack rounded the corner of the staircase, carrying the dining room table with Eve.

"We don't need a tech genius to record the video," Ford said. "Jack will be fine."

"I'm not leaving you while you bet your life on a bluff." Ari tapped his chin. "Hold still."

"It's not entirely a bluff," Jerek said from his spot at the coffee table Lincoln had dragged into the hall. He turned Ari's screen to face the rest of the group. "The current breakdown matching blackmail material to magician seems entirely accurate."

"I like collateral better than blackmail." Ford pulled the towel from around his neck, checking his blazer for any stray powder.

"So did the archivist," Eve said.

A hollow sort of pain swooped through Ford's gut. "Blackmail it is."

"The problem is, we've only found the blackmail four people handed over to the archivist. We've got one super dodgy birth certificate, one very compromising P.I.-vibe photo album, some epic proof of tax evasion, and a grimoire on necromancy the dumbass put an actual *this book belongs to* name plate in. Which all totaled adds up to"—Ari furrowed her brow—"that's right, a massive bluff."

"That doesn't need a super high-quality recording," Jack said as he and Eve set the table down. "Let us worry about this. You take care of you."

"I am taking care of me." Ari squinted at Ford's face, leaning back to catch him in a different light.

"You need to focus on getting to Regi," Ford said.

Everyone in the hall, even Eve, froze.

"I've got it handled." Ari set the tub of face powder on the coffee table.

"Ari—" Jerek began.

"If a shit ton of angry magicians storm this house, we're all dead," Ari said. "If we're all dead, who wants me dead in particular becomes a moot point."

"Ar—"

"Can I please focus on taking care of the people I love?" Ari rounded on Jerek. "I've got Regi covered. There's nothing I can do until 10:45 tomorrow morning, so let's focus on making Ford the new Don of all feu dirty laundry so we can start leaving breadcrumbs out for the archivist's patrons so they can actually find this video and start believing the blackmail bluff of the century so they don't all show up to kill us."

Jerek held Ari's gaze, like he dared to face her in a battle of wills.

"Gran would take you," Eve said. "I'm sure you've got better places to hide out, but the mountain is safe, and Gran would give you a bed and the protection of the pack."

"Thanks." Ari turned away from Jerek. "I'd never put that weight on your grandmother, but the offer feels really good right now."

"There wouldn't be any weight." Blazing, raw anger glinted in Eve's eyes. "Maree trying to come up the mountain would be the kind of fun the pack hasn't had in ages."

"Maybe consider not saying that in front of Lincoln," Jack whispered.

Eve shrugged.

"If everyone's so worried about me, can we actually record the video so I can start baiting the shadiest of the feu?" Ari took her laptop from Jerek without looking at him. "If shit goes sideways, I need to know you're all as safe as I can make you."

"Ari." Jerek grabbed her wrist.

"I'm not running, Jerek. I'm working." Ari still didn't look at him. "If you want me to hold on until tomorrow, let me work."

Jerek let go of her, yanking his hand away like her threat had stung him.

"Can we get this done?" Ari said.

"If our shield is ready, let's begin," Jerek said.

Jack gripped his end of the dining room table again. "On three?"

"One, two, three," Eve counted, working with Jack to rotate the table onto its side.

"Ladies and gentlemen, please keep your jugular, spine, and heart behind the barricade," Jack said as he and Eve lifted the table to protect them from waist to head. "If any boobytraps are triggered causing projectiles to shoot from the walls, please take cover behind your friendly neighborhood cryptid. You people heal too damn slowly."

"Annoyingly slowly," Eve said.

Ford took the spot closest to Jack as they lined up behind their thick, wooden tabletop shield.

"And go," Jack said.

Moving like an uncoordinated bug, the five of them shuffled into the library to record the video that would toss Ford off the edge of the somb world for the rest of his life.

17

Subject: The Return of Magic

Dear Feu,

We write to you in hopes of this information moving through our community too quickly to be silenced by the Council of the Feu or Knights Maree.

The Fracture has been mended. After twelve years, magic has returned to the world, but the darkness that haunts our people is far from lifted.

The Fracture was caused by a curse. A horrific piece of magic cast to weaken magicians and break the bonds of the feu.

The group that cast the curse has not been stopped. They are still lurking in the shadows. They have killed before. And we know they will attack again.

Protect your families. Protect your friends.

Protect the secrecy that has preserved our community for centuries.

Be slow to trust and quick to hide.
With hopes for a better tomorrow,
The Cursebreaker

———

New Post

Counting on your friend in Manhattan in these troubled times?
Our repository of resources is ready to help.
Click here for updated contact info.
Assistance provided to current patrons only.

Unique Visitors: 76

Password Attempts: 22
Passwords Accepted: Archives, Archivist, Archives in Manhattan, Archivist Piece of Shit
Successful Attempts: 10
Unique Video Plays: 10

A young, blond man fills the center of the screen, shelves of books barely peeping over the top of his high-backed chair.

The blond smiles.

"Welcome," he says. "If you've reached this video, I must assume you are a patron of the archives. You're probably hoping

the archivist will offer words of wisdom and promises of safety as we greet this post-Fracture world. I regret to inform you, you will never see the previous archivist again.

"I have procured the archives and all the information you" —he points at the screen—"have placed in the former archivist's care over the years. I am the new keeper of your secrets. And what glorious secrets they are."

The blond gives a faint laugh.

"First, I must assure you your arrangement with my predecessor continues. I am the guard standing between knowledge and survival. But it is a new day." He leans back in his chair, as though enjoying its comfort. "I understand we live in a dangerous time and believe in insurance fit for the digital age. Which is where you, my loyal patrons, come in.

"Records of the most...enticing pieces of my collection have been uploaded to a very special server. This server is far more secure than anything the Council of the Feu or Maree have ever created. The secrecy of my collection is fully preserved. However, should the need arise, the full contents of that server will be sent to every feu with an email address. Not to mention the Council of the Feu and the Knights Maree."

He smiles again, then wrinkles his nose in a dramatic cringe.

"But exposing your collateral is not my aim. I'd much prefer to avoid my patrons suffering such ruinous exposure. The key to keeping your secrets secret? My safety. It's quite a brilliant system. If anyone attacks the archives, the contents of the server will be released. If my associates are harmed, the contents of the server will be released. If I'm killed, the contents of the server will be released. If I so much as receive a malicious papercut, the contents of the server will be released.

"Simple, isn't it? Of course, the true beauty of the system is automation. Destroy the archives, murder me, your secrets zoom out into the world and there is nothing you can do to stop it.

"*The easiest choice would be to happily accept the archives transferring into my hands. Go about your lives and leave well enough alone.*

"*But*"—*he leans closer to the camera*—"*if you're genuinely worried about your deep, dark secrets flooding out among the feu, you had better pray none of the archives' other patrons are foolish enough to test my promise or my automation skills. All it takes is one member challenging my position, and whoosh, so many sandcastles swept away.*

"*That's a terrible risk for you to take, hoping my other patrons respect our new arrangement. One of you steps out of line, all of you fall. I encourage you to consider what you would do to protect your collateral and defend the archives and your new archivist with fitting resolve.*" *He laces his fingers together in his lap.* "*Remember, the safety of your secrets lies in your own hands.*"

The screen blinks to black.

18

Jerek

Imagining the short, mouse-brown wig on Ari only served to make Jerek feel more ridiculous as he sat perched on the bare box spring, his fists pressed together in front of him making a poor version of a fake head for Ari while she styled the back of the wig.

"The Milton Rayburn card needs to be taken out of the rotation." Ari leaned back, pursing her lips as she considered her work.

"Have I been reduced to abject poverty?" Jerek smiled as his lack of panic forged a tiny bead of joy inside him, promising he didn't actually care.

"Not even a little. But I've used it three times in the city." Ari left Jerek holding the wig, abandoning him to pull out the new clothes the courier had delivered with the massive batch of groceries Lincoln had ordered. "I also used it for operation Warbucks."

"Do I want to know?"

"Probably." Ari held up a green shirt, wrinkling her nose at the color.

"And?"

"Seventy-six people have found the archivist landing page." Ari set the green top down and pulled off her own pink shirt. "Of the seventy-six, fifty-four didn't answer anything for the login. Ten answered correctly and were taken to Ford's video, the rest have received a written message from Mr. Warbucks himself."

"And what does Mr. Warbucks say?"

"He offers help leaving the city to any feu in need." Ari switched into new, black pants. "I've been giving them a code to use to get a train ticket out of town. They can go anywhere they want, and Mr. Warbucks pays their way. On the Milton Rayburn card. Sorry for nixing one of your aliases."

"If it helps a single feu get somewhere safe while magic settles back into the world, you can burn any of my aliases you like."

"I know." Ari smiled at him. A genuine, non-panicked smile. "That's how I know we're the good guys."

Jerek watched as she pinned up her hair, carefully flattening its mass to fit under the wig. She checked her face in the mirror, adding another layer of eyeliner and more contour to her cheeks, then stepped back, tipping her head to catch different angles in the light.

"You don't look different enough," Jerek said.

"There's not much more I can do without going for clown paint."

"You can stay here and let me handle Regi," Jerek said.

"Oh really?" Ari lifted the wig off Jerek's fists, pointedly staring at the bag she'd draped over Jerek's hands, watching the paper turn from pink to black to red. "You're not leaving the house. And I can handle Regi."

"If it were only you and him, I still wouldn't agree with you. All of us are in danger right now. No one should be going anywhere alone."

"Wait." Ari stopped with her wig halfway on her head. "You actually think I couldn't handle Regi?"

"Poor choice of phrasing." Jerek took the now moss-green bag off his hands. "I think poor Regi has fallen desperately in love with you and finding you only to be rejected will break him. You, being the wonderful and caring person you are, will feel terrible for hurting him, and as your heart tears at the poor man's grief, I worry you may not be in top shape to watch out for people who want you dead."

Ari frowned. She stared at the wall just above Jerek's head, the look in her eyes holding such concentrated thought, it seemed almost as though Jerek could watch the cogs turning in her brilliant mind.

"I hate it when you're right about me." She yanked the wig the rest of the way on. "But I have to go meet Regi. If he's so worried about finding me, some random stranger telling him to stop looking isn't going to help."

"You need to take someone with you." Jerek stood, keeping his hands in front of him to avoid an accidental color change of the box spring he'd been sitting on.

"I'll ask Ford to come with me." Ari pulled on her new sneakers. "Jack can take a turn with the security cameras while we're gone."

"Ford's no good in a fight."

"I don't need someone who's good in a fight, just an extra set of eyes. Ford's a great lookout." She lifted the bottom of her green shirt and wrapped her new belt around her waist. "Honestly, just the lack of stuffed boobs is enough of a disguise to make people believe I'm not Juliet, the runaway girl from Greenwood Gardens. I'll be fine." She buckled the belt and took one of her daggers from the top of the dresser, tucking it into the sheath now hidden at the small of her back. She pulled her shirt down, twisting to examine her waist in the mirror.

"I can't see it. A clever new toy."

"I'll have to thank the fellow who bought it for me." She winked. "I'll find you a pair of gloves while we're out. Kitchen gloves may be enough to keep books legible, but you wearing those around the house gives too much of a horror vibe."

She turned around, checking herself in the mirror one more time before stepping toward Jerek as though ready to kiss his cheek and skip away with Ford.

"You have to take Lincoln." Jerek held up a hand, blocking her quick goodbye.

"No."

"It's either him or Eve, and I don't think either of us wants her out among the sombs right now."

"I'm taking Ford."

"I can't let that happen." Jerek took her arms, carefully avoiding touching the fabric of her shirt. "It's got to be Lincoln."

"We haven't heard from his family. We have no idea what's going on in the Maree compound."

"His staying in the house won't change that."

"But saying *Hey, Lincoln, want to come with me while I talk to the guy I almost had to have sex with while you were watching? But sharing a mattress with you tonight would still be great since I'm so freaked out by the corpse I dehydrated that's now hidden in the basement, I don't even want to try sleeping on my own, so after I break this dude's heart, do you want to tuck ourselves in bed and snuggle? That's really going to make things better for Lincoln.*"

"No, it won't." Jerek slid his hands down to lock fingers with

Ari. A brilliant, lung-tingling sense of absolute freedom filled his chest. He held Ari's gaze, tucking the bliss behind his worry. "But if things go wrong and Ford gets hurt, you'll never forgive yourself."

"I can protect Ford."

"Lincoln would experience more pain watching you terrorize yourself for having risked Ford's life than he ever could from watching you tell a man you knew for one night that he needs to leave you alone." Jerek bent down, kissing Ari's hand. He pictured her in his mind, the cursed girl caught in a web of those who loved her with exquisite devotion. His lips left behind a crimson kiss. "Take Lincoln with you. Be quick dealing with the somb, and come right back home."

"You just called this den of secrets and terrors *home*." Ari kissed Jerek's hand, turning her lips icy blue.

Jerek allowed himself a low laugh.

Ari winked at him and brushed the tip of her nose against his fingers, turning it icy blue as well.

He didn't try to stop that laugh.

"You're sure I can't just take Ford?" Ari asked.

"You can't risk that kind of regret."

Ari nodded, stepping away from Jerek, a deep worry dulling the sparkle in her eyes, as though regret had already taken hold.

19

Lincoln

Ari told their rideshare car to meet them three blocks east of the archives.

She didn't speak to Lincoln on the walk there. He'd been too busy examining every person they passed, searching for any hint of a threat, to think of something to say.

Other than a quick, "Thanks," for opening the door, she didn't speak to him on the ride, either.

Logical in such close proximity to their somb driver.

The car dropped them off in the center of a busy block with Lincoln's side nearest the curb.

"I've got it." Lincoln opened his door, hopping out then holding the door open for Ari.

She slid out after him.

"Thank you," she called to the driver as she stepped up onto the sidewalk.

Lincoln closed the door, waiting until the car had pulled away before asking, "Which way?"

Her neck tensed, like he'd broken some rule by speaking.

"What's wrong?" He stepped closer to her, placing himself between her and the street, scanning the crowd for any hint of a threat.

"You're not coming in with me," Ari said.

"Yes, I am."

"There's a hotdog stand at the end of the block."

"If that's where you're meeting him, that's where we'll go. Together."

"I'm going in there." She nodded to an older office building cattycorner from their position.

Rows of mostly empty desks took up what Lincoln could see of the space through the windows.

"You're going to stay out here, eat a hotdog, and watch for trouble." Ari pulled cash from her pocket and held it out to Lincoln.

"Will I be able to see you through the windows?"

"I rented a private conference room on the third floor."

"Then I'm going to the third floor." Lincoln gripped her hand, holding on to it, money and all. "I'm not letting you go someplace where I won't know if you're in danger."

"I'll be fine." Ari stepped away, sliding her hand from Lincoln's grasp.

"If Jerek had okayed me staying on the street, we'd both be wearing earpieces."

"I don't need Jerek's permission."

"Then I don't need yours. We're on the same side, Ari. It's my job to not let you put yourself in unnecessary danger."

Ari laid her hand on Lincoln's chest. "I'm going to be fine. Get a snack, and I'll be out in ten minutes."

"No."

"Lincoln, please." She closed the gap between them, leaving mere inches separating her body from his. "Stay out here."

"Give me one good reason." His fingers tingled as he took her hips.

"Do you want to kiss me?" She tipped her face up, her lips tantalizingly close to his.

"A kiss isn't going to convince me—"

"Answer me." She leaned closer to him.

The world around them started to blur, everything fading until there was nothing but her. He didn't want there to be anything but—but—

He shook his head, taking a step back.

A flash of pain flickered on her face.

"I want to kiss you"—he tucked his hands behind his back, farther from temptation—"more than I've ever wanted to be near anyone. But I can't focus on keeping you safe if I let myself wonder what it would be like to hold you again."

"Good." A tiny hint of teasing flickered through her eyes as she tucked the money into Lincoln's front pocket. "I don't want to break that. My life is teetering on the edge of disaster. You deciding you can't stand to be near me is one gut punch I'd really like to avoid."

"That's not going to happen." The lightening release of speaking pure truth spread warmth through Lincoln's chest. "Let's get this done and get back to the house. I would really like to be somewhere safe enough that I can think about kissing you without feeling like I'm endangering the fate of the feu."

"So dramatic." She studied his face for a moment before holding her hand out to him. "Just stay where Regi can't see you. If he thinks a guy who carries himself like a knight is making me tell him to back off, it'll make things worse."

"Let's get inside and find me a hiding place with a good sightline." His heart flipped as he kissed the back of her hand.

She nodded, like she was solidifying her resolve. "We're cutting under and up."

She freed her hand from his but didn't try to keep him from walking beside her as they headed toward the stairs that cut under the street to a subway station.

As they neared the steps, Lincoln glanced back three times, hoping he looked like a nervous tourist as he scanned the people walking behind them, noting their appearances just enough to be able to peg anyone who might be following them.

He looked back again as they reached the station and cut past the ticket machines, heading right to the stairs that led up to the far side of the street.

Daring to pause at the bottom of the steps, Lincoln checked for shadows one more time before following Ari up to the street.

At the top of the stairs, she didn't head left toward the building with all the desks, but went straight, cutting to the main entrance of a massive pharmacy.

As the pharmacy doors slid open, Lincoln chanced another glance behind. He checked again after they'd cut through the store, heading back toward the desk building, exiting the pharmacy through a smaller side door before going forty feet on the open sidewalk to reach the doors of their destination.

Collaborative Endeavour

The name on the door had been painted in letters too small to be read from across the street, almost as though the proprietors of the space hadn't wanted news of their treasure spreading to the common masses.

A wave of too-crisp air conditioning struck Lincoln as he stepped through the doors. Goose bumps rose on his arms as he followed Ari across the large open space toward the staircase in the far corner.

The desks had been laid out in perfect rows, with each

empty station prepared for its next inhabitant with identical furniture and basic office necessities.

Of the dozen people they passed, only two bothered to look Ari and Lincoln's way. Neither seemed overly interested in the newcomers. Still, Lincoln risked stopping at the door to the stairs, making sure all the desk people were still in their seats, checking for anyone lingering on the street watching through the windows.

Even through the tension in his body that screamed danger lurked near, he couldn't spot anything to interpret as a threat.

"You good?" Ari whispered.

"Fine." Lincoln closed the door to the concrete stairwell. "Though admittedly bothered by the lack of security."

"The noteworthy lack of cameras and guards is what makes this sterile, quasi-dystopian place our ideal location." Ari pulled out her phone, swiping over to an app with a desk-shaped icon as she led Lincoln up the stairs. "Also creates a perfect setup for criminals, but I'm not going to reject unintentional aid from bad guys."

"If there are criminals using this space, we need to meet Regi somewhere else. We can't get caught in a somb police raid with magic-wrought daggers."

"We'll be fine," Ari said. "Cops don't usually bother with places like this until the pot's boiling. Right now, it's still a warm little hot tub of inequity."

"How do you know about police raids?"

Roguish laughter glinted in Ari's eyes. "I don't think you're ready for that story."

Lincoln's toe caught on the stairs. He tripped up a step, catching himself with a thud that echoed through the stairwell.

"Don't worry, I currently have no outstanding arrest warrants with the somb police." The laughter in Ari's eyes grew. "It's okay, you can ask."

"Were there warrants?"

"Wouldn't you like to know?" She winked.

A swoop of quivering trepidation mixed with the thundering desire to hold Ari's hand and the anxious need to defend her from sombs and feu alike, forming a spiked ball that tried to punch out of his chest with every heartbeat.

She stopped at the door to the third floor. "We'll make a pass to find you a hidey hole and check for anyone waiting in the shadows."

"Let me go first. I have a better chance of recognizing a Maree."

"I've rented room 318C." Ari squeezed his hand and stepped aside to let him open the door.

20

Ari

The two sets of floorplans she'd found had been almost entirely accurate, close enough she didn't regret her choice of venue.

Most of the private offices on the third floor were little more than glass cubes with glass doors. But along the far wall, a set of three conference rooms had proper, solid walls. All three also had blinds on their single window set into their securely locked door.

Not that Ari could close the blinds. Not with Lincoln panicked about her safety.

With everyone panicked about your safety.

You're lucky to have people who care about you enough to bother worrying.

Try for gratitude, Ari.

A curl of self-loathing slithered through her stomach.

The first and largest of the three conference rooms had

been booked. The morning's occupants had left their door's window uncovered, giving Ari a clear view of the six people wearing VR headsets all moving as though dancing to the same music.

"Odd, but fun." Ari slowed her steps as she passed 318C.

Lights off, table clean—just as her booking had promised.

Around the corner, another row of terrarium offices led back to the staircase and elevator. There were no chairs in the hall. No nooks where a person could conveniently linger.

Five of the offices along that row had been taken by people who apparently enjoyed feeling like zoo animals while working. They all typed away on their computers, not even glancing up as Lincoln passed.

Ari pulled out her phone as she followed Lincoln around the rest of the loop. She swiped open the Collaborative Endeavor app, tapping through three screens before being excitedly thanked for spending Jerek's money.

Lincoln slowed as he reached the conference rooms on their second lap around the third floor, blatantly stopping to peer into the window of the VR dance party.

"There's no good line of sight," Lincoln said as Ari stopped, peeking over his shoulder, hoping she just looked like a curious patron. "You have to change the meeting place."

"So little faith," Ari whispered. "Pick up my phone and go to your office, Mr. Martel. You have a very important call to awkwardly sit on while watching my door."

She took two steps away from Lincoln before adding at a normal volume, "I wish that were the weirdest thing I'd seen today."

An odd sense of wrongness crawled across her skin as she shook her head and the short hair of her wig didn't move. She fixed her thoughts on that nerve-grating feeling, thankful for the petty distraction from the fear creeping into her stomach. She swiped to the first code in the app, holding her screen up to the scanner that served as the lock for room 318C.

With barely a hint of an electronic buzz, the lock clicked open.

She turned the knob, solidly wedging her foot in the doorway as she swiped over to the second code for the brand-new booking of office 321.

Gritting her teeth, she dropped her phone, instinctively wincing as the electronic hit the floor.

"Dammit." She bent down, palming the phone with her right hand as she mimed picking it up with the left. With one swift flick of the wrist, she slid the phone across the carpet to the door of office 321. Shaking her head at her own clumsiness, she pocketed the imaginary phone with her left hand and stepped into the conference room, closing the door behind her.

The rectangle of light coming through the door's window left the corners of the room thick with shadows.

Keeping her back to the door, Ari flicked on the lights.

Like a normal person going into a normal conference room.

No reason to glance out the window to make sure Lincoln had gotten into his office.

The conference room's table had been set with eight chairs, though the outlets running down the center of the table could provide power to three times as many devices.

A sign on the wall gave the password to *The Latest in Wifi Technology*.

"I need to up my workspace standards." Ari tried to make herself smile at her own glibness, but the next sign down, which read *This space has been soundproofed for your privacy*, dulled the spark of bravado she clung to.

"Keep it together. You don't have time to reassemble your soul right now, so just don't fall apart."

A sting burned at the back of her eyes.

She reached into her pocket, looking for her phone. The phone she'd just given Lincoln.

She had no computer with her, either.

Just cash and a credit card with a fake name. And a dagger hidden at the small of her back.

Turning back toward the door, she reread the signs.

Regi still hadn't arrived.

An itch started in her chest, both hovering over her skin and digging into her lungs at the same time.

She shook out her shoulders and began pacing beside the table, focusing on the feel of her feet touching the floor, ignoring the smooth, cool gleam calling from the back of her mind, reaching down to caress the itching in her soul, tempting comfort, promising freedom if she'd only obey.

You made a promise.

She circled the table instead.

You made a promise you're not allowed to break.

The itching in her chest changed, sharpening to prickles attacking her lungs.

"There's plenty of air." She stopped beside the door, leaning against the soundproof wall. "You know how to breathe on land, you've spent most of your life on land, you're getting plenty of air, so calm your ass down."

The prickles didn't ebb.

The gleaming promise of freedom pushed through her thoughts, growing larger and cooler all at once, clearing the tumbling panic from her mind like ice pressing against a throbbing wound.

"You're okay," she whispered to the empty room. "You don't have to panic. Fight or flight isn't necessary. You have options. You don't have to run."

She focused on the air flowing freely in and out of her lungs.

Plenty of air.

Nothing to run from.

Nothing to fear from staying on dry land.

The gleam at the back of her mind started to fade, retreating to an isolated corner where she could almost pretend not to feel it every moment of every day.

She closed her eyes, listening to the faint sounds in the room, waiting for a tiny electric buzz and the click of a lock opening.

Her heart had managed to settle back into its normal, inhumanly slow rhythm before the lock finally buzzed and clicked open.

Ari stayed pressed against the wall, one hand gripping the dagger on her back, as the door swung open.

The man who stepped into the room wore a baseball cap, sunglasses, and a boho scarf that covered most of his face.

Letting go of her dagger, Ari shoved the man, knocking him clear of the door as she slammed it shut behind him.

The man whipped around, hands held front, ready to defend himself.

He froze as he spotted Ari.

She reached behind her back, grabbing the hilt of her dagger.

"Juliet." He stepped toward her.

She yanked her dagger free.

The man fumbled back a step at the sight of the blade.

"Hat off," Ari said. "Glasses off. Scarf off."

"Jul—"

"Let me see your face." Ari sidestepped, planting herself in front of the door, blocking the man's exit.

"Okay." He moved slowly, taking off the scarf, then hat and glasses, shoving his pitiful disguise into his pockets as Ari examined his face.

Thick stubble covered his chin and cheeks. Worry had

replaced the joy in his eyes. His skin was paler and a touch gray, making the rings beneath his eyes seem to fit his face.

"It's me." Regi gave the smallest smile. "And you're alive. Thank god you're alive."

He stepped forward again, then paused, giving Ari time to stop him before pulling her into a tight hug. He rested his cheek against the top of her head. "I thought I'd never find you."

For a reason she couldn't have explained, she wrapped her arms around him, clinging to the boy who may have doomed her.

"Juliet, we need to go." Regi took her by the shoulders, stepping away from her to look through the window in the door.

"We can't."

"I stashed my car nearby." Regi pulled her sideways, out of view of the window. "Once we get off the island, we can figure out where to go."

"No."

"Juliet, we have to move."

"My name isn't Juliet." Ari slid her dagger back into its sheath and lifted his hands away from her shoulders. "And I can't go anywhere with you."

"Your name isn't important." Regi reached for her arm.

"I was at the gala to help a friend of mine." Ari stepped away from him, easing toward the door. "I should never have gotten you involved in any of this. It wasn't part of the plan, it just happened. It was wrong of me to be so careless, and I'm sorry."

"You're sorry?" Regi choked out a laugh. "Please, please explain to me what you're sorry about."

"Reg—"

"Was it leading me into the shadows like a goddess fallen to earth and giving me the best, most exciting and romantic night of my life?"

"I know it was wrong." Pain pinched the front of Ari's throat.

"As wrong as your fighting four security guards?" Regi side-stepped, planting himself in front of the door handle. "I've seen the video. You knocked the first two out like they were ragdolls."

"I took some martial arts when I was a kid."

"So you just run around kicking the shit out of guards?"

"I was helping my friend."

"And then two with clubs came after you. Juliet, you could have died."

"My name isn't Juliet."

"You ran across water." Regi stepped closer to her. "Your head was bleeding. You looked like you were going to pass out, but instead you sprinted across water!"

"It's not what you think."

"Are you sure? Because I've thought of a lot of things that might explain what the hell I saw." The last of the color drained from Regi's face.

"Just take a breath." Ari held out her hands, ready to catch him.

"You could be a mutant." Regi nodded. "The next step in human evolution. You could be an alien. It would be right on brand if a goddess swept into my life and she's an alien. Or maybe you are an actual goddess. I don't know!"

"Please don't shout." Ari grabbed his wrists.

"Or you could be a super spy with high-tech shoes. Or I could be trapped in the delusion from hell and you're not even real." Regi swayed. "How am I supposed to know what's real?"

"I am real." Ari let go of his wrists to take his face, making him look at her. "You gave me a ride to a gala, and I got you involved in something that has nothing to do with you. I'm so sorry for everything you've been through, but you're going to be okay."

"No, nothing is okay."

"It will be." She smoothed the wrinkles beside his eyes. "You're going to use your phone to pull down all your videos of me and posts about me. You're going to get rid of it all."

"No." He shook his head, knocking her hands aside.

"Once everything's been deleted, you're going to walk out of here, go home, and take a nap." Ari tried to give a comforting smile. "When you wake up, you're going to pretend it was all a dream. You're never going to talk about me or look for me again."

"I can't do that." Regi reached into his pocket.

"You have to." Ari lowered her hands, preparing to reach for her dagger.

"You could have been dead." Regi pulled out his phone.

Ari didn't relax.

"Take down the videos and just walk away?" Regi unlocked his phone. "I've been worried about you, searching for you."

"And I'm grateful." Ari reached for his phone with her left hand.

Regi lifted his phone out of her reach. "Your gratitude isn't going to make me feel better when you wind up dead."

No one wants me dead. Ari couldn't make herself speak the lie.

"You pulled me into this." Regi swiped on his phone. "I'm not going to spend the rest of my life wondering if they've gotten you, wondering if they're coming after me."

"No one is going to come after you."

He turned his phone's screen toward Ari.

The zoomed-in picture wasn't clear enough for her to recognize the two men's faces, but there was no mistaking the cut of their black suits.

"When did you take this?"

"That one was a few days ago." Regi swiped to the next

picture. "Across the street from my afternoon class." Two more in Maree suits. He swiped again. "Outside my apartment building." Two more Maree.

Panic dragged through Ari's chest, quickening her breath, shooting sharp tingles through her lungs. "When did you last see them?"

"This morning." Regi swiped to a closer picture. One of the two Maree had a shiny bald head. "I recognize that one from the gala."

"We need to get out of here." Ari pulled her dagger from its sheath.

"I lost them before I got here." Regi yanked his hat from his pocket and shoved it back on his head. "I parked my car then made a loop on the subway."

"Shit." She grabbed Regi's arm with her free hand. "You're going to stay close to me."

"I circled the block with my hat on before coming in."

"I say run, you run. I say hide, you hide."

Ari turned toward the door.

A streak of deep red stained the outside of the window.

21

Lincoln

The glass walls of the office seemed to have been designed to make the occupant feel as though they were being watched—scrutinized under the microscope of workplace demands, shrinking them down to nothing more than well-animated office equipment.

How do sombs survive like this?

Lincoln sat at the desk in office 321, holding Ari's phone to his ear, shaking his head as though the scowl on his face came from the speaker on the other end of the line, not the fact that he could barely see anything through the window of Ari's conference room.

"I agree with your assessment of the situation," Lincoln said to no one. "This setup is unacceptable."

He leaned forward in his seat, preparing to stand and pace beside his desk, hoping for a better view.

Ari passed by the conference room window.

He settled back into his chair as she passed the window again less than thirty seconds later, almost as though she were walking in circles.

She's okay.

The burning need to go to her twisted in his chest.

He should be holding her, making sure she knew she was safe.

"Make sure she doesn't run." Lincoln dragged his hand over his head. "Make sure she doesn't have to."

She stopped passing in front of the window.

"There's a way out. There's always a way out."

Martin's favorite phrase whenever he and Lincoln got into trouble as children. A promise to fix whatever chaos they'd caused before their parents found out. A comforting lie that often resulted in the boys creating an even worse disaster.

But Fredrick, he excelled in his role as the eldest of the Martel brood. He really would find a way to get his younger brothers out of trouble.

Lincoln lowered the phone from his ear. Ari had left it unlocked.

He couldn't call Fredrick or Martin. If the faction of Maree who'd tried to seize control of the compound hadn't been stopped, the slightest distraction could put his brothers in danger.

The fight hasn't ended. If it had, you'd know.

A pang of fear sliced through Lincoln's chest.

Rebellion within the Knights Maree. Blood being spilt in the compound he'd called home for most of his life.

He shoved the fear aside, ignoring its sharp ache to focus on the phone in his hand.

Ari's phone.

His mother knew more about Maree laws than most of his teachers ever had. His parents had fled the compound. They were away from the fighting. If he could get his mother on the phone for just a few minutes—

Movement at the elevator end of the corridor caught Lincoln's eye.

A man hurried down the hall, a patterned scarf around his face, the brim of his baseball cap tipped low, his shoulders creeping higher with every step.

Lincoln set Ari's phone on the desk, sliding a dagger from the sheath at his ankle as the man neared office 321. Lincoln tipped his head down, feigning reading from Ari's phone as the man passed.

The man didn't even slow his steps to take a second glance at Lincoln, didn't pause at all until he reached the door of Ari's conference room.

Lincoln kept his chin tucked, avoiding the man's gaze as the man turned in a circle twice and glanced to the elevator one more time before pulling out his phone and scanning to open the conference room's lock.

The man opened the door.

Ari's hand flashed into sight as she shoved the man forward.

The door slammed shut.

The back of Ari's head stayed in view through the window.

"It's Regi." Lincoln nodded to himself. "She's fine. It's just Regi."

Ari stumbled closer to the window, knocked back as the man, as Regi, threw his arms around her. He laid his cheek on top of her head.

She leaned into the embrace.

"Ari can take care of herself." Lincoln tightened his hold on his dagger as Regi grabbed Ari's shoulders, yanking her out of view.

She wasn't in danger. It had to be Regi locked in there with her. She wouldn't have embraced a Maree who'd come to hurt her.

But why would she let the somb who'd put her in so much danger touch her at all?

Lincoln pressed his forearm against the edge of the desk, letting the pressure on his bone jar his mind away from tumbling into a spiral of questions he had no right to ask.

A flicker of movement showed through the window, like someone waving their hand to emphasize a shout.

Lincoln turned his chair, angling himself toward the door of his glass cage. He picked up Ari's phone, holding it to his ear with one hand, while tucking his other by his side to hide the dagger in his grip.

A hand flicked past the window again.

Another movement caught the corner of Lincoln's eye. Coming up the corridor from the elevator, two Maree, both young, not much older than Lincoln.

The man, he knew. Brooks from Fredrick's year in school.

And the woman...Elizabeth? No, Olivia. Maybe a year or two ahead of them.

Lincoln tipped his head away as the Maree neared, heading right toward room 318C.

They split apart as they reached the door, placing themselves on either side of Ari's only exit.

Brooks leaned in, glancing through the window. He nodded to Olivia.

Ice-cold panic encased Lincoln's body as Olivia pulled a thin silver knife from her hip.

No!

The shout echoed through his mind as he pushed himself to his feet, lunging for the door of his cage, throwing it open as Olivia pressed the thin blade through the crack by the door handle. A blue shimmer glistened around her hands as she pulled the knife down.

No!

The scream tore through his thoughts.

Brooks spotted him. He raised his baton as Lincoln plowed toward him. "Martel?"

Lincoln slammed Brooks into the wall, knocking him over before he'd finished speaking Lincoln's name.

Olivia spun toward Lincoln, the thin blade in her hand still glowing a vicious blue. She lunged at Lincoln, slashing her knife at his arm.

He leapt back, dodging around the still-fallen Brooks, getting Olivia's back to the door.

"Where's Mariah?" She steadied her stance.

Lincoln raised his dagger.

"What the hell are you doing?" Brooks leapt to his feet.

"Mariah ran away," Lincoln said. "She wanted to come with us."

"Where is Mariah Chanler?" Olivia shifted her weight forward.

"Safe."

"Fine, don't tell me. I've been looking forward to questioning the div."

Rage consumed reason as Lincoln lunged forward, slashing his blade for Olivia's gut.

She leapt sideways, toward the perpendicular corridor, evading Lincoln's attack, pinning him between her and Brooks.

"Stand down, Martel." Brooks stepped toward Lincoln, holding his hand out as though expecting Lincoln to surrender his weapon. "You're not going to fight us."

Lincoln kicked out, catching Brooks in the hip, knocking him down again.

Olivia charged, slashing her knife, aiming for Lincoln's neck.

Lincoln blocked the blow with his forearm, not feeling the pain of the blade slicing through his flesh as he grabbed Olivia's arm, wrenching her sideways, slamming her back against the wall as he drove his dagger up under her ribs.

The blue blade fell from her hand. She opened her mouth like she wanted to scream, but the scream didn't come.

"No!" Brooks scrambled to his feet, horror contorting his face as he watched Lincoln rip his dagger from Olivia's gut.

She pressed her hands to the wound as she stumbled sideways, reaching for the blade she'd dropped.

Lincoln lunged after her, bracing himself against door as he kicked her knife down the hall.

"Drop the weapon." Brooks flicked his wrist. A faint, glowing sheen surrounded his baton.

The rumble of fleeing footsteps and the hollow thunk of fists banging on glass flickered at the edges of Lincoln's mind.

"Leave." Lincoln planted himself in front of Ari's door. "Just walk away."

"I can't do that, kid," Brooks said. "And a Martel knows that. A Martel also knows his duty to the Maree."

"You don't understand—"

"That you've been brainwashed by a div?" Brooks softened his stance. "I won't pretend to know what you've been through, but you've got to understand that none of this is your fault. The Maree can help you. We can get you to the other side of this. Whatever the div did to you—"

"She hasn't done anything to me."

"You just stabbed a fellow Maree." Brooks pointed to where Olivia lay on the ground, but neither he nor Lincoln dared to glance down at their wounded fellow. "No Martel I know would do that."

"You haven't heard about the compound?" Lincoln said.

Something pressed into Lincoln's back.

"Lincoln, let me out." Ari pushed on the door behind him.

Lincoln shifted his weight, wedging his heel against the door, keeping Ari from opening it.

"Maree are fighting Maree," Lincoln said. "There's a battle happening in our home."

"Stand down, Martel." Brooks tightened his grip on his baton. "I'm trying to help you."

"Ari hasn't brainwashed me."

"Let me out." Ari pushed on the door.

"There are things going on here you don't understand," Lincoln said. "The feu are in danger. We're—"

"The feu are in danger because of that div." Brooks stepped closer. "Don't let her twist your mind around. Think, Martel. She's a criminal. She attacked the Museum of Magic. She kidnapped Mariah Chanler. She jeopardized the secrecy that keeps all feu safe."

"She was defending herself against Maree who betrayed their vow of secrecy by attacking. She's done more to protect the feu than most Maree could ever dream of."

"She's feeding you lies," Brooks said. "But we can make this right. Put your weapon down now, and I'll tell the Council you helped capture the div. You'll get a commendation and the help you need to—"

"Let us go, Brooks. I give you my word as a Maree and a Martel, we are saving the feu."

The wailing of police sirens crept into the building.

"I'm taking the div." Brooks flicked his wrist again. The glowing sheen of the baton brightened to a crackle of white sparks that danced across its surface. "Dead or alive. No matter the cost. Those are my orders, Martel. Don't make your mother mourn her son."

"I'm sorry, Brooks."

Lincoln lunged forward, clearing Ari's path as he ducked below Brooks's baton. He jabbed his elbow, catching Brooks in the ribs, gaining a blow to the back in return.

Someone behind him screamed.

Not Ari. Too low.

That split second of distraction gave Brooks time to swing again. He caught Lincoln behind the knee. The crackling sparks of the baton sent a wave of numbing pain shooting through Lincoln's leg.

Lincoln stumbled forward, grabbing the glass wall, using his momentum to spin back around as the sound of fist striking flesh came from behind him.

Ari sliced her dagger down, aiming for Brooks's baton.

Brooks grinned as he knocked Ari's blow aside.

He raised his crackling baton.

Lincoln swung first, aiming the pommel of his dagger for the back of Brooks's skull.

Ari twisted out of Brooks's reach as Lincoln's blow hit Brooks with a sickening crack.

Brooks sagged forward and fell.

The sound of the sirens cut through the pounding in Lincoln's ears.

Ari stepped away from Brooks, still gripping her dagger, ready for Brooks to spring back to his feet, but he didn't move.

"We have to go." Ari shoved her dagger into its sheath at the small of her back. "Regi, grab her knife."

"No. No, this can't be happening." Regi stood in the doorway of conference room 318C, head shaking—whole body shaking.

"It is happening, and we can't leave their weapons behind." Ari grabbed Brooks's baton from the floor before patting around his hips. "Someone check the other one. Now!" She yanked something from Brooks's pocket before scrambling to his ankles.

Lincoln cut past her, heading toward Olivia.

Regi beat him there.

The somb stood beside Olivia—

Olivia's corpse.

The somb gripped Olivia's thin-bladed, magic-wrought knife, his eyes wide as he stared at the bloody weapon.

Lincoln checked her hips, taking her baton and standard issue knife then grabbing the wallet and phone from her pocket before pulling an extra blade from her boot.

The rumble of shouted commands came from the staircase at the far end of the hall.

"Dammit." Lincoln spun toward the noise.

"Lincoln, my phone." Ari reached for him.

A moment of panic sparked through his chest before he remembered he'd shoved the phone into his pocket. Digging past Olivia's things, Lincoln grabbed Ari's phone and tossed it to her.

"Steer Regi." Ari ran down the hall that cut along the row of conference rooms.

Lincoln shoved Olivia's baton into his belt and grabbed Regi's arm, dragging him after Ari.

"Come on, you little shit." Ari stopped in front of room 318A, swiping frantically at her phone as the rumble from the staircase changed, gaining clearer sounds Lincoln could almost distinguish as words.

22

Ari

"Come on, you little shit." Ari swiped her thumb across her phone's screen.

The surface had cracked, splintering enough the app didn't want to call up the code.

Booming, angry, male voices came from the far side of the floor.

"Just—" Ari dragged her finger across the screen. Tiny glass splinters lodged themselves in her skin as her phone opened the code. She held the broken screen up to the scanner. "Do not sass me," she muttered to the lock.

The lock clicked.

Ari wrenched the door open, holding it aside as Lincoln dragged Regi into the conference room.

"This is the NYPD—"

Ari dodged into the room and closed the door behind her. "Come on. Come on."

A buzzing came from inside the lock. The buzzing turned to a pained whirring as the lock jammed.

"Damn I'm good." Ari turned toward the boys, stepping out of view of the window in the door.

Both boys stared at the center of the room, eyes wide, mouths just a little bit open.

The group that had been dancing with the VR headsets on hadn't been bothered by the three people fleeing the cops. They all kept dancing, moving to the rhythm of a song Ari could almost hear as it blasted through the participants' headphones.

"Rave of the future." She cut around the boys, heading toward the front corner of the room where a gloriously discreet exit sign sat nestled in the soundproof padding of the walls.

"The police will be coming up the stairs," Lincoln whispered behind her.

"Oh ye of little faith." Ari pushed open the exit door, her heart catching for a split second as she waited for an alarm to sound.

Silence.

"I love riding on the back of criminal infrastructure." She held the door open, letting Lincoln and Regi reach the stairs before her. "Climb."

"What's happening?" Regi let Lincoln drag him up the stairs. "Can someone tell me what the hell is happening?"

Spots of red stained the stairs in front of Ari. "Someone's dripping blood."

"It's me," Lincoln said.

"Wrap it," Ari said. "Regi, don't you dare stop climbing."

Regi managed to keep moving on his own as Lincoln pulled off his shirt and wrapped it around his arm. The blood seeped through the fabric too quickly.

They neared the seventh-floor landing. "This is our stop."

Regi shoved the door open, dodging through like demons were nipping at his tail.

Ari checked the door on the landing for blood smears before following the boys onto the seventh floor.

The remains of an epic party littered the ground. Most of it had been swept to the side, as though someone had made a good attempt at cleaning before giving up on the hopeless task.

"Don't drip." Ari cut past Lincoln, heading to the opposite corner of the room, weaving between a wrecked DJ booth and a pile of empty liquor bottles.

"Ari, find a place to hide," Lincoln said. "I'll let the cops take me. Get back to Jerek and—"

"We're all getting back to Jerek," Ari said.

Thick, black fabric covered the walls in that corner of the room, hung in massive drapes like someone had wanted to create the feel of being in the wings of a theatre, ready to take the stage for the show of a lifetime.

Ari cut in at the edge of the curtains, squeezing behind the fabric, letting the weight of it press against her.

A new kind of siren joined the others already blaring outside.

Dragging her fingers along the wall, Ari plowed forward.

"I'm not wrong on this," she whispered. "I'm not wrong."

Her fingers found a recess in the wall.

"Ari, take the weapons," Lincoln said. "I'll go back down, buy you time—"

"I don't need time, I need a win." She felt down the edge of the recess, holding her breath until she found the lip at the bottom. "Give me a win." She dug her fingers in below the edge and pushed up.

A slit of daylight flooded the pure darkness behind the curtain as the blare of the sirens drove into Ari's ears.

She gripped the bottom of the window, ramming it up all the way.

The alley between her and the next building over was only four feet wide, but someone had already erased the need to jump the gap. A thin mesh platform had been rigged below the window, leaving less than a two-foot break between it and the ladder attached to the side of the neighboring building.

Ari ducked, keeping hidden as she peered out to the alley below.

Cops stood guard at the end of the alley, but none of them were looking up.

Ari turned back to Lincoln.

He had a grip on Regi's wrist. He'd bled through the fabric wrapped around his arm, but his face hadn't gone an awful shade of pale.

Yet.

"Lincoln, can you climb?" Ari asked.

"Yes."

She glanced to Regi. "Don't scream."

"No." Regi shook his head. "Whatever it is, no."

"You don't actually have a choice." Ari shoved the Maree baton in the side of her waistband and ducked through the window.

The shelf below her looked more like installation art designed to highlight the fragility of life than anything a person should stand on.

She tested its strength, leaning half her weight onto the platform before stepping out over the open air. She reached forward, grabbing a rung on the ladder across the street, transferring her weight onto the much more solid structure before even attempting to convince her lungs it was okay to take another breath.

She started climbing, not glancing down until she'd made it five rungs up, clearing the way for the boys.

Regi knelt on the platform, frozen, staring down at the ground.

"If the Maree catch you, they will kill you," Ari said over the sirens. "Do you want to give up or keep moving?"

Regi grabbed on to the ladder.

"Good." Ari climbed faster, getting halfway up before looking down again.

Lincoln had made it onto the platform, staying on his knees as he reached for the bottom rung of the ladder.

"Stay where you are!" The shout came from the alley below. "We will come to you."

"We've got people coming out of a seventh-floor window. I need rescue over here," another voice said before chaos devoured all words.

Ari reached the roof. She pulled herself over the ledge and onto the solid surface, stepping aside to let Regi scramble up after her.

"Help Lincoln," Ari said.

"Come on," Regi grunted.

Ari ran for the far side of the roof, not letting herself look back to make sure Lincoln had made it over the ledge.

The roof door had been propped open a crack with a broken brick.

She yanked the door fully open, dodging into the stairwell, peering down to the floors below.

"Move the brick and close the door," Ari said.

The door banged shut behind her.

She finally let herself glance back.

Lincoln shifted the fabric on his arm, trying to stop the bleeding.

Regi panted, his face sheet-white, pure panic filling his eyes.

"How opposed to scars are you?" Ari wiped the sweat from her hands onto her pants. "Lincoln, scars?"

"I don't care." Lincoln braced his hurt arm against his bare chest, pulling a knife from his belt with his free hand.

"Great." Ari grabbed his wounded arm.

Lincoln gasped through his teeth as she pulled away the bloody shirt.

"This might hurt, I've never tried it before." Ari grazed her finger along the gash, letting herself feel the movement of Lincoln's blood. "At the bottom of these stairs is a maintenance room." She closed her eyes, focusing on the blood at the very edge of Lincoln's wound. She called to the blood, wooing it, bidding the tiny bits of water within the plasma to leave Lincoln. To come to her. To let the wound clot and dry.

Lincoln sucked air in through his teeth again.

Dread rushed through Ari's thoughts, promising when she opened her eyes she would find Lincoln dead on the floor, desiccated by her touch.

But he stood in front of her, alive, breathing, staring down at the massive scab on his arm.

"How the hell did you do that?" Regi whispered.

"You okay?" Ari kept hold of Lincoln.

"Fine." Lincoln rolled his wrist. "Thanks."

"Good." Ari ran down the stairs, not giving Lincoln a chance to glimpse the relief in her eyes. "If the nasty little criminals on the web are right, we've got an epic escape route waiting for us."

"If?" Regi asked.

"It's the best I can give you."

23

Lincoln

Lincoln wiped the blood from his arm with the last dry bits of his shirt, carefully avoiding the wound Ari had just healed. Or dried.

Tended to.

He rammed the bloody shirt into his pocket, freeing his hands as they reached the landing on the second floor.

A squeeze of panic clamped around his neck as they passed the door. He tightened his grip on his knife, sending a rush of pain through his arm, but no police burst in to arrest the murderer.

You were defending yourself. You had to save Ari.

Ari didn't slow as they passed the door on the first floor.

The steps themselves changed as they headed down to the basement. The stair grips had worn away in places, and the concrete had cracked, as though not even a building inspector had been welcomed into the basement for a long while.

Ari reached the bottom of the steps. She held up a hand, warning the boys before switching to a walk.

The old florescent lights in the hall gave the peeling paint on the walls a patchy, yellow hue. The checkered pattern on the linoleum floor had been worn down in two strips along the center, as though the same thing had been dragged in the same way for years or even decades.

"Where are the cops?" Regi whispered. "Where are we going?"

"The cops are going to be right behind our happy little asses." Ari opened a door with a rectangle of missing paint where the room title should have been. She glanced inside before closing it and creeping to the next door down. "But we came down the third cop-free emergency staircase in the center of this building, which, according to the official city records, doesn't exist." She opened another door.

The stink of wet mop wafted out into the hall.

"What do you mean *doesn't exist*?" Regi said. "I'm here. I'm seeing this. Am I actually seeing this?"

"Yes, you are." Ari paused long enough to shoot a soothing smile Regi's way. "But city records are easy to hack."

"What?" Regi's voice wobbled. "That's not possible."

"I promise it is." Ari crossed the hall to check another door. "Anything below federal level is doable before coffee."

"Federal?" Regi said.

"That takes espresso," Ari said. "Lots of it."

"We're trapped," Regi said. "They're going to find the stairs. They're going to come after us. We should turn ourselves over to the police. We can explain everything. They can protect us from the agents."

"Not agents. Knights." Ari opened a door with a crooked, rusted handle, releasing the stench of motor oil. "Oh come on, you nasty assholes, help a girl out."

"I don't know how!" Regi said.

"Not you." Ari slipped into the room, pulling her phone from her pocket, using it as a flashlight.

Lincoln slid the baton from his belt and flicked his wrist, making the sparks on the Maree weapon crackle.

"How the hell did you do that?" Regi whispered.

Lincoln closed the door behind him, shutting them into the building's machine room.

"Why the hell is his stick glowing?" Regi said.

"That's more complicated than we have time for, and I don't want to shove you into a worse panic spiral, so explanations are going to have to wait." Ari stopped beside a long pipe, which ran the length of the room. She aimed her phone's light at the pipe and crouched low, looking for something on the bottom side. "All that matters right now is that the cops aren't an option for you. They can't protect you from the people who've been following you."

Ari stood, moving slowly along the pipe, still searching for something.

"If they can't protect me, can you?" Regi asked.

She stopped, freezing as though some catastrophic thought had seized control of her body.

Before Lincoln could drag something comforting to say from the chaos of his mind, she ran her fingers along the top of the pipe, tracing the outline of a poorly carved arrow pointing toward the right side of the room.

"I won't lie and promise to protect you"—Ari followed the arrow's path—"but, and I say this with total honestly and extreme regret for letting you get anywhere near this, you're in too deep and you have zero chance of surviving this on your own. So gloss over the details for now and just assume that choosing not to do what I tell you will result in your death."

Ari knelt beside the massive boiler. "Well, hopefully just a quick death. Depending on which of the four-plus groups who are after us catches you, they might torture you before they kill you, or lock you in a subterranean dungeon and gleefully watch you waste away day by day, suffering more and more until you finally die."

"Why would anyone want to torture me?" A tone of terror shook Regi's words, like panic might actually break him from the inside out.

"To see if you're hiding any information about me or my friends." Ari crawled beside the boiler. "Maybe just for funsies. Again, depends on who gets to you first."

The need to pull Ari into his arms, to shield her from every possible pain, to hold her and be sure she was safe, drove every other want from Lincoln's mind.

He tightened his grip on his weapons again, ignoring the pulling around his wound, trying to promise himself a baton and a blade would be enough to protect her.

Ari stopped, tipping her phone to focus the light on an arrow carved into the dusty concrete floor. "Sometimes simple works."

She looped back around the boiler, cutting past the door on her way to follow the arrow.

A thunder of boots pounded through the ceiling above them.

"Sooner than I'd hoped." Ari detoured from the path of the arrow, grabbing a worn welding jacket from a bench in the corner. She tossed the heavy leather jacket to Lincoln. "Better than half-naked and bloody."

"Thanks." Still gripping the dagger and sparking baton, Lincoln pulled on the jacket, trading pain from the leather dragging across his wound over tucking his weapons away even for a moment.

The grating whirr of aging machinery covered the sounds

coming from the floor above as they neared the back corner of the room.

Ari stopped, squinting as she shined her light on the back wall.

Metal doors covered the electrical control panels. Hand-written labels had been added to the doors, joining the official warning signs.

Ari swept her light from low to high. "Come on, you evil assholes, don't let me down now."

Lincoln kept his gaze fixed on the path of her light, searching for an arrow.

"In the graffiti." Regi pointed just above where Ari had been looking.

A coiled snake had been spraypainted on the wall. The red, monstrous eyes of the creature seemed to glow in the dim light, leaving its plain, arrow-shaped tail as a detail barely worth noting.

"I didn't know you liked art." Ari shoved her cellphone partway into her pocket, leaving the flashlight peeking over the fabric like a beacon on her hip, and dug her fingers into the side of the panel below the arrow. The door didn't budge. "Come on."

Fear seized Lincoln's spine as a muffled shout came from too close by.

"Lincoln, light." Ari twisted her hip toward him as she ran her fingers along the side of the panel.

He grabbed the phone from her pocket.

"Get it a little closer," Ari said.

Lincoln leaned in, focusing the light on her fingers.

A bang came from the front of the room.

Lincoln shoved the baton and phone into his welding jacket, wincing from the baton's sparks singeing his skin as light poured in through the machine room door.

24

Ari

The light from the hall invaded the machine room.
Trapped. Trapped like rats.
Exterminate the abomination.
A wave of panic roared through Ari's mind, adding to the chaos whipping through her thoughts, offering a thousand impossible solutions at once and dragging each idea away before she had a hope of grabbing on to it.

Either you get out, or you get dead.

She closed her eyes, still running her fingers along the edge of the metal electrical panel door.

You will not let them catch you. They don't get to catch you.

Her fingers snagged on a metal latch.

Please, please, please, please, please.

She flipped the latch and pulled on the door.

The metal swung silently open.

Keeping low, Ari crept forward, reaching into the black of

the electrical panel like she was on a quest to find a frost-bitten lion.

Her fingers found nothing.

She reached back, fumbling on the leather of Lincoln's stolen coat as she took his arm, pulling him in front of her. "Head down," she whispered as she shoved him into the darkness.

He didn't resist.

Regi gasped as she grabbed him.

Fighting her instinct to freeze, she steered him into the panel, pushing him to follow Lincoln.

A flashlight's beam swept down the aisle beside the boiler.

Ari knelt, twisting as she crawled into the panel, closing the door behind her.

She held her breath, waiting for someone to shout they'd seen the door move.

Nothing.

A gentle touch brushed Ari's shoulder, offering her a warning before a hand gripped her arm, pulling her to stand upright, guiding her farther into the darkness.

The ground beneath her feet stayed smooth, as though the creator of their path had understood the dangers of trip hazards in escape routes.

The hand disappeared from her arm, shifting down to her hip, moving her to squeeze between two bodies.

An arm wrapped around her waist, holding her close to a broad chest.

The scent of leather and motor oil surrounded Ari.

She allowed herself one moment in the shelter of Lincoln's arms, just enough to dull the edges of her panic.

He flicked his wrist, igniting the glowing sheen on the Maree baton, letting its dim light add shadowy definition to the darkness.

The brick-lined passageway was barely wider than the panel they'd entered through. The cement floor had no cracks or bumps as it reached deeper underground.

Lincoln looked to Ari, opening his hand, offering her his baton.

She shook her head and stepped away from him, pulling Brooks's baton from her waistband. A hum of energy flooded her hand as the baton's light sparked into being with a soft crackle. Holding it high enough to give the boys light, she followed the path farther down.

"—there's any way for—" The words broke through the mechanical rumble that filled the tunnel.

Lincoln turned, placing himself between the panel and Regi.

"—gonna like this. We should start taking bets on how fast the captain shits himself. I'll put forty—"

Ari took Regi's hand, pulling him down the passage as he stared open-mouthed at Lincoln guarding the panel.

The tunnel curved, cutting a sharp angle to the left.

Ari slowed to peer around the corner.

The empty passage sloped down at a steeper angle until a wide, metal door blocked the path.

Give me this win.

She dragged Regi with her as she ran to the door.

A handle had been set into the metal and a hole cut through the concrete right above it, giving just enough space for a hand to grip the lock made of a metal peg and vertical loops, which stopped the door from being pushed aside, like the serial killer version of a pocket door. Simple, but strong enough to keep the door from opening from the outside.

"Don't touch the light." Ari handed Regi the baton.

He tipped his face away from the gleam, holding the baton at arm's length as though terrified it might explode.

Gritting her teeth to stifle the threats she longed to spew at the lock, Ari grabbed the top of the peg.

It pulled free, as though regularly checked by a well-paid maintenance man.

She pocketed the peg and shoved the door aside, blinking in the low light of the room ahead.

A maintenance closet—brooms, tools, mops, orange cones—all treasures to behold.

Ari stepped through the door, beckoning Regi to follow.

He nodded and crept toward her.

"Lincoln," Ari whispered. "Lincoln."

He didn't appear.

"Stand here." Ari took Regi's shoulders, planting him with his back holding the door open.

She ran back up the tunnel, one hand on the wall, one in front of her searching for the curve in the passage.

Her outstretched hand smacked into the brick wall.

At the top of the tunnel, lights crept in around the edges of the panel, outlining Lincoln's silhouette, casting him as the noble warrior ready to meet his doom.

She sprinted to him, grabbed his wrist, and dragged him back without giving him a chance to argue.

Lincoln pulled against her grip, trying to return to his post as glorious, defensive, sacrificial offering.

She yanked him around the corner.

He stopped struggling as the magnificent light from the maintenance room came into view.

She shoved Lincoln through the pocket door and pivoted Regi out of the way.

The layer of panic that smothered Ari's mind popped and vanished as she slid the door closed, blocking out the tunnel.

"I don't"—Regi shook his head—"I don't know what's happening."

"Do you want to search Regi for trackers or block the door?" Ari glanced to Lincoln.

"Which kind of trackers?" Lincoln took the baton from Regi, stopping the sparks with a flick of his wrist.

"Start with his phone—" Ari shook her head, shuffling her thoughts back into order. "We have to make sure his and the Marees' phones can't be tracked, then check his clothes. I'll do Regi, you do the door. Have a peg. I recommend ramming it into the crack under the door as phase one of the barricade."

She tossed the peg she'd pulled from the door's lock to Lincoln, making sure he caught it before turning to Regi.

"Give me the phones and strip down to your briefs." Ari held out her hands. "I'm really hoping you don't have any hidden body jewelry."

25

Eve

The sounds of the city flicked at Eve's thoughts, distracting her from the book in her hands. She shook out her shoulders and started from the top of the page again.

When, if given the right provocation, a lycanthrope's obedience is won, the master of the beast has gained a mightier weapon than a hellhound straight from the fires. Violence may be the swiftest—

"Find anything?" Jerek asked.

Eve glared across the dining room table they'd left up in the second-floor hall so they could sit comfortably while reading the repulsive texts in the archivist's hoard.

"Should I take that as a no?" Jerek set his book down, holding his page with a kitchen-gloved finger.

"All I've found are reminders of why I hate leaving the mountain," Eve said.

"I'm sorry."

"That people are fear-mongering assholes, or that you convinced me to leave the mountain?"

"I wish I could say *both*. But I won't lie and pretend I'm not grateful you agreed to join our sorry crew."

"You sure about that?" Eve pushed the shit-filled book away and grabbed another from the stack Jerek had chosen for her.

"I can't see how I couldn't be." Jerek furrowed his brow, frowning like he actually had to work to remember her failings.

"I killed the archivist, Holden. And now if we never find the butcher, it's on my ass." Anger sparked heat in Eve's chest.

"We mended the Fracture—a feat deemed impossible by all. Now, we're hunting for murderers while in possession of a wealth of knowledge with the benefit of several solid leads. Our circumstances have improved considerably. We'll find the butcher." Jerek picked his book back up. "And I haven't forgotten my promise. You will be the one who gets to gut him."

The heat in Eve's chest twisted, winding into a ball of tension that pressed against her heart and lungs, promising relief would only come with the taste of blood.

"And whoever decides to attack this house first," she said. "Who gets to gut them?"

"I'm hoping it won't come to that."

"You think the archives' patrons will defend us?" Eve leaned across the table. "LeBlanc shows up, it's going to take more than a few magicians with flaring powers to stop him."

"I'm actually looking for a spell that might negate the need for either." Jerek turned his book toward Eve. "The protections my father placed around Holden House have never faltered."

"Which is why going there would have made all of this a lot easier." Anger flicked at the twisting tension.

"Until the Maree barricaded us in." Jerek shrugged. "The inconvenience of constantly changing locations was well worth the freedom of movement. Now that we've chosen to maintain control of the archives, the protections of Holden House are sorely missed."

"You want the Maree to barricade us in?"

"It may come to that, but I'm more concerned with shielding ourselves from the rest of the world than being penned in. And, with the artifacts available in the house and a contribution of yours and Jack's blood, I can begin building the kind of magical boundaries that protect my home."

Jerek tapped on a picture in his book. "This spell would only be the first part of the process. Truly protecting the archives will take layers upon layers of magic. To reach the level of safety Holden House enjoys took my father months. Without his training and experience in incantations, it could very well take me years."

"I'm not staying here for years."

"But every spell, every layer of protection, could prove invaluable when we're inevitably attacked." He pushed his book closer to Eve.

An image sprawled across both pages. Swirls of mist surrounded a castle. Two figures stood on top of the castle wall—one with a moon marked over their shoulder, the other with a dark droplet drawn over their head.

"Your dad used cryptid blood to protect Holden House?" Eve laid her hands flat against the table, pressing down on the wood to drive out the energy racing through her arms.

"Your grandmother's." Jerek turned the book back to himself. "I think she actually sent it as my birthday present."

The wood of the table groaned.

"From what I recall, my father sent her herbs from my mother's spell garden in thanks." Jerek held Eve's gaze, not flinching as the table groaned again. "That's how the feu should live. Helping each other. Living as a community, not as rats, hiding in our dark burrows, guarding whatever we've been able to hoard, terrified that helping others will either lead us to starvation or call predators to our den."

"Wolves are predators, Holden." Eve leaned across the table.

"Isolation is the most fearsome predator of all." Jerek sat for a moment, waiting, watching Eve like he could see her searching for weak points, ready to tear through his pretty words about using Gran's blood, blood that ran in Eve's veins. "I'm not asking this lightly. But if the archives are attacked, odds are you'll lose more than the eighth of a teaspoon of blood I'm requesting."

Eve stayed silent.

"Dealing with an attack would also create another distraction from our search for the butcher and the *they* behind him."

"And this spell of yours, it doesn't require magician blood? Only Jack and I have to slice ourselves open?"

"Magician blood would make things simpler." Jerek turned the book back to Eve and tapped the bottom of the image. A femur lay at the base of the flames. "The bone of a magician is necessary. Father took one from my great aunt's grave to protect Holden House. She loved the place, would've been happy to offer it."

"Do you want help ripping out a bone? I can pull off your leg without shifting." Eve leaned back in her seat, keeping her eyes fixed on Jerek's face, not letting her gaze wander to the joints that would be so easy to tear through.

"If anything, I'd ask for help amputating part of my pinky." Jerek smiled. "Luckily, the host of unsavory items in this place includes a few literal skeletons in the cupboards on the third floor. I only need to confirm which bones belonged to magicians."

"Think carefully before you ask for the next favor." Eve's anger thickened, gaining strength as it seeped out into her limbs.

Jerek frowned. "I'm not sure what other favor I'm supposed to ask."

"Not going to ask your dog to go sniff a bone?"

"I prefer my intestines inside my body, so I would never think of or refer to you as a dog, or as mine." He furrowed his brow. "And why would I ask you to sniff the bones?"

"Feu bones smell different." Eve shoved her chair back, knocking it into the wall as she stood, needing to be on her feet even if the house didn't give her any space to run. "Magician bones smell mostly human, but there's a scent of stale magic on them."

"Oh." Jerek looked down at his hands. "Hmm. Well then, may I request your expertise in selecting which...relic to utilize for the spell?"

"Should I deliver the right one in my teeth?"

Jerek's head snapped up, a hint of fear finally flickering through his eyes as he met Eve's gaze. "You can deliver it however you like, and I'll be grateful for your contribution to the protection of the crew and the archives. You can also vent as much of your anger at me as you wish. I'd rather it be me than any of the others. I deserve it. I asked you to leave the mountain. I asked you to slip into the archives. I brought you face to face with the archivist."

"You're not the one that killed him."

"Technically, Mariah and I *did* kill him, though I understand your meaning."

A growl rattled in Eve's throat. Heat surged to the tips of her fingers, begging them to become claws.

"I deserve your rage, but you don't," Jerek said. "You can't stay this angry. If you need to get out of the city and shift, I'll understand. We all will."

"I'm not leaving until we figure out how to find the butcher." Eve shut her eyes as the heat in her fingers seared her nerves, sending pain shooting up her arms.

"I don't suppose there's any sort of punching bag you can actually use."

A bit of the heat faded. "Not even a little."

"Ford should be able to research something sturdy enough to withstand a werewolf's strength. In Manhattan, you can have just about anything delivered to your door within an hour." Jerek's face stayed completely serious as he nodded. "Would other forms of exertion help?"

"We have to pour concrete to cover the grave in the basement. Locking the bigoted, hate-mongering shit head's corpse belowground might take the edge off."

"I'll ask Ford to order the supplies," Jerek said. "Have any of us actually used concrete before?"

"Ari probably has. Just random enough to be her sort of thing." Eve pushed her chair back into the table. The legs squeaked as they scraped against the wood. "Do you want me to go through the bones first or slice—"

A scream, a bang, and a crash came from upstairs.

26

Lincoln

Sweat slicked Lincoln's back as the sun beat down on his pilfered, heavy leather welding jacket. At least the sweltering coat had pockets large enough for him to keep the knife he clutched in his hand hidden.

A knife you stole from a corpse.

A sickening cold swooped through Lincoln's gut.

A Maree.

He let out a long breath, focusing on Ari leading their trio. On the people they passed who could be a threat to her. On Regi swaying slightly as he walked, as though ready to flee or faint at any moment. On the feeling of the hilt in his hand. On the cramping in his fingers as they begged him to cast the weapon aside.

Ari had taken them on the subway, not stopping until they'd gone too far uptown, passing the archives. They walked south, keeping to the quieter streets, giving Lincoln a better chance of spotting a threat.

She walked down to 85th street, passing the house again, before walking a long block east and looping back up around toward the house.

Her pace stayed steady as they neared the archives, but her posture changed, her shoulders stiffening, the swing of her arms shortening, keeping her hands closer to the weapons now hidden at her hips.

A couple sat on the stoop five houses down from the archives, eating ice cream and laughing as though enjoying a lovely afternoon. Cattycorner from the couple, a van for a painting company had parked in the shade of the trees.

Four houses farther down, two men flanked a small, above-ground flowerbed on their stoop. Both men held trowels and wore gloves, though there were no signs of loose dirt on either of them.

Ari didn't stop until she'd gone up the steps of the archives. She turned toward the boys, her gaze flicking to the gardeners for a split second. "You know the rule that three weird coincidences are no longer a coincidence?"

"I've never heard that rule." Regi shook his head, the movement so quick it looked almost as though his head were trembling.

"Either way, Ford will be pleased." She turned back toward the door.

"Who's Ford?" Regi said.

"You'll love him." Ari reached for the doorbell and froze.

A little note had been taped above the button.

Do NOT ring the bell OR knock.
   Text for entry.
   Or just wait, I can see you on camera.

"Creepy non-coincidences and foreboding phrasing," Ari said. "And I thought we'd already finished the interesting part of our day."

Regi whimpered.

Lincoln stepped past Regi, placing himself on the top stair beside Ari.

"We should leave," Regi whispered.

The first of the door's seven locks clicked open.

"Hop in a car and have them take us to Jersey," Regi whispered.

The second lock clicked, making an odd rasping sound as it turned, as though someone were trying to twist the bolt slowly.

"Once we hit Jersey, we hire a car." Regi nodded, his sweat-limped hair jostling on his forehead. "I have plenty of friends with empty shore houses. We can stay there without using a credit card."

The third and fourth locks clicked.

"I'd still be able to find you if you'd paid for the rideshare with a credit card," Ari said.

The fifth lock gave a heavy thunk. The rumble of a muttered curse came from inside.

"What the hell is going on?" Ari leaned over the railing toward the crack in the dining room curtains as the sixth and seventh locks turned quickly, like someone has chosen to rip off the proverbial band-aid.

"Quiet please." The whisper came as the door slowly opened.

Ford stepped into view, holding his finger to his lips before beckoning them in.

Ari entered, leaving Lincoln to drag Regi up the steps and into the house.

"What's happening?" Ari whispered.

"Why is he here?" Ford frowned at Regi.

"I asked first," Ari said.

Lincoln closed the door.

Ford winced at the click.

"Mariah woke up." Eve padded silently from the kitchen. She pointed to Regi. "What the hell is he doing here?"

"Shit happened." Ari shrugged.

"We can't keep collecting your lovesick castoffs. We're supposed to be—" Eve glared at Regi. "This isn't a halfway house for the heartbroken."

"Thanks, Eve." Ari smiled too brightly. "I didn't actually know that. I just thought it would be fun to drag an innocent somb into our shit show."

"Okay." Ford stepped between Eve and Ari, foolishly giving the werewolf access to his back. "The mess we're in here has to do with a certain somebody's *earache*."

"We were attacked by Maree." Ari pulled Olivia's and Brooks's phones from her back pockets. "Fairy's out of the flowerbed."

"Oh." Ford took the phones. "Glad you're not dead."

"What's wrong with Mariah?" Ari said.

"Her hearing's gone from cryptid good to crying in a closet with a comforter around her head because the sound of Ford chewing his sandwich in the basement was murdering her ears good," Eve said.

"Is she okay?" Ari pulled off her shoes.

"I left a glass of water by the door," Eve said.

"Does Jerek think he can help her?" Ari said.

"It's not a standard circumstance." Ford wrinkled his nose. "He's looking into it, but this...sort of reentry of...abilities has never occurred before. I've put in an order for earmuffs and—"

"Did you miss the part where the Maree attacked them?" Eve asked.

"Can we at least sedate her?" Ari looked to Eve. "Is there a potion you can make?"

"Potion?" Regi whispered.

"It's going to get worse before it gets better just keep breathing," Ari said without looking away from Eve.

"I'm not a potions master," Eve said.

"The one you made for Jerek worked," Ari said.

"Potion." Regi took a step back toward the door.

Lincoln gripped his shoulder, holding him in place.

"I've made one successful potion around you, so now you think I can make more?" Eve said.

"You just said *around you*, which implies more than one successful potion in your life, which makes you the potions master of the day," Ari said. "So can you sedate her?"

"I recommend Valium," Regi said.

"Do you have any?" Eve said.

"No," Regi said.

"Are you sure?" Eve fixed her anger-lit gaze on Regi.

"He really doesn't," Ari said. "I strip-searched him."

Eve turned and stalked up the stairs.

"Is that a yes?" Ari said.

"I'd rather look at potion books than be a part of this." Eve rounded the corner and disappeared onto the second floor.

"Great." Ari dug her fingers into her hair. "This is great."

"I assume you would have mentioned it, but are the Maree currently attacking us?" Ford said.

"Probably not," Ari said.

"Excellent." Ford stepped behind Lincoln and reached for the bottom lock. "I'm assuming Regi is staying for the moment?"

"Yes." Ari tangled her fingers deeper into her hair, pulling at the roots. "Can you take him...wherever in the house is least likely to cause disaster?"

"Kitchen's out." Ford started on the locks. "Basement's definitely out. There's a settee in the hall with Jerek, but—" Ford shook his head.

"The kitchen is the best bet." Lincoln rallied his remaining dregs of will. "It's away from the front door and easy to keep an eye on."

"Unless he tries to sneak out the back door." Ford turned the last of the locks.

Lincoln tightened his grip on Regi's shoulder and steered him down the hall toward the kitchen. "He's being followed by Maree and is wanted by the police. He's not going to run."

27

Ari

Mariah's mattress leaned crookedly against the bedframe, covering part of the pile of broken glass left behind by a lamp that had fallen victim to her panic.

"Mariah." Ari put barely a breath behind the word. She waited for a moment before inching silently toward the closet door. "It's Ari. If you want me to go, that's fine, but I wanted to check on you. Eve's working on something to help you sleep for a while. Is there anything else I can do for you?"

A rustle of movement was closely followed by a gasp of pain.

Ari reached forward, ready to yank open the closet door, stopping herself just before grabbing the knob.

The sound of a shuddering exhale came before the movement began again.

The knob turned, and the door pushed open.

A massive quilt covered most of Mariah, leaving only her face and hands showing. She pressed her hands over the layers of quilt, covering her ears as she retreated deeper into the walk-in closet.

Ari followed, holding her breath as she closed the door behind her.

Mariah scrunched her face, sending fresh tears down her cheeks.

"What can I do?" Ari knelt beside Mariah.

"I can't—" Mariah swallowed as though sick had flooded her mouth. "It's so loud and it's all the same and it's all squeezing my head. There are brakes squeaking, and a sink running, and someone's teeth touching their fork, and the glass won't stop clanking, and it all sounds so close."

"None of the sounds are here." Ari laid her hand on the side of Mariah's comforter cocoon. "Just you and me. All the other noises are far, far away."

"They're not. They're driving through my skull. I can't even tell which heartbeat is mine. There are too many. Hundreds and hundreds pounding beneath the other noise." Mariah curled in on herself, her tear-stained face disappearing into the mass of the comforter. "It's so loud and I can't make it stop. I just want it to stop."

"Give me your hand."

Mariah sank deeper into her cocoon.

"Please," Ari said, "just for a minute."

The comforter shuddered before Mariah's face reappeared. She lifted her hand away from her ear. Her breath caught in her throat. She pressed her hand to her head again.

"I think I can help," Ari whispered.

Mariah's jaw tightened, her breath quickening as she gave Ari her hand.

Ari dragged up the last bit of calm she could find, willing her body to relax as she laid Mariah's palm over her heart.

"Can you feel the rhythm?" Ari said.

Mariah gave a tiny nod.

"Can you hear it?"

Mariah shrank away.

"Just listen to my heartbeat." Ari pressed both her hands over Mariah's. "Find that rhythm. Nothing else matters."

Mariah screwed up her face as though pressing through some awful pain.

"Breathe and focus on the rhythm," Ari whispered.

Don't panic. Ari warned her own heart. *Calm, you are calm. You can be the peace she needs.*

Mariah bent her head forward, her nails digging into Ari's chest.

"My heart is right here," Ari whispered. "Everything else is far away."

Slowly, ever so slowly, Mariah's hand relaxed. She lifted her head, the pain on her face ebbing, though she kept her eyes closed.

"It doesn't match any of the others," Mariah said. "There's no other sound like it."

"Good."

"It's so slow." The wrinkles on Mariah's brow smoothed as she moved closer to Ari, tilting her uncovered ear toward Ari's heart.

Ari sat back on her heels, letting Mariah rest her quilt-covered head against Ari's chest.

"Why is it so slow?" Mariah asked.

Ari's heart gave an extra hard thump.

Mariah looked up at her, worry darkening her tear-reddened eyes.

"I'm a div." Ari's heart rammed against her ribs again. "Half-mer have slower heartbeats."

The tiniest smile curved Mariah's cracked lips. "I knew you were special."

She curled back into Ari's chest, nestling close to the sound of the abomination's heart.

28

Jack

The cool of the pipe did little to ease the nausea sloshing through Jack's stomach, but he kept his forehead pressed to the metal anyway, taking deep breaths through his nose, letting the scents of rust, vague moisture, and dirt dull the putrid stench of the basement.

He'd been able to bear the dust from Eve smashing through concrete just fine.

The addition of a desiccated body put his stomach on edge.

Filling out the aroma with werewolf blood, copper powder, iron powder, mashed up herb paste, a bone that reeked of old tomb, and topping it off with his own blood was too much for his vampire senses to endure.

"How much more blood do you need?" Eve whispered.

"The whole eighth of a teaspoon," Jerek said. "I'm sorry."

"No problem," Eve said. "I'll just slice down to the tendons, make sure it takes a little longer for me to heal."

"Thank you for helping me protect the archives," Jerek said.

"I know why we're doing this, Holden," Eve said.

The sound of slicing flesh came from behind Jack.

"The problem's not depth. It's blood flow. If you don't want to go for an artery, separate the cut skin with your fingers." Jack swallowed sour. "Hold it apart and jiggle a little. It'll slow your healing enough to let you bleed more."

"Sounds great," Eve said.

"Are you all right?" Ford said.

Keeping his cheek pressed to the pipe, Jack turned his head just enough to see Ford at the security monitors.

"Vampires can't puke," Jack said.

"Really?" Ford glanced to Jack, his face looking more intrigued than disgusted.

"New feu insight for you." Jack turned his nose back to the scent of the pipe.

"What's wrong with you?" Eve asked.

"Smell," Jack said.

"It's pretty rancid," Eve said.

"The bone." Jack pointed behind him to the table where Jerek had laid out the ingredients for the spell. "Do you really need that thing?"

"The spell requires a magician's bone," Jerek said.

"There's a dead magician over there." Jack turned away from the pipe, tormenting his stomach to point to the patch of packed dirt surrounded by broken concrete. "We could have used one of his bones."

Neither Jerek nor Eve looked to the grave that had become the centerpiece of Jack's living space.

"Old dead smells so much worse than new dead." Jack turned back to the pipe.

He'd taken three breaths of pipe-scented air before Jerek spoke.

"I thought it best not to involve him," Jerek said. "The former archivist served his purpose. Better for all if he stays buried."

"Fine." Jack shifted his head, giving his temple a turn at touching the cool pipe. "But once the spell is over, you're getting that nasty old bone out of this basement and we're locking the desiccated corpse under a fresh layer of concrete which has got to smell a hell of a lot better than this."

"The nasty old bone actually has to be crushed and scattered," Jerek said.

"Eve can do the crushing upstairs." Jack's stomach sloshed against his lungs. "Are you done bleeding yet?"

"Yep," Eve said. "Thanks for the tip."

"Cryptid blood play." Jack waved away her thanks. "That's Vegas, baby."

"Really?" Ford said.

"Didn't want to know that," Eve said.

"Think of it like sharing a nice meal, vampire style," Jack said.

"I believe I'm ready to begin the spell," Jerek said.

"Great." Eve hopped up to sit on a crate beside Jack. She licked her thumb and wiped away the stray bit of blood still smeared on her palm. "Are you sure you can't puke?"

"Unfortunately," Jack said.

"Here." Ford pulled off his shirt and tossed it to Jack. A delicious hint of pink bloomed in his cheeks. "You said you like the way it smells."

"Thanks." A warm, radiating peace dampened Jack's nausea as he held Ford's shirt up to his nose—a hint of sweat with just the right touch of musk and the earthy vanilla scent of the deodorant Ford had somehow managed to hold on to through all their packing up to run to the next location of doom.

Using the shirt to hide his blush, Jack turned toward the rancid ingredient-laden table.

"Theoretically, the spell itself shouldn't cause any noise." Jerek poured first Jack's then Eve's blood into the bowl with the herbs.

"Even if it does, Mariah might just have to suffer for a bit. We're on to our fourth set of lurkers," Ford said. "The same giant schnauzer has been walked past the house three times in the last hour."

"Same person?" Eve asked.

"No. But if your dog has a giant, white, Gandalf beard, you might as well not bother switching people," Ford said.

"On the bright side, Maree aren't known for using schnauzers." Jerek blended the blood and herbs with his purple, kitchen-gloved hands.

"What happened with Ari and Lincoln and the Maree?" Jack asked. "Other than landing a somb in the kitchen so you have to do the nasty ass spell in my living space."

"I'm not sure," Ford said. "Lincoln looked like he might murder me if I pressed too hard, and Ari's still in the closet with Mariah."

"I hate that sentence," Jack said.

"We can tackle the issue of Maree in Manhattan once the spell is finished." Jerek rubbed the blood-herb paste onto the bone.

"Sorry. I'll try to bleed faster next time," Eve said.

"Your ability to heal is too precious to present with apologies." Jerek wiped the extra blood paste off his now-red gradient gloves with a paper towel, then picked up the jar of copper dust.

He sprinkled that dust over the bone, patting it into the paste before moving on to the iron dust.

He set that jar down and stared at the putrid, defiled bone.

He furrowed his brow and leaned over to check the spell book.

Jack's fangs grew, piercing his bottom lip as the creases in Jerek's brow deepened. "Should we be worried about you doing this spell?"

He cut around the table, pretending to examine the bone while conveniently placing himself between the spell supplies and Ford.

Ford brushed his finger across the back of Jack's hand. The resulting blossom of joy had already retracted Jack's fangs before Jerek finally spoke.

"Not worried, no." Jerek stood up straight and pulled off his deep-orange kitchen gloves. "Simply aware of the potential dangers."

"Which are?" Jack asked.

"I'm not sure." Jerek picked up the bone.

Both ends of the aged femur had been left uncoated by the blood mash. The dull yellow of the bone turned a violent red as the paste shifted to a dark, greenish gray.

"That seems not great," Ford said.

"The color should be irrelevant," Jerek said as the red of the bone darkened to a shade just above black.

"*Should be,*" Eve said. "Perfect."

Jack backed closer to Ford, planting his feet and softening his knees, ready to shield Ford's fragile somb body.

Jerek closed his eyes and tipped his chin up as though speaking to the horizon.

"*En friena enboltza—*"

The bone shifted to absolute black while the mash flashed a blazing red.

"*—fortgiuno liantra.*"

A subtle shimmer began at the center of the bone, then stretched out to either end.

"Liantra fortgiuno—"

The shimmer didn't stop at Jerek's hands. It kept stretching toward the walls, broadening as it grew.

"—tri findo linituga."

The shimmer touched the walls and spread out over their surfaces, expanding to cover the floor, the ceiling, reaching up the stairs toward the kitchen.

"Briconax obsturnal—"

The shimmer began to vibrate, buzzing against the house itself. The sound drilled into Jack's teeth, tensing his jaw, digging into his head.

A panicked shout came from the kitchen.

"—enboltza friena fin."

With a crack, the shimmer flashed bright and disappeared, yanking away from the bone as though sucked into the walls of the house.

A squeal of brakes and the distinctive crash of a crumpling car bumper came right before a piercing scream from the top floor of the archives.

29

Jerek

A firetruck, an ambulance, and a police car all responded to the accident in front of the archives. Jerek leaned against the dining room wall, book in hand, pretending that glancing through the crack in the side of the curtains at the end of every paragraph wasn't making it impossible to absorb anything he'd just read.

The EMTs loaded the driver of the car into the ambulance. From the way he gesticulated, waving his arms and pointing toward the archives, the driver's death was not a weight Jerek would have to carry.

The police car and firetruck didn't follow the ambulance away.

"Damn." Jerek looked back to his book.

Soft footsteps came slowly down the stairs.

Jerek peeked through the curtain—a police officer and a firefighter stood together on the sidewalk on the far side of the street—before looking to the stairs.

Ari crept down the steps, wearing a fresh set of clothes sans bloodstains.

"Is she asleep?" Jerek asked softly.

"More like tranquilized out of her mind," Ari said. "She muttered something about a grinding noise before she started drooling."

"Mariah will owe Eve her thanks." Jerek peeked back out the window. The firefighter and the police officer were now staring at the archives. "Would you mind fetching Ford for me? Make sure he's presentable, too."

"This day is worse than most." Ari headed toward the kitchen, winding the shimmering sheet of her hair into a bun, exposing the nape of her neck.

Jerek tucked his book beneath his arm to focus on watching the street.

The Gandalf schnauzer and his current handler had stopped thirty feet west of the first responders, the handler giving a poor performance of worrying about the accident while the dog gleefully sniffed one of the same trees it had been circling past all afternoon.

A rumble of voices came from the kitchen before footsteps hurried down the hall.

Gandalf's handler frowned and shook his head, as though mourning the damage the rogue car had wrought upon the innocent tree it had attacked with its front bumper.

"What's going on?" Ford whispered close to Jerek's ear.

Jerek tightened his grip on his book, pretending his heart hadn't just vaulted into his throat.

"Mariah's zonked. Talking quietly won't hurt her," Ari said.

"Great." Ford sighed. "Whispering always makes everything seem worse than it is."

"Perform your role properly or everything will be worse than whispering made it seem," Jerek said.

"Why? What role?" Ford cut around Jerek to peer through the other side of the curtains.

The police officer and firefighter still stood on the sidewalk, the police officer talking into his radio while the firefighter shook his head.

"You're the archivist," Jerek said. "Assuming the groups watching the house are patrons of the archivist answering your demand for protection, if anyone but you should answer the door—"

"They might start questioning my authority." Ford nodded.

The police officer shook his head at the firefighter and started toward the house.

A bit of sweat tainted Jerek's palms as a childlike terror of the superhuman authority of a real somb policeman sped his heart. "Just tell him you didn't notice anything."

"You say that like it's my first time dealing with cops." Ford stepped away from the window.

"This is a large house," Jerek said as the police officer climbed the steps. "Tell him you've been in the kitchen on the alley side."

"Don't mention the kitchen," Ari said. "Eve's grinding a human bone in the kitchen."

"Calm down." Ford straightened his collar then began bouncing on his toes like he was getting ready for a race.

The loud and cheerful doorbell tune carried through the house.

"Shit." Ari whipped toward the stairs as though waiting for a pained shriek.

Ford kept bouncing.

No shriek came.

"Please don't let him ring it again," Ari said.

"It's almost time." Ford bounced twice more and ran for the door, starting from the bottom of the locks and zipping toward the top as though he'd been living in the archives for years.

Ari dodged over to stand beside Jerek, tucking herself out of sight as Ford opened the door.

"Oh," Ford said. "Hello, officer. Everything okay out there?"

"We'll have the car towed away soon," the officer said.

"No bother to me either way, I don't have a car to park," Ford said. "I appreciate your letting me know, though. Very kind of you."

"I actually wanted to speak to you about the cause of the accident," the officer said.

"The cause?" Ford said. "You mean that light?"

Jerek tensed.

Ari gripped his hand and shook her head.

"You saw a light?" the police officer said.

"I was upstairs and this bright light flashed through the window. I heard the crash right after. I thought they might be connected." Ford's voice dropped. "I don't want to tell you how to do your job, but I've been on my computer digging up information since the crash. You need to start looking at Manhattan colleges. The science departments."

"What would a science—"

"No, no, listen," Ford said. "Shh. Listen. They're going to try to say it was heat lightning, but the weather is all wrong. It's these students spawned by the malleable masses.

"They flood Manhattan's colleges. They're trying to create new ways to power the city using Tesla's research, but they're wrong. Tesla's work was pushed aside for a reason. Rogue lightning being called down from the sky, causing car accidents...this isn't even the beginning of it."

"Now, there's no need—"

"I know, it doesn't seem possible. Winning the technology

race isn't worth this kind of danger, no decent scientist would risk annihilating the entire population of Manhattan, but it's happening," Ford said. "That flash is proof."

"Do you have anyone home with you?" the officer asked. "Or does anyone come to check in on you?"

"Oh, sure. People are always in and out," Ford said. "Food delivery, cleaners, I even host a book club. We've been plowing through a reading list detailing the worst coverups this country has ever seen. I keep all the books from our list. I can bring you upstairs. You need to see the stacks of texts I've found on the dangers of Tesla's research. Well, if you don't mind taking off your shoes to keep the noise down, of course. A friend is staying with me, and the shock of the flash and the accident gave her a migraine."

Ari gripped Jerek's hand, pressing her side against his as though bracing for impact.

"I'm actually fine not seeing your books," the officer said. "But I'd like to give you a card for a colleague of mine. If you get scared and think the college kids doing Tesla research are coming after you, if you think you have to protect yourself or any of your friends from the Tesla people, any time you need someone to come here to make sure you're safe, you call this number first thing. This colleague is the one who's going to help you, got it?"

"But I haven't told you about Latimer," Ford said. "You can't say they'll help me with Tesla if you don't understand the connection to Latimer."

"Just save the number in your phone, sir. You need help, you call."

"I will," Ford said. "Thank you."

Ari relaxed.

"You have a nice evening, and don't forget to save that number," the officer said.

The door thumped closed behind him.

Jerek waited until the seventh lock had clicked before stepping away from his hiding place mashed against the dining room wall.

"That cop was so nice." Ford furrowed his brow, his mouth drooping into a frown. "If telling him the truth wouldn't have destroyed his career or worse, I would've felt bad lying to him."

"Yes, we should all feel very bad for the nice officer." Ari took Jerek's arm, steering him toward the kitchen. "But the fact that the current Gandalf dog guy isn't even trying to be sneaky is probably not a great thing for us."

"Should this be discussed in front of our guest?" Jerek asked.

"Shit." Ari stopped, letting go of Jerek's arm. "I forgot about Regi."

"Please don't tell him that." Ford cut around Jerek and Ari. "He's had a rough enough day without being told the girl of his dreams forgot he existed."

"In my defense, this has been a really crappy day for me, too," Ari said.

"Won't make him feel any better." Ford held the kitchen door open.

Regi sat at the table, a mixing bowl of cereal in front of him.

"Ari." Regi looked up at the girl he'd followed to his doom with lovestruck infatuation glinting through the fear in his eyes. "Did the police arrest the knights?"

"Right." Ari sat opposite Regi at the table. "The thing you need to remember is that panicking never helps."

30

Ari

"There's another reason to panic?" Regi pulled the mixing bowl of cereal toward him, clinging to the very bowl they'd used to soak the dead guy crust off the heliostone and amplifier like a security blanket.

"Let's just..." Ari stood, cut around the table, and pried the bowl from Regi's grip.

She turned to where Lincoln stood beside the kitchen sink, widening her eyes, not needing to see the slight stiffening of his neck to be sure he knew exactly what he'd done.

Lowering his gaze just enough to avoid meeting hers, he took the bowl and set it in the sink.

"Better." Ari settled back into her seat. She folded her hands on the table and willed her mind to calm, pushing all the chaos and danger aside to focus on the man whose life she'd destroyed. "First of all, I'd like to say again that I'm sorry for getting you dragged into this. It was careless of me, and I'm going to do everything I can to make sure you stay safe."

"As will I." Jerek pulled out the seat to Ari's right. "We haven't met yet, and I do hope you'll excuse the interruption, but I will not allow Ari to believe any guilt for your situation lies solely on her. Jerek Holden." Jerek reached for Regi's hand.

"Ari?" Regi looked to her, ignoring Jerek's hand.

"Ariel Love," Ari said, "but I prefer Ari."

"Ari." The corners of Regi's eyes lifted for a moment, as though a smile had tried and failed to pierce his panic.

"My friends and I aren't like normal people," Ari said.

"Ari." Lincoln's voice held a weighty tone of warning.

"Spells. I heard you say spells. And she's grinding up a dyed bone." He pointed to Eve. "I think it might be human."

"You didn't break it into smaller pieces downstairs?" Ari rounded on Eve, who stood beside the counter, a cleaver, cutting board, and mauled bone beside her, a stainless-steel mortar and pestle in hand.

"Jack can't take the smell, Mariah can't take the noise, there are cops near the front of the house, and at least the kitchen has a counter," Eve said. "I'm doing my best."

"Is she going to take my bones?" Regi whispered.

"If you give me a reason to," Eve said.

"Maybe we should move this somewhere else," Ari said.

"No," Lincoln said.

"Fine." Ari locked her fingers together, gripping hard. "But if anyone freaks Regi out and he faints or pukes, the one who pushed him over the edge has to clean up the mess."

"I'm not going to faint." Regi dug his nails into the top of the table. "And I have a very strong stomach."

"Great," Ari said, "because the ground-up bone is human, and Jerek needs it for a spell that's going to keep the house safe from the people who were stalking you. It's not the most pleasant sort of magic, but grinding up one old bone is nothing compared to what the stalkers would happily do to someone like you who found out about people like us."

"He was there," Lincoln said.

"What?" Ari focused on the flare of temper that flickered through her chest, letting her anger at his petty bowl distribution burn away the whisper in her mind that promised peace and salvation if she'd only toss the chaos aside.

"He was there. He already understands how far the Maree are willing to go," Lincoln said. "A knight died today. Maybe two, I don't even know."

"Lincoln, why didn't you—" Jerek began.

"I'm sorry." The heat of Ari's anger dwindled, sinking into fatigue and fear. "I thought I was careful. I knew they hadn't followed us. And they didn't track my message asking Regi to meet me."

"Don't blame yourself," Regi said. "I'm the one they followed. I knew they were after me. They had been for days."

"Then you should've stopped posting about Ari," Eve said.

"How could I?" Regi stood up, hands planted on the table as he shouted at Eve. "If they were following me, what would they do to her? If I just shut up and forgot I'd seen the most beautiful girl in existence run across water while being chased by the same creepy, lurking, black-suited assholes who'd been following me, how the hell would I ever sleep again?

"Just pretend I don't know something that isn't supposed to exist is happening? Try not to wonder if the girl who'd managed to steal my heart in an hour had died because I didn't find a way to warn her that agents in suits were looking for her?"

Eve watched Regi—leaning against the table, panting—like she was waiting to see if he'd faint. But he held her gaze, blissfully unaware of how easily she could kill him.

After most of a minute had passed, Eve shrugged.

"Thank you for trying to help me," Ari said.

"I had to." Regi sank back into his seat. "I'm sorry I led those knights to you. I thought I had lost them."

Jerek pushed Regi's waterglass closer to Regi's hand.

"It's not your fault. Losing a tail isn't something normal people know how to do. And I don't think any of us considered the"—Jerek paused for a moment, as though teetering between words—"knights would be wasting resources following you."

Regi winced.

"Not because of you. You aren't a waste of resources." Ari paused, selecting her own words as carefully as Jerek had. "But you aren't like us, so you wouldn't be involved in what's got them looking for us. And, since you were looking for me, they'd have no reason to think I was in the area, much less in Manhattan."

"Until we let Ford blast his location over the internet," Lincoln said.

"He was being followed before that." The anger in Ari's chest seethed.

Lincoln stepped closer to Regi. "By Brooks and Olivia?"

"You knew their names?" Ari asked.

Lincoln kept his gaze pinned on Regi.

"Was it them?" Lincoln said. "Or did it look like two high-schoolers were tailing you?"

"Lincoln." A heavy weight sank in Ari's stomach.

"Because Brooks and Olivia were well-trained, valuable assets," Lincoln said. "A child could have managed following you."

"I saw the woman the first day I noticed I was being followed," Regi said. "I don't remember when I first spotted the man. There were at least six of them. I think they rotated."

"Shit," Eve said.

"Six knights is rather extreme to be watching a plain

human," Jerek said. "With everything that's going on, why would that many be spared?"

"At least four of them are still alive to serve the feu," Lincoln said.

"You mean to hunt for Ari," Eve said. "With a bonus if we manage to end up dead, too."

"Knights Maree do not kill unless necessary," Lincoln shouted.

Ari cocked her head, tipping her ear toward the ceiling, listening for Mariah's scream, but Lincoln plowed on.

"This shouldn't have happened. None of today should have happened."

"Lincoln, breathe." Ari stood, reaching for his hand.

"We got penned in." Lincoln dug his fingers into his scalp. "They came after you, and I had no way to get you out."

"*I* had a way to get us out." Ari shoved her chair aside, steadying her stance as her body screamed for her to run. "I didn't happen upon a staircase the cops didn't know about because it had been wiped from the city's records. I went in with a backup plan. I knew about the hidden club and the owner's private entrance through the machine room.

"I actually pulled a list of four criminal shitwads with decent infrastructure I could borrow that I didn't mind serving up as a more tempting treat for the cops than me. But the club owner who pays the cost of his female employees coming to America so he can offer them as party favors to his patrons won the honor of being our sacrifice to the NYPD. I'm sorry you had to fight some of your own people. I won't pretend to know how awful you must feel. But do not make it sound like I didn't have my shit together."

"None of us would ever think that." Jerek was standing beside her. She hadn't noticed him move. He put his hand on her back and straightened her chair. "An escape route that brings down a vile criminal enterprise—a thing only you could achieve."

He nudged her toward her seat.

She let him.

"And while we all know I could spend an eternity praising you, Regi looks even paler than before," Jerek said.

"Right." Ari looked back to Regi. "Sorry again."

Regi silently shook his head.

"Lincoln's right." The cool, gleaming promise of bliss pressed against the back of her mind, forming tendrils that crept into her chest, taunting her with a pull that begged her to flee, hooking through the front of her ribs, making it harder for her lungs to expand. "Regi, if the knights were willing to devote six of their people to watching you, chances of them letting you slide back into your life after what happened today are nil. You're stuck in this mess, and I don't know for how long. We're going to take care of you, but we can't let you leave this kitchen until you understand why there are some things in this house that can kill you if you touch them."

Eve gave a low, single laugh.

"There are three kinds of people in this world." Ari locked her fingers together, resting her hands on the table. "The sombs, the feu, and the Knights Maree."

31

Eve

An arc of scrolls and books surrounded Eve. She'd laid them out on the bare dining room floor, keeping the scrolls flat with butter knives and the books open with potholders. Only the notebook right in front of her stayed open without being forced, like the handwritten text wanted to be sure its venom was properly displayed.

She made herself start at the beginning of the arc again.

A werewolf in the middle of their full moon transformation had been drawn at the top of the scroll, but the image was all wrong.

The wolf looked like a monster, wracked with pain, being punished for their sins with the torture of shifting into their twisted, hellish form.

Directions on how to properly hunt and kill a werewolf took up the rest of the parchment.

The book beside it didn't have any images.

...and in allowing the proliferation of moonstones among the lycanthropes, the monthly nuisance will become an all-consuming threat to the feu. The sterilization and removal of fangs...

The next three books held more of the same—rantings on the dangers of werewolves, filled with disgust and hatred for the packs who had learned to use moonstones to harness their power without the full moon.

Eve gripped the two moonstone pendants around her neck, half-hoping the authors would jump out of the books and try to snatch them from her.

The next author spread their hatred beyond werewolves, offering advice on how to hunt and kill several different kinds of cryptids, giving a potion that could stop any magic-fueled healing. The wanna-be mass murderer had even included a theoretical plan for the capture and slaughter of mermaids.

The final scroll in the arc looked too new for a scroll, like whoever had written the document thought spewing hate on fancy paper made them less worthy of evisceration and had traded in their notebook for parchment. The bloodhungry bastards had even decorated their manifesto with a sword slicing through a full moon at the top and *O.L.B.* in fancy swirling font at the bottom.

Tightly written text filled the center of the parchment.

We who stand against the darkness pledge our swords and lives to this quest.

United in a common goal, we seek freedom from the monsters who slaughter in the night. For the sake of our descendants, we vow to break—

Footsteps came down the stairs.

"Don't get onto me for putting old books on the floor, Holden," Eve said without even glancing toward the hall. "Consider yourself lucky I didn't burn them all."

"I appreciate your restraint." Jerek stopped beside Eve, just far enough forward to be in her peripheral vision. "Dare I ask what you're looking at?"

"More proof people are shit. Or maybe it's a hell of a lot worse." Eve pressed her palms to her legs. "I might be seeing what I want to see."

"And what's that?" Jerek sat beside her.

"A reason to be grateful I gutted the archivist." Eve pushed the notebook toward Jerek. "I found that when I was looking through his notebooks for a potion to make Mariah sleep."

"A potion to prevent a werewolf's full moon shift?" Jerek flipped to the second page of notes on the potion. "Is that even possible?"

"He kept updating his notes, so I don't think he managed it." Eve waited for anger to surge through her, but the cold, heavy hatred that filled her wouldn't budge. "Crossing shit out, adding new ingredients in. If he kept switching things, he must have used it."

"He experimented on wolves." A hatred to match her own darkened Jerek's voice.

"I can't make myself imagine how much it would hurt to not be able to shift at the full moon. It's what we're meant to do. To be trapped in human form with that much power trying to break out of your skin"—she finally looked to Jerek—"I don't know if a wolf could survive it."

"We should destroy those pages." He handed the notebook back to her. "Knowledge is sacred. Honing a tool for genocide is not."

"What about all of these?" She tossed the notebook into the center of the arc. "They're all anti-werewolf. Some want all cryptids dead, but wolves stay at the top of the list for slaughter, and I only searched a quarter of the collection for the archivist's favorites."

"Favorites?"

"The books and scrolls that have his scent from being handled. Some of them were about spells and laws and curses, but this is a third of them."

"A man involved in the Blood Mountain Massacre hated werewolves. While disturbing, I can't say I'm surprised."

The heavy hatred that filled Eve shattered, replaced by the burning anger that sizzled against the inside of her skin.

She was grateful.

"Decide werewolves are deadly vermin so you murder kids." The words rumbled in Eve's throat. "Funny how they don't understand they're the monsters."

"They don't," Jerek said. "But we do. And when we find the monsters, we'll destroy them and make sure the only legacy they leave behind is one of repulsive shame."

She grabbed the scroll the wolf haters had signed, wrinkling the parchment. "Can Ari find out about these names? The bigoted shits signed it like they were making a pact. If they had kids, I need to make sure they didn't inherit the family quest for werewolf annihilation."

"Absolutely." Jerek took the scroll from Eve, gently rolling it up. "I'll ask Ford to start on it."

"Is Ari still too busy with her harem?"

Jerek froze halfway to his knees. "Go easy on Ari."

"We have two sombs in the house because of her, Holden," Eve said. "Ford's useful, but he's not one of us, and the Maree already want Ari dead. If she's lucky, maybe she'll make it to a dungeon, but—"

"Nothing would be worse than a dungeon to Ari." Jerek sat back down.

"Then she needs to stop collecting sombs."

"It's not her fault, or theirs." He looked down at the scroll in his hands. "Sitting beside you...there's a feeling of power that emanates from your being—of danger, of warning. With you, I walk into a room and I can tell there's a predator nearby. Before you say or do anything, I can feel the force of your strength."

"Good."

"My mother used to tell me I was empathic and quick to notice things. I was too young to think much of it. But it's not as simple as being observant. The power inside me, it feels you. Your raw strength, your will. When the Fracture happened, that sense was smothered so completely, I'd forgotten what it truly was. How different the knowing I feel is from simple intuition."

"It's back now?"

"Yes." Jerek looked to Eve, giving a faint smile. "I can feel how close you are to breaking out of your skin. The power inside you thrums like a heartbeat, and it's crackling close to the surface."

"Should I go rampage through Manhattan?" The damn burning anger flashed brighter.

Jerek raised his eyebrows.

"I have it under control." Eve knocked the butter knives off one of the scrolls and began rolling it up with a less than gentle touch.

"For now."

"If you think I'm going to snap, don't push me, Holden."

"I'm not." Jerek moved the knives off the most fragile looking of the scrolls, taking it upon himself to protect the repulsive record. "But you're not the only one I can feel. Jack is like a paintbrush touching a deep blue canvas, dark and breathtaking, like candlelight, velvet, and the scent of orchids. Everything a vampire would need to lure you into the shadows."

The crackling eased away from Eve's skin. She turned to sit facing Jerek. "What does Ari feel like?"

"Freedom." Jerek's smile held a sadness Eve wanted no part of. "The sunlight glinting off the waves. The need that draws every sailor to the horizon. A promise of wonder so great, you want the feeling to wind around your heart, and you would gladly let that exquisite wonder drag you into the abyss if you had even the slightest chance of letting that glory consume you."

"Shit."

"*Shit* indeed." Jerek lifted the potholder from one of the books. "She doesn't know, and I have no intention of telling her."

"If her mer half is luring the heartbreak club in, she has to stop." Eve curled her hands into tight fists, pressing them into the floor on either side of her, uselessly trying to funnel some of the burning energy out of her body. "Not that I care, but Regi did just ruin his life chasing after a girl he didn't actually know."

"What would you have me tell her?" Jerek furrowed his brow. "That because of the magic flowing through her, the magic that's a part of her just as much as the power and strength of being a werewolf is a part of you, she should never let anyone near her again? Ari should spend the rest of her life wondering if anyone really loves her, or if it's just a trick of her blood? Regi, Mariah, Lincoln, Ford—"

"It sounds worse when you list them."

"—they're drawn to Ari, not by a spell, coercion, or force, but by the essence of who she is."

"And you just had to tell me this." Eve went back to the books, closing them with satisfying snaps. "Why the hell did you have to tell me?"

"In hopes of your understanding. Ari is what she was born to be. Just like you and me. Her attracting devotion isn't done out of malice or fun. She can't help people being drawn to her any more than you can help any person with a bit of sense being intimidated by you." Jerek stood, taking the scroll the werewolf haters had signed. "I'll run this to Ford."

"I'll do it. I can't look at these anymore." Eve closed the last of the books. She stood and took the scroll from him, giving the paper a satisfying extra crinkle. "The way you talk about her, I'm surprised you and Ari never got together."

"There was a brief moment we considered it." The sad smile returned. "But Ari will never be short on suitors, and only a monster would try to claim her heart knowing they could only bring her pain. Bad enough to know she'd grieve a friend. I'd never have been strong enough to make her mourn a lover."

32

Grace

Pain zinged through Grace's hand as her knuckles rammed into the car's bumper, knocking the screwdriver from her grip.

She sucked air in through her teeth, swallowing the curse she longed to shout at the damn car. She shook out her hand, glancing up and down the alley to make sure no one had decided a midnight stroll through a mugger haven would be fun.

A man walked down the street, head nodding to music Grace couldn't hear.

Good enough.

She wiped the sweat from her hands on the new, mostly clean pants she'd stolen.

So I can attach a stolen license plate to a stolen car.

She reached under the car and picked up the screwdriver, then made herself close her eyes, taking steadying breaths, tamping down the sparks that longed to leap from her skin.

Her grip on the screwdriver stayed firm as she finished attaching the license plate.

Blood rushed back into her legs as she stood, sending tingles through her feet with every step, like her body was begging her to stop as she walked out of the alley and into the lamplight that bathed the sidewalks.

I'm a good person.

Down the block and across the street, one house stood out from the rest.

While all the other buildings were rowhouses with only small alleys separating one set of homes from the next, Grace's destination had a full garden that wrapped around the sides of the house.

I'm a good person.

Willow trees and berry bushes gave the place an air of seclusion, even though people—maybe a hundred, maybe more—were sleeping close enough to hear an errant scream.

I'm a good person, making the best of a bad situation.

Tucking her screwdriver into her pocket, she strolled toward the house with the wraparound garden.

I'm making the best choice I can.

She stopped beside a blue blooming hydrangea, miming smelling the flowers while checking the street.

A couple walked together a few blocks down. Cattycorner to Grace, a woman hurried from her car to her front door.

Don't panic. Just get it done.

She rammed her shoulder into the hydrangea bush, shielding her face as she plowed through the flowers and into the garden, dodging to the shelter of a willow tree.

Holding her breath, she froze for a moment, listening for the faint sound of an alarm.

Nothing.

Yet.

She stayed crouched in the shadows as she crept closer to the house.

A branch snapped beneath her foot.

Shit.

She froze again, waiting for someone to shout about the intruder who'd crept into their garden.

Shit. Shit.

Nothing.

Getting on her hands and knees, she crawled to the very edge of the willow's shelter.

A security camera pointed directly at the back door. There were no other cameras in sight.

Jack would be disappointed.

A vague feeling that might have been a laugh loosened the knot of fear in Grace's chest.

You helped rob the Museum of Magic. You helped kidnap an heiress.

Get your shit together and do this, Grace Esther Lee-Weiss.

She bolted from the willow's cover, sprinting toward the window farthest from the back end of the security camera, cutting a wide arc through the garden, keeping out of the camera's view.

Her heart raced as though she'd run a mile when she finally pressed her back to the house.

Nothing.

No alarms. No screams.

Not so much as a rustling in the garden.

I'm a good person. I'm a good...

The thought faded from her mind as she reached for the radiant energy that lived inside her. Heat flared through her arm as she pushed all the fire that longed to burst from her body into her hand.

But the heat didn't burn her.

The heat was a part of her. The fire wanted to protect her.

Blue flames danced on Grace's palm.

She pressed her hand to the window and let her magic do its work.

33

Lincoln

Rubber ridges covered the handle of his toothbrush. A design created to make holding his toothbrush more comfortable. To make cleaning his teeth more comfortable.

No one had thought to put such effort into the design of his dagger's hilt. The weapon's maker hadn't thought of the comfort of the user. Hadn't thought to cushion the grip enough to dull the feel of blade slicing flesh.

Lincoln spat out his toothpaste as his throat spasmed, threatening him with illness if he let his mind linger on what he'd done.

He gripped the sides of the pedestal sink, focusing on the smooth, sturdy feel of the ceramic.

Like the sturdy feel of the weapons he'd trained with in the compound. Practicing the same series of movements over and over, spending hours honing his technique, sparring until pain no longer shocked his mind, training until fighting became instinctual.

He rinsed out his mouth and washed his face, ignoring the medicine cabinet where a stash of the archivist's little glass bottles of who knows what filled the shelves and taking his toothbrush back to the bedroom.

As he cut through the tiny hall, his fingers rubbed against the ridges on the toothbrush's handle. He switched his grip to pinch the plain plastic of the neck, aiming straight for the dresser as soon he reached the bedroom, dropping the toothbrush on top.

"Lincoln." Ari spoke from behind him.

He spun toward her.

She stood on the other side of the room by the closed bedroom door. "I didn't mean to spook you." She pulled the length of her hair free from the back of her shirt, like she'd just finished putting the top on.

"I didn't know you were in here."

"I sort of got that feeling."

Lincoln turned back to the dresser, opening the top drawer where he'd placed the items of clothing he'd managed to hang on to. He hesitated for a moment before grabbing the dinosaur pajama pants and tossing them beside his toothbrush.

The thwomp of a sheet being shaken came from behind him.

Lincoln shut his eyes, carefully plucking words from the storm of voices screaming into his thoughts. "Do you need help?"

"If Eve wants to haul a mattress up three flights of stairs, I can put sheets on it." Ari's voice tightened on the last few words, like she'd reached across the bed to tuck in the far side of the sheet. "I'm fine with her taking a turn sleeping at the front door, but why the hell did she switch mattresses?"

Lincoln reached deeper into the swirl of voices, searching his mind for words of comfort or wisdom. A void greeted him.

"What do you need?" Ari asked.

"Nothing." Lincoln shoved the dresser drawer closed. The dresser banged against the wall, tipping from the excess force. He winced and froze, waiting for a scream from Mariah.

"I put the big headphones on her," Ari said. "She was still muttering in her sleep, but the muttering got a lot more cheerful."

"Good. That's good."

"But what do *you* need?" The floor creaked as Ari walked slowly toward him, like she was afraid he might tell her to stay away.

"I'm fine." Lincoln knelt to untie his shoes. "I found a bunch of blankets. I'm going to pull the long cushion off the couch."

"The cushion won't even reach from your head to your hips."

"I don't mind."

"If you really don't want to share the bed with me, which is absurd since the mattress is more than big enough for two people, then I'll sleep on the cushion."

"Ari—"

"Where did you find the blankets?"

"I'm not letting you sleep on the floor."

"Well then, should I try to curl up with Eve or Jerek?"

Lincoln turned toward her before he could stop himself.

"There's no way you'd survive even asking if you could bunk with Eve." Ari shrugged. "And, as much as I love the idea of you and Jerek doing a nice buddy snuggle, you boys would be up all night creating brilliant plans to save our asses, which is, quite frankly, terrifying."

She paused, like she was offering him a chance to challenge her judgment of him and Jerek.

"Get some sleep." She turned toward the door.

"No, stay." Lincoln reached for his pajama pants, clinging to the safety of staring at the dresser. "You're right. The bed is plenty big. We'll be fine."

"If you're sure."

"I'm not sure you could survive Eve either, and Jerek said something about rubbing ash on the house."

"Sounds fun, but I'm happy to miss it."

The bed gave a soft sound, like she'd sat down.

Lincoln pulled off his shirt, gritting his teeth as burning pain jolted through the wound on his arm. He tossed the shirt by his shoes and switched into his dinosaur pants.

The clicking of Ari's keyboard began.

Keeping his gaze anywhere but on Ari, Lincoln headed toward the bed, wishing more than he ever had in his life that he had something in his hands he could focus on.

He sat on the edge of the bed. The wave of exhaustion he'd been hoping for didn't come.

The bed shifted as Ari moved. She closed her computer with a soft click.

"I'm sorry," she said. "I'm sorry I didn't fill you in on my plan or the escape route. I was trying to keep you out of it, but I was wrong."

"It wouldn't have ended any differently." A tightness began in Lincoln's chest, spiraling all the way up to his throat. "Waiting on the street, I watch Regi walk in. I see Olivia and Brooks following him. I come in after them. I try to stop them, we fight. I go in with you, knowing there's a way out. The fight still happens. It's all the same."

"I'm still sorry." The bed shifted again. "I don't have a huge family or a group that I've been raised in."

Heat burned in Lincoln's eyes.

"I can't imagine what the past few days have been like for

you," Ari said, "and I'm so sorry coming with me today made things worse."

"It didn't." The words sharpened the tightness running from Lincoln's throat to his chest, growing thorns that pained his lungs with every breath. "They were there for you. Under orders to kill you or drag you to a dungeon."

The bed shifted again.

Lincoln turned, diving across the mattress to grab Ari's wrist, terrified the walls themselves would rip her away.

She only stared at Lincoln with panic in her eyes.

"I told them they didn't understand," Lincoln said. "You were helping the feu. The guards at Greenwood were the ones at fault. But they wouldn't listen. They were going to hurt you. Olivia wanted to kill you, and I didn't even think about vows or loyalty. I had to protect you."

"I'm sorry." Tears gleamed in Ari's eyes.

"I don't think I am." The thorns grew, threatening to pierce his heart. "I killed a Maree today, maybe two. They were my brethren, and I didn't even hesitate. I am a Knight Maree. Everything I am is Maree. But I can't find a way to tell myself I wouldn't do the same thing over and over if it meant keeping you safe."

His tears spilled down his cheeks.

She slid closer to him, kissing the back of his hand.

"How am I supposed to grieve for someone I don't regret killing? How am I ever supposed to look another Maree in the eye? How am I supposed to call myself a Maree?"

"You are a Maree." Ari pulled on his hand, turning him to face her on the bed. "Right now, there are bad people doing awful things, and we're trying to stop them. I don't know which one of the monsters in the shadows sent Maree to attack a div in a building filled with sombs, but I am going to find out. And then we'll make sure the Knight's Council and the Council of the Feu understand exactly which asshole was pulling the strings today, and they'll understand that you aren't a villain. Lincoln Martel, you are a hero and a Knight Maree."

She moved closer, her knees nearly touching his as she brushed the tears from his cheeks.

He closed his eyes as she kissed his forehead.

"Thank you for protecting me," she whispered.

She rested her forehead against his.

He breathed in deep, taking in her scent, letting it sweep the pain in his chest away.

He reached for her, not out of conscious desire but a visceral instinct he didn't have the will to fight.

The instinct to be near her, to feel her safe in his arms, begged him to give in to the tiny but desperately strong surety anchored right above his heart that promised having her close would be the start to mending every part of his shattered soul.

She didn't back away as he rested his hands on her hips. She relaxed at his touch, as though she needed to be near him, too.

Panic flicked Lincoln's heart as she leaned away from him, but she only pulled back enough to look him in the eye.

She held his gaze, her teal eyes consuming him, asking him a question he couldn't understand, couldn't even make sense of, couldn't even make himself want to reason through because it couldn't matter.

Nothing mattered but being near her.

He leaned forward, his breath catching in his throat as he dared to brush his lips against hers.

Panic flicked his heart again as he waited for her to shove him away, screaming she could never want a disgraced knight to kiss her.

But she kissed him gently, carefully, like she too was afraid of being cast aside.

He kissed her again, and the world fell away.

The taste of her lips surged life into his veins, sending a vibrant energy dancing through his nerves, begging him to feel more.

She teased his lips apart with her tongue.

He gripped her hips, rising to his knees as he pulled her closer.

Her chest pressed against his, leaving only her thin shirt between them.

She wrapped her arms around his neck, anchoring herself to him.

The taste of her, the scent of her, washed everything else away. But there was more, so much more, yet to explore.

Her breath hitched, pressing her breasts against him in a maddening way that drove heat through his body as he touched the bare skin on the small of her back.

She gave the faintest sigh and the heat roared into flames, raging through him, snapping his last thin shred of control, surging into a pounding, undeniable betrayal of his desperate longing for her.

He shifted his hips—a useless attempt to hide his need—as she kept herself locked against him, like an unspoken dare for him to run.

She tipped her head, giving him access to the soft skin of her neck.

He moved his hand up to the center of her back, holding her against him as he kissed the side of her neck.

The softness of her skin. The feel of her chest arching against his as he trailed his lips out to her shoulder.

He shifted his other hand from her hip, sliding his fingers up to her ribs.

She gasped as his thumb found the side of her breast. She twisted her shoulder away from him, reclaiming his lips with hers, offering him more of her to explore.

Sparks danced through his soul as she pressed her hips against his.

More. He needed more.

"Lincoln." Her lips brushed his as she whispered his name.

With the gentlest touch, she teased circles down his spine, adding a shuddering, glorious desperation to the fire raging through him.

Her tiny moan quickened Lincoln's breathing.

She kissed him one more time, then leaned away from him.

He froze. A chill clawed at his skin as the warmth of her body abandoned his.

But teasing, joyful teasing, danced through her eyes as she lifted the bottom of her shirt, pulling the thin garment up over her head. She shook out her hair as she tossed the shirt aside, giving him a breath to behold the exquisite glory of her—the pale gold of her hair shimmering around her as though some fool had thought to highlight her perfection.

She took Lincoln's hand, lacing her fingers through his as she drew him toward the center of the bed. She kissed the back of his hand, then pressed gently on his chest, lying him down.

Lincoln's heart raced as she kissed his chest, his neck.

Her bare skin met his as she teased his ear.

He ran his hand up her side, not even attempting to swallow his moan as she pressed his hand above his head.

She kept her fingers laced through his, locking them together as though she were claiming Lincoln as her own.

The thundering in his body threatened to explode as she kissed him again—her chest against his, her hips against his.

All of her against him.

He slid his hand down her back, past her hips.

She shifted as he gripped her against him, rounding her back, stealing enough of her skin from him to lay her hand above his heart.

"Ari." Her name rumbled in his throat as she trailed her fingers down his chest. "Ari."

Bam!

A bright red light flashed through the curtained windows.

"What the hell?" Ari sat up, one hand still holding Lincoln's, the other still on his chest as she leaned toward the window.

No extra light shone through the crack at the side of the curtain.

"You saw that too, right?" Ari said.

A heavy, throbbing numbness muddied Lincoln's thoughts too much for him to do anything but nod.

"If the world is crumbling right now..." Ari crawled to the top corner of the bed, holding the curtain in front of her while she peeked outside. "Dammit." She tossed the curtain back into place and twisted to stand.

Lincoln sat up, the movement clearing just enough of his mind for him to ask, "What?"

"I don't know, but I really hope the homeowners across the street have good insurance. We need to"—Ari stopped, turning in a circle to search the floor before grabbing the shirt she'd tossed aside only a few blissful moments before—"see what the damage is before the cops get here."

She headed for the door.

"Ari." Lincoln scrambled off the bed, darting across the room to the door before she could reach it. "You can't do that."

"Did you look out the window?"

"I don't have to." Lincoln planted himself in front of the doorknob. "If Maree were willing to come after you in an office building during the day, they'll come after you on the street at night."

"Shit." Ari dug her fingers into her hair. "I'm so sick of this shit."

"Promise me you won't go out there?"

"You promise the same." Ari held out her hand as though ready to shake his. "We were both there this morning. We both stay inside."

The faint sound of sirens filled the moment before Lincoln spoke. "Deal."

She grabbed his hand, pulling him toward her, brushing a quick kiss across his lips before pivoting him away from the door.

She tossed the door open and bolted down the hall, leaving Lincoln alone in his dinosaur pajama pants.

34

Jack

The soft texture of the rug gave way to the smooth wooden floors, which met the cool tile of the kitchen.

Jack paused for a moment, sliding his bare feet across the tile before turning to make another pass. He pushed the kitchen door open, walked all the way to the front door, and looped back to the kitchen before the swinging door had settled into stillness.

"You don't have to wait for me." Ford didn't glance up from his computer. "I don't know how long this will take."

"I don't mind." Jack pushed back through the door, making another pass to the front of the house.

"It could be hours," Ford said as Jack pushed the kitchen door open and stepped back onto the tile.

"That's fine." Jack pivoted to begin another pass.

"You're making me nervous," Ford said.

Jack pivoted again, turning back toward the kitchen table.

Ford glanced up from his computer long enough to give Jack an apologetic wince and grab a pretzel from the mixing bowl of snacks.

"I'm making you nervous?" Jack leaned against the doorframe, crossing his arms in a pathetic attempt to look casual.

"I'm trying to hurry."

"I know."

"And you're pacing like I'm running late."

A tiny ping of nerves flickered through Jack's gut as he pushed away from the doorframe and cut around the table to stand behind Ford.

Ford didn't stop typing until Jack laid his hands on Ford's shoulders.

The pinging nerves returned, tensing Jack's throat as he bent down to kiss Ford's cheek.

"I'm not pacing because I'm waiting for you." Jack straightened up, careful not to squeeze Ford's shoulders as he pathetically feigned calm. "I'm enjoying feeling something other than cold, dusty concrete beneath my feet."

Ford's shoulders relaxed. "Understandable."

"Thank you." A flutter of rapturous butterflies tore around Jack's stomach and burst out of his chest.

"I hate that you're stuck in the basement all day." Ford laid one of his hands on top of Jack's while using the other to scroll down a webpage, seeming to still be reading as he spoke.

"I knew what I was getting into when I was turned."

"But you deserve an adaptive space." Ford shook his head, letting go of Jack's hand as he went back to typing. "This house is massive, and you're stuck with crates of quite possibly dangerous relics and a corpse we still haven't concreted over."

"Eve got distracted by the anti-cryptid propaganda section of this twisted library. I'll pour the concrete myself when the sun comes up. I want to enjoy the fresh, corpse-free air while I can."

"I'm going to look into sun-proofing at least the first floor," Ford said. "We can make a proper bedroom in the dining room. We'll have daytime access to a shower."

Jack's fangs pierced his bottom lip.

Ford kept typing. "This is where we've chosen to make our stand. No one can expect us to keep lurking in the basement while we fight to protect the fate of the feu."

"Us?" Another swarm of butterflies ricocheted through Jack's chest.

"I'm not going to sleep somewhere you can't." Ford looked up, the most honest and heartfelt confused frown on his face Jack had ever seen. "I'm not going to put the monitor bank somewhere you can't go during the day either."

"Thank you." Jack's fangs scraped his lip as he spoke.

"You're a part of this crew. You're valuable. You deserve better than being shoved under van seats and stuck in bathrooms." Ford shrugged, like the movement could distract Jack from the heat of the blood rushing to Ford's cheeks. "I think you'll be happier with more space. I want you to be happy, Jack."

Ford's typing picked up speed. He bent his head toward his computer, his focus locked on his screen like his work might shelter him from his own words.

Jack kissed the top of Ford's head, whispering, "Thank you."

Ford's heartrate jumped.

Jack carefully, casually, stepped away.

He opened his mouth.

He closed his mouth.

He went back to pacing.

Tile, wood, rug, wood, tile.

Ford wanted Jack to be happy.

Tile, wood, rug, wood, tile.

Ford wanted to stay where Jack could be.

Tile, wood, rug, wood, tile.

Ford, who could hack the Maree and would risk his neck to help people he barely knew and had the most adorable smile and the softest lips, wanted to sleep beside Jack.

Tile, wood, rug, wood, tile.

Don't do this to yourself. You know better.

Tile, wood, rug—

The rumble of Jerek's voice came from the kitchen.

Jack picked up his pace, reaching the kitchen door in four vampirically quick strides.

"How do you know it worked if nothing flashed or blew up?" Ford asked.

Jack's fangs tore into his bottom lip as he shoved the door open, letting it crash against the wall as he prepared to dive over the table to knock Ford away from whatever danger Holden had dragged into the kitchen.

"I felt my magic flowing into the spell." Jerek stood beside the counter, a small, gold, non-deadly looking bowl in hand. "Beyond that, I don't suppose we'll know for sure until someone tests our boundary."

"Ah," Ford said. "We'll know if it works after we're attacked. Comforting."

"What are you planning to do with that?" Jack pointed at the bowl.

"Smudge runes above the doors." Jerek dipped his gloved finger into the bowl, swirling it around for a moment before holding his now ash-covered finger out to Jack. "Old, but effec-tive magic."

"Great." Jack licked his blood from his bottom lip. "How's Eve doing on camera duty?"

"She's having a wonderful time," Jerek said. "She's watching the street, searching for someone to vent her rage upon. I think she was hoping the old lady with the puggle was going to attack."

A thud shook the kitchen floor.

Jerek tipped his head down, speaking as though he could see Eve through the tile. "Tell me I'm wrong, and I'll gladly apologize."

The kitchen floor stayed silent.

Jerek pursed his lips as he swallowed his laugh.

"You're lucky she likes you," Jack said.

"Truly. If you're not busy..." Jerek let the question hang.

"I am going to concrete over the corpse. I'm just waiting until after sunrise," Jack said.

"I was actually wondering how your copying skills are." Jerek set the bowl down and pulled a slip of paper from his pocket with his clean-gloved hand. He held the paper out to Jack. "The runes don't have to be written by a magician, and the faster we mark all the windows and—"

Jack took the paper.

A series of five runes had been drawn, each reaching between three parallel lines on the page like the special paper that children use when learning to write.

"I can paint silk." Jack handed the paper back. "I'll be fine."

"Perfect." Jerek opened the cupboard, searching for a moment before pulling down a teacup. "Don't worry about running out of ash." Jerek shook ash out of the gold bowl and into the teacup. "I have the supplies to make more."

A hint of what almost seemed like giddy excitement colored Jerek Holden's—*the* Jerek Holden's—voice.

"I'll paint an inch thick." Jack gave a sweeping bow as he accepted the teacup.

A faint huff of an actual, cheerful laugh bounced Jerek's chest.

Hell hath frozen over, and the angels doth sing.

"Would you like to start upstairs or downstairs?" Jerek asked.

"I'll start down here," Jack said. "The third floor smells about a third as bad as the basement. I don't know what dead people parts are up there, but it stinks."

"The same scent as the bone I used for the spell?" Jerek asked.

If Jack's fangs could have retracted fully into his gums, they would have burrowed up to his brain as he considered the two distinct odors of long-forgotten death.

"Downstairs is the stale, vintage, putrid, aged in oak barrels of death's own personal stench stink." Tension shook Jack's stomach as the old, plain human instinct to vomit begged to let loose. "Upstairs is the remnants of a kegger held in honor of death's asshole stink."

Jerek furrowed his brow. The expression held none of Ford's worried charm. "I take the term *kegger* to mean newer remains?"

Jack's stomach cramped. His mouth went dry. "That is the nauseating vibe I get, but with all the messed-up shit in this house, I wouldn't take my corpse dating as solid enough for spell use."

"We really should find a forensics contact," Ford said.

"I don't think the age of human remains—"

Bam!

The glasses in the cupboards tinkled as the tile floor gave a tiny tremble.

"What was that?" Ford snapped his laptop closed and clutched it to his chest, staring up at the ceiling as though expecting the sky to fall.

"It came from the street." Jack ran for the front of the house as another set of inhumanly quick steps pounded up the stairs from the basement.

He veered away from the front door at the last moment, forgoing the satisfaction of stepping out into the fresh, piss-tainted air of the dark street in favor of discreetly peering through a crack in the dining room curtains.

The streetlights didn't flicker. No flames leapt into the sky.

The door of the house across the street flew open. A man in a robe ran out onto the stoop, barely dodging the rain of bricks as the top of his doorway crumbled.

"What the hell?" Jack dared to push the curtains farther open, gaining a better view of the robe man's house.

A spiderweb of cracks radiated from the center of the man's stoop—reaching down to the sidewalk, streaking up the front wall—as though the whole house were carved from one piece of glass and someone had smashed the stoop with a hammer.

The damage hadn't stopped with the poor robed man's house, either. The cracks in the bricks stretched into the adjoining houses on either side, cutting through their front walls, stopping barely shy of those front doors.

"Oh, that repair bill is gonna suck," Jack said.

The robe man's hand shook as he pulled his cell phone from his pocket.

"He ran away." Eve skidded to a stop at the front door, racing through opening the locks from the top down.

"Who ran away?" Jack asked.

"The shit who punched the steps." Eve reached the seventh lock.

"Don't go out there!" Jerek and Ford's footsteps pounded up the hall from the kitchen.

A woman in boxers and a jersey joined the man on the stoop. The man held his phone to his ear as he pointed at his house, flailing his arm around like he thought the woman couldn't see the damage.

"There was a man sitting on the stoop. He punched the steps and broke the house," Eve said. "I'm pretty sure that counts as confirmation the shit is a magician who's been watching us."

"Which makes him not a Maree," Jerek said.

Eve growled.

Jack abandoned the dining room window, cutting around the corner to the front door.

Jerek had somehow planted himself between Eve and the door and for some reason didn't seem to think the look of rage blazing in her eyes was a sign of his impending doom.

"A magician watching the house is most likely one of the former archivist's patrons defending the archives to protect their secrets exactly as Ford requested," Jerek said. "We want LeBlanc, we want the *they*, we have to defend this house from the Maree, we can't risk unwanted attention for anything less."

The whining of sirens raced toward the house.

"That magician could be working for LeBlanc." Eve spoke through clenched teeth. "He could lead us to the people behind the Fracture."

"If you truly believe that, I'll step aside," Jerek said. "But at least consider the advantages of staying out of sight with the police coming."

Footsteps pounded down the stairs from the fourth floor.

"We'd be fools to hope the Maree won't come to investigate this," Jerek said. "Do you want to choose how and when we make our next move, or race after a magician, expose ourselves and our position, and hand the advantage to the Maree?"

"The cops are on their way." Ari sprinted down the last of the stairs, Lincoln right behind her.

"I know," Eve growled.

"Do we know how it happened?" Ari stopped beside Ford.

"A magician punched a staircase," Eve said. "After being stuck in this house waiting to be attacked, I can understand the urge."

"I wouldn't recommend it," Jerek said.

"Was anyone hurt?" Lincoln asked.

"Not that I can tell," Jack said.

"Someone needs to be at the monitor banks." Ari took Ford's shoulders, pivoting him to face her.

"Eve," Jerek said, "would you like to watch the cameras? Keep an eye out for anyone in a Maree suit?"

"The Knights Maree aren't our enemy," Lincoln said.

"Then who did you fight today?" Eve rounded on Lincoln.

"Not the time." Ari slid Ford's laptop from his grip and passed it to Lincoln. "Three of you weren't raised as sombs, so I'm going to make this as easy for you to understand as I can." She looked Ford over, grabbed the laptop back from Lincoln, and held it out to Jack. "Lincoln, I need your pants."

"None of us want a clearer understanding of that," Eve said.

Lights flashed through the cracks in the curtains as police cars wailed their way onto the street.

"Lincoln, pants." Ari forced the laptop into Jack's hands. "The shit just hit the fan in a massive way. This street is about to be flooded with every kind of law enforcement and first responder this city has to offer. There's going to be an army of sombs at our door who may very well force us to evacuate and/or want to check the house for gas leaks, or whatever other shit reason they decide the fronts of three houses just randomly cracked in the middle of the night. Lincoln, pants!"

Lincoln turned away from the group to pull off his dinosaur pajama pants.

"We have a corpse in the basement, and that would be the least shitty part of the cops searching this place. So let's play nice, kids, because blood on the walls isn't going to help our case for keeping New York's finest out of the archives of evil magic," Ari said.

Lincoln tossed his pants to Ari, who shoved them into Ford's hands.

Ford hung them over his shoulder as he unzipped his jeans.

More sirens blared through the door.

"This street is about to make national news, and there's nothing I can do to stop it." Ari ruffled Ford's hair, giving him a sleep-tousled look. "Anyone who doesn't want to end up on the Maree's *just kill them and get it over with* list with me needs to stay out of sight and work on hiding everything that could get us arrested."

Jack didn't need Ari's glance his way to sink fear deep into his undead veins.

His fangs pierced his bottom lip. "If the somb cops take us, we won't all make it past dawn."

Ford

If having to roll the waist of Lincoln's pajama pants so they didn't drag on the floor wasn't enough to shake Ford's confidence, the arrival of the bomb squad definitively tipped the scale in anxiety's favor.

The dining room lights glared around him, highlighting his well-staged tableau. He'd pushed the curtains wide open and pulled an armchair right beside the window where he sat, coffee cup in hand, watching the madness on the street.

The lights of the emergency vehicles glinted through the window, solidifying the theme of panic, as the police went door to door across the street, evacuating all the houses that could in any way be connected to the poor stoop at the center of the mayhem.

The residents obediently flocked out onto the street. Some seemed terrified, others intrigued, a few quite angry, but none of them resisted as the police herded them to the eastern end of the block.

When the residents had all been cleared away, an officer in a massive protective suit waddled toward the cracked stoop.

An important-looking man with a radio in hand called for the first responders to back farther away.

A knock pounded on the archives' front door.

Ford stood, snorting into his coffee as the officer in the puffy suit climbed the cracked stoop's steps, tipping side to side to raise their foot high enough to get to the next stair.

The knock pounded again.

"Coming." Ford backed away from the window, not looking toward the front door until the officer-made-stuffed animal reached the top of the damaged steps. "Good for you!"

Ford cheersed his coffee toward the street as he started on the door's locks.

The knock pounded on the door a third time.

"I'm working on it." Ford's stomach twisted along with the seventh lock. He swallowed the coffee-tainted sour trying to flood his mouth and opened the door.

The cop outside had already raised their hand to knock again.

"Good evening, officer." Speaking the familiar words soothed Ford's nerves.

The cop didn't smile at the greeting. "Sir, you need to prepare for evacuation."

Ford leaned sideways, peering past the grumpy cop to the broken stoop, watching as the stuffed animal turned toward the man with the radio.

The stuffed animal's whole torso twisted as he shook his head as though to emphasize, *I don't know what the hell you want me to look at. There aren't even any scorch marks on this shattered stoop, you pencil-pushing dimwit.*

Ford chuckled and sipped his coffee.

"Sir." The cop stepped closer to Ford. "Please gather any essential items, important documents, and medications you might need."

"Oh, sure, sure." Ford tapped his toe, pointing down at his sneaker-clad feet. "Ready to run when ordered. Just let me know when your bosses finally accept the truth."

"Truth? What truth, sir?"

Don't overplay it.

A gentle touch.

"Have you not read any of the reports about the other incident on this street?" Ford asked. "I very carefully explained the situation to that officer."

"What situation, sir?"

Ford furrowed his brow and sipped his coffee, pursing his lips as he swallowed in his best imitation of his mother's unmitigated disappointment.

He sighed. "May I please speak to your supervisor? If I'm going to have to repeat myself once, I'd rather not risk having to explain the whole thing a third time."

"Sir, if you have any information—"

"Could I at least speak to a detective?" Ford said. "Don't they all carry little recorders?"

"Little recorders," the cop muttered as they looked toward the street, searching for a moment before shouting, "Gene!"

A massive man with a normal shirt under his police vest jogged toward them.

"Perfect." Ford sipped his coffee, leaning against the doorframe as the stuffed animal man's squad made way for the firefighters. "You know, as much as I enjoy being right, I would prefer vindication at a more reasonable hour."

Ford stepped sideways, reaching toward the bureau beside the door.

"Stay where you are, sir," the cop said.

"Sorry." Ford set his coffee down and, holding his hands open in front of his chest, eased back toward the door.

"What's going on here?" The detective glanced between the cop and Ford then peered over Ford's head into the front hall of the archives.

A zap of fear shot up Ford's spine.

"Thank you so much for coming over." Ford offered the detective his hand, using the excuse to step properly into the doorframe, offering his body as a feeble barrier against invasion. "I explained this to a very fine officer before. The flash of light that caused the car accident just outside. The sudden gravity well practically sucking the houses across the street into a sinkhole. It's all connected."

"Connected to what?" The detective waved over his shoulder with his massive, meaty hand, beckoning to someone Ford couldn't see.

Too far. You've pushed too far.

You've doomed him.

It'll all fall apart.

He'll be dead before breakfast.

Shut up, you prick. You're better than this.

Get your shit together, buttercup.

No way out but through.

"College students trying to revive Tesla's work," Ford said.

Lean into it. Eccentricity terrifies the masses.

Ford mouthed, *The Tesla.*

"Tesla's work?" The detective frowned. "Have you seen people doing Tesla's work?"

"Of course not." Ford coughed a laugh. "They can't do their experiments out in the open."

An officer who had the same build as Eve, or at the very least definitely looked strong enough to snap Ford in half, climbed the steps, stopping right behind the massive detective's shoulder, completing the wall of New York's finest blocking Ford from escaping onto the street.

House searched.

Body found.

Jack arrested.

Jack burning in the sun.

"If you'd like me to explain everything to you, I'm happy to come down to the station." Ford twisted the panic in his voice, shading his words with rabid excitement. "I haven't spotted them yet, but if the news crews have arrived, we can stop by on our way. Make sure they understand the truth of what's happening here. The people of Manhattan have a right to know that our fine city is being used as a testing ground for experimental technology that could be catastrophic in the wrong hands."

"And how do you know about these experiments, sir?" The lines in the detective's brow deepened.

"I read about it online," Ford said. "And I looked closely at the websites, I did my due diligence, each of the sites swears their information is true."

The Eve-like cop's eyebrows pinched together as the first cop made a little noise in their throat that sounded like a cut-off laugh.

"That's interesting, sir," the detective said. "Thank you for the information."

"I'm happy to help." Ford beamed at the detective, letting every bit of the energy raging through his body consume his face.

The detective's eyes widened.

"Should I bring my wallet to the station with me?" Ford asked. "I've never been a key witness in a literal earth-shattering investigation before. I don't want to break protocol.

Will you be placing me in a safe house? Should I pack underwear?"

"I don't think we actually need you to come to the station," the detective said. "But I have noticed the security cameras on your roof and in your doorbell."

White-hot, razor-sharp, poison-laden terror coiled around Ford's throat.

He couldn't pull in air.

He couldn't speak.

I'm so sorry.

"Could we take a look at your footage?" the detective said. "Some of your cameras are aimed close enough to the damaged houses, they may provide vital information."

"No." Ford's voice caught on the word, making it two syllables.

"If you want people to know the truth about what happened here, those recordings cou—" the detective began.

"I know what cameras do." Ford fought the urge to back away. "They record things. They make recordings for people to watch."

"And we need to watch your recordings." The detective stepped aside, clearing the Eve-like, going to snap Ford's spine cop's path. "Officer Zapata can take a quick look at your videos. That would really help the investigation."

"No videos." The words spattered from Ford's mouth. "That's how they find you."

"Wha—"

"You think it's harmless, letting yourself be recorded like that?" Ford forced out a high, strangled laugh. "Everything gets uploaded to the master database. That's how they find you. All the cell phone pictures and security camera recordings, every video on social media, it's all training their database to recognize your face. The database pulls image after image after image after image until they can create a deep fake that looks more like you than you do.

"Listen to me." Ford leaned closer to the detective. "Just listen. You can't let them steal your face. You have to protect yourself. Put up security cameras around your house. Make it seem like your cameras are recording all the time. They'll think there are images of you constantly being sent to the master database, but there aren't. So when they try to copy your face, they'll be missing information. They won't be able to create a good fake."

"Who is *they*?" the detective asked.

"There are too many *theys* to count," Ford whispered. "But it's the master database that steers them all. You can't let the database create an algorithm of your face. There's no salvation once they replace you."

"Thank you for the warning." The detective pulled out a card. "If you ever think any *they* might be coming—"

"I already have one of the cards for the special unit." Ford dug into his pocket, whipping out the card he'd been given after the first catastrophic display of magic. "I didn't think I needed to call since there were already so many officers here keeping us safe."

"Good." The detective gave what was probably meant to be a kind smile as he backed toward the edge of the archives' stoop. "You hold on to that card. And remember to stay ready in case we have to evacuate this side of the street."

"Shoes on and ready for action." Ford clicked his heels. "When you're ready for me to come down to the station, you let me know. I'll pack for the safe house just in case."

"Goodnight, sir," the first cop of the evening said right before turning to hurry after their two compatriots.

"Night then." Ford closed the door.

He started at the top of the locks, letting out long, slow

breaths as he worked his way down, trying to ignore how badly his shaking hands slowed the process.

Keep going.

Don't crumble.

Homestretch. Don't screw it up.

He picked up his coffee cup, downing the rest of the hot liquid rather than risk his trembling hands sloshing coffee all over Lincoln's pajama pants.

The first of the reporters made it onto the street as Ford sank back into his armchair by the window, ready to be the intrigued voyeur clinging to his very own conspiracy theory.

"Masterfully done." Jerek's voice came from the hall. "I'll try not to be intimidated by your performance."

Ford lifted his empty mug, covering his mouth as he spoke. "Thanks. The key is unwavering confidence."

36

Ari

The heat of the coffee warmed Ari's hands, joining the scent of fresh-baked muffins that filled the kitchen to almost create a semi-plausible illusion of a quiet, peaceful morning.

She kept her computer on mute as she watched the news coverage of the houses across the street. The subtitles gave vague explanations for the *incident* on the upper west side.

A mini sinkhole had formed just below the ill-fated house's stoop.

A massive chunk of ice had fallen from the sky to crack through the concrete. None of the reporters seemed fussed about the lack of evidence of a piano-sized ice ball striking Manhattan.

The most common narrative blamed falling building standards and corrupt politicians who placed the maintenance of the city's vast network of underground tunnels in the hands of crooks who lined the pockets of the folks at City Hall rather than hiring contractors with actual safety records.

None of the reporters mentioned the dreaded word—

Magic.

A fresh set of workers appeared behind the reporter on the bottom left quadrant of Ari's screen.

All wore hardhats and orange vests. None bore any hint of magically wrought weapons at their hips.

The Maree aren't stupid.

Well, not that stupid.

The racks in the oven clanged as Ford pulled out the latest pan of muffins.

Mariah whimpered, curling over her coffee cup like it was taking every bit of will she had not to clamp her hands over her bright orange, noise-blocking earmuffs.

"Sorry," Ford whispered. "Sorry."

"It's fine." Mariah cringed as she spoke. "Whatever's grinding cement across the street was already stabbing through my temples."

Ford set the muffin pan on the cooling rack. "I'm not sure if I'm supposed to say *good* or *I'm sorry.*"

"Just tell me I can have a muffin and we'll forget the whole thing," Mariah said.

"One muffin, coming right up."

All four of the news reports on Ari's screen panned over to a group of three men in suits.

Ari's heart punched against her ribs.

"What?" Mariah's head snapped toward Ari.

Don't panic. Look at what's in front of you.

Ari zoomed in on the men.

Nice suits, but not Maree-cut. Two of the men weren't anywhere near Maree fitness level. The men kept shaking hands with the workers while maintaining a decent profile for the news cameras.

Not Maree.

"Nothing's wrong," Ari said. "Just keeping an eye on the street."

"Any feu being a bit too obvious?" Ford ran a butter knife around the edge of a muffin.

"Gandalf dog has made a few appearances," Ari said. "But there are so many people on the street, it's too hard to tell who's somb, who's feu—"

"And who are Maree waiting to attack?" Eve shoved the kitchen door open with her foot, using her back to hold it for Jerek while balancing three stacks of books in her arms.

"Don't get too excited," Ari said. "I spotted politicians, not knights."

"All for the best." Jerek set his stack of books down on the counter.

"Sick of the second floor?" Ari asked.

"More like need more eyes to get through all this." Eve set her books down on the kitchen table, ignoring Jerek's little cringing moan at the proximity of the books to Ari's and Mariah's coffees.

"Please don't ask me to read anything that involves entrails before breakfast," Mariah said.

"Then you can start with my pile." Eve shoved her stacks closer to Mariah. "If there are any entrails in these books, it'll be magicians murdering wolves."

"Eve," Ari said.

"Or Knights Maree murdering Knights Maree. Though I doubt any of the books are that recent." Ford pulled the last of the muffins from the tin.

"Explain," Eve said.

"The names you gave me last night." Ford set his butter

knife in the sink. "I have to do more digging, but all seven names seem to be Maree."

"Seem to be?" Eve's voice dropped low. "Why the hell are you baking when the people who signed a pact to murder wolves *seem to be* Maree?"

"Am I supposed to answer that?" Ford asked Ari as he handed her a plated muffin.

Ari began to shake her head.

"Yes," Eve said. "I'd really like to know how muffins got priority."

Ari gave up on the head shaking to cringe.

"Alright." Ford pulled three more plates from the cupboard. "We lured magicians here by demanding their protection in exchange for not exposing their secrets. But blackmail can only get you so far."

He held a plated muffin out to Eve.

She didn't so much as glance at the offering.

"Now that our street has become national news, fear of the horde of uniformed sombs, or even the inevitable attention of the Knights Maree, might drive some of our friendly, front-line, moderately blackmailed guards away." Ford handed the muffin to Mariah instead. "As useless at blending in as some of our feu friends on the street may be, I really don't think we want them abandoning their posts." Ford passed Jerek a muffin.

"Agreed." Jerek gave Ford a nod. "As much as I loathe luring magicians into a somb-packed area, we're too close to desperate to reject any protection. Even a spotty level of defense on the street could provide us an invaluable warning if an attack on the archives should come."

"When," Eve said. "When an attack comes."

"Which is why I prioritized the muffins." Ford held another muffin out to Eve. "If I stay hidden inside, our highly incentivized guards will think there's something to be afraid of. Any whiff of fear from me increases their temptation to run. But if I stroll down the street, giving out muffins to our suspected black-mail-induced allies—"

"You make it seem like this is all a passing inconvenience," Jerek said. "I'm impressed."

"If you think that's good, you should try the muffins." Ford winked. "Old family recipe I just found on the internet."

"If you're dumb enough to risk your neck passing out muffins while there could be Maree on the street waiting to snatch you—" Eve began.

"Why the hell are we even staying here when we know this street has become a Maree beacon!" Mariah winced, clamping her hands over her earmuffs. "We are literally sitting in the nightmare scenario. Magic got noticed, and the street flooded with sombs. This is exactly what feu are treaty-sworn not to do. If the Maree weren't after us before, they sure as hell are now."

Ford looked to Ari, his mouth just a bit open, as though the words were balancing on his lips.

She gave him a tiny shake of her head.

"The archives are protected," Jerek said. "With these books, I'll build better protections."

"So we can pen ourselves in?" Mariah said. "Am I the only one who can see that staying in the archives is the worst possible plan?"

"It's not." Ford added a stack of napkins to the side of his muffin platter. "We've been here for days. The invaluable and highly dangerous information in the archives is still under our protection, everyone's awake and ambulatory this morning, and no one's been stabbed or attacked, at least not while inside the house. All things considered, by this crew's standards, this is the best plan we've ever had."

Ford turned to Mariah, his calm smile not faltering. "And yes, it was my idea. And yes, you can thank me for having the opportunity to recover from regaining your magic in a bed instead of on the floor of a van. Ari, can you take out the next batch of muffins in three minutes?"

"Sure," Ari said.

"Thanks. I'll be back around to collect them, because when you've seized information that could endanger the lives of hundreds or even thousands, you don't abandon the literal archives of irreplaceable texts that could hold the feu's doom and just cross your fingers and wish real hard that the guys who seem to enjoy mass murder don't get it.

"You stand your ground. Whether you defend your fortress with moats or muffins, you stand your damn ground." Ford turned on his heel and strode out of the kitchen.

The faint sound of clapping carried up from the basement.

Ari tipped her head down to speak at the floor. "Isn't he sexy when he's determined?"

"Yes."

Ari laughed at Jack's single, muffled word.

"And he's right. We don't hand weapons to murderers." Eve planted her palms on the table, leaning toward Mariah. "And a Chanler doesn't get a say in how we protect anything in this hell hole."

"Eve," Jerek said, his face placid despite the warning in his tone.

"A *Chanler?*" Mariah leaned toward Eve. "You say that like I didn't put my ass on the line to help mend the Fracture."

Eve's shoulders tensed.

"Since Ford is busy, do you want to give me the list of names he was working on?" Ari asked in a too-bright voice.

"You did one spell that benefited you," Eve said.

"I can listen to the news coverage while I dig around," Ari said. "Who has the list?"

"It's on top of the fridge." Eve kept her glare pinned on Mariah. "I can smell it."

"Then why don't you—" Mariah froze.

Ari's heart knocked up into her throat, staying lodged, blocking her air while Mariah tipped her head as though considering how painful being torn apart by a werewolf would actually be.

"Why is someone ca-cawing and rawring in the basement?" Mariah asked.

Love of my life.

"That's for me." Ari's heart settled back into its normal position. "Be right down." She spoke to the floor. "Need me to bring anything with me?"

"Jack says no," Mariah said.

"Great." Ari closed her laptop.

"Why don't I take these books and go downstairs with you?" Jerek picked up his pile.

"No, no." Ari widened her eyes at him. "Don't want it to get too crowded down there. You should stay in the kitchen."

"Did everyone lack this much subtlety before we mended the Fracture and I just didn't notice?" Mariah asked.

"Probably." Ari skirted around the table, heading toward the basement door. "Have fun with your book club."

"You forgot the scroll." Jerek tightened his lips into a flat line, sucking in his cheeks to hide his smile. "And your muffin."

"Thanks, Jerek." Ari grabbed her plate and took one step toward the scroll before her phone rang.

37

Jerek

Brrrink-dinka-dinka-dink

The plate fell from Ari's hand, smashing against the tile floor before the last note of the ringtone had played.

Mariah gasped, her hands flying to her earmuffs as Eve vaulted over the table, landing in front of the kitchen door as though preparing for an attack.

Hands shaking, Ari set her laptop on the counter and dug into her pocket.

The thunder of footsteps pounded down the stairs.

"Everyone okay?" Jack shouted up from the basement.

Mariah gasped again.

"Ari?" Jerek took a step toward her, holding his hands out to catch her. Whether she fell or tried to run didn't matter.

She tapped her phone and held it up to her ear.

"Hello?" Ari tensed. "This is she."

Jerek took another step toward her, ignoring the crunch of the broken ceramic beneath his shoes.

"I'm sorry, what?" Unfamiliar lines pinched between Ari's eyebrows. "How is that even possible?"

Eve's head snapped toward Ari.

"He's the only one?" A dark anger settled over Ari's face. "Don't call me back. I'm on my way to you." Ari grabbed her laptop from the counter. "Every effort isn't going to cut it."

She hung up and shoved her phone back into her pocket.

"Who's Casanova?" Mariah asked.

An oddly light pang of disquiet flickered through Jerek's gut. "And how did this admirer reach your phone?"

"Jerek, it's Cas." Ari took his hand.

"Cas?" The flicker in Jerek's gut strengthened, solidifying into a dazed foreboding that pummeled his stomach up into his lungs. "My Cas?"

"Someone took him." Ari locked her fingers through his. "They broke into Pet's Paradise and stole Cas."

"Why?" A strange silence draped over Jerek's mind. "Why would someone take my cat?"

"Cas is a cat?" Mariah said.

"The woman said Cas is the only one missing." Ari tightened her grip on Jerek's hand as though afraid he might topple over. "She called the police—"

"The likelihood of a somb taking Cas?" Lincoln cut around the table, stepping into Jerek's view.

Jerek couldn't remember when Lincoln had gotten to the kitchen.

He swallowed the pain in his throat. "The police won't be able to help."

"Who the hell would want to steal a cat?" Mariah asked.

"The Maree," Ari said. "*They*, the butcher, LeBlanc."

"If they hurt the fucking cat." Eve swung for the wall, ramming her knuckles into the white paint.

A deep resonant ringing, like a hundred gongs hidden within the walls had been struck at once, echoed through the house.

Mariah screamed and toppled sideways, falling off her chair as Eve shouted, "Son of a bitch!"

She turned back toward the table, cradling her hand to her chest.

Blood seeped from her knuckles, highlighting her now-crooked bones with scarlet.

"The house is protected." Jerek reached for Eve, quickly yanking his hand back as Eve growled. "It's part of the spell I used your blood for."

"You could have warned me." Eve pinched one of the bones in her hand, straightening it out with a sharp crack.

"I didn't know you were going to punch the wall," Jerek said.

"Who would know where Cas was?" Lincoln asked.

A sickening hollow sank in Jerek's gut.

"I used Ari's real name." He met her gaze. "I gave them your S.O.S. number."

"Good." Ari let go of Jerek's hand.

The world wobbled.

"I've had a really shitty week," Ari said. "I would love to take it out on the filth who kidnapped your cat."

"Ari, no," Lincoln said.

"Give me the van keys," Ari said.

"We don't know who took Cas." Lincoln stepped between Ari and the door.

"That's why I'm going to Pet's Paradise to figure it out." Ari held Jerek's gaze. "Keys, Jerek."

"The Maree are after you," Lincoln said. "They've already come for you once."

"I'm aware."

"You promised to stay inside," Lincoln said.

"Things changed." Ari kept her eyes locked on Jerek. "Whoever took Cas crossed a line. I don't care if they're luring us out or just stupid. I'm not letting those shits get away with it."

"Tell me you're not even thinking about going after a cat while the archives are surrounded by sombs with a horde of Maree probably hiding in the crowd." Mariah rubbed the already growing bruise on her arm.

"I have no problem fighting my way through the crowd." Eve cracked another of her bones back into place. "Maree would just add to the fun."

"Wait a damn minute." Jack's muffled shout came from downstairs. "If we couldn't send anyone to help Grace, we can't spare anyone to go after a cat."

"The cat matters," Eve shouted at the floor.

Mariah whimpered.

"We can spare someone to get Cas back because taking him was an attack on this crew," Ari said. "When we're attacked, we respond."

"And Cas isn't a coward who made the choice to walk out," Eve said.

"We're not even sure who half our enemies are. Whoever was ballsy enough to take Cas just tipped their hand. How much information do we risk losing if we let them slip away with Cas? Who also happens to be an innocent animal that needs our protection in case anyone is unclear on that point," Ari said.

Jerek shut his eyes, trying to think back to sitting with Cas in Holden House only a few weeks before. Cas purring as he listened to the plans Jerek didn't dare share with another being capable of comprehensible speech.

"Don't pretend I'm not right, Jerek," Ari said.

"Someone is trying to lure us in," Lincoln said.

"Which is why we're going to figure out who it is," Eve said. "And tear the catnapping, soon-to-be-dead asshat apart."

"And try to take whoever they're working with or for or whatever down with them," Ari said.

"You are actively being hunted by Knights Maree who have been granted the authority to kill you," Lincoln said.

"What?" Mariah leveraged herself against the table to stand, gripping the edge of the wood like it was the only thing keeping her upright.

"You can't risk your ass for a cat," Jack shouted from the basement.

"So we wait for the asshole to go after Lydia? Or my mom? Or Ford's mom?" Ari said. "If they stooped low enough to kidnap a cat, they're not just going to skip off into the sunset brushing Cas's luxurious fur."

No one argued with her.

Jerek wanted to reach for her hand, but he couldn't get his arms to move.

The cold that had draped over his mind added weight to his limbs, winding around him, taunting him.

The cold whispered that it was his fault. He had let the darkness creep in around him, sneaking into his life, clawing at things he had never agreed to risk.

Ari took Jerek's face in her hands, making him meet her eyes. "Give me the van keys."

The cold wrapped around his heart as he summoned the strength to shake his head.

"You're still not safe to go out in public, Jer Bear." Ari lifted her hands away from his face. Her palms had been turned a painfully beautiful shade of sea-blue. "I'm Cas's emergency contact, and I'm going."

She reached into Jerek's pocket and pulled out the keys.

Your duty to protect.

They can't—

There are some sacrifices the world doesn't get to demand.

Ari brushed a kiss against Jerek's cheek.

Her lips turned an icy, lavender-tinged blue.

"Save me some dinner." Ari cut past Jerek and strode out of the kitchen.

"Jerek, you can't let this happen," Lincoln said. "The second any Maree spot her—"

"Let her go." Jerek let the pain of the cold dig into his flesh.

"Jer—"

"I said, let her go." Jerek made himself stay on his feet as the smell of burned muffins filled the air.

38

Eve

Heat danced through Eve's skin, brightening with each stair she climbed. She jumped the last six steps to the fourth floor, giving her body a taste of the relief to come.

Ari hurried out of her bedroom, pink pack in one hand, baseball cap in the other as she cut right toward the stairs. "Keep the boys safe."

"Stop." Eve held up a hand, blocking Ari's path.

"If you've suddenly left team save Cas—"

"I'm going with you." Eve grinned. "But we're not going out the front door."

"Well, that sounds fun."

Eve led Ari toward the bedroom at the end of the hall.

"Is this a jail break?" Ari asked.

"Would it matter?"

"Nope. Just curious."

Eve focused on her hand as she turned the bedroom's door-knob, keeping her grip light, gentle.

She eased the door open, holding on to the knob until the door stopped moving, not letting it crash into the wall.

The scent of the living archivist still filled the room that had been his, even though his sheets had been thrown away and his piles of clothes bagged up and tossed into the closet.

"At the risk of sounding like I doubt you," Ari said, "you do know I can only fall long distances into water without lots of pain and potential death? Concrete is a big no for me."

"I've got you." Eve jumped up, catching the lip of the skylight.

Holding on with one hand, she pushed the loose pane of glass up and over with the other before letting go and dropping back to the floor.

"I love an escape route with a view," Ari said. "Can I get a boost?"

"Should be soon." Eve cocked her head, listening beyond the sounds of construction from across the street. "Stay low and be ready for me to grab you."

"Sounds great."

The wailing of sirens approached the archives.

"Up you go." Eve grabbed Ari by the hips and lifted her straight up, letting Ari get her elbows planted on the roof before grabbing her feet to shove her the rest of the way through the skylight.

As soon as Ari's legs cleared her path, Eve leapt up, gripping the window ledge just enough to leverage herself to land silently on the roof.

"What the hell is happening now?" Ari looked toward the flashing lights racing to the front of the archives.

"An anonymous report of a new sink hole from one of Ford's

burner phones." Eve scooped Ari into her arms, not bothering to wait for Ari to hold on before taking two long strides and vaulting to the next roof over.

"Oh wow." Ari's voice came out pinched as Eve bolted across the roof, heading away from the archives. "Love using the cops as a distrac—"

A gasp ate Ari's words as Eve leapt off the roof, and let them plumet toward the ground.

39

Lincoln

The fresh chaos on the street only lasted an hour. Plenty of time for Eve and Ari to slip away, not nearly long enough to distract Lincoln from the ever-widening hollow consuming his chest.

"You really don't have to do that," Ford said.

Lincoln glanced up from his book.

Ford had stopped typing and, though not going so far as to close his laptop, turned to Regi, who had a wooden spoon in one hand and a whiskey in the other.

Regi looked from the spoon to the whiskey.

"I meant baking," Ford said.

"So, you'll let me look at the books with everyone else?" Regi asked.

"No," Lincoln said.

"Then I might as well take over muffin duty," Regi said. "At least the scary redhead is gone."

With Ari.

Lincoln fixed his mind back on his book.

Spells, some in a language he didn't recognize, filled the pages.

The person who'd cobbled the collection together had left notes in the margins of the handwritten text.

To halt the advancement had been written beside a spell that seemed, as far as Lincoln could tell, to give temporary life to plants—like a dancing flower, or a shrub growing into a wall—

Or a cursed forest worthy of nightmares.

"Huh," Ford said.

"Me?" Regi asked.

"No," Ford said. "*Huh* to the seven people who were dumb enough to sign their real names."

"You found them?" Lincoln didn't bother marking his page as he set the spell book down.

"If I'd been looking for them a few days ago, I could have confirmed their identities and pulled their files in an hour, probably less. But with the Maree database down, I had to find other crumbs to follow." Ford turned his laptop to face Lincoln.

"Maree?" Lincoln reached across the table, grabbing the laptop and dragging it toward him.

"All seven of them," Ford said. "And not lowly grunt Maree. All seven signees of the werewolf hate scroll achieved high honors during their service to the Maree."

"You can't be right." Lincoln scrolled down the page, stopping as he reached a photo of a woman with cropped gray hair. "That's Isabella Schmitt. I know her."

"You do?" Ford stood, cutting around the table to peer over Lincoln's shoulder.

"All the kids in the Maree compound do. She helps organize the youth events. She mentors young knights." Lincoln scrolled further down the page. "Nielsen." He pointed to the picture of a man with a burn scar on his cheek. "He lives in the compound, too. My father hates him, thinks his arrogance is a liability to the Maree."

"Signing a scroll vowing to eradicate werewolves would make someone a liability," Ford said.

"The signatures must have been forged." Lincoln kept scrolling. "Werewolves fall under the Maree treaty. The Knights Maree are sworn to protect cryptids."

"Swearing to protect someone and actually doing it are two different things," Regi said. "At least I assume that tracks for magic people as much as for normal people."

"It does," Ford said. "And not that I'm as good as a forensic specialist, which I've been saying we need, but the pen pressures of the signatures are all different. The pen strokes are consistent and fluid. And, though sources have been scarce, the comparisons to known samples have all been a match. I'm going to give it a ninety-eight percent chance those signatures are genuine. Sorry."

"Why?" Regi stopped stirring the muffin batter. "Why the hell do you know all that?"

"A love of true crime documentaries and an obsessive personality."

The hollow in Lincoln's chest grew jagged edges. "I don't care what you think you know about forgery. Isaac Zara can't be on the list."

"He is," Ford said. "His handwriting actually has more unique traits than most of the others."

"Then he must have changed his mind." Lincoln pushed the computer away. "How long ago was the scroll even signed anyway?"

"That one's a lot harder." Ford grimaced. "More than one decade, less than four?"

"Then it was probably something stupid they all signed when they were kids," Lincoln said.

An expression almost like anger wrinkled Ford's brow. "Tell me you're not saying it's okay to believe in genocide as long as it's just a youthful phase?"

"I'm saying people can be redeemed." Lincoln stood, his chair pushing away from the table with an ear-grating squeak. "Whatever this scroll was meant to start, Zara has no part in it."

"Why do you care so much about this Zara?" Regi pulled on his oven mitt. "I know I'm not supposed to ask questions, and I honestly don't want to know any more about werewolves or knights, but this much worry over one man's moral leanings seems absurd given your current issues."

Lincoln dragged his hands over his head. "Zara isn't just any man. He's a Maree legend. He commands the most elite company of knights the Maree have."

"There are a lot of assholes in power positions in this world," Regi said. "It's sad but undeniable."

"If Zara willingly signed that scroll, what else is he capable of?" Lincoln grabbed his book from the table. "He betrayed his vow as a Knight Maree by signing that manifesto. What if he's betrayed the Maree again? If Zara sided with the traitors who started the insurrection in the compound, my brother is up against the best warriors with the most powerful weapons the Maree have." He strode toward the kitchen doors.

"You're not supposed to go outside," Ford called after him.

"I'm not going outside," Lincoln said. "I need to send an email."

40

Ari

The van swerved suddenly to the left—again—as Eve dodged around a car whose driver had chosen to only drive seven miles an hour over the speed limit.

Eve switched back into the right lane.

"Do you want me to drive?" Ari asked.

"I hate driving," Eve said. "It feels unnatural."

"I don't mind taking over." Ari gripped her laptop as Eve swerved left again, cutting around a beat-up jeep that looked in no way capable of surviving a fight with the van.

"What are you doing on the computer?" Eve turned to Ari, keeping her eyes away from the road long enough Ari truly hoped werewolves had some magnificent kind of peripheral vision she'd simply never heard of. "Ari?"

"Trying not to feel too guilty for trolling the people who are saying the video of me is real," Ari said. "Killing clicks for a video of a little girl in Maine doing impossible backflips. Digging through two Maree phones, trying to break enough of the encryption to see who the hell is commanding the Maree these days."

"I don't know how to do any of those things." Eve veered between two cars, cutting through a gap barely longer than the van. "Stop panicking. I'll get us there alive."

"Sorry."

They drifted into silence, with only the rumble of the wheels and Ari's occasional stifled gasp for company.

Brooks's phone opened first—emails, contact, pictures.

Lots of pictures of an orange cat. Everything a normal somb's phone should have.

Ari held her breath as she swiped over to the symbol of the Maree crest.

"I didn't do anything," Eve said.

"Not you."

Ari tapped on the Maree App.

Update Required

"Damn." Ari tucked her phone back into the front pocket of her bag.

"Can't get into the Murderers' App?"

"How dare you doubt my skills. I can hack an out-of-date app, but it's not going to help much with gaining current information."

She closed her eyes, trying to place her next steps in order as the map app told Eve to leave the highway.

Work on Maree phone number two.

Hope Olivia was better about updating her apps.

Post spoof video of myself.

Feed aliens take the upper west side *conspiracy theories.*

Create timelines tracking archivist, LeBlanc, the mysterious they—

"When we find the catnapper," Eve said, "you get Cas, I'll take care of the one who took him."

"Was that a request or an order?" Ari closed her laptop and slid it into her pink backpack.

"Both. The muscle gets point on a two-man team. And I'd love the chance to tear the catnapping asshole apart. Also, cats don't really like me."

"Hmm. Surprising."

"Because I'm a wolf?"

Ari twisted in her seat, leaning against the wall of the van to face Eve. "You're straightforward, skeptical of strangers, more dangerous than you look, and really quite lovely once you peel away the layers of distrust and false love of isolation. With such a catlike personality, I thought you and Cas would get along well."

"Nice save."

"Wasn't a save."

Eve turned onto the main street of the town.

"Most cats can recognize predators," Eve said. "If Cas is as smart as Jerek always claims, he'll be able to tell I could rip him apart for lunch."

"I'll grab Cas, you tear intestines. Sounds like a great plan."

They drove down a long row of shops. Every storefront had the quiet, tidy feel of an upscale neighborhood trying to preserve its main street charm. An older couple sat outside an ice cream shop. A mother tried to comfort a wailing infant, the fatigue on her face making her look almost as desperate as the child sounded.

Nothing to imply Maree or murderers waiting to attack.

The shops gave way to brick rowhouses.

With low stoops and none of the dug-in basement entrances

so common on the upper west side, this sidewalk offered nowhere to hide.

"You know you have to be discreet, right?" Ari said. "With the intestine ripping?"

"I'm a wolf, not an idiot." Eve slowed as they neared a house with willow trees in the lawn.

"I don't think you're an idiot." Ari tucked her own phone into her pocket. "But I'm on the Maree *go ahead and kill them* list. I'd really like to keep the rest of the crew on the *capture them and drag them before the Council of the Feu* list."

"What those Maree tried to do to you is shit." Eve stopped in front of the willow tree house.

A subtle sign out front read *Pet's Paradise. A home away from home for the discerning pet.*

"But you've got to understand, Ari"—Eve turned in her seat, facing Ari with an uncharacteristic sincerity in her eyes—"not everyone is going to look at what you've done to help the feu and only see a div that got caught running on water. You're a badass hero. And if the bigots with swords forget it, we get the joy of reminding them." Eve's eyes glinted as she grinned.

"Thanks." A hint of heat pressed on Ari's eyes. She pulled the dagger from her pack and slipped it into the sheath already in place on her back. "Want to go find a throat to tear?"

"Hell yes."

41

Eve

A dozen different sets of footprints had trampled the grass of Pet's Paradise's front lawn. One idiot had even stomped straight through a flowerbed.

If someone stomped through Gran's flowerbed, Gran would tear their leg off and make them hop home.

No, she wouldn't.

Gran isn't you.

A woman in a pale pink polo with a Pet's Paradise logo on the chest opened the front door before Ari and Eve had reached the top of the porch steps.

"Hi, thank you so much for dropping by Pet's Paradise today. Unfortunately, we can't take day of reservations." The woman spoke without any air between her words even as she thrust a flyer at Ari. "You can find out more about our services online and we'd love to take care of your furry friend the next time the need arises, with twenty-four hours advance booking, of course. Have a nice day."

The woman began to shut the door.

Ari leapt forward, planting herself in the doorframe.

Let it close. I'll knock it down.

"My name is Ariel Love." Ari laid a palm on the door, slowly pushing it farther open. "You lost my godcat. So unless your insurance covers that level of stupid, I suggest you walk back a second and try that greeting again."

"Miss Love." The woman fully opened the door, a hint of terror showing through the well-painted remorse on her face. "I'm so sorry. We've had local kids knocking on the door since the police left."

"Kids can be assholes," Ari said. "Where's Cas's room?"

The woman peeked over Ari's shoulder, waving her and Eve into the building, not speaking until she'd closed the door firmly behind them.

The combined stench of cat, bleach, and cheap gravy slammed into Eve's face. Her stomach quivered.

"At this point, we can guarantee he's not in the building," the woman said. "My nephew is still small. I made him crawl through every nook in this place, and there is no sign of Casanova. Not even a stray white hair."

"While I respect your attention to detail, Cas can't open doors," Ari said. "If he's not in his room, someone let him out or took him. Since you mentioned someone smashing through one of your windows, I'm going to bet catnapped, so where the hell is Cas's room?"

"This way." The woman nodded them down a long, white-painted hall. "The police have blocked the room off, though I don't know why. We don't have locks on the cat room doors."

"So anyone can just walk in and take a cat?" Eve stayed on Ari's heels as they followed the woman down the corridor.

Every door had a chest-high window, giving a view of the room beyond, as though Pet's Paradise's owners had understood the absurdity of having Paris, robot, and whiskey-themed rooms for cats and wanted to lean into the quirky schtick instead of taming it.

As Eve passed the cats' rooms, their meowing changed. Most cats fell silent. A few brave felines gave warning yowls.

The woman stopped in front of a book-themed room with police tape across the door. A fake fireplace with a flame-shaped scratching post took up the left-hand wall and a bookcase-like cat tree the right. Someone had even taken the time to paint books on the wall behind the cat tree, completing the look.

Lord of the Felines, Cats of Wrath, and *The Great Catsby* were among the titles.

"The lack of locks on the cat room doors is for the safety of our feline guests." The woman pushed her shoulders back, attempting a glare in Eve's direction before sinking back into angst. "The outside doors are kept locked at all times. Pet parents have to ring for entry even in the middle of the day.

"At maximum capacity, we can accommodate up to fifty-seven guests in Pet's Paradise. If an emergency were to happen, evacuating our fifteen private rooms and twenty-one double occupancies would mean thirty-six locked doors between emergency workers and getting these precious babes to safety. If anything, the damage from last night's break-in proves Pet's Paradise's no-lock policy is correct."

"Wow." Ari blinked at the woman. "Show us this damage and get yourself a glass of water. You need to sit and breathe for a second."

"Yes. I really do." The woman nodded, her voice gaining a high, strangled pitch as she spoke. "This way."

She waved them farther down the hallway, past the double

occupancy suites with themes like the beach, space, red high-heeled shoes, and vampires.

The vampire room even offered a coffin bed draped with a Halloween-style black cape.

Sombs.

Jerek left his cat here?

Eve dug past the quivering in her stomach where anger and hunger begged her to attack, searching for a hint of humor at Holden's expense.

The scent of burned plastic distracted her before she could find even a speck of laughter.

"The firemen were here all morning." The woman stopped in front of a door marked *exit* and pointed to the left where another room had been blocked off with police tape.

The bright, glitter-covered walls had been plastered with cartoon cats, dogs, unicorns, and leopards, giving the frighteningly cheerful room the look of a 90's dream gone wrong.

The pane in the room's one window to the outside had bowed in around the edges then shattered, leaving warped glass littering the floor. The paint on the windowsill had charred and bubbled like an over-roasted hot dog.

Beside the window, a chest-high plastic unicorn housed a cat bed in its stomach. The unicorn's horn had melted, curling in on itself as it tipped toward the creature's misshapen nose.

"They're still trying to figure out how it happened." The woman stepped aside as Ari leaned through the door. "I had a bit of a breakdown this morning, just terrified I'd done something to endanger the guests, but the fire inspector assured me he found no sign of faulty wiring or any mistake I might have made."

"What does he think did it?" Ari asked.

"No ruling yet," the woman said. "I was hoping it had been ball lightning or something natural, but a person did this."

"Really?" Ari asked. "From the way the glass is bowed, ball lightning sounds like a better bet to me."

"The guest in this room had been moved when I arrived this morning," the woman said. "I found her sleeping in the staff room. Meteors and lightning can't move cats. But I went to senior prom with the Chief of Police, and there are some things that man really doesn't want his wife to know. I assure you, Miss Love, whoever endangered the lives of my guests and dared to yank a beloved feline from my care will be prosecuted to the fullest extent of the law. Whatever it takes."

Lincoln

The latest construction truck pulled up in front of the archives, moving from one screen in the monitor bank to the next as it passed by the security cameras.

Lincoln leaned closer to the screens, watching two men get out of the truck. One wore a tie and would never pass the Maree physical, the other had a beard hanging well below his chin.

It could be a disguise.

Because they know there's a traitor in Manhattan.

Ford's computer dinged.

"Not for you," Ford said as Lincoln straightened up, daring to glance away from the screens for a heartbeat. "Ari's email warning system has a more fire alarm beep, beep, beep to it."

"Right," Lincoln said. "Sorry."

"How much lavender is too much lavender?" Jack asked. "I don't want covering the fresh concrete musk to end up leaving the basement smelling like a candle shop."

"I'd say you can never have too much fresh-cut lavender, but I don't have vampire senses," Ford said.

Lincoln glanced back again, just long enough to see Jack standing on a chair, six bundles of fresh lavender in hand.

"Don't glance judgmentally in my direction," Jack said. "If this house gets attacked, you at least have a chance of surviving. If I get dragged up those stairs, I die. One layer of old wood and some potentially toxic insulation are all that stand between me and an agonizing death."

"Jack," Ford said.

"If I'm going to be facing a horrific end to my afterlife every moment of the day, not smelling rot would really help keep the anxiety at bay. Even at night when I don't have to worry about being sun burned, the constant nausea from this basement's stench without the ability to actually vomit slows down my productivity. I've already been getting more done sans corpse stench."

"He really has," Ford said.

"Imagine what I could achieve once the concrete smell dissipates."

"Sorry. I'm just..." Lincoln's mind raced through the index of words that could describe him.

He couldn't pick one word to encompass the panicked, guilt-ridden, useless mess he'd withered into.

The new construction worker with the beard set up a tripod with an unfamiliar device on top.

Lincoln's heart stopped as he leaned toward the screen, waiting for the world to explode.

"It's a surveyor thingy." Ford spoke from right behind Lincoln's shoulder. "I've seen them used before."

"Right." Lincoln leaned back in his seat. "Sorry."

"Please don't apologize to me." Ford's voice held a hint of regret-laced worry. "At least, not in this moment."

"Why?" Lincoln glanced away from the monitors for a third time.

"The Maree server is still offline," Ford said. "So, digging into Zara and the other names on the scroll has been rough. I've had to get inventive with my sources."

"If you've found out my brother is in even more danger—"

"No," Ford cut in. "I can't find any word on what's going on inside the Maree compound, who started the insurrection, or where your family currently is. While it may not feel like it, that last part is actually a really good thing.

"If I can't track down your parents or their five kids under the age of ten, they're probably all holed up at your grandparents and being smart enough to stay quiet about it. And not to sound like a total dick, but if I can't find them, unless they turned in a forwarding address, the evil Maree don't have a chance of tracking your family."

"Confidence isn't a dick move," Jack said.

"Can you still keep an eye out for them?" Lincoln blinked back the heat stinging his eyes.

"Absolutely," Ford said.

A new set of reporters was granted the prime spot in front of the damaged houses.

"I still have to tell you the thing I needed to tell you," Ford said. "Switch with me."

Lincoln welcomed the painful ball of worry pulsing in his gut as he slid out of the seat, keeping his eyes on the monitors until Ford had taken his place.

Ford held up his tablet, passing it to Lincoln. "Swipe right for more screenshots."

"What am I looking at?" Lincoln scanned through the contents of an email.

Demand whoever you think can get the job done.

I'm putting millions into this. I want the best.
-C

"That is the end of the email chain where LeBlanc nudges Chanler toward giving an ultimatum," Ford said. "He'd only fund Maree quests to search for the origin of the Fracture if LeBlanc got to handpick the knights for the mission."

"The Maree must not have agreed," Lincoln said. "They must have found another way to convince Chanler to supply the funds."

"Oh, the Maree happily agreed," Ford said. "Only fifteen minutes between the ultimatum being given and accepted."

Anger consumed Lincoln's worry. "All three quests Chanler funded were total losses. If LeBlanc chose the knights—"

"We have to assume LeBlanc knew the Maree he named weren't coming back alive," Jack said.

Lincoln swiped to the next screen.

Three lists of twelve names in an email signed off on by Chanler.

"LeBlanc condemned thirty-six Maree." Lincoln swiped over to the next screen. "He chose thirty-six knights and sent them to die."

The screen showed the same list but with the top name of each column highlighted.

Adrian Müller, Marcus Andersen, Andrea Jensen.

"Did you get to the highlighted names?" Ford asked. "I can hear you grinding your teeth, so I'm going to assume you have."

Lincoln tried to loosen his jaw.

He failed.

"All three names are from the scroll," Ford said. "All three were chosen to lead their quest."

"Three out of the seven makes shit odds for being a coincidence," Jack said. "And believe me, I love gambling a long shot."

"LeBlanc trying to sabotage the quests makes sense," Ford said. "He couldn't risk the Maree finding out he'd been involved with the curse that caused the Fracture. But why choose were-wolf haters?"

Lincoln swiped to the next screen—a map of the United States with four dots along the east coast and two on the west.

"Gandalf dog!" Ford smacked his desk. "We're up to five trips past the house today."

"That poor dog has got to be sick of sniffing the same damn trees," Jack said. "I should have guessed higher."

"Definitely." Ford drew a hashmark on a piece of paper. "Wait, Lincoln did you spot Gandalf? We have to keep everything in order for the betting pool."

"We're under siege, and you're betting on a dog?" Lincoln swiped the screen again.

"I don't think you can call it a siege if you can have fresh flowers delivered in twenty minutes or less." Jack hopped off the chair and turned to examine the bundles of lavender he'd hung from the ceiling.

"Ordering flowers—"

"Portrays an even greater air of confidence to our street guards. Keeps the troops loyal and raises crew morale all for the low price of some of Jerek's money," Ford said. "People who are abandoning their homes and all the deadly secrets therein don't have fresh flowers delivered. The second our reluctant defenders smell panic, we're doomed, so let them smell lavender instead."

"It's a little scary how good you are at this," Jack said.

Lincoln tightened his grip on the tablet, wishing he could shatter the screen and destroy the picture of a young LeBlanc sitting on top of a bar, smiling with three others that all held their glasses out as though cheersing the photographer.

The woman sitting on the bar beside LeBlanc had brown hair and a familiar face, though Lincoln couldn't place it.

The two standing in front of them, Lincoln needed no help in recognizing—Isaac Zara and Isabella Schmitt.

"Are you trying to find another argument against maintaining a calm façade, or is something on the tablet making your blood pump that hard?" Jack asked.

"Who's the woman sitting on the bar with LeBlanc?" Lincoln asked.

"That would be Andrea Jensen," Ford said. "One of the three handpicked by LeBlanc to lead a doomed quest."

"And we hit the three-times-gives-shit-odds-of-a-coincidence rule again." Jack slid his notebook down the table and pulled open a yet-to-be-searched crate.

"I only found that picture because it turned up in my Andrea Jensen searches," Ford said. "The picture was contributed to her memorial by Zara."

Lincoln zoomed in on the picture, focusing on LeBlanc's face. He couldn't find any hint of a murderer hidden in his eyes. "It looks like they were all friends."

"And you said the word of the hour." Jack set the top of the crate aside. "A *they* orchestrated the Blood Mountain Massacre, murdering most of a pack of werewolves. Seven assholes, which would constitute a *they*, signed a manifesto promising to exterminate werewolves. No way in hell would I bet on two different werewolf-hating *theys* being linked to the archives."

"If the Maree *they* are responsible for Blood Mountain, did that *they* also cause the Fracture?" Ford asked.

"Maree wouldn't do that," Lincoln said.

"Based on the scroll seven Maree signed, I think I have to disagree with your assumption of Maree morals," Jack said.

"Then they couldn't," Lincoln said. "Orchestrating something like causing the Fracture—"

"Would imply a rot within the Knights Maree big enough to cause an insurrection?" Jack said. "Call it a bitter upbringing, but when people flaunt how shitty they are, you should always assume their evil digs about ten levels deeper."

"Then it was LeBlanc," Lincoln said. "He was in D.C. when the Fracture began. He was near the incidents of feu casualties in Ireland, Massachusetts, and Pennsylvania. He sent the thirty-six knights on Chanler's quests to die. He's the one controlling the *they*."

"Controlling seven knights who outranked him?" Jack said. "And he kept control of the seven wolf haters even after he was kicked out of the Maree?"

"LeBlanc sent three of those seven to die." Ford held up a hand before Jack could speak. "I'm just saying we shouldn't try to condense our problems. Knowing the seven who signed the scroll are evil doesn't mean there weren't other evil Maree conspiring with LeBlanc to cause the Fracture or trying to cover their tracks by dooming three quests."

"Did you have to pick now to be right?"

"Stop." Heavy, cold, bleak anger settled in Lincoln's chest. "Both of you are looking for reasons to accuse Maree."

"Signing a murder manifesto does the accusing for itself," Jack said.

"The actions of a few knights does not imply corruption within the Maree," Lincoln said.

"I hope I'm wrong," Jack said. "But I wouldn't bet against me."

"We're missing something." Lincoln set the tablet beside Ford. "There's another connection between LeBlanc and the butcher—"

"And the seven and the *they*?" Jack said.

"We just haven't found it yet." Lincoln forced the words

through the cold smothering his chest. "You have to find out how LeBlanc connects to the seven traitors."

"Traitors is an improvement," Jack said.

"I've been trying to find another link starting with where and when the bar picture was taken," Ford said, "but with the Maree server down, I can't trace any of their movements well enough to figure out where their paths crossed when."

"Then you have to get into the server." Lincoln tried to swipe again, but the picture of the four Maree traitors bounced back into place.

"It's actually not possible," Ford said. "At all."

"Can Ari do it?"

"Not even our goddess of tech can hack something that's just not there." Ford leaned closer to the monitors. "For all we can tell, the server may not actually exist anymore."

"Meaning?" Lincoln balled his hands into fists, stifling his need to scream.

"Don't panic about it." Ford ran his finger across one of the screens, tracking the movement of a couple dressed for a run in the park. "A blowtorch could kill a server. So could water. Or heat. Or an axe if you aren't fussed about electrical safety. The server might not even be in the Maree compound. Don't link its demise to your family's wellbeing."

"Thanks," Lincoln said.

"Our wellbeing may be another matter," Ford said.

Jack knocked the top of the crate over with a bang as Ford tapped on the monitor.

"Two joggers, choosing to walk through construction hell, breathing in dust before their run." Ford shook his head.

The couple slowed as though watching the workers, but both kept glancing away from the ruined houses as though eyeing the archives.

"Damn," Jack said.

The woman knelt to tie her shoe while the man stepped behind a tree, hiding himself from Ford's cameras from the torso up.

"We need to get Regi off the first floor," Lincoln said. "Jack, can you hide in one of the crates? They can't drag you into the sun if they don't know you're here."

"I won't—" Jack cut off as the man stepped out from behind the tree, a massive hammer in one hand, an axe in the other. "Those would not have fit in his running shorts."

The man handed the woman the axe. He gave her a nod as she stood, and they both started toward the house.

Lincoln shifted his weight, ready to bolt up the stairs, but a dark blur hurdled across the screen, cracking right into the man's head.

"What the—look out!" Ford winced as another blur shot across the screen. "What the hell was that? Oh, shit!"

The woman ducked, dodging the blow, letting the thing shoot past her to the archives as she spun toward the source of the attack.

"That's a brick!" Jack yelped as the brick struck the front of the archives but didn't fall to the ground.

Silently, without any damage from colliding with the house, the brick bounced back, rocketing right toward the woman and cracking her in the back of the head.

The woman's knees buckled, and she toppled to the ground.

"Shit." Lincoln finally ran for the stairs.

43

Ari

What kind of sick son of a shit breaks in and screws with somebody's cat?

Oh, I'll tell you what kind of ass-brained dick would endanger a building full of animals.

The kind that's going to get my foot shoved so far down their throat, my toes will tickle their kidney, that's who!

Ari screamed the words in her mind as she waited for Carrie, the owner of Pet's Paradise, to photocopy the forms she'd gotten from the police.

"I have people searching the streets in the area." Carrie handed Ari the second batch of forms. "And I put the litter box Casanova has been using out in the garden in case he's searching for a way back."

"You think Cas gave his kidnappers the slip?" Eve stepped closer to Carrie, towering over the poor woman.

"I just…" Carrie's gaze darted around the room while somehow managing to avoid flicking in Eve's direction. "I've been in this business for years. The flea incident of 2019 was the worst thing we'd ever dealt with. I don't"—Carrie shook her head—"I never created a plan for this."

"And there's no reason you should have." Ari grabbed the last stack of papers from the copier. "Just do me a favor. If you find Cas, post it on your website."

"The website?" Carrie's flustered worry snapped into a sharp tone of perturbance. "I can't post about a lost cat on our website."

"Yeah," Eve said, "you can."

"The number you called to reach me was a one and done. It won't work a second time." Ari grinned, not bothering to hide her hint of joy at Carrie backing into the desk as she inched away from Eve. "Since you can't call me, if you find Cas, you'll post it on your website.

"And please don't even daydream about pulling his litter box back inside or not telling me if he shows up." Ari stepped closer to Carrie, pinning her between Ari and Eve. "Someone kidnapped my godcat."

"And I'm very sorry," Carrie said. "But Pet's Paradise is not at fault for—"

"Before you consider arguing, remember that an asshole targeted Cas and stole him," Ari said. "If Cas's family has the kind of enemies who will break in to take a cat, picture what Cas's godmother would do to someone foolish enough to not do everything in their power to get Cas home."

Ari reached down and took Carrie's hand, doing all the work of shaking it while Carrie's arm flopped up and down like terror had stolen her bones. "Thank you for all the information and for helping us bring Cas home. I highly suggest you invest in at least seven more security cameras."

Ari turned and walked out into the hall, locking her teeth together to keep from screaming.

The Maree are crumbling, magic is being noticed, Cas got snatched, you've got a target on your back...shit, shit, shitty McShits.

"Shit," Eve said as she shut Pet's Paradise's front door.

"An abbreviated version of my internal monologue." Ari pulled her phone from her pocket as she climbed down the porch steps, heading toward the black van.

"You wanted us to get attacked in there, too?" Eve said.

"What? No." Ari checked her phone.

No S.O.S. call from Jerek. No warning of Jerek's impending doom from Ford.

"Getting ambushed would be a hell of a lot better than trying to hunt down a catnapper," Eve said.

"We'll be fine." Ari unlocked the van, climbing into the driver's seat without giving Eve a chance to argue. "We'll find some decent coffee and take a nice stroll."

Eve gripped the driver's side door, stopping Ari from closing it.

"The stroll is to subtly search for security cameras to hack," Ari said. "The coffee is for the extreme lack of sleep."

"And the note?" Eve nodded toward the windshield.

A receipt with words scrawled across it in purple pen had been shoved under the windshield wiper.

"Doesn't look like any parking ticket I've ever gotten." Ari slid out of the driver's seat.

Eve snatched the receipt out from under the windshield wiper, scanning the paper before cursing under her breath and shoving it Ari's way.

Meet me in the parking lot at the eastern entrance of South Square Park.

Do not come armed.
Please don't attack me.

"Please don't attack me?" Ari crammed the note into her pocket and pulled out her phone.

"Now I just want to tear their spleen out," Eve said.

"Love a good spleen tearing." Ari hopped back into the driver's seat as she pulled up a map of South Square Park.

44

Jack

J ack cringed as he reached into the bottom of the crate, trying to ignore the stench of mildew, grateful to find an old, relatively non-foul odored, wooden jewelry box in the depths of this particular niche of the archivist's hoard.

"How do I know if I'm doing this right?" Mariah asked from her seat in front of the monitor bank.

"Have you been watching for signs of impending doom?" Jack lifted the jewelry box from the crate, keeping it far from his face as he gave the box a moment to attack.

"Yes."

"Then you're doing a great job." He gave the box a little shake.

"You okay over there?" Mariah asked.

"A book had attack spines in its bindings. Not fatal, but painful enough to make me suspicious of everything in this place." Jack set the box down and dusted his hands off on his pants before spotting the filth-packed engraving on the top.

He rubbed his finger across the ornamentation, knocking bits of the debris free.

"Are you sure you wouldn't do a better job with the monitors than me?" Mariah asked.

"Did you miss the part where a book attacked me? I heal faster than you."

L'ordre de la lame lunaire.

"Do you speak French?" Jack asked. "I ran away long before French class did me any good."

"French, Italian, Greek, and a hint of Mandarin. Why does Ford have a dog?"

"What?" Jack set the box aside.

"Ford is leading the Gandalf dog toward the house." Mariah pointed at the farthest left screen.

"Did he just kidnap a dog?" Jack leaned over Mariah. "Ford, you can't take a dog!"

Jack squinted at the monitor as though his vampire sight had somehow mistaken Ford happily holding Gandalf's leash as he stopped to watch the EMTs and police officers who'd shown up to take care of the two who'd taken bricks to the head. "We're all mad because someone kidnapped Jerek's cat. We can't be mad about catnapping while actively dognapping."

"I'm going to leave the dog between you and your boyfriend," Mariah said.

A swirl of delight closely followed by a pang of panic streaked up Jack's spine.

"Oof." Mariah leaned away from the screens. "The EMTs gave up on Mr. Brick Head pretty quick."

Ford strolled up to the edge of the police barrier, holding

Gandalf's leash with one hand while beckoning a police officer toward him with the other. An officer cut around the EMTs, heading Ford's way.

The EMTs who'd been working on the male bricking victim had all backed away, making room for a body bag, but the ones working on the bricked woman had finally started loading her onto a gurney.

Ford pointed from the woman being rolled away to the house across the street. He dodged side to side as though demonstrating the brick attack.

The officer spoke into the radio on his shoulder.

Ford nodded, pointing at Mr. Brick being shrouded in a body bag.

Ford whipped his head to the side.

So did the police officer.

And everyone else on the street.

All of them looked up toward the sky.

"What are they looking at?" Mariah stood, leaning closer to the top-right screen where everyone seemed to be staring. "What the hell are they looking at?"

"In the sky." Jack spoke the words before his brain had properly processed exactly what stage of the apocalypse he was witnessing.

A flying mass dove into the camera's view, streaking toward the ambulance.

But the form wasn't solid. It split into hundreds of parts—some surrounding the bricked woman, others swooping right at the people on the street.

"Are those birds?" Jack looked down at the screen where Ford had been a second before.

Through the storm of black-striped-gray wings, he couldn't find Ford or the police officer he'd been talking to.

Jack turned toward the stairs, his fangs tearing into his bottom lip as instinct screamed for him to protect.

He froze, his hands shaking as fear squashed instinct. "I can't go up there."

"Take the cameras." Mariah dodged past Jack, tearing up the stairs to the kitchen.

Jack slipped into the chair, scanning the screen where he'd last seen Ford, ignoring the knot clenching his throat as he moved on to the cameras closer to the house.

A hint of white broke through the gray of the wings.

"Come on, Ford," Jack whispered. "Come on home."

The bit of white broke free from the storm as Ford sprinted toward the archives, a massive, white-bearded schnauzer huddled in his arms.

Jack tipped his head, resisting the urge to close his eyes as he listened for the front door through the growing cacophony of the mayhem on the street.

As soon as Ford reached the top of the stairs on the screens, the front door opened with a creak, slamming shut the instant after.

A dog whined.

"It's okay. You're okay, Gandalf," Ford panted. "I hate pigeons, too."

45

Eve

South Square Park was less a park and more a span of flat grass someone had decided would be fun to sit on. No tree cover. Nowhere to hide.

No chance of hiding from sombs.

"One or both?" Ari asked.

"What?"

"Do we go out and meet the catnapper together, or does one of us watch from the sidelines, waiting for the moment when the big reveal happens and the catnapper snaps their sincerely badly planned trap?" Ari unfastened her seatbelt. "I'm fine either way—"

"We'll go together." Eve unfastened her own seatbelt. "Just promise if things get bloody, you're not going to blame yourself."

Eve opened her door and hopped out before Ari could answer.

There were four other cars in the eastern parking lot, and a few across the flat grass on the northern side of the *park*.

Taking a deep breath, Eve searched past the stench of chemical weedkiller and too much dog pee. A hint of cat carried on the wind.

None of the park people prowled toward them. None of the cars in their parking lot moved.

She leaned against the front of the van.

Ari closed her door and cut around to Eve, scanning the park for a moment before leaning against the van beside her. "Thanks."

"Don't mention it," Eve said.

"Coming from you, I'll take that literally."

"Good."

A man on a bike sped through the middle of the park.

A dog peed on an unsuspecting woman's foot.

A kid made himself dizzy and cried when he fell down.

A ripple of tension raced up Eve's spine. She pushed away from the van, taking a deep breath, scenting the air as she scanned the park.

She whipped toward the east.

A girl wearing an unreasonably warm sweatshirt hurried toward the park. She'd pulled her hood up, hiding her face even though her head twisted back and forth like a metronome as she searched the street. She had a backpack on her front, and she clung to the pack, gripping it like it might be torn away.

The backpack moved.

"I won't even need claws to tear that shit apart," Eve said.

Ari stepped forward, giving Eve her right flank as she watched the girl approach.

The pack yowled.

Ari reached behind her back, gripping the hilt of her dagger.

"Please don't hurt me," the girl whimpered.

The pack hissed as the girl pushed her hood back and raised her chin.

Grace.

Fire-starting, mission-abandoning Grace.

Grace stood in front of them with Jerek's cat in a backpack.

Grace had the nerve to let her lip wobble as she glanced between Ari and Eve.

"I know you're angry." Grace backed a step away. "And you have every right to be. But please, please listen before you tear my entrails out."

"Glad you understand who you just pissed off." Eve grinned, savoring Grace's shudder.

"Give me Cas." Ari reached for Grace.

"I can't do that." Grace tightened her grip on Cas.

Cas yowled.

"Give me the cat," Ari said.

"I need sanctuary," Grace said, "or asylum. Whatever you want to call it."

"I call it hand over the cat and be thankful if I let you walk away with all your limbs," Eve said.

"I was awful, and I know it." Grace matched Ari's distance as Ari prowled toward her. "I said some terrible things and pretended I knew what was at stake when I didn't. I didn't understand what you've been fighting against."

"And now suddenly you do, so you kidnap a cat?" Ari said. "Give me Cas now, or Eve will take him from you."

Grace glanced between Ari and Eve.

Eve reached for her pendants.

"I'm sorry about kidnapping Cas." Grace slid the backpack off, keeping as far from Ari as she could while carefully handing the cat over. "It was the only way I knew how to get ahold of you."

"And now that you've realized this isn't all some game Jerek and I just made up for funsies, you want to rejoin the cause?" Ari slid the pack onto her front.

"It's not that noble." Eve stepped closer to Grace, taking Ari's place as she backed away, peering into a tiny slit in the pack's zipper.

"You're okay, sweet boy," Ari cooed.

Cas merped in response.

"He good?" Eve asked.

"Pissed off, but alert and gorgeous," Ari said.

"Then what do we do to the catnapping traitor who walked out on us?" Heat simmered beneath Eve's skin.

"I have nowhere else to go," Grace said.

"Do we let her walk away, or do we make sure she understands the consequences of putting innocent animals in danger?" Eve asked.

"I never put Cas in danger!" Grace backed farther away, stumbling as her heel caught on a crack in the sidewalk. "The backpack looks bad, but he's only been in there for a few minutes."

"And the rest of the cats?" Ari said. "You almost burned the whole Pet's Paradise down!"

"No, I didn't."

Eve stalked closer to Grace. "You melted through a window. You melted through plastic. One stray flame, and you'd have been an animal killer."

"There were no stray flames." Grace backed into a tree, trapping herself between Ari and Eve. "I never put any of the animals in danger."

"Your hands spark when you panic," Ari said.

"Not anymore," Grace said. "I learned to control it when the Maree took me."

The heat under Eve's skin solidified with a tension that threatened to tear through her flesh.

"They captured me and tortured me." Tears streamed down Grace's cheeks. "Then they started killing each other, so I managed to get away, and I've been running for days trying to find a way to get back to you."

Grace swiped her tears with her sleeve, leaving a streak of dirt behind. "Please. I need help. I can't go home because the Maree are after me. And I don't have any money. And I had to steal a car and clothes and food."

Grace's shoulders shook as she gave up on speaking to lean against the tree and cry.

"You saw Maree fighting each other?" Ari asked.

"Wh—when they had me in the blue cage," Grace said. "A few phones rang, and then they just started fighting."

Ari looked to Eve. "If she was there when the fighting started…"

"Please don't leave me," Grace said. "They'll find me again."

"Take her back with us, find out everything she knows, make her look Jerek in the eye and apologize for taking Cas, then figure out if we should dump her?" Ari asked.

"Fine." Eve stepped right up to Grace, towering over the coward. "But the second she says one shitty, rude ass, bigoted thing, the right to decide what to do with her goes to me."

"Deal," Ari said.

46

Lincoln

Five young faces smiled up at Lincoln from Ford's tablet. The youngest of the Martels were caked in mud in the picture, though Lincoln didn't know on which muddy occasion the picture had been taken.

He tapped away from the image and pulled up the list of files in his parents' personal cloud account. He scrolled down past the milestones in the family timeline his mother had used to label the images.

William joins the crew marked the birth of his youngest brother right before the file his mother had labeled *The last baby* when Nelson, the second youngest, had been born.

He kept scrolling past the births of the youngest five Martels until he reached the file labeled *Italy*, his mother's way of writing *when our family fled to the Maree compound in Italy after the Fracture ripped magic from the world.*

He opened the file and scrolled down to start at the oldest of the pictures.

Lincoln, Martin, and Fredrick camping in their bedroom in the compound before the furniture had arrived.

A group of adults smiling together as they gathered around a bonfire.

A posed picture of the first knights to take their vow after the Fracture.

Zara stood on the platform at the head of the ceremony, his face proud and determined as he enjoyed a place of honor right behind the members of the Knight's Council.

And on either side of Zara, Christian Nielsen and Isabella Schmitt shared in the glory of being chosen to symbolize what the young knights should strive to become.

"Traitors," Lincoln whispered.

"Sorry, what?" Regi whispered back. He leaned across the kitchen table as he waited for Lincoln to respond, clutching the old plank of wood Jerek had given him with a promise that the poor weapon would let Regi defend himself from any attack. "Are we getting attacked now?"

Lincoln dug his heels into the kitchen floor, barely resisting the temptation to test Jerek's lie.

"If we were getting attacked, you'd know it." Lincoln swiped to the next picture. He was giving Martin bunny ears as Martin blew out his birthday candles.

"A legion of pigeons just bombarded the street," Regi said. "I'm not even sure what an attack would look like."

"Just wait for one of us to tell you to run," Lincoln said. "If we do, hide in the closet and do not call the police."

"Because the police would be attacked by murder birds." Regi sat back in his seat.

"Because three of our crew can't risk being taken to a hospital, somb police searching the house could trigger magic or booby traps, and Eve coming back with blood all over her face from ripping out the catnapper's jugular with her teeth could cause a lot of problematic questions." Lincoln moved on to the next picture.

The oldest three Martel boys and their parents, Lincoln's father's face barely in the picture as he tried to capture his family all lying on a picnic blanket.

"But what if I'm willing to promise a $200 tip?" Ford shoved the kitchen door open, holding it aside as he ushered the dog in.

The dog bolted straight for Regi, begging for attention despite the dribble of bird poop in his fur.

"I'll make it $300." Ford opened the fridge door.

"You don't know how you ended up here either, do you buddy?" Regi scratched a clean patch of the dog's head.

Gandalf licked Regi's face in response.

Ford sighed. He closed his eyes, and his shoulders sank. "No, I understand. Safety first. Let animal control do their work. Yep." Ford nodded. "You, too."

The dog abandoned Regi to scramble toward Ford, his claws clicking against the kitchen floor as he slid on the well-scrubbed tile.

Ford hung up his phone and tucked it into his back pocket. "It's okay, Gandalf. We'll find you a snack."

Lincoln moved on to the next picture. He couldn't remember when Fredrick had gotten a cut bad enough for someone to draw a smiley face in the blood dried on his cheek.

"What human food can you give dogs?" Ford snapped the fridge shut.

"I had embarrassingly little to do with my dog growing up." Regi clutched his board of protection to his chest, like Lincoln might steal it from him for having been a distracted child.

Gandalf dove for Lincoln, licking Lincoln's chin as Lincoln dodged the worst of the mess in the dog's fur.

"I'm no help, either." Lincoln lifted the tablet out of Gandalf's reach. "We had a strict no people food rule for all animals in our house."

"Harsh." Mariah opened the door from the basement, dodging right for the door to the hall, out of reach of the still-leashed Gandalf.

"My parents have survived a herd of kids that's included teenagers and toddlers for a long time." Lincoln scrunched his face, protecting his eyes from Gandalf's renewed affection. "Teenager sneaks the dog a piece of sausage. Toddler sees it and thinks, *chocolate's brown, close enough*, the dog gets sick, and everything ends in tears."

"Did your mother give you that speech?" Ford asked.

"At least once a week," Lincoln said.

Gandalf abandoned Lincoln to prance in front of the sink.

"The army of pigeons is still patrolling the street, but the ambulance and police backed off," Mariah said.

"Animal control is going to take care of it." Ford pulled a carrot from the fridge.

"I definitely saw my nanny give my dog carrots," Regi said as Gandalf snatched the carrot from Ford's hand.

"Great," Mariah said. "Someone else has to take over the cameras. Jack needs to get back to sorting crates, and Jerek wants me on the second floor to practice basic spellwork. How did I end up in magician kindergarten taught by a Holden?"

Not waiting for a reply, Mariah pushed open the kitchen door and abandoned the boys to Gandalf's gratitude.

"It's like—" Ford began before snapping his mouth shut and shaking his head.

"I can watch the security cameras," Regi said.

Ford wrinkled his nose. "That's a kind offer, but there's no way."

Lincoln moved on to the next picture—his mother with a twig tangled through her hair. A smile twinkled in her eyes, even though Lincoln felt sure she'd had to cut her hair to free the twig.

Martin smiling with his class after his first day of blade work.

Zara stood behind the group. He'd been Martin's teacher.

"I can't just sit here waiting to be attacked," Regi said. "And please don't hand me another magic board or tell me to watch the dog."

The next picture didn't have any smiling faces.

Lincoln remembered the night captured in the image.

A ceremony of mourning and honor.

"Well, you could..." Ford began.

It was the first major loss since the quests to mend the Facture had been stopped. A werewolf colony had gotten out of hand. Started grabbing locals during the full moon.

Ten knights had been sent to stop the killings. Only three returned—Zara, Nielsen, and Schmitt.

"How would you feel about working on a list of supplies we need?" Ford said. "Not like dead magician bone—"

Regi gagged.

"Like bread, dog food, more bleach. Think of it like being the quartermaster of the crew. Ari usually..." Ford's voice trailed away. His shoulders sank. "I need more sleep. My brain isn't keeping up with my mouth anymore."

Gandalf barked.

"Where can I find a pen and paper?" Regi said. "I'll put dog shampoo first on the list."

"Great." Ford pulled another carrot from the fridge. "Can

you aim for hypoallergenic? Poor puppy's been through enough. He doesn't need a rash."

"Of course," Regi said. "Wouldn't want the dog to have a hard day."

Gandalf snatched the carrot from Ford.

"Lincoln, can you watch the cameras for a few minutes while I wipe the poop from our sweet boy's fur?" Ford asked.

"He's not *our* dog," Jack shouted from the basement.

"And get him a few blankets to curl up on," Ford said.

"You can't keep a dog you dognapped!" Jack called back.

"I'll stay on the cameras." Lincoln set the tablet onto the table, zooming in on the three honored knights' faces before turning the screen toward Ford.

"Oh, shit." Ford picked up the tablet. "I don't think I've seen this one."

"No reason it would have come up. My mother took this picture." Lincoln dragged his hands over his face, trying to regain some of the blissful numbness that was so much better than the guilt and anger rolling through his stomach. "They're the heroes who defeated the Coos Bay Pack."

"How do I not recognize that name?" Ford zoomed in closer, focusing on Zara's face.

"The Knight's Council didn't shout that success, and the feu were so distracted by the Fracture, they didn't notice." Lincoln stood, not bothering to keep his chair legs from squeaking against the floor. He swallowed the bile rising in his throat, locking his arms against his sides to keep from taking a swing at the wall. "The three heroes of Coos Bay signed that werewolf-hating manifesto, and they got their wish. An entire lycanthrope bloodline was taken out at Coos Bay. They wanted to kill wolves, and the Maree gave them the chance."

47

Grace

The back seat of the van looked the same as it had before she'd run from the crew. The same worn upholstery. The same carpet. The same black curtains around Jack's little niche.

It should have looked different. There should've been tears through the fabric and dried blood on the windows.

It should have been the stink of singed flesh and death twisting Grace's stomach, not rancid self-loathing because she knew, absolutely knew she'd earned every glare Eve shot her way. But Ari still looked perfect as she nestled Cas's new supplies in the back of the van, and Eve still looked terrifying and undefeatable as she drove away from the pet store, heading toward the highway.

Ari pulled out her pink laptop. The crack in the corner had gotten a little bigger.

Grace tried not to feel relieved.

"Assuming we're getting back into the archives the way we got out," Ari said, "should I prepare a request for another distraction?"

"Not sure," Eve said.

"If we wait until dark, do you think Jack would be able to make the same jumps as you?" Ari looked to Eve. "It would save you from having to make two trips."

Eve tightened her grip on the wheel.

"Or if you prefer to be the only one leaping between buildings, I can wait while you carry flight-risk-McGee first," Ari said.

"Maybe." Eve's neck tensed.

Cas yowled.

Grace slid to the seat at the very back of the van.

"I'm going to assume there's a good reason you're being cagey," Ari said. "But can you at least tell me if Ford needs to prepare a homecoming bonanza to keep people from noticing you leaping over the rooftops?"

"We don't need Ford," Eve said.

"Great." Ari pulled a black phone from her pack. "Don't make me regret not pushing for answers."

Cas leapt up onto the seat beside Grace, nipping at her shirtsleeve before curling up beside her.

"Thanks, Cas." Grace scratched the cat's long-haired chin. "I really am sorry for catnapping you."

Cas rolled onto his back and purred.

"Enjoy Cas's quick forgiveness." Ari didn't look up from the black phone. "The rest of us are much better at remembering who's betrayed us."

"I never meant to betray anyone." Tension cinched around Grace's lungs.

"You committed to a cause. You ran," Eve said. "That makes you traitor."

"I'm sorry. I really am." Grace measured her breathing, keeping it calm. "I know I said some awful things and I shouldn't have walked away. I know that now, I promise I do."

"Please don't start begging." Ari swapped the phone for her computer. "I trusted you. You broke that trust. Saying you're sorry isn't going to make me or anyone else on the crew trust you again." Ari glanced back at Grace. "And in this game, trust is everything."

"I know I'll have to earn back your trust, but—" Grace sild across the back seat of the van as Eve veered off the road, then flew off the seat and onto the floor as Eve slammed on the breaks.

Cas yowled as his new food and water bowls tipped, spilling his lunch.

"What is it?" Ari had set her computer down and unbuckled her seatbelt before she'd finished speaking. She yanked a dagger out of nowhere.

Grace scrambled up onto the back seat, cowering like the terrified little traitor she'd proven herself to be.

"You're my friend, Ari," Eve said. "We're all your friends."

"That's great, but why did you veer off the road?" Ari said.

"And I know this is going to be hard for you, but we're doing this because we love you," Eve said.

How did I end up at an inter—

"Why does this sound like an intervention?" Ari asked.

"Because Ford told me what to say." Eve shoved her curls away from her face. "I'm not taking you back to the archives. I'm taking you to Gran's in North Carolina."

"Is Gran okay?" Ari asked.

"She's fine," Eve said, "but you're not. We can't protect you in the city."

"I never asked to be protected." Ari's knuckles paled as she tightened her grip on her blade.

"But Gran can keep you safe," Eve said. "The mountain is safe from Maree."

"Until it's not."

"Then you'll have an entire pack defending you from any asshole who dares to breach our boundary." Eve reached for Ari's dagger. "You'll be safe with Gran."

"While you all stay in the archives with who knows what fresh hell tightening around your necks?" Ari tucked her blade away. "I'm a member of the crew. I stay with the crew."

"You can help us from Gran's. I've seen you use your computer there before."

"Whether or not I can access a sliver of bandwidth has nothing to do with me going back to the archives." Ari refastened her seatbelt. "I appreciate how much you all care for me. You have no idea how much it means to have people actively wanting to keep me alive. But I'm not going to North Carolina."

Eve slowly laid her hands on the steering wheel, staring at her fingers as she lowered them one by one like she was forcefully manipulating their movement.

"Will you be needing a distraction from Ford or not?" Ari pulled the black phone back out of her pack.

"You don't get a choice." Eve started the van. "You're going to North Carolina."

Ari looked slowly up at Eve.

Grace backed herself into the corner of the seats, fumbling along the cracks, searching for a seatbelt.

"You're kidding me," Ari said.

"I'm not. I was really hoping it would take longer to find the catnapper and eviscerate them, and something in this shit show would have changed and I'd never even have to mention you going to Gran's. But it didn't." Eve pulled out onto the road. "We made the decision. If you won't protect yourself, we'll do it for you."

"*We'll?*" Ari said. "Who's in this *we?*"

"Everyone but Regi." Eve merged onto the highway heading south.

"Wait," Grace said before her brain could stop her. "Like Regi from Greenwoods Gardens Regi?"

48

Ari

R*un.*
   Run.
      Open the door and run.
"So not that Regi?" Grace asked.

Ari slid Maree Olivia's phone back into her pack. "You're going to drag me to North Carolina whether I like it or not?"

"It's for your own protection," Eve said.

"You're kidnapping me," Ari said. "You get that, right?"

"The Maree want you dead, Ari," Eve said.

"What?" Grace said.

Ari reached for the loop on the top of her pack.

Eve snatched it first, whisking Ari's pack out of her reach and setting it on the far side of the driver's seat.

"The fact that the Maree want me dead slightly more than they want the rest of you dead is fine with me," Ari said.

"That's not true, and you know it," Eve said.

Ari gripped the sides of her seat. "It doesn't matter if there's only a capture order on you. You can't tell me you wouldn't die fighting before letting those shits take you."

A growl rattled in Eve's throat.

"Take me back to the archives," Ari said.

"And what if the Maree decide to capture you instead? You wouldn't even get a trial. They wouldn't bother bringing you before the Council of the Feu. They'd dump you in a dungeon and let you rot."

"Dungeon?" Grace said.

"Shut the hell up," Eve said.

Pain clawed at Ari's throat. The cool gleam promising freedom pressed on her mind.

The feu. Jerek. Ford. Lincoln. Vengeance. Freedom.

Shit.

Ari dug her nails into her thighs, racking her mind for a reason to stay.

"You being in North Carolina also leaves one of us outside the archives in case we get trapped," Eve said.

"I can stay in North Carolina," Grace said.

"Like hell I'm letting my pack risk their necks for you," Eve said.

Because your traitor friends need you, Ariel Love.

"I'm not going to North Carolina." Ari turned forward in her seat.

"Unless you leap out of the van and into a river, yes you are," Eve said. "You can't outpace me on land."

"You're right." Ari settled her hands comfortably in her lap, letting thoughts of strategy, hidden files, and screaming at Jerek Holden compress the gleam, shoving it further from the front of her mind, giving herself room to think. "I can't. Which is why you're going to pull over at the next patch of forest."

"No," Eve said.

"You've been shift-starved since you killed the archivist," Ari said.

A sound like the beginning of a swallowed question came from the back of the van.

Eve bared her teeth.

"You pull over and take some time to shift," Ari said. "Run. Eat woodland creatures. Live the wolf life."

Eve's neck tensed. For a tiny moment, her skin seemed to ripple.

"While you shift, I'll finish digging through nasty Maree Olivia's phone. See, this phone is taking more time than Maree Brooks's because there are sneaky shadow files hiding with her normal somb-vibe apps. A lesser hacker might not have noticed the difference between what I'd found and how much data was there, but you're *lucky* enough to have me."

"And we want to keep you alive to help us." Eve kept speeding down the highway, heading south.

"Give me another hour with the phone and I can find those files," Ari said.

"You can look at them on the way to Gran's," Eve said.

"Take the hour to shift," Ari said. "Let me dig through the phone."

"No."

"And if Maree attack the archives in the, what, twenty hours it'll take you to drive to North Carolina and back?"

"The archives are protected."

"And what if LeBlanc shows up at the fight?" Ari said.

"He's too cowardly." Eve's skin seemed to ripple again as she spoke through gritted teeth.

"And he's too involved in the underbelly of this mess to not have allies in the Maree. If we capture one—"

"No."

"Fine." Ari shrugged. "If you want to drag me to North

Carolina, there's shit I can do about it. You can hold my bag hostage until we get to your Gran's and we'll just hope the fate of the feu isn't impacted by our road trip."

"The archives are protected." Eve rolled her shoulders back, tipping her head side to side as though trying to keep the tension in her neck from seizing the rest of her body.

"The archives are bait," Ari laughed. "Ford's little gaggle of feu scum hanging out on the street, watching the front door, only makes the bait better."

"Bait for who?" Eve said. "Ford's shitty plan has been working."

"For the Maree," Ari said.

"The Maree aren't going to start a fight, out in the open, on the upper west side."

"If the Maree were still sticking to the treaty, I'd agree with you," Ari said. "But they've proven they don't care."

"Which Maree?" Grace asked from the back. "And don't tell me to shut up. When I was in the cage, half the Maree holding me attacked the other half. They were killing each other."

"There's been fighting at the compound, too," Ari said. "The Knights Maree have been contaminated. Eve, can you honestly tell me you don't think the shitty Maree who have turned to the dark side will happily attack the archives in broad daylight? Tell me you don't believe LeBlanc is at least the tiniest bit involved with the Maree who tried to murder me."

Eve rolled her shoulders back again. "All the more reason for you to go to North Carolina."

"The Maree are closing in around us, and I don't think there's a chance in hell LeBlanc is going to miss the show. Vengeance, Eve. That's why you joined us in the first place. After everything you've been through, are you really going to risk missing your opportunity to eviscerate LeBlanc?"

Grace whimpered.

Cas yowled.

"One hour, Eve." Ari kept her speech slow, not allowing pleading to taint her voice. "If I don't find something on that phone worth going back to Manhattan, I won't fight you. I'll be escorted to Gran's like a good little girl. But if I find something, anything that proves I'm right and we're going to miss a chance to get closer to LeBlanc or the *they* who started all this shit while you're literally kidnapping me, you take me back to the city.

"This could be it. The right piece of information, and we could connect LeBlanc to the *they* to the Maree tearing themselves apart and the monsters who signed that scroll. We're so close. Once we have that link, we can figure out who murdered your family, Eve."

Eve lifted her fingers from the wheel, only steering with her palms like she was trying not to break the van.

"Don't risk missing your chance to avenge your family trying to protect me." Ari twisted in her seat, daring to lay her hand on Eve's shoulder.

Eve's skin really did ripple beneath Ari's touch.

"Let my safety be my choice," Ari said. "I'm not going to hide from this fight. After everything LeBlanc has done, after everything the Fracture stole from us, I want to be there when we tear the heads off the monsters who caused all this pain. Please. One hour, Eve. That's all I'm asking."

"You really think there's something on that phone?" Eve asked.

"You don't hide your grocery list, and normal Maree programmers aren't savvy enough to use shadow files."

Ari slid slideways in her seat, slamming her back against the passenger door as Grace screamed, Cas yowled, cat litter flew, and Eve cut a sharper turn than a VW van should ever attempt, diving right for the break in the divider between sides of the highway.

"If there's even a shred of a chance—" Eve's hands shuddered. She loosened her grip on the wheel again. "I'm not wasting time shifting or driving the wrong direction. If you don't have something in an hour, I'm making another U-turn."

"More gently, please," Grace whimpered from the back.

"Jerek is going to kill me for this," Eve said.

Ari held out her hand for her pack. "Not if I kill him first."

49

Jerek

J erek set down his book, looking out the second-story window, watching the sky flash red as animal control tried scaring the pigeons away with flares for the fourth time that hour.

The birds grunted, a sound that had barely lost any of its startling novelty despite its repetition, as a battalion of pigeons dove down from the archives' roof, attacking the poor animal control team who couldn't figure out why the birds had suddenly been called upon to lay siege to the street.

Animal control fled.

The pigeons settled back into their normal cacophonous cooing.

"Better luck next time." Jerek looked back down at his book.

...and in making the sanctuary consecrated by sacrifice, any with an intent to harm those who have sought refuge will be

caught within the spell, their power adding to the spell's potency, strengthening the protection paid for in blood.

Jerek linked his hands together behind his neck, leaning back against them as he closed his eyes.

"Should I worry?" Lincoln asked.

"Just trying to figure out how bad it would really be if I used five gills of my blood for a spell," Jerek said.

"No," Lincoln said. "Just no."

A piercing, screeching wail blared from the street.

A scream of pain carried up from the basement.

Jerek clamped his hands over his ears, not bothering to even attempt thinking beyond the birds diving past the window until the sound finally stopped.

The ringing in his ears hadn't ebbed before the pigeons settled back into their cooing.

"Poor Mariah." Jerek rubbed at the itching in his ears. "The consequences of my still learning to control my full magic are inconvenient. I can't imagine how betrayed I'd feel if finally regaining my magic caused such pain."

"You almost died twice mending the Fracture."

"The curse hurt me, not magic itself." Jerek looked back down to his book.

He could start saving his blood now. Take a few days to stockpile five gills to complete the protection spell. Not ideal to wait, but—

Jerek flinched as a high siren blasted to life. He looked to the window as Mariah screamed in the basement.

"Jerek, phone." Lincoln leapt to his feet, knocking his chair over, bolting around to Jerek's side of the table.

Jerek grabbed his phone, tapping to stop the horrible sound before actually reading the screen.

"Is it my family?" Lincoln leaned over Jerek's shoulder.

Ari's name flashed across Jerek's screen.

A shock of fear jolted through his stomach. If Cas was hurt, or Eve, or Ari.

If she ran—

Jerek answered the phone. "Yes?"

"That's how you answer a call from the friend you tried to ship away?" Ari said. "North Carolina was a desperate bid. I'm disappointed."

"Ari, I'm sorry." Jerek stood. "But I can't let you sacrifice any more for the feu."

"Rich coming from you," Ari said.

"You have every right to be angry. But please, please understand I can't risk losing you."

The phone stayed silent.

Jerek stepped away from the table as panic promised his body he was trapped and drowning. "I will beg your forgiveness every day for the rest of my life."

"Better start practicing your apology speech now, Jer Bear," Ari said. "I'm on my way back to Manhattan."

"Ari, I'm begging—"

"Don't bother. There's no chance I'm missing Mariah's Manhattan reunion with Daddy Dearest and his right-hand man."

50

Lincoln

"We're not doing this." Lincoln dug his fingers into the basement table, trying to convince himself not to flip the whole damn thing over.

"*You* don't have to do anything." Ari's voice came from the phone in the center of the table. "*I* am giving the courtesy of an explanation to people I don't actually owe anything to at the moment."

A muffled shout came from upstairs.

"Can someone shut him up?" Mariah spoke through gritted teeth.

"I'm sorry the somb didn't take well to being tied up." Jerek paced beside the stairs.

"You could have locked *Regi* in the bathroom." Ford chanced a moment of not staring at the monitor bank to shoot a glare Jerek's way.

"You tied Regi up?" Ari asked through the phone.

"Jerek did," Ford said.

"Temporarily," Jerek said. "Letting him wander the house would be making him a danger to himself. Being a part of this conversation wasn't an option—"

"So you decided to remove him from the situation against his will," Ari said. "I see you've chosen a theme for the day."

"Can you snip at each other later?" Mariah said.

"Sure," Ari said. "I love letting anger fester."

"Ari, I'm sorry," Jerek said.

Lincoln shifted his hands, digging his knuckles into the table, letting his bones bruise as he tried to drown out the desperate, panicked scream pounding through his mind.

"Start making it up to me by accepting the brilliance of my plan," Ari said.

The wound on Lincoln's arm stung as the barely healed skin tugged apart.

"No." Jack snatched the phone off the table, holding it near his mouth even though it was still on speaker. "If you think I'm a shit friend, fine, but I'm still the career criminal in this crew. I'm telling you, no. We don't rush plans. We don't run into things because we're mad. We wait until we're ready."

"We're not asking," Eve said.

"Stay out of this, Eve," Jack shouted.

Mariah gasped and clapped her hands over her earmuffs.

Gandalf huffed and snuggled closer to Ford's feet.

"Sorry," Jack mouthed.

"I'm going into that courtyard in two hours," Ari said. "Eve has agreed to come with me. The rest of you can do what you want."

"Please don't do this." The warmth of blood trailed down Lincoln's arm. "You've given us the information. We can find a way to use it—"

"While I run away to North Carolina?" Ari asked.

"Come back to the archives," Jack said. "We'll work on a plan together."

"And you'll tie me up beside Regi?" Ari asked.

Mariah reached for the phone.

Jack didn't fight as she took it.

"Let me make the call instead." Mariah turned her back to the group. "Do some fancy tech magic so I can call from here."

The phone stayed silent.

"You don't have to be the bait. I can do it," Mariah said. "I'm the runaway princess. Let me play the part."

"I'm not asking you to do that."

"We both know it's safer," Mariah said.

"There's no such thing as *safe*," Ari said. "Not with LeBlanc involved."

"I don't care."

"Have you ever even been in a fight?"

"No. But if things go wrong, I'd survive long enough for you to rescue me." Mariah's voice hitched. "Please don't make me spend the rest of my life wishing I'd been able to save you. Let me do this."

The phone stayed silent again.

"Ari?" Mariah said.

"If shit gets bad, we'll get her out," Eve said.

"Eve," Ari said.

"I'm being nice," Eve said. "You have to admit she's better bait."

"Shit," Ari said. "The second it looks like there's any chance swords might come out, you run like hell. If you can't run, hide. If hiding doesn't work, play nice and let the Maree take you. One of us will come for you."

"Ari—"

"You do not try to fight, Mariah," Ari said. "Promise me."

"I promise." Mariah turned back to the group, dipping her chin as she swiped the back of her free hand across her cheeks. "If two hours is our time frame, what the hell do we have to get done first?"

"Ford," Ari said. "I've got security footage and a blueprint coming your way."

"On it." Ford slid out of the seat at the security monitors, giving Jack his place.

"Jack," Ari said.

"Yep." Jack switched out of the seat, giving it to Mariah, claiming the phone.

"Snatching a room key sounds easier than duping one," Ari said. "Can you look at the footage and see if I'm right?"

"Love a plan that starts after dark," Jack said.

"Me too," Ari said.

Lincoln shut his eyes, waiting for Ari to say his name.

Whatever it takes to keep you safe.

"Jer Bear," Ari said. "Before someone starts on the apology of the century, I've got a little surprise for you."

"Go on," Eve whispered.

"Purrt-merow." The sound came through the phone.

"Cas!" Jerek grabbed the phone from Jack. "You were coming back. You'd tracked LeBlanc. I didn't think you'd found Cas."

"Go on," Eve whispered again, her tone gaining a harsh edge.

"Hi Jerek," a familiar voice came over the phone. "I'm really sorry I kidnapped your cat."

51

Jerek

Mariah's eye twitched in time with the printer's humming.

"Two thousand dollars." Regi paced beside the sink, one hand tucked casually into his pocket. "No, there's nothing wrong with the cat. I just need it delivered safely."

Jerek wrinkled his nose, pressing slowly to try and minimize the thump of his stapler.

Mariah's shoulders still tightened at the sound. She adjusted her headphones.

"I'll make it twenty-five hundred if you can be at the door in thirty minutes, cat in hand with enough safety gear to get four people through the horror show and into your van," Regi said.

"Dog food," Jerek whispered.

"Bring a bag of dog food and a bottle of hypoallergenic dog shampoo with you and I'll make it three thousand." Regi stopped pacing. "If you'd seen what's in this dog's fur, you wouldn't laugh at paying that much for shampoo."

"I can see everything from here." Jack strolled into the kitchen and hopped up onto the counter, gaze locked on the screen of the tablet he carried where all the archives' security feeds had been compressed into squares so tiny, only a person with cryptid sight could hope to make any use of the videos.

"Pleasure doing business." Regi hung up the phone. "Your animal control chariot will arrive in thirty minutes." He gave a sweeping bow then dodged through the basement door as though terrified Jerek might tie him back up.

Mariah passed Jerek another stack of papers to staple.

"Sorry for the sound." Jerek wrinkled his nose as he pressed on the stapler.

"The stapler is unavoidable," Mariah said. "Bringing a dog into the house was just plain cruel."

"Gandalf is more than a dog." Ford slid into the seat beside Jerek at the kitchen table, abandoning Lincoln and Regi to carry the security monitors up from the basement.

Ford flipped open his laptop, typing and swiping for three pages' worth of printing before looking up at Mariah. "You're going to have to keep the call quick. Under twenty seconds would be my preference."

"Twenty seconds?" Mariah handed Jerek another packet of papers.

"Hiding the location of an active cellphone is a shit ton harder than it looks in the movies." Ford shrugged, not bothering to look at Mariah. "I'm good at playing hide-the-signal-screw-you-this-is-a-fake-too, but I'm not *Ari* good. Keep it short."

Lincoln pushed open the basement door, using his foot to hold it aside for Regi, even as he balanced two monitors under each arm.

"What if Daddy doesn't answer? What if he's not actually

in Manhattan?" Mariah wrinkled the papers in her hand. "What if this puts him in danger?"

"He's your father." Jerek eased the papers from Mariah's grip. "If we asked him to participate in this mayhem, would he do it for your sake?"

Mariah took a breath as though preparing to speak, but closed her mouth instead, biting her lips together as her eyes began to glisten. She stepped away from the printer, tucking her hands into her back pockets. "I want to say Daddy would do anything to protect me, but he let a murderer live in our home for years."

"Your father has never had access to the information we've found on LeBlanc," Jerek said.

"But he knows LeBlanc is a controlling dick." Proper tears formed in Mariah's eyes. "He let LeBlanc make me a prisoner in our home. He practically handed control of our lives to a monster."

"Daddy issues should be taken to Ari," Jack said. "Parental rejection and revulsion comes to me. Dead parents goes to Jerek...I would say Eve, but we all know she gets a little murdery sometimes. We also offer services for nicked moral compasses, abandonment issues, and revenge obsessions."

"Which one am I?" Ford said.

"The sole bastion of sanity in a world gone mad." Jack's lips lifted into a tiny grin as though he could sense Ford's blush without needing to glance up from his tablet.

"Your father is in Manhattan." Jerek slid in front of Mariah, taking the still-warm papers from the printer tray. "He wouldn't be here if he wasn't looking for you."

"I didn't say Daddy doesn't love me. But wondering if your father is an idiot or a coward isn't fun." Mariah held her hand out to Ford.

Ford pressed one of the burner phones into Mariah's palm. "Keep it quick."

"I know." Mariah began dialing the number.

Jerek grabbed her wrist. "You missed a third option."

Mariah froze.

"Your father got sucked into his grief and drowned. He lost the woman he loved, and he's never taken another full breath." He let go of her. "Judge him however you like, but love breaks people more easily than evil ever could."

Mariah didn't bother brushing the tear from her cheek before she finished dialing.

She closed her eyes as the phone rang, sending two more tears down her cheeks.

"Hello?" a gravelly male voice answer.

"Daddy." The word cracked in Mariah's throat. "Daddy, it's me. I'm in Manhattan."

52

Jack

The rancid stench of the alley didn't quite reach the level of awful required to make Jack miss the stink of the basement.

Beyond the dumpster, from which emanated a soft scratching sound that seemed to imply a well-attended rodent gala, a barely open door spilled a harsh slit of florescent light into the night.

His stomach quivered as he stepped over a pile of gooey, meat-ish rot that seemed tossed into the alley by the fates as a gentle reminder that temporarily calling the archives home was not the worst option Manhattan had to offer.

Trying not to breathe through his nose, Jack straightened his collar and checked his fly. "Lights, camera, action."

He paused for a moment, waiting for Ford to laugh, but no comforting voice spoke in his ear.

He gripped the cell phone in his pocket, trying to take

comfort in his sole connection to the crew, even though the phone somehow felt far flimsier than his earpiece ever had.

"This is such a bad idea," Jack whispered as he threw open the door.

The stink of bleach slammed into his face, instantly erasing the stench of the alley while simultaneously lessening the probability of Jack being able to smell properly ever again.

To his right, a staircase leading down and a set of double doors at the end of the corridor offered shit chances of escape. To his left, a beefy security guard at a fake wooden desk blocked his path to a long hall with a worn linoleum floor.

"Can I help you?" the beefy guard asked.

"Oh, it's Anthony that needs the help." Jack rounded on the guard. "Four times he's stood me up. Four times he's humiliated me in public like the love-struck idiot I am. Well, if I'm going to have to book extra therapy sessions to deal with this fatal blow to my self-esteem, that overconfident, eight-packed, Adonis from hell is going to feel my pain."

The guard stood. "Sir, I don't think—"

"Anthony!" Jack shouted. "Anthony Graves, come out, come out wherever you are!"

"I'm going to have to ask you to leave." The guard stepped around his desk.

"Anthony!" Jack cupped his hands around his mouth, sending his shout bouncing down the long hall. "Where are you, you cowardly little prick?"

"Sir, you need to vacate the premises." The guard sidestepped, planting his hands on his hips, reaffirming his blockade of the hall.

"Do your work friends know what you say about them?" Jack turned to shout toward the swinging doors on the right.

The doors flew open, flung by an angry chef with two trembling servers in her wake.

"Who the hell is shouting near my kitchen?" The chef stormed toward the guard.

"I'm not going to ask you again, sir." The guard moved toward Jack, ignoring the chef, holding his arms wide like he could sweep Jack out the door.

"Does your boss know about your side hustle?" Jack shouted. "Do you think you'll be able to keep your job after what you've done in this hotel? I'll tell them. Hell, I'll even call the cops for them!"

"Sir, if you have information about something illegal going on in this hotel—"

"Information?" Jack threw his head back and laughed. "Hell, I have the videos."

"The only one allowed to shout in this hotel is me." Red crept up the chef's sweat-slicked face. "Connie, fetch my boning knife."

"Chef, please let me handle this." The guard reached for the radio on his hip.

"Knife. Now," the chef ordered.

Connie ran to get the knife, abandoning her fellow server in the hall.

"I'm going to need assistance by the employee entrance." The guard spoke into his radio.

"You're going to need an ambulance by the employee entrance." The chef stalked closer to Jack.

So much drama.

"Why are you treating me like *I'm* the villain?" Jack wobbled the words in his throat, tensing his shoulders and trembling his lips. "I'm not the one who breaks hearts. Why can't I just find a good man?"

Jack buried his face in his hands, allowing himself a flicker of a grin at the sound of the guard's sigh.

"Alright, son, take a breath." The guard stepped slowly closer to Jack. "Getting your heart broken is a terrible thing."

"You've got to be kidding me," the chef muttered.

"I just want to be loved," Jack wailed. "Why does nobody ever want to love me?"

"You just haven't found the right person yet." The guard laid a hand on Jack's shoulder as the distant sound of heavy footsteps pounded closer.

"Why me?" Jack threw his arms around the guard, burying his face on the man's shoulder as he shook with mock sobs. "I'm such a good boyfriend."

"I'm sure you are." The guard patted his back.

The doors from the kitchen burst open, and the ones with the heavy footsteps raced into the hall.

"We're okay," the guard said softly.

The footstep people froze.

"I paid his rent last month." Jack let his knees buckle, leaning his weight against the guard as he slowly slid lower. "I let him name our dog Mr. Melvin Pudding Pants the Fourth!"

"Wow," the chef said.

"Why?" Jack threw himself backward, collapsing to the unfortunately sticky floor with such exquisite drama, not a single hotel stooge noticed the guard's keycard disappearing up Jack's sleeve.

53

Jerek

The lights of the city racing by the car's windows added an extra thrum to the nerves rolling through Jerek's stomach.

"Are you clear on the plan?" Jerek straightened the stack of papers on his lap.

"Yes," Mariah said.

"If you need to go through it again—"

"Don't make me regret sharing a car with you."

"Sorry." Jerek turned his attention back out the window.

The car slowed as they reached the more crowded avenues.

"What if he knows?" Mariah's tone held a note of quiet, child-like vulnerability Jerek had never noticed in her before. "What if my father has known about LeBlanc and the Fracture and my mother? What if he's a monster and I was too damaged to notice?"

"Then we make a new plan." Jerek held his hand out to her.

"We take the information we gain and figure out the next step, then another step, and another, the same way we've always done."

"Right." Mariah nodded, ignoring Jerek's hand.

"And, if your father isn't the man you hope him to be, we'll figure out the next step for you, too. I truly hope your heart isn't broken tonight. But if it is, you won't be alone. Even if you want to be." Jerek allowed the warmth in his chest to still the nerves in his gut. "Like it or not, you've become a member of this crew, and I'm afraid we're awful at staying out of each other's troubles.

"You'll be comforted and coddled against your will. You'll have food forced upon you. Probably tea and soft blankets, too. But worst of all, however cumbersome you find it, you're doomed to never be abandoned, even when you think you might deserve it. I offer you my deepest apologies, Mariah, but I'm afraid you won't be rid of us."

Mariah slipped her hand into Jerek's.

They sat in silence as the car pulled up in front of the Mirage Hotel.

Ari

The packs of people bustling by did nothing to ease the tension scraping down the back of Ari's neck, promising she was being watched.

That's the point, Ari. Keep your shit together.

Smile. Calm. Poised.

Shit.

She pinched the muscles between her shoulder blades together, adding even more emphasis to her breasts, burning some of the energy that slammed against the gleam in her mind, battering the thin barrier that kept her from kicking off her black, sparkling heels and disappearing to a blissful place where there was no one to stare.

"Nice, baby." A man licked his lips, ogling her as he passed.

"Not enough money in the world, asshole." Ari gave the man a smile and a pleasant little wave.

An uncomfortable feeling of unfortunate vindication

seeped bitterness into Ari's mouth as the dress she'd purchased on her ten-minute shopping spree did exactly what she'd assumed. The sparkling, red fabric of the low-cut, form-fitting dress drew the attention of five more catcalling creeps before a familiar face appeared at the end of the block.

With a swagger to his step that distracted Ari from her spiral of doubt over the worth of the human race, sombs and feu alike, Jack strode toward Ari.

He slowed his steps as he neared her, taking the time to study her, from her sparkling stilettos to her pixie-cut black wig, letting his gaze linger on her cleavage as he pulled a card from his pocket.

"Call me when you have a free night." Jack held the card out to Ari.

Ari grabbed the card, locking eyes with Jack as she slid it down the top of her dress. "You just changed your life."

"Good." Jack tucked his hands into his pockets and joined the ever-flowing crowd passing by, leaving Ari to savor the chill of the keycard tucked beside her breast.

55

Lincoln

An itch that pressed the boundaries of irritating prickled around Lincoln's scalp, reminding him every moment that he'd fallen further than he'd ever imagined, plummeting past betraying his vows to participating in actions that could shake the very foundations of the Knights Maree.

He rammed his hands into his pockets, gritting his teeth as the urge to rip off his black wig, storm into the lobby of the Hotel Mirage, go find the Maree, and let the plan be damned threatened to break through all reason.

Traitors in the shadows are more dangerous than any truth.

He couldn't even sell himself his own lie.

To be a Knight Maree was to swear fealty to deceit.

That's what the Maree had spent centuries protecting—the worst lie Lincoln had ever heard—there's no such thing as magic.

Generations upon generations dedicated to hiding magic.

Spending their whole lives working toward that singular goal, passing their mission on to their children for hundreds of years.

A lie defended by a sea of Maree blood.

Thousands of knights had sacrificed their lives to hide the feu from the sombs. One plot by Jerek Holden, and Lincoln had helped shove the secret of the feu to the brink of discovery.

It's not just Jerek.

A biting pain pinched between Lincoln's eyes.

This is on your hands, Martel.

A black car pulled up in front of the Hotel Mirage.

Lincoln tensed, pushing away from the building he'd been leaning against, feigning boredom in a pathetic attempt to hide his need to scream.

An older couple got out of the car, the man opening the door and offering his hand to the woman.

A simple act of chivalry.

A simple act of kindness society had somehow linked to being a knight—completely ignoring the reality of living and breathing to serve a cause that may, in fact, be so contaminated the very core of the Knights Maree might crumble, destroying a centuries-old treaty that had protected the sombs from the feu even if the sombs didn't know to be grateful, making every sacrifice demanded of the knights completely pointless—romancing a fair maiden in need of aid.

The older couple entered the hotel, not even nodding to the doorman as they passed.

Lincoln's heart kicked up into his throat as Jack appeared on the far side of the street, a length to his stride that screamed of confidence. Giving a poor attempt to match Jack's poise, Lincoln crossed the street, heading toward the wide glass doors of the Hotel Mirage.

He held his breath as he approached the threshold and fear began to whisper in the back of his mind, slithering into his thoughts, promising with every step that he was throwing himself into a trap.

You know I'm right, the voice whispered. *You'll be penned in. You'll be outnumbered. You're going to be captured.*

You're going to lose everything.

"Good evening, sir." The doorman bowed to Lincoln as the automatic glass doors slid open.

"Evening." Lincoln pitched his voice toward the top of his normal speaking range, adding a hint of unnecessary breath to the word as though that could somehow make up for his bad British accent.

What the hell are you doing?

Heat rushed to Lincoln's face as he stepped into the hotel.

The white marble floor and white walls served as a blank canvas for the collection of colorful, abstract art displayed in the lobby.

A settee with a shape Lincoln couldn't help but compare to a distinctive bit of anatomy held the place of honor as the only piece of furniture in the space other than the white concierge desks.

The heat in Lincoln's cheeks doubled as he cut right past the concierge desks, where the older couple spoke to a hotel employee.

Forcefully ignoring the discreetly tucked away hall beside the desk, he cut around the settee to a second set of double doors at the far side of the lobby.

"That's why you never make eye contact with the living statues," one of the concierges laughed.

Lincoln picked up his pace, keeping his gaze locked on the doors ahead of him.

The white doors with swirling white handles swung silently open as Lincoln approached.

His breath fought to burst from his lungs as he fled the well-lit lobby and escaped into...

The vines that twined around the pillars, reaching all the way up to the fourth-floor balconies, seemed to somehow dampen the noise of the city, allowing the rustling of the fountain at the center of the square to add to the calm of the illogical haven.

The cobblestone of the square and stone of the walls looked for all the world to be from one of the old villas his mother had made the family tour in Italy. Lanterns with real flames provided the light for the square, giving the night a soft, romantic quality that defied the neon chaos of Manhattan.

Café tables dotted the space, with a few fainting couches tucked into the shadows, completing the façade of romantic seclusion.

A faint ding carried across the square as the elevator on the far side opened.

Lincoln changed his path, heading right toward the elevator, not allowing himself to flee as six Maree charged through the still-opening doors, cutting across the square and out to the lobby as though the world had caught fire.

56

Ford

"Do it," Regi whispered.

"Wait for it." Ford kept his finger hovering over the enter button.

"Do it," Regi whispered.

"Not yet." Ford's leg began to bounce.

"Something's gone wrong." Regi leaned closer to the monitors, earning a huff from Gandalf as he studied the video feeds like they might actually be useful. "Just do it."

"We wait for the signal." Ford let out a slow breath, stilling his shaking hand.

Regi stood up, backing away from the computers. "This is ridiculous."

"Which is why it has to be precise."

"Her phone doesn't have reception." Regi paced across the center of the dining room. "She's been captured."

"No, she hasn't." Ford rolled his shoulders. "Patience,

padawan. The dude on the computer always has to wait in agony while the crew does dangerous things."

"But what if our part of the plan doesn't work?"

"Then we improvise and try to keep everyone alive."

"What?" Regi froze.

"Don't worry about it."

"I'm never going to get my life back, you know." Regi picked up his pacing again. "Even if the knights stop hunting me, I can't just go back to class and pretend everything is fine. I'm never going to be able to walk down the street without wondering if I'm surrounded by vampires and werewolves."

"Would you want to?"

Again, Regi froze.

"Knowing what's actually out there, that magic is real and so are cryptids and knights and quests..." The trembling of Ford's hand stilled. "That's the kind of truth that lifts a veil off the world, and you realize everything before was tainted with a shade of gray you were too foolish to notice. Once you've seen the astounding beauty of a world filled with magic, how could you ever want to walk away?"

"Shit." Regi buried his face in his hands. "Shit, you're right. How the hell did this happen?"

"Ariel Love."

Cas gave a yearning yowl from his chosen spot on top of the curtain rod, where he'd fled as soon as the well-paid, if very confused, animal control officer had delivered him to the archives. Cas's yowl ended with a defeated merp.

"As have we all." Ford shook out his shoulders, fixing his attention back on his laptop.

"Dammit." Regi returned to his position hovering right behind Ford, looming over him like an anvil about to fall from the sky. "What if we call the hotel? Ask if anyone's come to see Louis Chanler."

"Wait for it."

"If we don't move soon—"

Ford's phone buzzed.

Game on.

"Yes!" Ford punched the enter key.

A live feed flashed to life on his computer screen.

The chaos of Times Square. Thousands of tourists, street performers, ticket hawkers, and self-loathing locals all packed onto one, neon-lit stage, perfectly placed to enjoy the evening's entertainment.

"Step one." Ford leaned back in his seat. "Light the beacon. Distract the herd."

New words appeared on one of the massive screens that surrounded Times Square.

This is the night that will make you a believer.
The magic begins in...

A timer flashed into being, starting its countdown at thirty minutes.

"Holy shit, it worked." Regi leaned against the desk beside Ford.

"I may not be Ari, but I am good." Ford pulled out his phone and hit *send*.

One night.
One winner.
One million dollars cash prize.
See you in Times Square.
May the best magician win.

57

Eve

Car horns blared on the streets far below, adding to the hell of Manhattan.

Sombs are different. Gran's whisper barely cut through the chaos. *Wolves need to run, sombs need to feel special. Can't feel special with no one to praise you. Can't run in a horde of strangers. Nature gave us separate places to be happy for a reason.*

The fifth siren in the past ten minutes roared by.

Let the sombs keep their hell.

Eve gripped the two pendants around her neck, focusing on the feel of their metal in her hand as she knelt on the edge of the roof, staring down into the Hotel Mirage.

Only four stories below, the Hotel Mirage's roof begged her to make the tantalizingly easy jump from her perch on top of the neighboring building.

Ten seconds, no six, and she'd be in the hotel's courtyard.

Her prey had boxed itself in. No need to wait for the pack.

A man crossed through the stone square at the center of the hotel. His steps wobbled, but his shoulders stayed stiff as though he actually believed his poor imitation of sobriety would fool anyone.

Eve grinned, the taste of her prey's blood already teasing her tongue.

Patience, Evelyn, Gran whispered.

Eve unfurled her fingers, letting go of her pendants.

It's time, Gran. I promise you. It'll be done tonight.

A man with black hair entered the hotel's square.

The set of his shoulders betrayed Lincoln as a Maree even before Eve caught the unnatural glint of the lantern light on his plastic hair.

Lincoln kept his pace steady as he crossed the square, conspicuously ignoring the six Maree who bolted past him, running toward the catastrophe that would shatter their little Maree world.

58

Ari

Three catcalls, one ass graze, four whistles, and one vow to put lots of fat babies in her later, Ari reached the entrance of the Hotel Mirage.

"Miss." The doorman stepped to the center of the glass doors, blocking Ari's path even as the doors slid open. "Can I help you?"

"Would you like to take care of the client who's invited me to the fourth floor?" Ari stepped right up to the doorman, leaving mere inches between their bodies as she leaned close to whisper, "Nice enough lady as far as my clients go. You just have to get used to her...perfume."

The doorman took a definitive step to the side. "We at the Hotel Mirage value our guests' privacy, but we do request discretion. It is our policy to respectfully avoid speculation."

"No need to speculate." Ari winked. "Next time I'll wear a sign. *Accepts digital payment.*"

The color drained from the doorman's face as Ari stepped around him and strode through the still-open doors.

Watching the hotel's security feeds had almost prepared Ari for the stark white floor and overtly anatomical décor of the hotel's lobby. But the echo of her heels clacking on the marble hadn't occurred to her.

A vague satisfaction dampened the ping of panic that reverberated through Ari's thoughts.

The clack of her shoes daring people not to look her way.

The clack of her shoes proving her confidence with every step.

The clack of her shoes making sure everyone knew what description to give when the Maree started asking questions about the girl who'd dicked up their night.

The doors on the far side of the lobby swung open with a soft swoosh.

Earthy moisture in the air, soft lighting, the deep, blue-hued green of the ivy growing up the balconies—the video hadn't prepared Ari for the lure of the hotel's square.

"Oh, to be Holden rich," Ari whispered.

Fear flickered through her chest. There was no voice in her ear to whisper back.

Giving her steps a little extra saunter, Ari started across the cobblestones.

In the center of the space, a tiered fountain of elegantly cut stone almost blocked her view of Lincoln walking ahead of her.

Someone had given him a black wig with a cut comically similar to the one she wore.

What did he do to piss off Jack?

The elevator doors opened before Lincoln reached the far side of the square. He changed his path, walking straight toward the six Maree who bolted out of the elevator before the doors had fully opened.

A fist of panic punched through Ari's chest as the knights charged straight at her.

Run.

No. Can't run.

Still in heels.

Kicking them off would cost too much time.

But the knights weren't focused on her.

None of them stopped her as she stepped out of their path, taking the long way around the fountain, letting them keep running all the way through the doors to the lobby.

Thank you, Ford.

It had to be Ford.

If the crew was at the hotel and Ford was creating a distraction, there couldn't be anything else in Manhattan worth the Maree prying themselves away from their precious Chanler.

Ari's fingers itched to reached for the phone tucked beside her breast.

One quick search and she'd know if a bigger magical problem had seized the city. Or if the archives had been raided. Or if the world in general had decided to end.

You have a job to do, Ariel Love.

First, do the job, then worry about everything else.

She reached the elevator.

The etched-stone call button in the discreet brass setting aided the hotel's attempts to lure her into the kind of calm that could never exist in Manhattan.

She jabbed the button.

"Ari," a voice whispered from the shadows.

Her heart stuttered. She dropped her hand to her side, closer to the blade strapped to her thigh.

"It's me. It's Lincoln."

Her heart regained its rhythm even as a vice tightened around her lungs.

"I know you can't answer and that's fine," Lincoln whispered.

Ari jabbed the button again.

"I'm sorry I tried to send you away," Lincoln said. "But I'm not sorry for trying to protect you. I didn't have a choice. It's self-preservation. If something happened to you, it would break me, and I'm not strong enough to face that kind of pain."

Ari rammed her thumb against the button, keeping her gaze fixed on her finger as the tip of her thumb turned red.

"If wanting to keep you alive because I'm terrified of losing you makes you think I'm a selfish ass, then I'm happy to accept your anger. And I know I may never be able to earn back your trust, but even if you despise me, I'm begging you to believe me. You are strong and capable, and you can defend yourself. No one could argue that."

The glorious rumble of the elevator approached.

"I'm the weak one, Ari. I met a girl in Vegas. She was sitting beside a fountain surrounded by a crowd, with a sort of peace I've never felt filling her face, and my heart stopped. And she smiled and it started again, and I tried to pretend it would have happened with any girl half as beautiful as her but that's a lie, because my heart's never gone back to beating the way it did before I met you."

Heat pressed against Ari's eyes.

"You tore through my life and stole every part of me—"

The elevator doors swooshed open with a ding.

Three women wearing thousand-dollar shoes and even better jewelry flocked out of the elevator, only pausing their chatter long enough to toss knowing glares at Ari before whispering their way to the lobby.

The elevator doors began to close.

Ari pressed her hand against the doors, keeping them open as she stepped through.

"...yours."

The faint whisper of the word was all Ari heard as the doors swished shut with a ding.

59

Jerek

"This is ridiculous." Mariah fidgeted with her earmuffs. "I can't go out in public. I look ridiculous."

"Would you like to take them off?" Jerek leaned forward, peering through the window on Mariah's side of the car.

"No." Mariah clasped her hands in her lap. "But I'm seething with envy for your gloves."

"*Seething with envy?*" Jerek said.

"Is this really the moment to mock me?"

Ari, red dress sparkling in the city lights, strode toward the Hotel Mirage.

"No time to mock." Jerek nodded out the window. "You're up."

Mariah reached for the handle, then froze for a moment before looking back at Jerek. "What if this goes to hell? What if we're wrong and we're tossing ourselves into a monster's jaws for no reason?"

"Signatures and photographs rarely lie." Jerek adjusted the stack of papers in his arms, carefully keeping the corners aligned despite the encumbrance of his double-layered gloves. "However, if fate has chosen to taunt us again, we'll do as we have before and—"

"Take the information and make a new plan?" Mariah swallowed hard.

"Survive, regroup, and charge back into battle, stronger and better prepared than before."

"Your talent for motivational speaking is literally nauseating."

"But you admit it's a talent." Jerek winked.

"Just watch my back." Mariah opened the door and slid out of the car, slamming the door shut behind her.

"I'll be waiting just one more moment." Jerek leaned forward to speak to the driver. "Please double the fare as compensation for your time."

"If you're sure."

"Very sure." Jerek sat back in his seat. "The value of a few extra moments should never be underestimated."

60

Lincoln

*D**ing.*

The elevator doors swished closed, whisking Ari away.

Lincoln backed farther into the shadows of the corner where the elevator met the vine-covered wall.

We weren't trying to trap you.

I didn't mean to hurt you.

Lincoln's mind raced through all the things he should have said. Better words. More convincing words that could somehow prove he was sorry and how much he cared for her and convince her to keep herself out of danger all at the same time.

It's not our fault the world is so awful.

All I want is to keep you safe.

The world is a better place with you in it.

I need you alive.

I need you.

"I messed up," Lincoln whispered to whatever ghost, spirit, or fairy was willing to listen. "Please let there be a way to fix this, because I really messed up."

He dug his fingers into the lace of his wig, dragging his thoughts toward the sounds of the present, away from the horde of angry voices roaring in his mind, screaming his failures loud enough to crack through his reason.

I can't lose her.

The doors on the far side of the square opened.

Mariah walked through, the tension in her shoulders the only betrayal of her fear. She kept her path straight, heading right to the fountain. Reaching down, she trailed her fingers through the water in the basin, only watching the water, ignoring the carved stone of the fountain itself.

After a moment, she stood up straight, shaking the water off her hand as she looked toward the balconies on the northern side of the square.

"Hiding from little old me?" Mariah spoke toward the balcony. "I don't know if I should be honored or disgusted."

Lincoln tipped his head, listening for a response.

"I'm here to see my father. Let him come to me or I'll make a fuss." Mariah grinned. "Have you been taking bets on what kind of fuss I can cause now?"

She shook her head. "You should've started the betting higher than a measly hundred dollars."

Mariah paused for a moment, then whipped toward the western balconies, pointing up, winking as though wanting to be sure whoever she'd found knew it.

"Did you bother betting on anything else? Like if Chanler's little brat had gained anything besides..." Mariah pointed to her headphones. "Unless you think now is the moment to find out, send my father down."

Lincoln held his breath, straining to hear anything beyond

the racing of his own heart, rustling of the fountain, and sounds of the city drifting in to ruin the square's façade of peace.

A horn blasted out on the street. Music came from somewhere.

Nothing else. Nothing closer.

"If you insist." Mariah reached for the fountain. "Don't pretend I didn't warn you."

She trailed her fingers through the water.

"Mariah!" The shout came from the north. "Mariah."

"Daddy." Mariah backed away from the fountain, looking up toward her father's voice.

"I've been looking for you, lamb," Mr. Chanler said. "I've been—"

"Sir, I must insist."

The sound of LeBlanc's voice flared a loathing in Lincoln that brushed every other thought aside. He reached for his hip where he'd hidden the best of his three daggers.

"You filthy bastard." Mariah spat the words. "I had barely let myself hope you'd be stupid enough to stick around."

"Mariah, stop," Chanler said.

"All of you, down here now." Mariah flicked her wrist. A sphere of water shimmered into being, balancing on the tips of her fingers. "My mother taught me that trick. It's easy really. Want to see what happens next?"

"Mariah, this stops now," Chanler said.

Lincoln untucked the back of his shirt, slipping his hand beneath the fabric to grip the hilt of the blade he'd hidden there.

"Unless you'd like to see what a temper tantrum looks like in our newly mended world, all of you will come downstairs now," Mariah said. "Irrevocable damage to the treaty will be caused in five, four, three—"

"Let me go to my daughter," Chanler shouted.

"Sir," LeBlanc said.

"Let me go to my daughter!"

The elevator dinged open.

Lincoln pressed his back to the wall, sacrificing his view of the square in favor of concealment.

A terrible, quiet minute ticked past.

Bam!

He lunged out of the shadows, yanking his blades from their sheaths, steadying his stance, reminding himself to keep breathing as he prepared to run into battle.

"Smart." Mariah threw the sphere of water into the air.

She didn't try to catch her ball of blatant magic. Didn't even glance its way.

Mariah Chanler simply smiled as the ball and its water vanished with a pop before it could hit the ground.

61

Jerek

"Let me go to my daughter!"

Well-taught manners begged Jerek to turn around and cut straight back through the lobby as Chanler's shout greeted him before Jerek had even managed to step into the vine-draped square.

"Sir." A voice that dug coals into Jerek's lungs spoke from above.

"Let me go to my daughter." Chanler gripped the balcony rail on the third floor, panic twisting his pale face as he stared down at Mariah.

Jerek hurried through the doors and into the courtyard, his genuine wish to flee bleeding into his movements as he dipped his chin, clutched his stack of papers to his chest, and darted onto the path behind the pillars, deepening his portrayal of an innocent hotel guest trying to avoid an awkward encounter.

The western wall of the square left few choices for hiding

places, but if he could meander to the southern wall where hotel room doors offered extra niches—

Ding.

The elevator doors slid open.

Jerek dove behind a pillar. He pressed his back to the ivy-covered stone, shoving the leaves away from his eyes as he twisted to catch a glimpse of the square.

Mariah stood beside the fountain, one hand up as though carrying a tray, a transparent sphere balanced on her fingers.

A mother and son bustled out of the elevator, both holding their phones, their gazes darting from the screens to Mariah, to the doors that offered them the sweet hope of escaping into the lobby, both so intent on not paying attention to the scene in the square, neither noticed as Mariah's sphere began to shimmer, glimmering with a light no reasonable person could mistake for anything but magic.

The lobby doors swooshed shut behind the two sombs, sparing them from a danger they'd no hope of comprehending.

Bam!

Mariah grinned. "Smart."

She threw the shimmering sphere into the air, whisking it out of existence with a soft pop before it could hit the ground.

"Well done," Jerek murmured as he studied Mariah's face, searching for any hint of exhaustion.

She blinked a few too many times in a row, almost as though her vision had blurred, but her smile didn't slip as she turned toward the corner where the door to the emergency staircase blended into the square's décor.

The door burst open, crashing into the wall with another bam.

"Daddy!" Mariah took two steps toward the corner, then froze.

Her smile twisted, hardening into a fiery look of absolute, untainted hatred.

"Daddy, come here." She reached out her hand.

Jerek tensed, cringing at the faint sound of the ivy sweeping against his clothes as he inched toward the other side of his pillar, losing sight of the door to the lobby, gaining a view of Louis Chanler standing beside Callen LeBlanc.

"Daddy." Mariah kept her hand out. "I need you to come here."

Chanler stayed at LeBlanc's side, keeping just a few inches behind LeBlanc like a dog called to heel.

"Mariah," LeBlanc said. "We've been worried about you."

"Don't bother," Mariah said. "I don't have to pretend you're not a monster anymore, and neither does Daddy."

"Such strong words." LeBlanc furrowed his brow. "Mr. Chanler, I fear I may have been correct."

"My daughter is the victim in all this." It wasn't the gravel in Chanler's voice, but the utter fatigue that allowed a thread of pity for the fool to burrow through the nauseous disgust that seized Jerek's gut as LeBlanc shook his head, daring to lay a sympathetic hand on Chanler's shoulder.

"Don't touch my father!" Mariah started toward LeBlanc, making it to the far side of the fountain before she froze, then looked up to the balconies above. "I'm not in the mood to play. You are all going to come down here right now." She looked back to LeBlanc. "My father is going to come stand with me. If anyone tries to argue with me, I'll throw a tantrum the likes of which the knights haven't cleaned up in a century."

LeBlanc looked to Chanler, smug assurance filling his face.

Chanler worked his lips together for a moment before speaking. "Mariah, stop this nonsense at once. Mr. LeBlanc has been kind enough to arrange amnesty—"

"LeBlanc can shove his kind amnesty up his traitorous, murdering asshole," Mariah said.

A door slammed shut on one of the floors above. The sound of overly bright laughter came right after.

"A gem like you always needs to shine," a female voice said. "No, lovey, I'm not—No, what I'm saying is I'm not—" The clacking of heels followed the voice along the southern balcony toward the elevator. "Well you know what, Carol? Not letting people finish their sentences isn't very attractive, either."

Mariah shrugged and stepped back, reaching for the basin of the fountain. She trailed her fingers through the water, lifting out strands of droplets that clung to her fingers.

"Have you ever bothered listening to yourself speak?" the woman said as the elevator dinged open on the third floor.

Jerek shut his eyes, tearing through all the logical arguments he knew should be stopping him, not finding any worthwhile as he bit the fingers of his glove, pulling both layers off with his teeth.

"You are being such a nightmare," the woman said.

Jerek laced his bare fingers through the ivy.

He shut his eyes, tenderly caressing the core of the magic that burned inside him.

The force of the power scraped against his being, begging to be let loose.

That danger made him love it more.

Just a bit.

Touch the surface of the power, don't reach too deep.

A kiss. A soft graze.

The leaves around his hand shimmered, turning a pale, radiant gold.

A tiny bit more.

The gold grew, consuming the green of the vines as it

spread, reaching up the balconies. The lamplight glinted off the leaves as a wind born of his magic swept around the square.

A bit too much.

Jerek bit his lips together, focusing on that delicate balance of maintaining control while allowing his magic to flow from his body.

"We'll come down," a man called from above.

LeBlanc snapped his head toward the voice.

The elevator dinged open.

Careful.

Jerek closed his eyes, focusing on the tension that connected him to his magic as he guided the gold toward him, not yanking it, letting it roll back like a wave pulling away from shore.

"I agreed to be a part of this because I thought you were my friend," the elevator woman said.

Jerek opened his eyes and jerked his hand away from the ivy. The leaves had returned to green. Almost the right green. Too purple, but close.

The woman stormed out of the elevator, making it halfway across the square before stopping. She stumbled back a step, her eyes wide.

Jerek dodged to the other side of his pillar, trying to see what she'd spotted.

The new, purple hue to the ivy gave the square a darker, rather mysterious gothic look, but didn't scream of magic.

Unless she remembers the color the vines were when she got on the damn elevator.

"I'm sick of hearing about how it's *your day*, Ca-rol." The woman emphasized both syllables of the name. "Asking me to wear a ball of fluff knocked off by a secondhand designer is not a sign of everlasting friendship."

The woman narrowed her eyes. "Being told I can be pretty in anything isn't a compliment, Carol. You are mocking the burden I bear." She stormed toward the lobby doors. "Yes, Carol, I know what the word *burden* means." She grabbed the door, yanking it open before the automatic system could finish its work. "My face is not printed in the dictionary, you vindictive little twat!"

The sound of footsteps in the corner of the square caught Jerek's ear before the woman's rant had fully faded.

Dodging back to the other side of the pillar, Jerek yanked his gloves back on, barely daring to lean over far enough to watch the seven Maree file out of the stairwell door.

"So much better." Mariah waved to the Maree. "Now let Daddy come stand by me and we can talk like reasonable people."

"There is nothing to discuss, Mariah," LeBlanc said. "The Maree have been very generous with their lenience. Do not test their goodwill."

"I don't give a shit about the Maree or you."

"Mariah." Chanler finally moved, making it a whole step in front of LeBlanc before LeBlanc grabbed his arm, holding Chanler in place.

"Let go of my father." Mariah walked toward them, the rage on her face not matching her easy saunter.

The Maree flanked LeBlanc, each of them keeping their hand close to the baton at their hip.

"Can't even keep two Chanlers in line by yourself anymore?" Mariah asked. "Is it wise to let your traitor knight minions see how badly you've slipped?"

"You will be escorted to your father's suite, where you will remain while travel back to Newport can be arranged," LeBlanc said. "You will behave. You will be grateful to the Knights Maree. You will grovel in thanks for my aid in securing mercy from the Knight's Council and the Council of the Feu."

"Daddy, don't listen to him. Everything will be fine, just

come to me." Mariah held her hands out to him. "LeBlanc doesn't get to control you anymore."

"Louis, have I ever controlled you?" LeBlanc's smile didn't falter.

"Shut up," Mariah said.

"Of course not." Chanler stepped back, taking his place as LeBlanc's trained dog. "We should go upstairs, Mariah."

Mariah didn't move. "Daddy, I need you to listen to me, okay?"

"Mariah—" LeBlanc began.

"It's not your fault he stole our lives." Tears glistened on Mariah's cheeks. "I know you're scared of him, I've been terrified of him for years, but we don't have to live like that anymore."

LeBlanc nodded toward the Maree on his right. "Take her upstairs."

"Don't even think of touching me." Mariah pressed her palm toward the Maree in a very convincing, though probably empty, threat.

A tickle shocked Jerek's thigh as his phone gave a faint buzz.

If we've any touch of luck left...

He edged to the very back of the column, wrinkling his nose against the sound as his phone buzzed again.

"You have your magic back, Daddy," Mariah said. "So do I."

"This conversation will move to a private location," a male voice, one of the Maree, said.

A message lit Jerek's phone screen.

Time for study hall.

He let his brief burst of relief bring a smile to his lips as he drew his shoulders back and stepped around the pillar. "Actually, I find this kind of conversation generally goes best with a very public sort of privacy."

"Jerek Holden." The Maree who'd spoken stepped forward, already gripping the handle of his baton.

"You might want both hands free for reading through this packet." Jerek held up his stack of papers as he crossed the square. "For that is the beauty of information, isn't it? Years of the Chanlers and their resources being controlled by LeBlanc, a festering wound of betrayal rotting the very core of the Maree, a plot to destroy the feu coming from within the Maree—it may seem as though triumph over these horrors can only be bought with blood, but we are fortunate enough to merely need ink."

Jerek lifted the top packet of papers from the stack. "There is quite a bit of material to go through. Shall we begin with the plot to commit werewolf genocide, or would you prefer a brief account of how exactly the Fracture began?"

62

Ari

The Hotel Mirage hadn't bothered extending the faux villa façade to the emergency stairs.

The linoleum on the fourth-floor landing stuck to the bottom of Ari's stilettos as she peered up to the locked roof door at the very top of the steps, checking for anyone lurking in the shadows before reaching down the top of her dress.

"Just once"—Ari pulled out the practically useless ballet flat she'd hidden on the left side of her ribs—"I'd love to dive into doing something"—she pulled out the shoe tucked on the other side—"stupid with decent-sized pockets."

She leaned against the wall, switching from the heels to the flats without letting her bare feet touch the ground.

She set her stilettos aside and pulled off her wig, taking a moment to listen for impending doom before beginning the skin-scraping process of shimmying the red, sparkling dress over her head.

"Do you know what I could accomplish with pockets?"

She tossed the red dress aside, leaving herself in spankies and a bra, with an accordion-folded square of black fabric covering her stomach, one small dagger on her thigh and another beside her breast. "So much easier with pockets."

She pulled the top of the black fabric from the bottom of her bra.

"The number of times Mom warned me I'd end up stripping in hotels." Ari shook out the black material, unfolding the thin fabric of her sundress. "You're going to ruin your life, Ariel." She pulled the black dress on. "That's how arrest records begin, Ariel."

She reached into her bra again, pulling a key card out from the right breast, a black bandana from the left, and her phone from the center.

"You know what would help prevent arrest, Mom?" Ari tucked the phone and keycard into the pockets of her black dress. "Pockets."

She tied the bandana over her pin-curled hair and grabbed her clothes from the floor.

"Nobody ever suspects the sex worker. Nobody says *are you here to do crimes?*" Ari opened the door to the fourth floor just a crack.

No hotel room doors open. No one on the balcony.

"Nope, not here to do crimes. How could I be? I'm in a sparkly, tight-ass dress with no damn pockets." Ari eased the door farther open. "Little old no-pockets me is just here to bounce on—"

"Let me go to my daughter!" Louis Chanler's voice echoed up from below.

"That went faster than I expected," Ari whispered.

Bam!

The sound echoed up the staircase.

Ari slipped onto the fourth-floor balcony, easing the door closed behind her, dampening the pounding of the footsteps racing down the stairwell. She scanned the shadows on the balconies, checking again for anyone lurking, waiting to pounce.

Bam.

The sound came from the courtyard far below.

"Daddy!" Joy and relief filled Mariah's voice.

Keeping against the wall, Ari headed toward the northern side of the balconies.

"Daddy, come here." The relief had left Mariah's voice. "Daddy, I need you to come here."

One of the guests had left a stack of trash beside their door.

Ari knelt, shoving her heels into the empty wine crate and her dress into the largest of the fast-food takeout bags.

"Don't touch my father!" Mariah shouted.

Ari set the trash back in place and made a dash for the center of the northern balcony, tucking herself into the shadows behind a pillar before checking to see if she'd been spotted.

"I'm not in the mood to play. You are all going to come down here right now," Mariah said.

Ari knelt, hiding behind the slim bit of cover the balcony rail offered as she peered down at the center of the square.

"My father is going to come stand with me." Mariah faced Chanler and LeBlanc. "If anyone tries to argue with me, I'll throw a tantrum the likes of which the knights haven't cleaned up in a century."

Movement on the third floor caught Ari's eye.

Two Maree had been stationed along the eastern balcony. The younger moved closer to the older, glancing between his elder and the square as though expecting the older Maree to race in and stop Mariah.

"Mariah, stop this nonsense at once," Chanler said. "Mr. LeBlanc has been kind enough to arrange amnesty—"

"LeBlanc can shove his kind amnesty up his traitorous, murdering asshole," Mariah said.

Two Maree had been stationed along the western side of the balcony and two more along the southern.

Bang.

Fear punched Ari's throat as the sound pounded from right behind her.

She twisted, springing to her feet, planting her back against the pillar, reaching for the blade beside her breast.

A woman stopped just outside her hotel room door, purse in one hand, phone held to her ear with the other. "A gem like you always needs to shine."

Ari yanked her phone from her pocket, swiping the screen open as the woman walked her way.

"No, lovey, I'm not—" the woman said.

Ari glanced up in time to see the woman roll her eyes.

She gave Ari a look that could either have been *some people, am I right* or her impression of a drunken platypus.

Ari gave a commiserating wince.

"No, what I'm saying is I'm not—" Apparently satisfied with the interaction, the woman headed toward the elevator. "Well, you know what, Carol? Not letting people finish their sentences isn't very attractive, either."

"Wow, Carol," Ari whispered. "How could you not know that?"

She waited for the elevator to ding closed, whisking the Carol hater away, before peering around the column.

Gold. Gleaming gold.

Pale, shimmering, pure gold shone around the square, dancing up the vines, painting the ivy with a dazzling shade so beautiful, not even an asshat, skeptic somb could manage not to notice its wonder.

The gold grew up the vines, climbing toward Ari.

She touched the leaves, holding her breath, waiting for the glorious moment when mundane and magical met.

"We'll come down," a man shouted from below.

The gold pulled away, surging back to the place it had begun, leaving the leaves it had devoured a deeper green, marking them as something that had been touched by magic and could never be fully normal again.

The older Maree below nodded toward the stairs. The baby Maree followed right on the elder's heels. The other four Maree on the third-floor balconies obeyed as well. A seventh Maree joined the line, coming out from under the balcony where Ari crouched, fingers still laced through the ivy.

"I'm sick of hearing about how it's *your day*, Ca-rol." The Carol hater's voice grated back into being as the elevator opened in the square.

Keeping low, Ari ran for the eastern corner of the balcony.

A sharp sting caught the top of her head.

She dropped to her knees, feeling her scalp for blood as she drew the dagger from beside her breast.

Clack.

Something hit the wall behind her. She shifted to crouch on her toes, ready for attack.

Clack.

Another thing struck the wall.

Not exploding. Not flaming.

Gray. Small.

A piece of gravel.

Ari spun toward the rail.

"Yes, Carol, I know what the word *burden* means," Carol hater said.

A shadow high above caught Ari's eye.

Eve knelt on the roof of the neighboring building, the lights of the city catching her just enough to make her red hair a magnificent beacon as she held up one finger, then pointed down and to the right of Ari.

Ari held up a finger, mouthing *only one?*

"My face is not printed in the dictionary, you vindictive little twat!"

Eve nodded and sank back, her beacon hair retreating from view.

"This is why you make a plan, Ari." She shut her eyes, running through a hundred different options before standing up and tucking her dagger-wielding hand into her pocket as she strode toward the emergency stairs. "You make a plan so it can go to shit."

63

Eve

L eBlanc had a stench.

Not a sweat-dripping odor, or a stink of too much perfume.

Coward.

Coward.

A growl rumbled in Eve's throat.

The rancid stench of cowardice, of a man so rotted by evil and fear not even a vulture would touch his soul.

Mariah stepped toward LeBlanc.

"Don't even think about it." Eve crouched low, daring to inch even closer to the edge of the roof.

"About what?" Jack whispered, his voice barely carrying over the squeak of the roof's door closing.

"LeBlanc is mine." Eve planted her hands on the gravel-covered, tarpaper ground, rocking forward, savoring the rumbling growl in her chest.

"Eve, as a friend and fellow cryptid, I'm asking you to listen without attacking."

Eve let her rage dance through her eyes as she rounded on Jack, her lips pulling back as she snarled.

"No biting." Jack took a step back. "But what we're doing here, the point isn't to kill LeBlanc."

"Ha." Eve's rage ebbed. She turned back toward the hotel square.

"We all agreed to Ari's plan." The gravel of the roof crunched under Jack's feet. "We expose LeBlanc as the murdering monster we know him to be and let the Maree arrest him."

"I know," Eve said.

"Then you know there are Maree down there." Jack crept closer. "Maree who haven't hurt anyone."

The rattle of Eve's growl shifted the tension in her shoulders, twisting anger into strength, preparing her to attack as every nerve in her body begged for blood.

"Once they've captured LeBlanc—"

"They won't." Eve sneered. "He's a cowardly piece of shit, but he'll fight back. He'll refuse to be taken. The Maree might try to stop him. But they will fail. It's all the worthless shits know how to do. Then it's my turn."

Far below, LeBlanc grabbed Chanler's arm, holding him in place.

"LeBlanc needs to be arrested." Jack stopped four feet behind Eve.

"I'm not going to give him the chance to hurt anyone ever again."

"I agree."

Jack's footsteps changed to a nerve-grating scrape as he crouched, walking like a damn chicken as he neared the edge of the roof.

A wave of gold swept around the square.

A swirling burst of wind lifted the scent of piss-gripping fear up from the Hotel Mirage.

"We'll come down."

The gold retreated.

"Can you do me one favor?" Jack asked.

A woman crossed the square, ignoring the murderer glaring at her back.

"Eve?" Jack said.

"What?"

"Don't let bloodlust make you forget who you are."

"I'm not a vampire."

The Maree filed into the stairwell on the fourth floor.

"Which makes me worry more," Jack said.

Ari peered up over the railing on the other side of the building.

"Let's get this done." Eve dug her fingers into the gravel on the roof.

Ari started moving toward the fourth-floor stairwell.

A figure on the third floor moved as well.

A Maree.

"I won't pretend to know what being a werewolf is like," Jack said.

Ari kept moving toward the staircase.

Eve dragged her fingers through the gravel.

Ari still hadn't stopped moving.

"But I know what it's like to be further from human than the rest of them can understand," Jack said.

Eve grabbed a piece of gravel. She pelted it at the top of Ari's head.

Ari staggered as the stone struck.

"What the hell?" Jack dropped to his stomach, cowering,

hands protecting his head like the Maree could swoop down from the sky to grab him.

Ari peered up over the railing.

Eve grabbed another piece of gravel.

Friend. She's a friend.

She hurled the stone, striking the wall just behind Ari.

"Eve." Jack gripped her ankle.

Eve growled.

Ari looked toward the roof of the Hotel Mirage.

The Maree looked up too, like the worthless shit had actually noticed something beyond his yearning to hide in the corner like every other coward with a Maree tattoo.

"There are seventeen people in this world I would love to see dead." Jack tightened his grip on Eve's ankle. "And when I think of tasting their blood, killing puppies seems like a fair price."

Seven Maree ran out into the square. They flanked LeBlanc and Chanler, lining up like they hadn't realized they'd filed right into a box.

"But the other side of bloodlust holds a shit ton of regret. LeBlanc deserves to die, but what if he can lead us to the *they*? What if he—"

"This isn't like the archivist. We don't need LeBlanc."

"Yes, we do. We still don't know about his missing time, or his connection to the seven Maree from hell, or—"

"Information is Ari's department. She doesn't need him breathing."

He let go of her. "Then can we at least make sure it's done right? LeBlanc surviving for another few minutes won't help him any. But waiting until we're ready could end up saving a hell of a lot of lives."

She didn't need minutes. She didn't need waiting.

One leap. Let her claws grow as she fell. Slice through LeBlanc's throat before her feet touched the ground.

Two Maree down before they knew what had happened.

"No one who signed that werewolf scroll is in the square," Jack said. "*They* aren't in the square."

Eve threw another stone, striking the wall beside Ari.

Ari looked up into the shadows high above the roof of the Hotel Mirage.

Eve crept forward, placing herself in the brightest patch of light the neighboring buildings provided.

Ari's teal eyes widened as she spotted Eve.

Patience, Gran.

Eve held up one finger, then pointed to the Maree lurking on the third-floor balcony.

Ari furrowed her brow, holding up one finger as she mouthed *only one.*

I'm trying, Gran.

Eve nodded and slunk back into the shadows.

"Thank you," Jack said.

Ari ran across the fourth-floor balcony, her steps light enough Eve almost missed them beneath the nerve-tearing racket blaring up from the sombs on the street.

"You're wrong about the regret," Eve said.

Ari disappeared into the stairwell on the fourth floor.

"I really don't think so," Jack said.

"You talk about wanting blood like it's unnatural."

Ari pushed open the stairwell door on the third floor.

Jack pulled himself forward, peeking over the edge of the roof to watch Ari.

"I'm not a vampire." Eve dug her fingers into the gravel. "I was born a wolf."

Ari held her phone to her ear, chattering about something—presses, no classes—as she walked toward the last Maree on the third floor.

"I know I wasn't born feu," Jack said.

"I am as much wolf as I am human."

Ari laughed as she approached the sole Maree.

"I can regret not getting the chance to dig more answers out of the archivist," Eve said. "But wolves are meant to hunt."

Ari locked her arm around the Maree's throat. He jerked once before going limp. She leaned the Maree's weight against her body as she lowered him to the ground.

She looked up at the roof, winking as she pulled a room key from her pocket. She pressed it to the door two rooms away from the downed Maree. The door opened.

Eve pulled the phone from her pocket, sending the pre-typed message.

Time for study hall.

"LeBlanc dies tonight." Eve tucked the phone back into her pocket. "Anyone who gets in my way is fair game."

64

Jerek

"One for each of you." Jerek strode straight toward the Maree, packets in hand.

"Jerek Holden." LeBlanc gave him a mildly interested look.

An unfamiliar, burning, seething loathing clamped around Jerek's chest.

"Congratulations, Mariah," LeBlanc said. "You've taken falling from grace to a level of mastery."

"Careful," Mariah said. "A drowning man shouldn't waste his time flailing."

"No indeed." Jerek offered Mariah a packet. "Would you like to read along?"

"I can look on with daddy." Mariah stepped closer to her father and LeBlanc.

The Maree moved forward, tightening their position, preparing to attack.

"A bit fearful." Jerek pursed his lips and wrinkled his brow, cocking his head for added effect as red crept up LeBlanc's neck, marring his performance of the calm, respected, innocent man. "That's quite all right. Caution is prudent when we face such horrors as Maree betraying and slaughtering their brethren."

"Mr. Holden"—LeBlanc smiled even as the red of his face deepened—"you are wanted by the Council of the Feu for the crimes of theft, arson, and what were the other charges?" LeBlanc spoke over his right shoulder.

"The murder of a Knight Maree," the nearest knight said.

"Mariah, come here." Chanler kept his voice low, as though that could save him from the glare LeBlanc shot his way. Chanler stepped back, placing himself behind the Maree. "Mariah is an innocent child."

LeBlanc swiveled his glare to Mariah, the red leaving his face as his smile gained a vicious edge.

"Mariah is innocent." Jerek took three steps forward, placing himself between LeBlanc and Mariah, leaving him only ten feet from LeBlanc—less from the Maree as they edged in front of the demon, all of them gripping their batons. "As, fortunately for me, am I."

Jerek shifted his mind inward, his focus on LeBlanc wavering for a moment as he reached for the energy that begged to burst free, grazing the edges of his magic just enough to keep his papers perfectly aligned as he threw the stack at LeBlanc's favored Maree.

The stack struck the Maree in the shins and thumped down onto his foot.

The Maree narrowed his eyes at Jerek.

"Apologies." Jerek gave as much of a bow as he could while keeping LeBlanc in view. "You needn't pass out the packets for us to begin going through the material."

LeBlanc stepped forward, raising his hand as though preparing to order an attack.

Six feet. LeBlanc stopped six feet away from Jerek.

If LeBlanc had been the one to plant the bombs, if he was the butcher—

I'm closer to my mother's murderer than he had to get to kill her.

"Mariah." Chanler held his hand out to his daughter.

"And don't worry about needing more copies," Mariah said. "There are backups of backups."

"Mariah," Chanler said.

"This packet, along with a few exciting extras, was also sent to the Council of the Feu and the Knight's Council. Once things calm down, I'm sure they'll be interested." Jerek flipped open the cover page of his packet.

"Restrain them, and take them upstairs," LeBlanc said.

"Before we've gone over page one?" Jerek turned the packet, displaying the photo of LeBlanc sitting on a bar, smiling with three others. "While consorting with knights who have broken their vow to the Maree by signing a manifesto declaring their intent to slaughter werewolves en masse may seem a mere source of deep shame, paired with your direct hand in the deaths of thirty-six Maree and involvement with the creation of the Fracture and death of Katie Chanler, we've built a case well above what is necessary for the Council of the Feu to take action."

"Such time you've wasted," LeBlanc said.

"Callen LeBlanc, you are a traitor, bigot, and murderer," Jerek said. "You will surrender to the Knights Maree."

"Take them," LeBlanc said.

The knights moved forward, flicking their wrists, sending skin-searing sparks dancing along their batons.

"LeBlanc is the one you need to capture." Mariah grabbed

Jerek's arm. "The evidence is there. We made a packet." She kept hold of him, pulling him along as she backed away.

"We are happy to surrender to you," Jerek said.

"What?" Mariah tightened her hold.

Jerek dropped the last of his papers, keeping his hands open as he held them forward. "Under the condition you arrest LeBlanc as well."

"Dammit, Jerek."

"A peaceful end to the evening." The side of Jerek's leg knocked into the rim of the fountain. "No blood will be spilt, and you get to be the heroes who brought in one of the monsters behind the Fracture. What greater victory could a Knight Maree hope for?"

Callen LeBlanc smiled.

A cold, jagged understanding tore through Jerek's mind, stilling his rage as his heartbeat thundered in his ears.

"Kill them both." LeBlanc turned, passing the gray-faced Chanler as he strode toward the elevator. "Keep the mess to a minimum."

"Not likely," Jerek said as a shadow fell from the sky.

Ford

"Not an event I ever thought I would be covering, but a thrilling night, nonetheless"—the blond reporter spoke into her handheld microphone—"as magicians and illusionists, both amateur and professional, continue pouring into Times Square, all trying to impress the mysterious Mr. Magic."

"Mr. Magic?" Ford frowned at the tablet he'd propped up with the security monitors.

"It's a good name." Regi scooted his chair closer to the desk.

"But while this evening of unending rainbow scarves and disappearing assistants may be a dream for these hopeful winners of Mr. Magic's one million dollars," the reporter continued, "the NYPD is finding this flash event less than ideal."

"It's a brilliant event, that's what it is." Ford swiped on his tablet, switching to a different news station.

"I'm just trying to stand out from the crowd." A man in a

bright blue, sparkling suit spoke into the camera. *"I've toured my act twice, and I am ready to wow Mr. Magic. I'm on the corner of 42nd and 7th."*

"For now," a voice shouted.

"Dibs means dibs," sparkle suit shouted back.

Ford looked up to the security monitors.

Barricades still blocked traffic on the archives' street and the construction workers had yet to return, but animal control had finally managed to catch most of the pigeons, lovingly taking the enchanted, living projectiles away.

A squeaked scream blared from the tablet.

The camera had backed away from sparkle suit and his foe, giving a better view of the two pummeling each other.

The foe knocked sparkle suit into a woman with three bowling pins balanced on her head. The woman stumbled back, sending the pins tumbling down.

One landed on sparkle suit, who ignored the blood on his cheek as he launched himself at his foe. The other two fell on a woman in a black unitard who rounded on pin woman, a crystal ball in each hand.

"Does that look like the beginning of a mob to you?" Regi asked.

"Sure does." Ford checked the security monitors again, scanning them all before opening his laptop.

"Ooh!" Regi covered his mouth with the side of his fist, shrinking back in his chair.

Ford risked glancing down.

A man in a black unitard had joined the fray, grabbing pin woman and lifting her over his head before tossing her at sparkle suit.

"Perfect for a viral hit." Ford snipped the video, dragged the clip to the waiting browser window, and hit *post*. "And so ends the reign of real magic on social media. Flying cereal, backflipping children, freak snow squalls—all meaningless foreplay to the final evening of magical mayhem in Times Square. An event so epic, everything else fades away."

"Any PR firm would be lucky to have y—ooh that's bad." Regi cringed as the camera panned to the other side of the street where, though the fight hadn't reached those illusionists, one seemed to have gotten stuck halfway into shoving his body through a small hula-hoop. The man toppled sideways, crashing to the ground. "I really hope he stretched first."

Upload complete.

"The time for massive congratulations is nigh." Ford closed his laptop and pushed it aside. "Check the channels."

Regi swiped on the tablet.

Ford checked the monitors.

A cluster of bystanders had gathered by the blockade on the eastern end of the street. A few gawkers. A few with cameras.

"Found it." Regi sat back, giving Ford a view of the massive screen over Times Square where Ford's first message had been replaced by a video slideshow.

In the first, a picture Regi had taken of his Maree stalkers, Ford had blurred out both the knights' faces and added *The Uniform* in large print above their heads with arrows pointing to their classic Maree suits.

The next image, borrowed from the Museum of Magic promotional materials, showed an old sketch of a woman levitating a prone man. The original page had included the wording for the necessary incantation. Erasing that had given Ford a conveniently bare place to write, *The Task.*

The third and fourth pictures, and Ford's favorites, had been carefully composed, taking images of Times Square at night, layering in pictures of Maree blending in with the crowd.

After a moment, the third image shifted, darkening everything but the Maree until the six Ford had pasted in shone like beacons as the words *The Judges* appeared on the screen, completing the glory of the fourth image.

Finally, Ford's instructions appeared.

Make sure the judges see you shine.

The sounds from the newscast changed as the mob of illusionists began searching for their own life-sized, black-suited Waldo.

Gandalf growled as an airhorn blasted in the video feed.

"You're okay." Ford patted the dog's head, leaning down even as he stood to get a better view of the top-left security camera.

"They can't trace Mr. Magic back to you, right?" Regi asked.

"That's the least of my worries."

A police officer stood at the barricade on the eastern end of the block, abandoning his birdproof car to talk to the cluster of onlookers.

"*—at the end of the day—*" a woman belted into a reporter's mic on the tablet, her voice bouncing as she lunged sideways, blocking the reporter's escape as she tried to steal a few more seconds of camera time. "*If you want a quintuple threat, I can do that, Mr. Magic! The sun'll come out—*"

Ford's phone dinged.

"What, what is it?" Regi reached for the phone.

Ford batted him out of the way, grabbing his phone first.

"What is it?" Regi leapt to his feet, peering over Ford's shoulder.

"Let me open it." Ford leaned away from Regi as he unlocked his phone.

Cas yowled from his roost on top of the curtain rod.

"Send in the clowns," Ford read the text.

Regi sank back into his seat.

A second message popped up with a ding.

Ford stared at the phone, waiting for the text to change.

It didn't.

He set the phone down and flipped his laptop back open.

"What did it say?" Regi dug his knuckles into his eyes.

Ford hit *enter,* sending one hundred and twenty-seven text messages at once.

"What order did you get?" Regi asked.

"With candles."

"Shit."

66

Jack

If he hadn't been so used to seeing the Eiffel Tower in the desert, Jack might have been astounded or at least intrigued as he stared down into what seemed from the street to be a hip, modern hotel but actually hid a villa vibe that contrasted with the neon-glowing, ever-rushing, never-silent reality of Manhattan in a way that had either plunged past absurd to let them eat cake, or displayed a brilliant, money-making angle for a hotelier.

As Vegas had the ability to out-absurd everyone up to and including the freemasons, glitter-strewn nudist colonies, and cryptocurrency crime lords, all Jack felt was the growing desire to tear the hotel apart along with any idiot who got between his fangs and LeBlanc's throat.

A flash of something bordering on guilt curled through Jack's gut.

"Quiet." Eve didn't shift from her position at the very edge of the roof, where she lay, shirt yanked up in back to hide her hair, staring down into the courtyard, the gleam in her eyes promising *he'd* be the idiot if he dared get between *her* and LeBlanc's throat.

"I didn't make any sound," Jack whispered.

"You fidgeted."

"Sorry."

Jack kept just behind Eve, avoiding the worst of her predator's gaze.

Jerek threw his stack of packets, striking one of the knights in the shin.

Eve pushed herself up onto her hands and knees.

"Take a breath," Jack whispered.

Eve growled.

Jack's fangs grew, piercing his bottom lip.

LeBlanc grabbed Chanler's arm, keeping him from reaching Mariah.

"Send the message," Eve said.

"We can't rush this." Jack pulled out the phone he'd been given.

"Twelve years isn't rushing."

"We're in Manhattan. We're surrounded by millions of sombs."

"Then send the damn message."

Send in the clowns.

Jack hit *send* and shoved the phone back into his pocket.

Chanler held his hand out to Mariah. She didn't run forward to take it.

Jack barely registered the tensing of Eve's muscles before she vaulted off the roof, plunging toward the square below.

"Really?" Jack yanked the phone back out.

With candles.

He shoved the phone back into his pocket and stood.

Plain human fear clenched his heart as he took the first step toward the edge of the roof.

"Jack!" The shout came from below.

Jack leapt back, baring his fangs as he searched for his enemy.

"Jack!" Ari stood at the rail of the third-floor balcony, waving for him.

A scream came from the square below.

"Jack." Ari held up a black case.

"Well shit." Ignoring the taste of his own blood in his mouth, Jack turned, running back twenty feet.

He pivoted and sprinted for the edge of the roof, not giving himself time to plan or consider the distance or wonder how badly missing would hurt, as he launched himself into the air.

His stomach dropped as he flew—no fell—toward the square. The balconies across the way raced toward him. He reached forward, begging the skills bought by every dodge ball bruise he'd ever suffered to save him.

He caught sight of Ari, her eyes wide as she dove sideways, clearing Jack's path as he crashed into the railing, flipped over it onto the balcony, and landed on his ass with a soul-crushing crash.

"Jack." Ari knelt beside him.

"Don't know if that was dumb or badass." Pain shot from his tailbone up his spine and down to his heels, warning him of all the ways his plain human body would have shattered.

"You need to take this and go." Ari pressed the black case to his chest.

Another scream carried up from the square.

"Get back up to the roof and run," Ari said.

"I'm not running." Jack didn't take the case as he pushed himself to his feet, shaking out his shoulders as the pain in his back ebbed.

"Take the case and go." Ari shoved it against his chest again.

"You take—"

"I'm a swimmer, not a jumper." Ari grabbed Jack's hand, forcing his fingers around the handle of the case. "Get this back to the archives."

A door banged open at the far corner of the balcony.

A sweat-faced Maree charged toward them.

"Now, Jack." Ari shoved Jack behind her as she drew her two daggers.

Jack leapt onto the balcony railing, twisting and jumping for the next balcony up before he'd even heard the swish of Ari's dagger flying toward the Maree.

67

Grace

*T*his is real.

This is real.

You are not hallucinating.

You are just fine.

You are not locked in a cell having the most therapy-inducing dream of your life.

The massive, pink kitten pulled off its head. The woman inside the cat suit wiped the sweat from her brow with her furry arm, then reached down the front of her fursuit and pulled out a flask.

What the hell has my life become?

The pink kitten handed the flask to the dragon, who'd removed his head after the crowd of waiting horses, foxes, cats, and more had reached the ten-minute mark and the chatter about lurking outside a hotel on the invitation of a mystery fursuit-loving, party-throwing benefactor had gone from intrigued to impatient.

Grace stuck out her bottom lip, blowing the sweat from the tip of her nose, trying not to think about how many other people had sweat in the squirrel costume that had somehow become a part of her penance.

Another cat, something like a robot, and a unicorn joined the crowd next.

"I'm just tired of defending a perfectly legitimate pastime," the new cat said, their latex nose moving perfectly with their words.

A muffled, "Huh?" came from within the robot.

"Forget the haters, focus on the fur," the unicorn, whose face wasn't covered by her fursuit, said.

"Huh?" the robot repeated.

"This party is going to be massive." The unicorn raised the robot's ear flap to repeat herself. "The party is going to be massive."

The robot nodded with their whole body.

"Anyone know when this is going to get started?" the unicorn asked the headless, pink kitten.

"There are door prizes, honey," the dragon said. "It's every fursona for themselves."

This is real.

This is real.

Grace blew another drop of sweat from the tip of her nose.

Ding.

Ding.

Ding. Beep. Ding. Bleep.

The crowd's phones started beeping.

Ding. Blink-a-link

Grace reached for the phone tucked inside her paw as the costumed crowd seemed to freeze for a moment, like all seventy gathered fursonas had taken a breath at once, before bolting for the doors of the Hotel Mirage.

Fumbling her phone, Grace followed the crowd. She squinted through the mesh of her head to read the message.

Send in the clowns.

"Stop!" The doorman stood in front of the sliding doors, waving his arms in a vain attempt to defend his station from the oncoming fur storm.

A six-foot ladybug knocked him aside, clearing the way for the stampede.

Grace's phone dinged again.

With candles.

Her throat tensed as she waited for fear to seize her.

A dinosaur crashed into a jaguar. Both tumbled to the ground.

The woman behind the concierge desk screamed as the unicorn joined the pileup.

Grace cut around the fur pile, weaving between a downed teddy bear and an oddly suggestive couch, still well behind the fox that reached the doors to the courtyard first, but far enough from the back of the menagerie no one tried to stop the squirrel as she cut left—darting behind the security guards as they ran toward the pileup—and into the discreetly placed corridor.

Something rammed into her back.

Grace stumbled forward, grabbing her head to hold it in place as it threatened to twist far enough to steal the small patch of mouth mesh she could see through.

She whipped around, daring to let go of her head with one

hand, raising it toward her attacker instead, ready to let her magic burn.

"Sorry." The red fuzzy bear who'd smacked into her straightened his own head.

A crash came from the lobby.

"Don't follow me." Grace shooed the bear away. "Go to the square. The door prizes are in the square."

The bear turned, knocking into the corridor wall twice before finally managing to run back to the lobby.

"This is real." Grace hurried to the middle of the three doors at the end of the corridor.

The ornamental windowpane marked *security* gave the center door a helpless look that pinged a tinge of regret through Grace's conscience as she ripped off her paw and pressed her finger to the old-fashioned keyhole.

The air around the lock rippled as the metal began to warp, bending from the heat of her hand.

"Come on." She surged more heat into her finger, not stopping until the metal began to glow a faint red.

She flung off her other paw and gripped the knob with both hands.

Gritting her teeth against the strain, she twisted the knob as hard as she could. "Come on, you stubborn shit."

A faint crackling came from within the lock.

"Yes." Grace leveraged her weight against the knob, ramming her shoulder into the wall with bone-bruising force as the lock finally gave. She yanked the door to the security room open. "Hell yes."

The two security guards she'd passed had been eating takeout before the furry invasion. A puddle of spilled soda dripped from the desk onto one of the two chairs.

"Good. This is good."

Three screens rotated through videos of the hotel.

The concierge pulled the unicorn to her feet.

Empty balconies on the third and fourth floors.

Chaos in the courtyard.

Jerek with a glowing sword. Lincoln fighting two Maree, his back pinned against a column.

A panda chasing a cat.

Two headless creatures screaming at each other.

The screens switched cameras.

LeBlanc.

Sword in hand, a knight beside him, LeBlanc faced Eve.

Grace pressed her hands to the rack of mounted electrical boxes, covering the knobs and little lights with her palms, letting the searing heat within her flow from her hands, watching Eve's claws grow as the video blacked out.

68

Eve

The wind raced past Eve as she plummeted toward the ground.

LeBlanc didn't even look up.

Unaware. Fragile. Breakable. Human.

Power rippled through Eve's limbs as she landed in the square. Her body demanded more.

More strength. More hunger. More wolf.

LeBlanc's eyes widened, like prey.

Small. Helpless. Terrified of their inevitable fate.

The rat hid his fear as he lifted his chin. "Step out of my way."

Tiny beads of sweat swelled on his forehead even as four of his knights ran to his side.

"Remove her," LeBlanc said.

All four knights dared to approach, raising their batons like the sticks would protect them.

"You don't have to do this." Lincoln appeared, keeping his hands out as he approached from the side. "LeBlanc is a monster. There are traitors hiding within the Maree. I swear to you we're telling the truth. Let me show you the proof."

"Keep Louis alive if you can," LeBlanc said. "Get rid of the rest."

Two of the knights went for Lincoln.

A shout came from behind LeBlanc.

Eve grinned.

One of the knights charged Eve, baton in one hand while he reached for his dagger with the other.

Eve lunged forward, catching the knight's wrist before he'd raised his blade.

A sting shocked along her spine as the knight slammed his baton across her back. The blow didn't affect her aim as she flung him into a pillar.

A high scream pinged in Eve's ears as she stalked toward LeBlanc.

The terrified rat pulled a knife from his belt. The filth steadied his stance as the blade grew, gleaming as it lengthened into a sword.

Flickers of color darted behind LeBlanc as he nodded his last pawn forward.

Eve held the knight's gaze as she flicked open her pendant, letting claws take the place of fingers as her shoulders strengthened and her teeth lengthened.

The knight faltered back a step.

Eve made up the distance, stalking toward the knight, letting him raise his blade before she attacked, slicing her claws across his ribs with one hand while knocking his baton aside with the other.

The knight dove forward, ramming his shoulder into Eve's hip, gaining one moment of her stumbling back in exchange for his life as she swung her arm around, slashing her claws through the air, tearing the knight's throat.

The sounds around Eve changed, crisping as the scent of blood filled the square.

LeBlanc attacked.

He swung first for her neck.

She dodged.

He sliced sideways, aiming for her spine.

She twisted out of the way.

He swung for her wrists.

Perfect. Every blow aimed for her weak points as though the rat had learned a werewolf-murdering dance.

Eve ducked, kicking back.

Leblanc swung, slashing his blade down, giving in to the lure of her ankle.

Pain narrowed Eve's vision as LeBlanc sliced through her Achilles, but she didn't let her momentum stop, twisting as she slashed below LeBlanc's sword, driving her claws into his gut.

Fear danced through his eyes again as she raised her arm, letting his weight plunge her claws deeper into his torso. His throat spasmed. Blood stained his lips as he tried to breathe.

She grabbed him by the throat, breaking his neck as she ripped her hand from his gut and tossed him aside, ending the life of a murderer.

Callen LeBlanc's corpse crumpled to the ground. Eyes blank. Heart stopped.

A halo of blood surrounded his head.

Not the monster's blood.

A unicorn's.

Fear flickered through the unicorn's eyes as she pressed her hands to the four long wounds in her stomach, and the prey realized death had come for her.

69

Grace

Sweat dripped into Grace's eyes, blurring her vision as she bolted through the lobby, dodging between a fairy and a llama to reach the doors to the hotel's square.

"All of you, just leave!" The desperate wail carried over the chaos.

Grace ignored the plea as she ran into the mayhem.

The flock of fursonas searched the square, looking for the non-existent door prizes.

Most kept to the edges of the space, scouring the shadows and digging through the vines, but enough invaders had stayed in the center of the square, wading into the fountain and searching the cobblestones, to muddy what Grace could understand of the fight.

Jerek faced a Maree on the far side of the square, his glowing sword slashing through the air with smooth strokes.

Fine, he's fine.

Lincoln had gotten away from the pillar. He bled from a gash on one arm, but he was still fighting.

On his feet. Not dead.

Ari had taken one of Lincoln's Maree.

She slashed her dagger up, slicing through the Maree's thigh.

The Maree stumbled forward.

Ari managed another blow across the Maree's chest, but he grabbed her, twisting her arm behind her back as he shoved her face-first into the fountain, pinning her head below the water.

Grace shoved the ladybug aside, running toward Ari.

An earsplitting scream came from the other side of the square.

Eve spun, ramming her claws into LeBlanc's gut as the unicorn behind her struggled to sit up, wide-eyed as she looked down at her bleeding stomach.

Grace glanced back toward Ari.

The Maree still had her face pinned under the water.

Ari reached back, grabbing the knight's arm.

He screamed as something—something awful—twisted his face in agony.

But the twisting didn't stop.

His cheeks sank in, graying, hardening under Ari's attack.

More screams pulled Grace's attention the other way just in time to watch Eve toss LeBlanc to the ground.

He landed beside the unicorn, his limp limbs splayed out, his head in the unicorn's blood.

The unicorn didn't notice. She was too busy grasping at her stomach, trying to stop the bleeding from four horrible gashes.

Eve stalked toward LeBlanc, her face twisting like that of the Maree attacking Ari, but different. Terrifyingly different.

Her jaw lengthened as her teeth sharpened. Her face darkened as deep, mahogany-brown fur grew on her cheeks.

Her shoulders widened. Her spine curved.

"Eve!" Grace shouted.

Eve stood over LeBlanc, the back of her shirt splitting open as her leg bones snapped into a horrifying angle.

Grace glanced toward Ari again.

Ari kicked back, catching her Maree in the knee.

The Maree toppled over, crashing to the ground, like she had knocked over a statue.

Grace ran toward Eve.

Eve threw her head back, howling at the sky as the shape of her neck changed.

"Eve!"

Eve ignored Grace's shout.

"Eve, stop." Grace held her hands out as she reached Eve, her voice wavering even as she fought to keep it calm.

Eve's face sank lower, out of Grace's view.

Grace stumbled back, trying to see Eve through the hole in her squirrel suit.

But Eve wasn't there.

Yes, she is.

A massive, brown-furred wolf with long, dagger-sharp teeth snarled at Grace. The wolf's rounded shoulders and sharp, black claws marked the creature as unnatural, wrapping a fear born of ancient instinct around Grace's spine.

"Eve." Grace forced the word from her throat. "It's me." Grace kept her hands up, palms toward the wolf that was Eve. "It's Grace, okay? I need you to take a breath. Just calm down and be human again."

The wolf's growl deepened.

"There are sombs here," Grace said. "You have to shift back."

The wolf dropped its head, almost like it was looking toward LeBlanc and the unicorn.

"LeBlanc is gone. Everyth—"

The unicorn had gone still. Deathly still.

Without a twitch of a warning, the wolf leapt over Grace.

"Eve!" Grace spun around, holding her squirrel head steady, barely catching a glimpse of Eve as she ripped through the doors and disappeared into the lobby. "Eve, come back! Eve!"

Still gripping her head, Grace sprinted after Eve, chasing a werewolf out onto the somb-filled streets of Manhattan.

70

Jerek

The blade slicing across his shoulder caused barely any pain. Worryingly little pain.

Jerek dodged left, cutting behind the Maree, risking glancing away from his foe for a split second to check his torso for any damage he might not have noticed.

None of the bloodstains on his shirt seemed large enough to kill him.

He lunged toward the Maree, anticipating the knight's next attack, swiping his left arm up beneath the Maree's while stabbing with the blade in his right hand, knocking the Maree's blow aside, but not quickly enough.

As his blade plunged into the Maree's flank, a faint sting touched Jerek's back.

Wrenching his sword from the Maree's gut, he leapt away, losing ground but gaining the chance to choose his next blow.

The Maree toppled forward, his knees striking the ground,

his eyes rolling with unconsciousness Jerek's sword shouldn't have caused.

Lincoln stood behind the Maree—blood on his face, his hand still raised from the blow to the Maree's head.

Jerek spun around, planting his back to Lincoln as he searched for the next enemy.

The horde of brightly colored fur creatures still filled the square, but their manner had changed, fear taking the place of excitement as the first batch of them fled back toward the lobby.

A headless hippo knelt by one of the downed Maree, a cellphone pressed to their ear.

A cat knelt beside a unicorn, sobbing, ignoring the miracle right beside them.

Callen LeBlanc dead.

His eyes wide, blood staining his mouth.

The monster who had helped tear magic from the world, who had started the years of pain and loss that had stolen Jerek's parents, and Eve's parents, and so many other innocent lives, could never so much as utter an evil word again.

Jerek ripped his gaze away from LeBlanc, turning toward the elevator as a panicked scream cut through the pounding in his head.

"Jerek, we have to go."

Pressure pinched Jerek's arm, keeping him from running toward the scream.

The pressure wrenched him back.

"They're down, Jerek." The pressure tightened as Lincoln spun Jerek to face him. "The Maree are down. We have to go!"

Jerek nodded, making his feet take the first steps toward the lobby. "Where are the others?"

Lincoln let go of Jerek's arm, leaving him to move on his own as he ran toward the fountain.

Jerek followed before he knew why.

Ari gripped the edge of the fountain, using the stone to leverage herself to her feet.

"Ari." Lincoln grabbed her under the arm, yanking her the rest of the way up. "Come on."

"You go." Ari planted a hand on Lincoln's chest as though pushing him away, only managing to make herself stumble. "Get back to the archives."

"The police are coming." Lincoln switched his grip, wrapping his arm around Ari, steadying her, propelling her toward the lobby. "Where are you hurt?"

Ari twisted out of his hold. "I'll find Mariah, you go."

"There's no time." Jerek reached for her.

Ari backed away, swiping her soaked hair from her face. "Get Eve and Gra—"

"They aren't here." Jerek batted Ari's hand aside, gripping her around the waist and dragging her toward the lobby.

"Stop, Jerek." She rammed her elbow into his gut, sending pain spasming through a wound he hadn't noticed as she broke free. "Find them. Make sure they got out. Run. Now!"

She turned away from them, stepping back toward the fountain.

"Ari." Jerek grabbed her wrist, whipping her around, catching her as she stumbled toward him.

"Jer Bear." She pushed against his chest. "G—go."

Her breath caught in her throat. Her ribs spasmed.

"Ari?" Jerek held her tighter as her knees buckled.

Her ribs kept spasming.

He shifted his hold on her, bending down, ready to scoop her into his arms.

The world froze.

Time shattered.

Gray froth foamed from her mouth. Pain filled her eyes as she fought for air.

"Ari."

Her throat tensed as she gagged on the darkening foam.

She pushed against him, fighting as Jerek lifted her, trying to break away even as her chest went still.

"Ari!" The scream tore from Jerek's throat as Ariel Love's eyes fluttered shut.

Lincoln

A high, piercing scream swallowed Lincoln's thoughts as Ari sagged toward the ground.

Terror filled Jerek's face as he lifted her, clutching her to his chest, shouting something Lincoln couldn't hear.

Lincoln reached for Ari, needing to support her head as it tipped back.

Foam spilled from her mouth.

The screaming in his head grew louder.

Her eyes closed.

Jerek pushed Ari toward Lincoln. He held her against Lincoln's chest, shouting something. The fear in his eyes promised it was important, but nothing could be as important as Ari limp and unmoving. No laughter in her eyes. No quick word on her lips.

No. No. No. No.

Pain burst through Lincoln's shin.

"Can you carry her or not?" Jerek held Lincoln's gaze as he lifted his foot to kick Lincoln again. "We can't let the sombs near her. Lincoln. Lincoln!"

Lincoln nodded.

He lifted Ari from Jerek's arms.

She didn't weigh enough. She needed to be heavier.

She should hold the weight of the universe, of everything that had ever existed. She shouldn't feel so delicate and breakable in Lincoln's arms.

Jerek planted his palm in the center of Lincoln's back, forcing him toward the lobby of the Hotel Mirage. "We have to get her to the river."

Lincoln shook his head, digging through the screaming in his mind, searching for the meaning of Jerek's words.

The flashing of police lights glared off the white walls of the lobby.

"Shit." Jerek's pace faltered, like he was searching for an escape that didn't exist. "Shit." He pushed Lincoln faster, shoving him toward the street. "Get her past the police. Get her to the river."

"No." The syllable caught in Lincoln's throat. "Jerek, she's not—"

"She needs to be in the water."

"She's not breathing, Jerek."

"Do you understand exactly how a div's body works?"

A swarm of police officers ran through the hotel's doors.

"Help!" Jerek shouted, plowing forward even as the police ordered everyone to stop. "She needs an ambulance!"

"No." Lincoln clung to Ari, twisting to shield her from the police officer who ran their way. "They can't touch her. I won't let them touch her."

Jerek blocked the police officer's path. "Is there an ambulance? Please, she needs help."

"Outside." The police officer planted herself between Jerek and the chaos as she waved for them to run for the door. "Move!"

Jerek grabbed Lincoln's arm, dragging him forward.

"We can't give her to the sombs." The words came too easily. The screaming in Lincoln's mind had been better. "Their doctors will butcher her."

"Ari's heart is slow. Her lungs are different." Jerek spun Lincoln toward him, stopping just before the hell that had broken out on the street. "Neither of us knows how her body works, so neither of us can know if she's dead."

Dead.

Gone.

Gone forever.

Cold, hollow pain sliced into Lincoln's chest, cutting all the way up to his throat.

"We have to get her into the river." Fire and fear mixed in Jerek's eyes. "If there's any chance we can help her—"

Lincoln shoved past Jerek, running onto the street.

EMTs sprinted toward them, carrying their tools and medicine that could kill a div.

"Clear a path," Lincoln bellowed, mimicking courage and authority as he ran past the EMTs, heading west. "Clear a path."

"Lincoln!"

He ignored the call as he dodged past a downed peacock, heading toward the police at the edge of the chaos.

"Lincoln!"

An officer at the perimeter spotted Lincoln. "Stop."

Lincoln didn't.

"Ari!"

The panicked shriek broke Lincoln's stride.

Mariah ran toward them, hand pressed to the bloody stain on her side. "Ari."

"We need medical," the officer shouted as they stepped into Lincoln's path.

"Let me pass," Lincoln said.

"Ari." Mariah swiped the foam away from Ari's mouth. "Ari."

"What the hell is that?" the officer dodged back.

"We have to get her out," Jerek said.

"Officer Sullivan on scene. We have a possible biohazard situation. Request immediate backup, hazmat, and EMS on the west side of the Hotel Mirage perimeter." The officer spoke into their radio even as they drew their weapon. "All of you, step back."

"Mariah," Jerek said.

"Save her." Mariah turned toward the officer. "Get the hell out of their way."

"This area may need to be quarantined," the officer said.

"Can't say I didn't ask." Mariah lifted her hand away from the wound on her side.

"All of you need medical attention," the officer said.

Mariah traced her finger through the blood on her palm, drawing lines and curves.

A rune.

"*Heletza,*" Mariah said.

The officer staggered back, doubling over like they'd taken a terrible blow to the gut.

"Run." Mariah grinned as she sauntered toward the officer.

Lincoln charged past the barrier before Mariah landed her next blow.

A crowd had gathered beyond the police, enjoying the spectacle of bloodshed and pain.

"Is she okay?" an onlooker called even as they raised their phone to record.

"Out of the way!" Jerek cut in front of Lincoln, sprinting toward the horde.

The crowd parted, stumbling back, falling onto each other as though the force of Jerek's fear had formed an invisible plow.

Lincoln shifted his hold on Ari, curling her in on herself, protecting her head as he followed Jerek across the street.

Cars blared their horns. A driver started shouting.

Lincoln didn't slow to hear the man's words or apologize to the people Jerek shoved out of their path.

Please. Please.

His lungs began to ache as they reached the next cross street.

Just get her to the water, that's all they had to do.

The pain in Lincoln's chest twisted, squeezing around his lungs, making him fight for every breath.

She's not breathing.

Her arm hung loosely at her side, bouncing with every step.

It's not possible.

How is this possible?

"Do you need help?"

Lincoln ignored the somb, pushing his legs harder as the cars on the street slammed to a stop, keeping Lincoln and Jerek's way clear.

Please. Anything. I'll do anything.

Up ahead, the lights of the city dimmed, leading to a stretch of dark nothing.

Ari slipped in Lincoln's arms, her shoulders twisting toward the ground.

He looked down, hope taunting his panic as it promised him Ari's eyes would be open.

The deep gray foam in her mouth had slipped onto her chin, dripping onto her chest as Lincoln ran.

He shifted his grip on her again, ignoring the burning in his arms and the pain in his chest as the bottoms of his lungs pinched closed, refusing to let him breathe, promising breathing no longer mattered.

You failed her. You should have protected her.

There were no cars for Jerek to stop at the next cross street.

The muscles in Lincoln's legs cramped, tightening his gait as the sidewalk slanted down, leading them toward the river.

It should be you. That Maree was fighting you.

She's not even bleeding.

Sirens sliced into Lincoln's mind, igniting the screaming that drowned out his thoughts.

Jerek picked up speed, outpacing Lincoln as they reached a pier at the edge of the Hudson.

Locked gates blocked the gangways, but only chest-high railings filled the stretches in between.

Lincoln slowed to a stop, his entire body trembling as he stepped closer to the rail.

"Lincoln. Lincoln!" Jerek called from a hundred feet down the ramp, waving Lincoln toward a gate that had tipped out over the water, barely hanging on to its broken hinges.

Lincoln's legs didn't stop trembling as he ran toward Jerek, reaching the top of the ramp as Jerek tossed aside the rope that had tethered the powerboat to the dock.

"Lincoln, now!" Jerek darted to the boat's wheel, frantically digging through the shadows as Lincoln ran down the boat ramp.

I'm sorry.

The screaming in Lincoln's mind let the words break through.

I'm so sorry.

Whatever trade you want, I'll make it.

He jumped down into the boat, stumbling as the deck shifted beneath him.

"Just once." Jerek spoke to the darkness. "Give me this one."

"Jer"—the word cracked in Lincoln's throat—"Jerek, we reached the river. If you want to put her in the water—"

"Not here." Jerek yanked his hand out of the dark, gripping something that jingled. "Thank you."

He flipped through the keyring, rejecting one before choosing a key to shove into the boat's ignition.

The boat rumbled to life.

"Jerek, we don't need a boat." Lincoln tipped forward as the boat lurched back, falling to his knees with a bang rather than risk dropping her.

"She's not safe close to the banks." The back of the boat rammed into a piling. "Shit."

She didn't flinch. Didn't breathe.

"Jerek." Lincoln slid her onto the bench along the side of the boat.

Her head lolled to the side. Vivid red tinged the foam in her mouth.

A heavy darkness stole the heat from Lincoln's limbs.

"Jerek, stop."

The boat hit the piling again.

"Jerek, stop!" Lincoln stood, rounding on Jerek as he finally backed the boat past the piling. "She's not breathing. She hasn't been breathing."

"Which is why we're getting away from the pier."

The boat tilted as Jerek turned, steering them toward the center of the Hudson River.

"I don't know how long it will take her to heal from this. We can't risk someone finding her before she wakes up." Jerek pushed the throttle forward. "Find something to weigh her down."

Lincoln gripped the handrail, keeping on his feet as his body begged to collapse. "Feu can't heal if they're dead."

"Find a weight, or I'll get it myself." Jerek angled the boat south. "Now!"

Lincoln searched the shadows, looking for something, anything heavy enough to sink.

To hold her down. Keep her trapped in the dark.

I'm so sorry.

The city lights glinted off the silver of a metal toolbox at the back of the boat.

He stumbled toward it. Not letting himself think as he grabbed the toolbox and a heavy stretch of rope. He tied the rope around the black handle of the toolbox, yanking it tight as the boat began to slow.

Ari had lost one of her shoes.

He didn't know if he'd dropped it.

Sour rose in his mouth as he reached for her ankle.

Her skin held no heat.

"Did you find something?" Jerek said.

"We can't do this."

"We're almost there."

"We can't dump her like trash!" The screaming in Lincoln's mind snapped away, leaving a deafening silence in its wake. "She's gone, Jerek. She died defending the feu."

"She's not dead!" The boat rocked as Jerek slammed it to a stop. "If there's anything I have faith in, it's Ariel Love." He ripped the rope from Lincoln's hands, wrapping it around Ari's ankle without hesitation. "We've seen each other through worse, and I'm not giving up on her now."

"Jer—"

"Do you really want to have to admit that you gave up on

her when she gets back?" Jerek tied the rope tight. "Will you be able to look her in the eye if you gave her up as dead?"

A burning, deadly sharp hook drove into Lincoln's heart, promising to drown him in pain.

"Jere—"

"The world has taken too much from me. I will not let it take her." Jerek searched Ari's pockets, pulling out her phone.

"I need a pen." Lincoln scrambled toward the front of the boat, ripping through the box of maps until he found a marker.

Jerek pulled the dagger from his own belt, tucking it into the empty sheath on Ari's thigh as Lincoln tore off a corner of a map.

He let his hand scrawl the words on the scrap of weathered paper, writing quickly, not giving the pain in his chest a chance to stop him.

"Ready." Jerek bundled the rope into his arms and grabbed the toolbox.

Lincoln slid the note into Ari's pocket.

Say goodbye.

"Lincoln."

You owe her a goodbye.

"Lincoln!" Jerek kicked Lincoln in the hip, the spike in pain slamming into Lincoln's mind just enough to allow him to command his body to move.

To pick her up.

To carry her to the railing.

To hold her out over the water.

To let go of her.

To watch her fall.

To hold in his scream as she hit the river with a splash.

To watch the last shimmer of her golden hair fade as Ariel Love disappeared into the darkness.

Thank you for reading *The Bloodbound Knight*. If you enjoyed the book, please consider leaving a review to help other readers find this story.

As always, thanks for reading,
    Megan O'Russell

Never miss a moment of the magic and romance.

Join the Megan O'Russell Readers Community to stay up to date on all the action by scanning the QR code below with your smart device.

THE JOURNEY CONCLUDES IN...

The Fatebound Wraith. Coming Summer 2024.

HOW I MAGICALLY MESSED UP MY LIFE IN FOUR FREAKIN' DAYS

We walked uptown toward my dad's. I don't know if it was instinct, habit, or the fact that my keys to Mom's place had been melted by a fire. Either way, Le Chateau seemed like the best bet.

A cab would have been faster, but since I smelled like a barbeque gone wrong, I figured it was better to walk.

Devon started by giving me a blow-by-blow of what the firemen had been doing: running in and out and a lot of hauling hoses mostly. "And then Linda May, sweet little Linda May, was so terrified she needed comfort, and of course she ran to me. I'm telling you man, the fire made 8th Ave crazy."

"You do remember I was there, right?" I asked, trying not to sound snarky even though I was tired enough to curl up on a subway grate and sleep. "I was the one who saw the fire start and pulled the alarm to get everyone out."

"Really?" Devon asked, looking surprised for a second but trying to cover up his shock by punching me in the arm. "Good for you, man! Elizabeth must think you're a hero. This could be the break you've been waiting for. Did you ask her out?"

"What? No, I didn't ask her out!" I ran my hands through my hair. It was gritty from the smoke and orange paint.

Devon grimaced and shook his head, looking down at the sidewalk.

"What?" I asked again, trying not to get angry. "What did you want me to do? Was I supposed to look down, see a fire, and stop on the way to the alarm to ask Elizabeth to be my girlfriend?"

"I mean, *girlfriend* might have been pushing it, but it would have been better than nothing," Devon said.

"Sorry, I was trying to make sure everyone didn't burn to death."

"What about when you two were talking once everyone was out of the theatre then?" Devon said, nodding and winking at a random dog walker.

The poor girl had two mastiffs, three Chihuahuas, and one drooling pug. Their leashes had all gotten tangled, and one of the Chihuahuas was dangling over the bigger mastiff's back. Being a dog walker was on my top ten list for jobs I never wanted in Manhattan.

"I don't know how many more chances you can hope to get with Elizabeth."

"I've never had a single chance," I said as we turned onto Central Park West, "and now she probably thinks I'm a freak, so...." I was screwed. There was something about knowing she thought I had magically started a fire with a cellphone and was now afraid of me that made it seem more true than years of her never speaking to me ever had. My stomach felt heavy and gross.

"Why does she think you're a freak?" Devon asked. "I mean, you just saved the whole theatre class."

I pulled the little black demon out of my pocket.

"She's thinks you're a freak because you forgot to return the phone? Which, by the way, is not cool, man. You don't leave a guy phoneless in Manhattan."

"If you remember, before you *had* to tell me all about how you made out with Linda May while our school was on fire, Elizabeth wants me to get rid of the phone." I slid it back into my pocket. Somehow having it out in my hand made me feel exposed, like a big eye in a creepy tower was watching me as I ran toward a pit of lava.

"So then let's get rid of the phone," Devon said. "We'll take it to the purple restaurant and make it their problem to find the vampire dude, and you can tell her you did what she wanted."

"She doesn't want me to return the phone," I sighed, knowing full well Devon was going to laugh at me. "She wants me to throw it into the Hudson to destroy it. She thinks the phone started the fire."

I started counting to three in my head. Before I got past two, Devon had tossed his head back and roared with laughter. People stared as they walked by.

It took Devon a full minute to speak. "I'm sorry." He wiped the tears from his eyes. "Was there a stray ray of sunlight you reflected off the screen to ignite the mounds of dried grass in the set shop?"

"No." I pushed Devon in the back to make him start walking again, and he promptly skidded on sidewalk goop. "There's an app on the phone, and she thinks I started the fire with it."

"An app. She thinks you started a fire with an app on a phone you can't even open?"

"I did open the phone," I said, "and a fire app thing."

"How did you open the phone? It should have a password." Devon turned to me, his laughter fading a little. "Do you have like post-traumatic stress or something from the fire? Because I mean, we could call your mom."

"I don't have traumatic stress." I pulled Devon into the

shade of a coffee shop awning. The place smelled like vegan food and almond milk. "And I didn't use a password." I glanced around before pulling the phone back out of my pocket. I didn't know what I was looking for. No one seemed to care about the two teenagers hanging out by the vegan coffee shop. But I still couldn't shake the feeling that someone was following me. Or that the evil eye was gazing down at me from the Empire State building. "I used my thumbprint." I pressed my thumb to the button, and the phone opened, showing the same funny symbols as before.

"Whoa!" Devon took it from me, but as soon as it left my hands, the thing turned back off. "Aw, come on." He pressed his thumb to the sensor, but the screen stayed dark. "Damn. Battery must have died."

I took the phone back and pressed my thumb back on the button. The screen popped back up. Devon grabbed the phone again, and it was the same thing. Him—phone off. Me—phone on.

"Bryant." Devon's voice was barely above a whisper. "Did you buy a phone and rig it to do that to freak me out? Because I mean, good for you, but that's a lot of trouble for a prank."

"You found this in the cab. And I would never prank you. I know better." And really I did. Devon would take any reason to punk you. If you were five minutes late when you were supposed to meet him, you had to spend the next week wondering what his revenge would be. Pulling a prank on him would be the worst idea anyone in Hell's Kitchen had ever had. Except maybe the next thing I did. That may have been the worst idea anyone in New York had ever had.

Devon was still giving me the *I don't believe you* stare with his eyebrows raised and his arms crossed. And Elizabeth thought I had a possessed phone, and my mom's theatre had burned down, and I had sort of had enough.

"Fine." I dragged him over to a trashcan by the side of the street, then tapped on the app that showed the picture of the fire. There it was—the still flames with the bar below balancing perfectly centered. I held the phone out like I was going to take a picture of the can and tapped the bar, tipping it all the way to the right.

Big mistake.

Flames shot out of the can and flew ten feet into the air like the sanitation department had decided collecting trash was too hard and installing a giant blowtorch was a better use of resources.

People behind us started to scream. Devon cursed and backed away. I stood there, frozen by the sudden heat. I couldn't move. I mean, I know I had gone to the fire app to prove to Devon that I wasn't wandering the city in some PTSD haze. But finding myself in front of a ten-foot-tall pillar of fire, holding a possessed cellphone in my hands, I sort of felt like maybe I had lost my mind. Maybe this wasn't even New York and I was locked in a cell. Or even better, and less scary maybe, I was still in bed, and this whole thing was a dream. I hadn't even gotten out of bed yet, and soon I would wake up with cat ass on my face.

I squeezed my eyes tightly shut and opened them again. There was still a fire right in front of me. No padded white room. No stinky cat ass.

I tapped the left side of the bar and pulled it all the way down. Just like it had sprung up without warning, in an instant, the fire disappeared with nothing but a melted trashcan to show for itself. Well, that and the sour, nose hair-burning stench of flaming crap.

I turned to Devon who stared, petrified, at where the flames had been.

"See? Not a prank."

"What the hell?" he muttered. "Not okay. That is definitely not okay. Burning trashcans is not okay."

The rubberneckers behind us chattered noisily. One woman shouted into her cellphone, "The fire's gone out, but I think it's a gas line!" She paused for a second. "Back away. 9-1-1 says everybody back away."

People immediately scurried down the street or hugged next to the building, still transfixed in fascinated horror.

"You need to move, boys!" the cellphone lady shouted at us as sirens echoed between the buildings.

"Go!" I pushed Devon so hard his feet finally started to work again. I grabbed his arm and dragged him onto a side street out of view of the fire trucks as they pulled up to the melted trashcan.

Two run-ins with the fire department in one day is not a good thing. Especially not when you might have caused the fires. Even if it was by accident.

We cut back around the block and to my dad's building. The fire trucks had parked down the street, but from here we couldn't even see what all the firemen were staring at.

Drake was behind the desk like always. "Mr. Adams." He smiled. "I wasn't expecting to see you here today."

"Yeah." I tried to put my thoughts into an order that didn't involve a possessed demon phone with the ability to make things spontaneously combust that was currently burning a hole in my back pocket. Not literally. I hoped. "There was a fire at school. Everybody's okay, but I lost my house key, so I'm gonna hang out here until my mom gets home." If my mom still had a house key.

"Of course, Mr. Adams." Drake unlocked the safe beneath the desk. "I would be more than happy to let you into the apartment. I am so relieved you're safe. Have you called your father?"

Drake led us to the elevator and turned the key to go up.

"No." It hadn't occurred to me to call my dad. I mean, how could he be worried about me when he didn't even know my school had been on fire? Never mind the fact that the more time passed, the more convinced I was that I had caused the fire in the first place. But Drake was still looking at me all concerned, so I said, "Not yet. I'm going to call before I shower." And I did need to shower. Even though the elevator was a big one, it was still small enough to trap in the horrible smoke and burning trash smell that was stuck to me.

The door opened to my dad's apartment, and Drake waved us in. "Shall I call for a pizza?"

"Two." Devon half-stumbled into the apartment.

"Very well." Drake closed the elevator doors and was gone.

Devon walked into the living room and collapsed onto the couch. I followed him, a little afraid he might be panicked enough to start throwing up onto the carpet. And having to call the cleaning lady to tell her you got puke in the carpet was never a fun time.

I sat on the metal rim of the glass coffee table and stared at Devon, waiting for him to speak. If he could still speak. I wasn't too sure about that.

"The fire," Devon said finally, his hands shaking as he dragged them over his face. "The phone started the fire."

Elizabeth had been right. She had seen it right away.

"Both fires. And the one at school didn't go out till I put it out with the app."

Devon scrunched his face and let out the longest string of muttered curses I had ever heard. "We have to get rid of it."

"Same thing Elizabeth said. I can take it down to the restaurant and leave it with them."

"No way in *Hell!*" Devon shook his head, looking as pale as I had ever seen him. "You just burned down half the school with that thing. You can't keep it. It's arson evidence, Bry."

"So we give it—"

"We are not giving the damn phone to people who might want to do more damage with it than you've already done! That guy we saw looked evil. He looked like a vampire or demon or something. We can't give an evil dude something this dangerous. What if he lights us on fire? Or decides to take out Times Square. I can't have that on my head, man."

"So, we do what Elizabeth said and dump it into the Hudson," I said, wondering if I could convince Drake to find a guy to take the phone to the river.

No, it couldn't be trusted to a courier. I mean, who wouldn't want to open a package they had been hired to dump into a river. We'd have to do it ourselves.

I turned my wrist over, making my watch blink on. Nearly seven PM. "If we head to the water in a few hours, we should be able to find a place to dump it without getting noticed."

"No way." Devon pushed himself to sit up. "The river's way too risky. What if it washes up and someone finds it?"

"It's a phone. It'll be dead from the water."

"A demon phone that starts fires, and you think water is going to hurt it?" Devon stood up, color coming back into his determined face. "We have to destroy it ourselves. It's the only way to make sure it's done."

Order How I Magically Messed Up My Life in Four Freakin'
Days *to continue the journey!*

ABOUT THE AUTHOR

Megan O'Russell is the author of several Young Adult series that invite readers to escape into worlds of adventure. From *Girl of Glass*, which blends dystopian darkness with the heart-pounding danger of vampires, to *Ena of Ilbrea*, which draws readers into an epic world of magic and assassins.

With the *Girl of Glass* series, *The Tethering* series, *The Chronicles of Maggie Trent*, *The Tale of Bryant Adams*, the *Ena of Ilbrea* series, and several more projects planned, there are always exciting new books on the horizon. To be the first to hear about new releases, free short stories, and giveaways, sign up for Megan's newsletter by visiting the following:

https://www.meganorussell.com/book-signup

Originally from Upstate New York, Megan is a professional musical theatre performer whose work has taken her across North America. Her chronic wanderlust has led her from Alaska to Thailand and many places in between. Wanting to travel has fostered Megan's love of books that allow her to visit countless new worlds from her favorite reading nook. Megan is also a lyricist and playwright. Information on her theatrical works can be found at RussellCompositions.com.

She would be thrilled to chat with you on Facebook or Twitter @MeganORussell, elated if you'd visit her website MeganORussell.com, and over the moon if you'd like the pictures of her adventures on Instagram @ORussellMegan.

ALSO BY MEGAN O'RUSSELL

<u>The Girl of Glass Series</u>

Girl of Glass

Boy of Blood

Night of Never

Son of Sun

<u>The Tale of Bryant Adams</u>

How I Magically Messed Up My Life in Four Freakin' Days

Seven Things Not to Do When Everyone's Trying to Kill You

Three Simple Steps to Wizarding Domination

Five Spellbinding Laws of International Larceny

<u>The Tethering Series</u>

The Tethering

The Siren's Realm

The Dragon Unbound

The Blood Heir

<u>The Chronicles of Maggie Trent</u>

The Girl Without Magic

The Girl Locked With Gold

The Girl Cloaked in Shadow

<u>Ena of Ilbrea</u>

Wrath and Wing

Ember and Stone

Mountain and Ash

Ice and Sky

Feather and Flame

Guilds of Ilbrea

Inker and Crown

Myth and Storm

Viper and Steel

Tower and Grave

Siege and Sparrow

The Heart of Smoke Series

Heart of Smoke

Soul of Glass

Eye of Stone

Ash of Ages

Fracture Pact

The Cursebound Thief

The Oathbound Blade

The Bloodbound Knight

The Fatebound Wraith

Sorcerers of Ilbrea

Spell and Secret

www.ingramcontent.com/pod-product-compliance
Lightning Source LLC
Chambersburg PA
CBHW030143200726
48285CB00004BC/1354